PUFFIN BOOKS

EXTRATERRESTRIAL TALES

Nicholas Fisk is an outstanding writer of science fiction for children, and this volume brings together three of his most popular stories.

TRILLIONS: Falling out of the sky come millions and millions of hard, shiny objects, whose appearance no one can explain. Are they a blessing, as their beauty suggests, or a deadly, inexplicable threat?

SPACE HOSTAGES: A crazed, dying Flight Lieutenant, nine frightened children, and a top secret spacecraft – all of them out of control and adrift in space!

ON THE FLIP SIDE: As animals everywhere begin to act strangely, a tale of real terror and menace unfolds. Will Lettice's uncanny understanding of animal behaviour be enough to avert the horror?

Nicholas Fisk has been an actor, jazz musician, illustrator, photographer, copy-writer, publisher and always a writer. His favourite work is writing science fiction for children and he believes that almost any imaginable possibility may become a reality within the lifetime of someone who is young now. He lives in Bushey Heath, Hertfordshire.

Nicholas Fisk

Extraterrestrial Tales

PUFFIN BOOKS

PUFFIN BOOKS

Published by the Penguin Group
Penguin Books Ltd, 27 Wrights Lane, London w8 5tz, England
Viking Penguin, a division of Penguin Books USA Inc.
375 Hudson Street, New York, New York 10014, USA
Penguin Books Australia Ltd, Ringwood, Victoria, Australia
Penguin Books Canada Ltd, 2801 John Street, Markham, Ontario, Canada l3r 1b4
Penguin Books (NZ) Ltd, 182–190 Wairau Road, Auckland 10, New Zealand

Penguin Books Ltd, Registered Offices: Harmondsworth, Middlesex, England

Trillions first published by Hamish Hamilton 1971; published in Puffin Books 1973
Space Hostages first published by Hamish Hamilton 1967; published in Puffin Books 1970
On the Flip Side first published by Kestrel Books 1983; published in Puffin Books 1985
First published in one volume 1991
10 9 8 7 6 5 4 3 2 1

Text copyright © Nicholas Fisk, 1971, 1967, 1983, 1991
All rights reserved

Printed in England by Clays Ltd, St Ives plc

Contents

TRILLIONS   7

SPACE HOSTAGES   125

ON THE FLIP SIDE   265

Trillions

Written for Nim

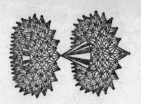

No one can tell you exactly who it was now, but it was quite certainly one of the youngest children that invented the name 'Trillions' You can imagine a group of children squatting on the ground, scraping together heaps of brightly coloured, mysterious grit that had fallen from the sky . . .

'I've got millions!'

'I've got billions!'

'I've got *trillions*!'

Trillions it was from then on. The name fitted perfectly. It had the right hard, bright sound to it – and Trillions were hard and bright. It suggests millions upon millions – and the Trillions were everywhere, sprinkling roads and gardens and roofs and even the firesides of people's homes with a glittery dusting of tiny jewels (but Trillions were not jewels).

And the name Trillions had a foreign sound to it – a suggestion of other worlds, star-studded skies, the cold emptiness of space. That was right, too. For wherever Trillions came from, it was not this world.

So everyone – the children, then the adults, then the local newspapers, then the national newspapers and TV stations and at last the world authorities – came to call the strange, jewel-like dust by the name the children invented: Trillions.

It is strange about names. Ten years before the Trillions came, Mr and Mrs Harding had christened their well behaved, sandy-haired baby 'James'. When he was five, it was found that he would have to wear spectacles, so James Harding became Specs. When he was six or seven, his school-friends began to call him Prof, because his appearance reminded them of an absent-minded professor.

But this name was wrong too: James turned out to be anything but absent-minded. In fact, he was the very opposite. He was the sort of boy who wanted a place for everything and everything in its place. He wanted hard facts, not soft opinions. When he had got the facts right, he would act.

It was James who solemnly, earnestly and thoroughly cleared the name of the oil-delivery man who was accused – wrongly – of stealing central-heating oil from the tanker he drove, then selling it. (The local newspaper called James *The Boy Detective*, which made him furious. 'I am not a boy detective,' he said, 'I am someone who can do arithmetic.')

By then, James' name had already become Bem. Bem suited him perfectly. It had the solid, sober sound of 'Ben'. In addition, it meant B.E.M. or Bug-Eyed Monster. For James, with his round face, round spectacles and passion for science, 'Bem' was the name that made sense.

Or – still talking about names – take Panda. Bem's eight-year-old sister was christened Penelope, rather a grand name. But even as a baby, she had been tiny, burning-eyed, round-faced yet spiky. Very soon her 'real' name suggested itself. Her eyes were black, and slightly shadowed; her skin was white; her face was round. What other name was there for her but Panda?

Mina, the Olivellis' girl who lived next door, needed no nickname. Mina – you say it 'Meena' – suited her perfectly. She was nine and a half, olive-skinned, black-haired, very slightly plump – Italian-looking. You could call her a female girl. If you dressed Mina in a top hat, lumberjack coat, riding breeches and coalminer's boots and finished off with a burnt-cork moustache, everyone would still say 'What a pretty girl!'

You can imagine for yourself how Mina responded to the Trillions. When they arrived, her large, dark-brown eyes widened and glistened. Her neat, long-nailed, tapered fingers began to prod and pick. By the end of that day, she had found out how to use Trillions. She used them to decorate herself.

Which leaves Scott Houghton.

Scott is the most important person in this story after the Trillions themselves, yet it is hard to find the right things to say about him. He was of average height for his age – thirteen. His hair was average brown. So were his eyes. His school record was average or above average. He was averagely popular. He never had a nickname – you can hardly count 'Scotty' – because he was too average to need one.

He was also extraordinary. The things that made him so unusual were unknown to his friends and barely noticed by his parents, who took him for granted (which suited Scott very well). His extraordinary qualities are hard to explain. Is it extraordinary for a schoolboy to keep bees? Scott did and had done so for four years. To Mr Bygrave, the strange old man who had first interested him in bees, Scott was extraordinary because he came to know more than his teacher. At first, the man had said, 'Ah, you've got an instinct for them! That's what it is, an instinct!' Later, he changed his mind. It wasn't instinct that Scott had: it was ability to observe, study, think, compare, invent.

Most modern beekeepers nowadays use a gadget called the Bygrave Controlled Demand Winter Feeder. Only one beekeeper, Mr Bygrave, knows that it should have been called the 'Houghton' Feeder. For the invention was Scott's, made when he was eleven.

His other interests were just as extraordinary. Scott was

given a toy star telescope – made a real one from a kit of parts – rapidly became an expert observer – quickly tired of observing – and spent hours, from then on, in comparing astronomy and astrology; he was trying to make sense of the battle between science and mysticism.

When there was a craze for guitars and folk singing at his school, Scott tried to find a form of guitar amplification that did not spoil the sound of the guitar. He failed, but found instead a method for making very small loudspeaker enclosures that could still deliver a good bass tone. The little transistor radio Scott had in his bedroom sounded like a big set with a twelve-inch speaker. His mother complained about the booming of the bass, so he turned a switch and cut it down. Now the set sounded like any other portable radio. It never occurred to Scott's mother to ask him how such a small radio could produce such big tone – mothers are not curious about such things. Nor did it ever occur to Scott to do anything about his loudspeaker invention – he had lost interest in the thing when he had got it working properly and had become interested instead in four-wheel drive for motor-cars. His room became a maze of Meccano and the little radio's batteries ran flat.

Scott never spoke about his ideas and inventions, not even to his father. He was, after all, a schoolboy. Why should his father, a grown man, be interested in schoolboy ideas? In fact, his interests were shared by only one other person – Bem. But Bem was younger than Scott and also perhaps a smaller-minded person. Bem had an 'old' mind, Scott had an ageless mind. So Scott was really alone with his extraordinariness.

Meanwhile, the ordinary world went on. Scott suffered cut knees, punches in the nose, sarcasm from the English teacher and falls off bicycles, just like everyone else; he enjoyed chocolate ice-cream, certain funny programmes on TV, air rifles and all the things that thousands and millions of other boys liked. He did not think himself extraordinary. He knew only that certain things that interested him might bore other people. So he kept his mouth shut. It seemed the simplest thing to do.

But when the Trillions came, everything about him and around him became complicated. For the Trillions were very extraordinary indeed and it was to take more than ordinary ways of thinking and acting to deal with them.

Much more.

Just what were the Trillions?

Start at the beginning. Scott, Mina, Panda and Bem all lived in the same road in Harbourtown West. Once, this town had been a fishing village. Now, it was just a pleasant place to live, with pleasure boats of all shapes, sizes and colours filling the harbour. Scott's father ran the yachting marina and made a comfortable living from it.

The important thing about Harbourtown West, as far as the Trillions were concerned, was that the place was situated on a narrow spur of land sticking out into the ocean. Harbourtown could be a windy, stormy place to live. It could get weather that no one else got.

On a sunny but windy day in May, Harbourtown and Harbourtown alone received a heavy shower of Trillions.

There was no rain and no cloud. In the windy, open sky there was a slight darkening – a cloudy patch that glittered in the sunlight. Then there was the sandstormy, rattling hiss as the Trillions came. Their showering lasted perhaps fifteen minutes. When it was over, there were drifts of Trillions everywhere. Trillions packed inches deep against a garden fence; Trillions glittering in drifts over roads and gardens; Trillions caught between the windows and window frames of houses and cars; Trillions edging the gutters, sparkling in the clefts of branches, lying thinly on the roofs of cars.

A few people were frightened by the Trillions. Most were puzzled and curious. The children were excited. 'I've got millions . . . billions . . . Trillions!' they cried.

While the other children squeaked and jumped or sifted and sorted the Trillions, Bem collected a single jar full of them and walked down the road to Scott's house – and nearly collided with Scott, who was just leaving his house to visit Bem.

'Come inside, Bem,' said Scott. 'What do you make of it?'

Bem did not answer for some time, then he said, 'Can we have a sheet of your father's layout paper from the big pad?'

'Sure. Hold on.'

Bem looked closely at his handful of Trillions.

'Make it four sheets.'

Scott came back with four large sheets of the half-transparent white paper and spread them on the floor.

'What are you going to do – sort them into sizes, or colours, or what?' he asked Bem.

'Sizes first. We could use strainers – '

'Yes, a wire coffee strainer and a nylon strainer. Two different sizes of mesh to begin with.'

Scott got the strainers from the kitchen. Bem took one strainer, then the other, and poured Trillions through them to grade them into two sizes. While he did this, he and Scott said nothing. They were used to doing things together.

They lay on the floor and studied the two heaps. A shaft of sunlight lit them and they glittered fiercely.

'They're beautiful,' said Scott, softly.

'Bigs and smalls. Most of the pale colours are smalls: most of the darker colours are bigs,' said Bem, without bothering to reply to Scott.

'Look at this sapphire one –'

'We need the microscope.'

'*I'll* get it,' said Scott, raising one eyebrow at Bem and smiling slightly.

'Yes, get it,' said Bem simply. Scott laughed to himself and went to get the microscope. It was always like this. Though Scott was older than Bem, it was Scott who fetched and carried. Not because Bem was selfish or rude, but because it never occurred to him to concentrate on more than one thing at a time. At this moment, he was concentrating on Trillions.

'Let's have it,' said Bem when Scott came back. Again Scott smiled. The microscope was his, Scott's.

'Here you are, you bossy little squirt,' said Scott.

For the first time, Bem looked up at him, startled. 'What did I – ?'

'Never mind,' said Scott. 'Get on with it.'

Bem put a few Trillions on a dished glass slide, set up the microscope rapidly and peered into it.

'Two!' he said. 'That's odd. You look.'

'Two what?'

'Two sorts. See for yourself.'

Scott put his eye to the microscope. What he saw amazed and dazzled him. 'They're beaut –' he said, then remembered he had said it before. But they were beautiful all the same. It was as if he looked at priceless jewels, cut and facetted into superb circular gem-stones. Under the microscope, the colours were even more startling than they were under normal light. He increased the magnification to concentrate on one particular Trillion. It looked like a great ruby. Then he shifted the slide to what appeared as a giant emerald, with a thousand geometrical faces cut in it.

'Do you notice? Two sorts?' said Bem.

Scott looked again, comparing one Trillion with another.

'You're right, Bem. Two sorts Only two ... One like a doughnut, with a hollow in the centre –'

'Not a hollow, a complete hole,' interrupted Bem.

'And the other with –'

'The other like a doughnut again, but with a spike sticking out of the centre. I suppose it's the same on both sides?'

Bem silently handed him a needle. Scott licked the point of it to make it sticky, touched the point to the Trillion and turned it over on the glass slide.

'Yes, the same both sides. Just the same. Like a jewelled doughnut with jewelled pyramids coming out of the centre. You could spin it like a top.'

'While the other sort has a hole in the centre ... do you notice something else?'

'What about?'

'About the edges. Look at the way the outside edges are cut.'

Scott peered down the microscope, then lifted his head. His eye was watering.

'You should keep both eyes open, I've often told you –' said Bem.

'Oh, shut up. What do you mean about the edges? All I can see is a whole lot of regular triangular cuttings, like teeth in a gear wheel. The cuttings cover the whole of the outside of the doughnut shape –'

'Let me look for a moment,' said Bem, butting his head against Scott so that Scott had to move. Bem fiddled with the needle as he looked, then said 'Keep still. Don't jog me. Nearly there!'

He licked the needle again, and picked at the Trillions on the glass slide for a long time. Then said, 'Whatever you do, don't jog. But have a look!'

Scott carefully put his eye to the microscope. Bem, he saw, had moved two Trillions together so that they touched. Although the Trillions were of different size, they 'geared' together perfectly.

'They're like interlocking bricks – you know, those children's construction things!' said Scott. 'If you put a whole lot of Trillions they'd lock together!'

'That's not all. They fit together edge to edge, but they also fit together on top of each other. You can see how the ones with pyramids in the middle could lock into the ones with doughnut holes. You could *build* with them!'

Scott sat back and stared at Bem. Bem stared owlishly back at him.

'What does it mean?' said Scott at last.

'I don't know.'

'Well, have you ever seen anything like it before? In nature, I mean?'

'I suppose there must be lots of things like it,' said Bem. 'But I just can't think of them. I mean, there's honeycomb, and crystals, and molecular structures – they all have shapes that fit together. But I can't think of anything just like this . . .'

Scott was about to look through the microscope again, when Bem's sister Panda came rushing in, trampling over the sheets of paper on the floor and shaking the microscope.

'Mind out!' shouted Bem, too late.

'They're *fantastic*!' shouted Panda. 'Oh, never mind the microscope, who cares about – they're *marvellous*!' She went on, 'I bet you don't know about them!'

'Know *what* about *what*?'

'About the Trillion things! They can do tricks! All on their own! Come and see!'

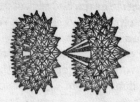

It turned out that Panda – along with most of the children in Harbourtown West – had already discovered the most important and startling thing about Trillions. Just as she said, they could do tricks. All on their own.

'Watch!' she told Bem and Scott.

She squatted down on the stones of the patio, holding a piece of chalk. With this she made a simple squiggle – a rough 'S'. She scattered Trillions loosely over the 'S': then she sat back on her heels, looking triumphant.

'Well, what happens now?' demanded Bem.

'Wait!' said Panda. Everyone waited, silently.

It took about three minutes to happen.

Very slowly, piece by piece, the Trillions began to move. Looking closely, you could see one Trillion nudge another – gear with it – turn it – move it!

Then more Trillions would combine to form a geared-together mass. The process would go faster now. Some Trillions would lock with more Trillions, and still more, until the whole collection would shift and tumble like sand.

Scott looked quickly at Bem. His eyes and mouth were wide open.

At last, the Trillions finished their work. And now, replacing the 'S' that Panda had made, was another 'S' made entirely of Trillions. An 'S' correct in every detail, however tiny: where Panda's finger had slipped slightly and made a jerky curve, the Trillions' curve was jerky too. Where the chalk line was grainy, the Trillions' line was grainy.

The youngest children were shouting and laughing and

pushing as they imitated Panda and made shapes of their own for the Trillions to imitate. Bem and Scott did not hear them. They stood in their own silence, staring and wondering. They walked back together, in silence, to Scott's house.

'Dad will be back about six,' said Bem at last. 'Perhaps he'll know something.'

Scott shook his head. 'He won't, nobody will. There's never been anything like this before. There just can't have been . . .'

There was silence for another minute or so. And then the cars started arriving.

'Your flash lead is pulled out,' Bem told the photographer.

'Thanks, son. Move over to one side a bit, would you? Thanks.'

Bem shrugged and walked on. There were cars everywhere, journalists and photographers everywhere, TV men everywhere. And everyone was in a hurry. The light was fading, the photographers were beginning to use flash to get their pictures.

'And what's your name, dear?'

Bem turned a cold eye on the TV woman and said 'Bem, what's yours?' She turned away hurriedly and trapped Mina.

'And what's your name, dear?'

'Mina Olivelli, and I'm nine and a half in one month's time.'

A camera lurched overhead on its gantry, with a tough looking young man in control, and swooped on to Mina. 'And how do you feel about what's been happening here today in Harbourtown, Mina?'

'I'm collecting all the prettiest ones to make a bracelet!'

The camera came in still closer. Mina fluttered her eyelids at it, put her head on one side and beamed.

21

'And tell me, Mimi –'

'Mina. Mina Olivelli.'

'Tell me, Mina, how do you think the Trillions will change things in this little town?'

'Well, my *Daddy* says it's fan-tas-tic and my *Mummy* says oh dear what a mess to clear up, but *I* say –'

Bem groaned aloud and the TV woman looked furious. A sound engineer shouted, 'We picked up that groan, better forget it!'

Bem cheered up and walked on. *Bracelets* . . .!

A few hundred yards away, Scott and Panda were among a group centred on a TV commentator, who was talking in preacher-like tones into his microphone, 'From the clear sky above us fell today a strange dust – a dust that could be a threat or a promise, a mysterious messenger from outer space or just the accidental sweepings of the universe . . .'

'Waffle,' said Scott.

The TV man extended the microphone to a white-haired but quite young-looking man in a trench coat, who seemed embarrassed.

'Well, we can't possibly give an explanation for a phenomenon that no one has had time to evaluate or examine . . .' he said, miserably.

'But tell me, Professor – with your unrivalled knowledge of conditions in outer space –'

'I haven't any unrivalled knowledge of outer space. No one has. I prefer not to be called "Professor".'

'What should I call you, sir? Flight Commander? – your rank when you –'

' – Never mind, forget it. I don't want to talk.'

The Professor or Flight Commander or whatever he was looked pitifully embarrassed now. He moved jerkily away and in doing so bumped into Panda.

He said, 'Oh, I am sorry.'

For some reason Scott wanted to talk to this odd-looking

man, who seemed one of the few 'real' people there. He found courage to say to him,

'Excuse me, but I've looked at the Trillions under my microscope and they're very strange. I wish you could let me show you. Oh, I'm called Scott –'

'My name is Blythe –'

'This is Panda. Why don't you come and look for yourself?'

A few minutes later, there were more introductions when Blythe met Scott's parents and still more when Bem called in.

The man Blythe setttled down with the microscope and for the first time, Scott had the chance to study him closely. What he saw puzzled him. He somehow knew the face but could not place it. Professor, Flight Commander or Mister Blythe was a strange mixture of youth and age. His eyes were remarkable: pale but dark-lashed, and brilliant. His hands were firm, hard and young – yet he used them nervously, sometimes clumsily. One hand moved woodenly as if it did not belong to the arm. The skin on his face and hands was strangely untidy in texture and colour – patchy – but smooth and unlined, except for a deep crease, a seam, on either side of his mouth. And this seam deepened whenever his mouth twitched, which was quite often. It was almost as if the professor was constantly biting back an unpleasant remark. Scott remembered a schoolmaster who had the same tight, nervous mouth, apparently bursting to say something that would never be said. But the schoolmaster had been a much older man.

Scott noticed another thing. Twice, Blythe put his right eye to the microscope, muttered something, peevishly – then used his left eye instead. Scott's father must have noticed too, for he asked. 'Can you handle the focusing all right? The coarse adjustment is on the lower wheel –'

Blythe replied, almost rudely, 'I know, I know!' Then, as

if realizing he had sounded rude, said to Scott, 'This is a nice little instrument. Do you happen to have any polarizing screens? No? Well, never mind.'

After a long time, he took his eye from the microscope and sat upright, frowning.

Scott said, 'Well?'

Blythe looked blankly back at Scott and said, 'I could send you some polarizing screens, if you would like me to.'

'To make pretty coloured pictures? Thanks,' said Scott, coldly.

Blythe stared at him, then chuckled.

'Sorry,' he said.

'What do you think of them? The Trillions?' Scott insisted.

'Very interesting. Most unusual.'

Now he looked furtive – even shifty. Yet Scott still liked him, if 'like' is the word. There was a feeling of power about Blythe.

'The two shapes – and the toothed edges so that they can lock with each other – ' said Scott, 'surely you noticed that?'

Blythe stood up, then sat down again. He rubbed his forehead and said, 'How old are you?'

'Thirteen. But I don't see –'

'And your friend – Ben, isn't it?'

'Bem. For Bug-eyed Monster. He's two years younger.'

'Well, your friend Panda's gone,' said Blythe, as if this was a good thing. 'So there's only us and you look sensible enough. And in any case, the papers, television – they'll all be full of it tomorrow. So what I think or say can't matter much . . .'

'What do you think?' said Scott's father, leaning forward.

'It's the fact that they form . . . make shapes . . . that's so extraordinary,' said Blythe. 'Extraordinary and frightening.

Yes, I'm sorry, but I mean frightening. There's no parallel that I can think of, none at all. Sponges, great boulders said to move by themselves in the desert (did you hear about that? Fascinating) – coral reefs, molecules ... There's nothing uncommon in things *forming* – in their developing shapes and structures.'

'But the Trillions *imitate!*'

'Yes, I was coming to that. As I was saying, there's nothing uncommon in things forming and growing – nature is full of elaborate structures. All quite usual. But then there's this question of mimicry. Almost instant mimicry. The Trillions can mimic and imitate. So can parrots. So can death-head moths. But they have taken countless years to learn their simple little tricks! While the Trillions – '

'Chameleons,' said Bem, suddenly.

'Quite right, chameleons. But it would be useless to expect a chameleon, for instance – and they are very advanced mimics, very good at it – to disguise themselves as a letter "S". Chameleons haven't many tricks. They don't have many ways of adapting themselves, camouflaging themselves. They just change colour. And chameleons – several fish and insects, too, for that matter – always alter their colour or pattern or shape for a limited purpose. Generally defence. But Trillions are doing exactly the opposite. They are doing something I have never heard of before, except in the higher animals. They're using mimicry and imitation in immediate response to whatever is done to them – even though the things we give them to mimic are new each time!'

'Have Trillions got brains?' said Bem.

'I don't know. That's what worries me most.

Then Mina scampered in, cheeks glowing. 'Excuse me, Mr and Mrs Houghton; but I had to show you! My lovely bracelet!'

She held out her golden-brown wrist. On it there was a

bracelet made of rosettes of glittering Trillions; a perfect pattern of flower shapes, repeated again and again, in glowing red, emerald and diamond white.

'Beautiful, Mina!' said Mrs Houghton. 'It must have taken you hours!'

'Oh, *they* did it! The Trillions! I made one pattern, and put it down on the ground in the middle of a whole heap of Trillions, and they just *did* it! You could watch them doing it! They just *formed* and I put sticky paper down on the patterns as they made them! Who are you?' Mina interrupted herself. She had noticed the stranger.

'This is Mr Blythe, Mina.'

'How do you do,' said Mina, politely. She shook hands uncertainly with him, then said – 'You're the space man! I saw your picture in a magazine! You went to the moon or somewhere in a spaceship!'

Scott and Bem exchanged looks. 'Blythe!' whispered Bem. 'Of course!'

'Why is your hair white? It wasn't white then. And you've got thinner,' burst out Mina.

Scott's father leaned forward in his chair. 'You are – were – Flight Commander Blythe . . .?'

'Just Blythe now. And I've hung up my space unit. That's all over.'

Scott's father whistled quietly and said, 'Well . . .!'

'You've changed quite a lot,' said Scott's mother, quietly. 'I don't think I'd know you as the same man we all watched on TV that terrible time. You must have been through – '

'Well, that's all over,' repeated Blythe. 'And I'm not the same man. Not all over, anyhow.' He touched his face. Skin grafts, thought Scott. Skin grafts on his hands and face – and what else?

'Let me look at the bracelet again, Mina.'

She held it out to him, and asked, 'How old are you, Mister – I mean Commander – what you said?'

'That's not a polite thing to ask, Mina dear – ' said Mrs Houghton. But for the first time, Blythe smiled. 'Forty-one. You can call me Icarus. It's simpler.'

There was an awkward silence while everyone waited for Mina to say, 'You look much older than that!'

But Mina said, 'That's a funny name, *Icarus*. I've never heard of anyone called *Icarus*. Is it a joke?'

Bem was just about to explain to Mina that Icarus was the man who tried to fly to the sun with wax wings, but the sun melted his wings and Icarus plunged to his death. Scott gave Bem a warning glance and Bem shut up.

Blythe carefully examined the bracelet without answering Mina. 'It's very pretty,' he said at last. 'You know what you should do now?'

Mina shook her head.'

'You should get them to make you a necklace to match!'

They watched Mina run from the room, delighted with the idea.

Bem said, 'You think Trillions are safe, then?'

'Safe enough to make pretty things for Mina. But the rest of us ... I wonder what they mean to the rest of the world?'

Alone in his bedroom, Scott watched the 'forming' of Trillions through the low-power lenses of the microscope. They were easy to watch now; they moved no faster than ants, though sometimes, when they had 'work' to do, they were too quick to follow. He could not get used to them, could not get over them. He watched the outer, geared surfaces join and mesh, jostle and nudge, link and interlink, and imitate the simple pattern he had drawn on a sheet of paper. He watched one Trillion climb another, with tiny, shaking jerks as the teeth meshed; then the settling of the pyramid-like spike of one Trillion into the matching hole in the centre of another. He watched the mistakes the Trillions sometimes made – a pyramid Trillion would try to engage with another pyramid; discover the error; cog itself away; be replaced by the right sort of Trillion with a hollow centre.

After a time, he began to imagine he could hear the sounds the Trillions made. The little clicks as gear-tooth engaged with gear-tooth, the tiny sounds of falling as pyramid engaged in hold and locked there, the microscopic turnings and rollings and linkings and climbings.

At last he tired, got into bed and turned out the light. Now the room was almost dark, but he could not take his eyes from the dully glittering Trillions on the white paper by the window and still he could hear the sounds that did not exist – the little movements of the restless Trillions.

He slept, and dreamed Trillions. Do they *understand*?

He awoke to a world that was all Trillions. There were Trillions in Poland, Portugal, Pakistan; Trillions on the radio, in the newspapers, on TV. And in Harbourtown, there were helicopters in the sky, cars jamming the roads, motor cruisers rubbing the paint off each other's sides in the harbour, and, everywhere, men with cameras; still cameras, TV cameras, movie cameras.

The children went to school and found they could not get in: reporters and cameramen blocked the gates.

'Just a minute, sonny – what were you doing when the Trillions arrived?'

'What's your name? How old are you?'

'Who thought of calling them Trillions? You? Well, was it her, the little girl over there? What's your name, little girl? What's that? Louder! . . .'

'Were you scared? You weren't scared? Well, were you pleased? Both pleased and scared? Well, thank *you*, that's very helpful, I suppose . . .'

'What's your name? What's your age?'

They asked Bem questions like this. He answered stony-faced, staring straight back at the questioner.

'What's your name, sonny?'

'Sonny.'

'How old are you?'

'Twenty-seven. I'm a midget.'

'Be serious. What did you feel when you first saw the Trillions?'

'Thrillions.'

'Now listen, sonny, answer straight. Millions of people are watching you, you know . . .'

Bem stared blankly at the nearest TV camera then made himself squint. 'I can't see anyone,' he replied.

Mina showed the reporters her bracelet: the volley of flashbulbs almost blinded her.

But it was Scott the reporters wanted.

'You've talked with Mr Blythe, haven't you?'

'Yes. A little.'

'Did you know who he was? Did you know he was the spaceman?'

'Not at once, later –'

'Did you know he's here acting for the government – that he's one of our greatest authorities on space pheno-menons?'

'Phenomena,' Bem interrupted. 'The plural of pheno-menon is phenomena.'

'Get that kid out of here. Now listen, Scott, don't go away . . .'

Miss Wolfe and Mr Clark, teachers, tried to get the chil-dren into the school. They tried for half an hour, then gave up. 'No school today!' they shouted, over the crowd. 'You can all go home! Go home, do you hear?' But Mina had found someone else to show her bracelet to, and Scott was in the clutches of a hard, blonde, tanned girl reporter in an expensive suede jacket decorated with three expensive cameras.

'Tell me, Scott,' she whispered – or it felt like being whispered to, in spite of the noise – 'Tell me *all about yourself.* Now, your father: what does he do?' She made her eyes pop open wide as she waited for the answer.

'Builds boats. Runs the marina here.'

'Boats! A *wonderful* way of life!' The eyes popped again. 'And your *mother*, Scott, what does she do?'

'Runs the house. All sorts of things.'

'What *sort* of things, Scott?'

'Oh, she does pottery and textile designs. As a freelance.'

'Oh, an *artist.* So your mother is an *artist . . .?*'

She gave him the same sort of feeling you get when you go to pick up a jar of jam and someone has left it sticky. Scott escaped but was caught straight away by an elderly reporter with a tape recorder and a bright purple face, glistening with sweat.

This reporter jabbed questions at Scott as if they were friendly punches from a flyweight boxer. They didn't hurt but you could not escape them.

'So why was Mr Blythe in your home? What did he say about Trillions? What did he reply? What did he mean by that? Was he looking worried? Well, how was he looking? What do you mean, normal? How do you know he looked normal if this was the first time you met him? So he was looking a little anxious? You said a little anxious? Anxious was the word you used? Now, why do you think he was anxious? What do *you* think anyone's got to be anxious about?'

'All right, that's enough,' a voice said in Scott's ear. It was 'Icarus' Blythe. 'Come with me. No more questions. Come on, Scott.'

Scott was delighted to find himself being towed away. 'In here,' said Blythe, pushing open the back door of the school house. It was empty inside, of course. They sat down, each in a desk, and were silent for a minute.

'Wow,' said Blythe. 'I thought I was over all this.'

'You mean, after that moonshot? All the reporters?'

'Yes, all the reporters. It's a funny thing: you can't stop yourself answering them. And the more people there are, the more answers they get out of you. It's catching. Everyone gets the questions and answers disease, everyone behaves the same way.'

'I know, I felt like that. You don't want to, but you have to,' said Scott. He yawned. He was blazing with excitement yet numb with lack of sleep. He felt like two people having a quarrel.

'Didn't you sleep well last night?' asked Blythe.

'Oh yes, fine. Well, I slept all right. It's just that I couldn't get to sleep. I'd been looking at the Trillions again, at low power. You know, the microscope. And couldn't stop thinking about them.'

'What do you think about them?' asked Blythe sharply. Then he laughed, and said, 'Just like a reporter.'

'I don't – I don't know. I don't understand why you ask me, my opinions aren't worth – '

'Nobody's opinion is worth anything so far. That's why I ask you. You probably know as much about Trillions as anyone else in the world. Why assume that I know any more than you?'

'But you are a Professor or a Flight Commander or . . . I mean, you're *qualified*.'

Blythe stood up and stretched, then sat down again. 'I am Icarus – the one who got his wings singed. All the other titles mean nothing.' Scott stared at him, expressionlessly.

'Scott, once, not so long ago, I was the greatest expert in the world on a certain surface of the Moon. I was the greatest expert because I was the only expert. No one had been there but me. And do you know what all my expert knowledge amounted to?'

Scott shook his head.

'It amounted to this. I was alone, my suit was overheating, I was feeling a bit sick, and the Moon wasn't made of green cheese. That's what being the greatest expert in the world meant then. And that's very much the position with Trillions. We're world experts, both of us – and a hundred per cent ignorant. So tell me what you think!'

'If I do, will you tell me what *you* think?' Scott answered.

'Yes, certainly.' He met Scott's eyes and added, 'I mean it.'

'All right. I think Trillions are invaders of some sort from another planet. Or from space. I think they're intelligent. Probably more intelligent than ... than bees, say ...'

'Why bees? Why did you pick on bees? Are bees intelligent?'

'I suppose because Trillions can do all sorts of things that you could call "clever". So can bees. But is it "cleverness" or is it just instinct, or habit, or something that just developed over millions of years?'

'Bees make choices,' said Blythe.

'I know. They decide whether they're going to stand guard duty, or fan the hive to ventilate it, or look after the queen bee, or go and collect pollen, or work on the honeycombs. And they can give each other messages. Instinct or intelligence?'

'You seem to know a lot about bees,' said Blythe, raising an eyebrow.

'It's all instinct with bees, I suppose,' said Scott, ignoring the raised eyebrow. 'At least, that's what they teach us.'

'And now we have Trillions. Things the world has never seen before. "Clever" things, or things with instincts developed for situations that are never met with on our planet. For heaven's sake!' he broke off, 'Let's move!'

A face had appeared at the window, then more faces, all behind cameras. Scott and Icarus Blythe took seats right against the wall where no one could see them.

Icarus leaned down and scooped together the bright dust that had collected along the skirting of the wall. 'Look,' he said, holding out the palm of his hand, loaded with dust, for Scott to inspect. 'Trillions! A handful of Trillions. You and I look at them and wonder about them . . .

'Do you think,' he continued, 'that they are looking right back at us?'

Outside in the streets, there was a new commotion. The morning editions of the evening newspapers had arrived. As fast as the men and boys in the vans could unload, hands grabbed. The headlines screamed –

TRILLIONS!
World scientists probe invaders from space
Friend—or deadly foe?

Bem, Mina and Panda shared the only copy they could get with three other children. The front-page pictures showed magnified Trillions like great gem stones, and a street scene in Harbourtown West.

'Turn over!' said Bem, impatiently.

' "WORLD REACTION TO OTHER-WORLD INVADERS". Stop there a minute . . .' Frowning, he read the short paragraphs, each headed with the name of a capital city. Moscow, Paris, Rome, New York, London . . .

'They don't say anything!' said Panda, crossly.

'They don't know anything,' answered Bem. 'That's why.'

'Ooo! Look! Me!' squeaked Mina. And there, sure enough,

33

she was. The photographer had caught her at the moment when she held out her bracelet. The caption read, 'THE TRUST OF A LITTLE CHILD'.

'Urggh!' said Bem.

'*I am* a little child,' said Mina. 'Quite little. And anyhow, why shouldn't I trust them?' She admired the bracelet on her arm. 'They're only Trillions,' she said.

Next day, however, there was real news in the newspapers: the Trillions had 'formed' in a new and sinister way.

Harbourtown was once again the first place where it happened. Two local youths, whose hobby was skin-diving, reported. 'There's something strange down there in the water. Something huge. Like a – a *fortress*, all made of Trillions.'

Their underwater photographs showed great untidy blocks with holes like windows, dark towers and turrets looming in the dim waters; caves like great entrance halls, black and terrifying, that the swimmers dared not penetrate. Looking at the photographs, 'fortress' seemed as good a word as any for the structure. But a child playing in the sand with bucket and spade could have done better than the Trillions . . .

Very soon, there were more Trillion structures – a vast 'aeroplane' in a Vietnam jungle – a 'factory' (or was it a 'battleship'?) near Houston, Texas – a tower rather like an enormous gun barrel in Holland – and many others.

'These structures,' Scott said to Icarus, 'they simply don't make sense. What good are they? What could the Trillions *use* them for?'

'The more you look at them the less sense they make,' said Icarus, prodding a newspaper photograph of a 'fortress' in Japan.

Scott shrugged and stared at the picture in silence. He found himself remembering Blythe's words – 'Do you think

34

they are looking right back at us?' The thought made him shiver.

'They haven't got eyes,' he said at last.

'What was that?'

'Trillions haven't got eyes,' said Scott. 'Nor anything that looks like eyes. How could they look at us?'

'Perhaps the whole Trillion construction is an optical system. All those jewel-like facets may add up to an "eye", just as a fly's eye is made up of thousands of lenses.'

'And brains ... I wonder about the brains,' said Scott. 'Bees have brains, but they run their lives by a bigger brain – the brain of the hive.'

'Good description,' said Blythe. 'Mind you, human beings do much the same thing. We act as single, individual persons, but we also act as groups, or mobs, or races, or whole nations.'

'Suppose they do have brains. What have they been thinking? Did they think of coming to our planet – or just arrive by accident?'

'And when they make patterns, when they "form", are they thinking – or just behaving?' said Blythe.

'I suppose the most important question is, what do they want?' said Scott, speaking slowly. 'What do they hope for here?'

'Assuming they can hope or think at all,' Blythe reminded him.

Scott thought for a long minute, then looked up at Blythe and said, 'You're worried, aren't you? You're afraid that they can think, and they've come here for a purpose.'

'Yes, of course I'm worried. I am one of the people who has got to try and find out what Trillions are, what they mean to us, how we must treat them. You see, it's not simply a matter of scientific facts. It's more like ... well, it's like waking up in the middle of the night because you've heard a noise downstairs. So you go downstairs. The noise is coming from the kitchen. You open the door, and there's this enormous dog. He's got great white teeth. When you go near to him, he snarls at you – but wags his tail at the same time!'

Scott laughed.

'What do you do with a dog like that?' Blythe said. 'Throw him into the cold? But that's cruel. And anyhow, he might bite you. Give him food? But do you really want an enormous dog in your house from then on?'

'So what *do* you do?' said Scott.

There was a short, dry, rattling sound, like rice being thrown against a window. The man and the boy scrambled to their feet. There was a cloud over the blue sky – a cloud that glittered and twinkled in its depths.

The light, dry rattling sounded again against the window pane.

'More Trillions,' said Blythe.

And now the streets were suddenly filled by another invasion. This time, it was the Army. While the Trillions rained down from a clear sky, the streets of Harbourtown West became blocked with trucks carrying steel-helmeted men, with staff cars, with soldiers carrying walkie-talkies, with white-gaitered military policemen directing traffic, with special road signs. There was even an Army helicopter overhead making such a din that no one on the ground could hear all the orders and counter-orders and directions and commands that the soldiers gave each other.

Mina soon got herself a soldier. His name was Billy. He was over six feet tall and had freckles and bright yellow hair. He called Mina 'little lady' and carried her about on his shoulder until an officer told him not to.

'What are you going to do about the Trillions, Billy?' Mina asked. She looked very pretty with her necklace and bracelet.

'That's a good question, little lady,' said Billy, not answering it. His voice was deep and vague. When he spoke, he sounded rather like a cow mooing.

'Do you like Trillions?' said Mina, flashing her eyes and her bracelet at him.

'Don't know one way or the other, little lady,' said Billy. 'No orders yet.'

'I bet you're stronger than the Trillions,' said Mina.

'Could be,' said the soldier, screwing up his eyes and sticking out his chin. 'Could be,' he repeated, in a tough voice.

'I bet you're stronger than all the Trillions in the world!' said Mina, squeezing his hand. 'I bet you could smash them and bash them and mash them and hash them – '

'Could be,' said Billy, nodding his head menacingly.

'Well, I bet you could,' said Mina, adoringly.

Billy looked around him, saw no officers, and put Mina back on his shoulders.

'Vroom! Ker-Bang!' she shouted. 'Pow! Bam! Splat!'

In Scott Houghton's house, the Army seemed to have formed a sort of headquarters. There were officers and soldiers everywhere, under the command of an Army Major.

'Glad to meet you, sir,' said the Major, 'And not only glad: honoured.' He pumped Blythe's hand up and down vigorously and stuck out his chin, just like Billy.

Blythe mumbled something but couldn't get his hand away.

'Your achievement, sir,' the Major went on, 'was an inspiration to ...' Suddenly he dropped Blythe's hand and yelled 'Hey, SOLDIER! Yes, YOU! Over here at the double!'

Billy the soldier sheepishly put Mina down, and doubled over. 'SIR!' he mooed, saluting smartly.

'Your mission here, soldier, is a military mission,' began the Major, sticking out his chin still further. 'MILITARY, you understand?

'At ease soldier,' grated the Major. 'Stand by to run messages.'

Billy stood at ease. The Major scratched his grizzled grey hair under his field cap and started again.

'My duty is plain enough. In fact, it's all here in Orders,' he said, tapping a leather folder significantly with a large, clean finger. 'My duty is to protect the citizens of this town, this country, this nation, against their foes. Sounds simple enough, but is it?' The Major stopped dramatically and stared into Blythe's face with rounded eyes. 'Trouble is, we don't know what we're up against. You follow me?'

'I follow you,' said Blythe patiently.

'I want some lemonade,' said Mina, and skipped out of the room.

'The Trillions ...' said Blythe.

'Yes, the Trillions,' said the Major. 'Now we've dealt with the lemonade question, perhaps we could talk about the Trillions. Sir,' he said, making himself look soldierly again by puffing out his chest and thrusting forward his chin, 'I've got just one simple question to put to you – and I need hardly say that a great deal depends on your answer ...

'These Trillions: are they Friend – or Foe? Do we bless them – or do we BLAST THEM OFF THE FACE OF THE EARTH!'

'Guess which he'd rather do!' whispered Bem to Scott.

Blythe took a deep, slow breath before he replied.

'Major,' he said, 'I don't know what fire-power you've got here – '

'38's, 75's, napalm and all the usual small arms,' interrupted the Major, happily.

Blythe lifted a hand. 'Major, as I was about to say, I don't know what weapons you've got – any more than I know if Trillions are friend or foe – but I do know one thing. I found it out last night. Scott,' he said, 'Would you get me a hammer and something to use as an anvil? Thanks . . .

'Now, while Scott gets them, I want you, Major, to pick out just one Trillion from this collection here. Give him the saucer, Bem.' Bem took the saucerful of Trillions he kept by the microscope and held it out before the Major. The Major took one.

'Put it in this,' said Blythe, opening out a white paper envelope. The Major dropped in the Trillion. Scott came back with the hammer and an anvil in the shape of a rusty old anchor blade. He looked at Bem as if to say 'What is happening?' Bem shrugged.

'Now, Major, you talk about blasting Trillions off the face of the earth, and smashing them and so on. And you are a man of action. Well, let's see you go into action and smash just one single Trillion. Here's a Trillion. I place it, in its envelope, on the anvil. Here's the anvil. And here's the hammer. Right?'

Uncertainly, the Major took the hammer. He pushed a finger on to the envelope and the little bump of the Trillion showed through. He took aim with the hammer and brought it down hard. The little bump was flat. The Major handed the hammer to Blythe and said, 'Well?'

'Look inside the envelope.'

The Major looked.

'It's smashed! Smithereens! Beat into powder!' he laughed loudly. 'Well, there you are, Sir!'

'Now come over to the microscope, Major. Is it set up, Bem? Focused? Good. Sit down, Major. Take a look.'

The Major silently peered through the microscope. A minute passed. 'Nothing to report,' he said. 'Not a thing!'

'Nothing?' said Blythe. 'You're sure?'

Bem and Scott looked at each other.

'Nothing. Just stuff like powdered glass.'

'Right! So you have smashed a Trillion. But now watch this . . .'

He increased the magnification of the microscope, used the fine focus, and invited the Major to look. 'See anything?'

The Major peered into the microscope for some time in silence. Then looked up and said, 'Strange. Thought I saw something move!'

'Keep looking, Major,' said Blythe.

The Major kept looking, sometimes dabbing impatiently at the fine-focus wheel.

'Have trouble keeping them in focus, Major?'

'Damn things seem to be moving all the time. Something wrong with the microscope?'

'I'll make a little adjustment. Bem, where's the high-power objective? Thanks . . .'

He screwed the highest-power lens into place, carefully re-focused and invited the Major to look.

As he looked, the Major's neck seemed to swell in his collar, as if it were a red rubber ring being blown up, puff by puff. 'Blast them!' he roared, swivelling his head to glare at Blythe, 'Blast them! Know what they're doing? The broken bits are meshing together! Climbing! Gearing! *That Trillion I smashed has become more Trillions!*'

The expression on his face was so outraged, so childishly peevish, that Scott knew he would have to laugh. The arrival of General Hartman saved him.

The door was thrown open by Billy. He suddenly looked a
soldier.

'SAH!' yelled Billy. He raised his right knee and brought
the heel of his boot down with a crashing thump on Mrs
Houghton's polished floor. He tucked his chin into his
Adam's apple, braced his shoulders back so hard that his
whole body quivered, and yelled, 'General Hartman –
SAH!'

General Hartman strode into the room, stopped exactly in
the centre and said, very quietly, 'At ease.'

'SAH!' screeched Billy.

'Major?' said General Hartman.

'SIR!' bellowed the Major, standing rigidly to attention.
Mrs Houghton came in, glancing anxiously at the mark
Billy's heel left in the floor, then at the General.

'Major, introduce us,' said the General.

'This is Mrs Houghton, General, who has kindly
allowed – '

'Mrs Houghton. Honoured. Grateful.' The General extended a hand that might have been part of a machine. Scott
and Bem also shook for a second the dry, hard hand that
exerted no pressure whatsoever.

Mina came in with her glass of lemonade. 'This is Mina,'
said Mrs Houghton, rather faintly.

'Charmed. Pretty. Thank you,' said the General, taking the
glass of lemonade from her and draining it. Mina stared at
him round-eyed, said 'But! . . .' and shut up.

For there was very little you could say to the General. He
stood precisely five feet five inches tall. Every inch was

41

covered in expensive material. His cavalry boots were of a leather so old and beautiful that the various shades of mahogany seemed to be lit from within. His cavalry breeches were of a light tan whipcord in which every thread seemed to be formed into ranks and all the ranks stood at attention. His tunic, of a much darker brown, had pleated pockets that might have been carved from a hard, dark wood. His medal ribbons, straps, belts, buckles, tabs, collar and tie seemed so permanently perfect that it was possible to imagine that the single drop of moisture that had fallen from Mina's glass on his lapel would shortly sizzle and evaporate itself, out of shame.

Even his hair and skin seemed to be made of some costly inhuman material. The grey hairs were perfectly grey, the white hairs were perfectly white, and each colour was sharply divided from the other – white at the temples, grey elsewhere. His eyes were blue marbles made of the finest and most highly polished glass, while his skin was of that beautiful, parchment-like leather found only in the suitcases of. millionaires.

'Major,' continued the General, 'Want your report, now. Outside. My compliments, Mrs Houghton, and truly grateful. Come.'

He left the room, and everyone seemed suddenly able to breathe.

'Wow . . .!' said Bem.

Scott looked at Blythe. He was fingering a scar on his cheek and staring at nothing.

'First that rather stupid Major,' said Mrs Houghton weakly, 'And now . . .'

'Now, the General. General Hartman. Now *him*,' said Blythe. 'It would have to be *him* . . .' Blythe suddenly looked ill. Scott felt sorry for him.

'Well, I'd rather have the General in charge than that Major,' said Scott.

'The Major is moronic,' said Bem. 'Moron Major. Major Disaster.'

'But the General – well, he's quite something,' said Scott. 'Isn't he, Icarus?' The nickname slipped out.

Blythe appeared not to have heard for a moment. Then he stopped fingering his scar and said, 'Oh, the General. General Hartman. General Hartman, Scott, is' as you said – quite something. Quite something. "Heartless Hartman", no less . . . I think he is the most dangerous man I've ever met.'

Mrs Houghton smiled and said, 'Surely, Mr Blythe, you don't really mean that?'

'I do.'

'But why?'

'Because he never has doubts. And he always gets action.'

'But I still don't see –'

'Suppose, Mrs Houghton, that the General was absolutely wrong about something very important.'

The General was efficient. The General was a leader. The General was an organizer. And the General was everywhere.

Under his command, Harbourtown West became overnight a barracks and everyone in the town a conscript. Suddenly, it seemed, you could no longer park your car outside the library – the space was sealed off with white ropes and filled with brown Army vehicles. So you tried the little square, where there were parking meters. But now there were never any meters vacant – the spaces that had been yours were painted with new yellow lines and the meters themselves had their heads in bags marked 'OUT OF ORDER'.

There seemed suddenly to be quite a number of loud-speakers in the town. They blossomed overnight, growing on lamp posts and telegraph poles. Music came out of them but also mysterious messages: 'B company personnel report HQ oblique Three Seven I will repeat that HQ oblique THUR-REE SEV-ENN. Out.'

Everyone said, 'Well, I suppose there is good reason for it.'

Or suppose you were Billy, Mina's soldier. Billy played the guitar. For years now, Billy and his friends had practised whenever they could. Wherever the Army sent him, Billy always found friends to play the guitar with. In Harbourtown West, he met a young man called Bert, a garage mechanic.

One night, Bert was walking along through the sleeping streets after a guitar session with Billy – it was three in the morning – when a huge shape moved out of the shadows and a hard voice said, 'Halt! Who goes there?' It was a soldier in a glinting steel helmet and a wicked looking rifle.

Bert was so frightened he dropped his guitar case. The guitar case made a hollow sound as it hit the pavement – but a far worse sound came from within the case. Bert knew what it was: it was his guitar, the guitar, the finest and most expensive guitar in Harbourtown West, breaking its neck with the shock of the fall.

'—!' said Bert, and instinctively lunged forward towards the guitar.

The soldier jabbed with his rifle and broke one of Bert's teeth.

Bert must have gone a little mad. He kept pushing the soldier away from the place where the guitar lay, then kicking and punching. The soldier, who had not meant to hurt anyone, had to defend himself. Bert spent the night in jail.

Next morning, Bert appeared in the court of justice and gave his evidence as clearly as he could through a swollen mouth. The Chief Magistrate of the three, an old man in a thoroughly bad temper, kept shuffling his papers impatiently and muttering 'Can't *hear*. Can't *hear*.' The Clerk of the Court barked 'SPEAK UP!' and Bert mumbled louder. Then the sentry was called to give evidence.

But at this moment, a soldier's voice bellowed 'SAH!' and the General was striding up the centre of the Court, and Bert and the soldier were quite forgotten. Could the General be granted the privilege of saying a few words? The magistrate supposed so, but it was most irregular. Could the General ask the Court to allow the military forces to take what action was necessary? The Court hummed and hawed. Might the General remind the Court that the soldier was under military discipline and it was only proper that he be tried by the military authorities? The Court uneasily agreed. Could the General draw the Court's attention to the very serious nature of the situation in Harbourtown West and ask all possible cooperation in maintaining discipline, both civil and military, during the present emergency? The Court was not quite clear as to what the General meant either by 'cooperation' or 'emergency', but supposed there was no objection. Might the General approach the magistrates and speak to them privately?

The magistrates obviously disliked this idea, but there seemed no way of stopping the General. He was already marching towards the Bench. They surrendered to the determined, spotless, disciplined figure approaching them and listened while he spoke to them so quietly that no one else could hear.

Then the Chief Magistrate growled 'Case dismissed!' The soldier saluted: a Sergeant standing near him told him he shouldn't have done: the soldier turned red, thumped clumsily down the stairs and was gone. The General bowed to the magistrates, about-turned and left the court, his heels echoing on the floor. The clerk of the Court shouted, 'Order in court!' quite needlessly, for no one had made a sound. The affair was over.

Yet no one could stop talking about it. Some people took it very badly. Mr Houghton was furious and his wife uneasy.

'What does he mean, that General, walking into our courthouse and running our affairs for us?'

'You'd think we had a military government . . .'

A day or so after, everyone had cooled down. 'Well,' they said, 'There must be a good reason for it. That General seems to know what he's doing . . .'

But Icarus Blythe, white-faced, would not discuss the matter at all.

'I suppose there must be a good reason for it,' said Scott uncertainly.

Bem said, '*What* good reason?'

'Well, the General's idea of cleaning up the place. The Trillions are everywhere. All over the place. Someone's got to get rid of them. It may as well be us. It might even be fun, going around with a little barrow and brooms and shovels –'

'Fun . . .!' said Bem.

'Well, there's our barrow,' said Scott. And there it was indeed. An Army-brown metal wheelbarrow with hooks on the side to carry the Broom (1) Army Issue, and Shovels (2) Army Issue.

'G stroke One Eleven stroke A Two, Double-you Dee,' said Panda, reading out the number stencilled on the side of the barrow. 'Proper old hot-rod.'

'They say we've got to make up teams,' said Scott.

'You make up a team,' replied Bem. 'You're the leader. You're the biggest and oldest. Make up a team.' He made a small rude noise.

'All right, I will!' said Scott, jumping to his feet. 'You, me, Panda – '

' – And Mina,' said Panda.

'Why Mina? For goodness' sake, why her?'

'Because if anyone can find a way of getting us out of pushing a barrow – Mina can!'

'All right, all right!' said Bem gloomily. 'Barrows . . . Shovels . . . *Mina* . . .'

The streets were filled with barrows, boys and girls. The barrows squeaked and thumped and clanged. The boys yelled, bumped barrows and dropped spades on people's feet. The girls screamed 'Don't!' and 'Stop it!' or just stood bending forward from the hips, shouting gossip into each other's faces.

Yet, slowly, order came from this chaos. Someone discovered that the only way to keep his team together was to invent a rallying call: someone else made a rival call; and soon, every team had its own cry.

So while one boy shouted, 'TRILLy-willy-willions!' you could hear another farther down the road hooting, 'Yodel-AY-EE-TEE!' like a Swiss shepherd. Scott's call was quite simply, 'HI HO TRILLIONS!'

Quite soon, the teams actually went to work. You crashed

your barrow against everyone else's, made your way to any place where there were drifts of Trillions – Trillions were everywhere – and shovelled them up. The shovels made a good loud scraping noise, the Trillions were clean and light and easy to swing into the barrow (the smaller children used plastic buckets and spades) so everyone was kept busy. When the barrow was something like full, you shouted your rallying cry and hurtled the barrow along the road to the dumping ground, crashing into any other barrows you met on the way. Finally, you tipped out the load of Trillions on to the fast-growing heap.

Soon this heap became a pyramid of considerable size and some soldiers constructed a raised walk from planks and steel tubing. This made the tipping more amusing – it was quite dramatic to trundle your barrow along the echoing planks, then stop with a jerk – thrust the handles up and forward – and watch the glistening, twinkling Trillions fall away from you, in a glittering curve, to spill over the top of the pyramid. Some children jumped in on top of the pile, whooping with joy, but the soldiers soon stopped this.

Meanwhile, a whole team of soldiers was bulldozing a site right beside the Trillions dump. This was worth watching. The giant yellow bulldozers chuntered and thundered, screamed and yelped. Tons of earth were pushed this way and that by vast, curved blades, their steel polished by the work. Nonchalant soldiers perched on top of these yellow monsters, pulling levers, baring biceps, lighting cigarettes and twisting the peaks of their caps into rakish shapes.

'What are you doing?' Panda asked one of them.

'Trillion trap!' shouted the soldier. 'Make a big hole, then a special machine to get rid of the Trillions. General's orders. Now stand clear, sweetheart!'

'Special machine?' said Bem to Scott. 'What can he mean, special machine?'

'What can he mean, special machine!' sang Mina, prancing about to the rhythm of the words. 'Special machine! What can he mean!'

Bem scowled. Scott decided to have another talk with Icarus.

Icarus was always surprisingly easy to find and surprisingly easy to talk to. Before Scott had come to accept Blythe – before Mr Blythe had become Icarus to Scott and his friends – this had been a puzzle. After all, Icarus Blythe was an important and famous man who had been sent by the government to examine and report on a matter of world importance – the coming of the Trillions. Telephones rang and voices asked for Mr Blythe. Big cars whisked Mr Blythe to airports. Military and civil aircraft carried Mr Blythe to London, Washington, Paris, anywhere. Yet somehow he managed to return frequently to Harbourtown, where he spent most of his time in the public library. Scott asked him why. Icarus pointed to a sign that read, NO TALKING.

'Oh, I'm sorry,' said Scott.

'I didn't mean you,' said Icarus, smiling slightly. 'I meant *them*. I escape them here.'

Scott did not like to ask the next question, but asked it all the same. 'Why?' he said. 'What have you got against them? Which them?'

'I mean the people who don't know,' said Icarus, 'and the people who think they know. I mean most people who ask questions, and everyone who asks the wrong questions.'

He had raised his voice. Now, he pointed again at the notice; gave a small smile; and said, 'Let's get out of here. I need a walk. And you've got something on your mind.'

They walked, fast but without purpose. Scott was on Icarus's blind side. He could look up at the expressionless face and study the small scars round the blinded eye, the tight mouth with the firm-set creases at its corners, the hand that had been broken and repaired. He felt as if he were spying but continued to observe. Soon he found himself running out of breath: Icarus was walking faster and faster, with no apparent effort. Scott set himself to keep up and thought, 'This man looks like an athlete and a college professor and a soldier and an invalid and a success and a failure . . . I don't understand him at all.'

Suddenly Icarus stopped. 'It's the reporters I can't stand. Do you know what "human interest" means, Scott? I'm "human interest". So are you, but not so much as that little girl, Mina. I am "human interest" because I was once a spaceman, a pioneer, a hero. I went up there and the whole world watched with one eye and ate TV snacks. And then things went wrong up there and they forgot all about the snacks. They watched with both eyes – watched like hawks – when things went wrong. I suppose all sorts of dear old people said all sorts of dear old prayers and all the children said "Wow!" and "Gee!" and "Gosh!" And I suppose not one person in a million saw what it was all about . . .'

'What was it all about?' said Scott at last.

'Whatever it was, it wasn't "human interest". It wasn't about a man in space, or what his wife thought about it, or whether his mother worried, or how he ate his meals – '

'Or what happened when the heat shield failed and you got your – your – '

'You're just the same as the rest, Scott. You want to hear the gory details, the "human interest", don't you?'

'No. Yes, I suppose so. But not so much as I want to understand what you are talking about.' Scott found himself losing his temper. The words rushed out. 'You ought to try and explain! It's not fair, doing what you do. You just complain and sound bitter and start saying something and then shut yourself up and then criticize *me*! . . .'

Blythe, for the first time since Scott had known him, suddenly looked human and ordinary – and ashamed. When he began talking again, even his voice had changed. It was urgent, interested, warm.

'You're right. Absolutely right. I apologize, and now I'm going to explain. And first, I'll tell you why I am explaining to you, and not to anyone else. It's because you have an open mind. It's because you are *not an adult* . . .'

He seemed unable to continue with this thought and started again.

'Scott,' he said, 'tell me what would happen if your father lost all his business. No money, nothing. What would happen?'

'I don't know. I suppose he would have to begin all over again – find ways of raising money, paying his debts – '

'Fine. He would start all over again – but he would start along the same road, wouldn't he? He wouldn't say to himself, "Well, I am completely lost. I am not *me* any more." Right?'

'All right.'

'But now take a child. A very young child, with a smiling mother and a kind father. They take that child, put it in the family car, drive out to a desert. Then the mother, still smiling, throws the child out of the car. The father, still smiling, begins to drive off. The child tries to follow. It's in pain, it's crying, it's hysterical, screaming – it tries to follow the car. But the car just keeps going and the mother keeps smiling and the father turns round to wave. And then the car gathers speed and is gone. The child is alone in a strange place. What happens to that child, Scott?'

'It must die. It will starve or go mad or . . . look, I don't understand, I don't like this idea about the child – '

'Does it frighten you, Scott?'

'All right, it frightens me. Is that what you are after?'

'No, I want to explain to you. Scott, just once or twice in your life, you have felt what the child in the desert must feel. Perhaps you had no reason to feel it, but you felt it all the same and you are young enough to remember it. Right?'

'Yes ... Once I got locked in the tool shed. After a time I knew I was going to die there. I just knew it was the end. That was after I had finished screaming and yelling ... It was when I was quiet that I *knew* ...'

Scott shook himself.

'And it still makes you shudder. Later, Scott, you will remember that time without shuddering. You will remember it as something that happens to small boys if they are not careful in garden sheds. By then, you will be like any other adult. You will have learned all kinds of rules and ways of doing things, thinking about things, just as I did when I was being trained for space.

'Then one day, you *are* in space. In a capsule. You know everything there is to know about what you are doing. You know that whatever happens, there is a button to push, a procedure, a course of action. You know you are in danger. You know you may die – but your training covers that too. More buttons. In case of death, push button B.

'Suddenly, things go wrong. The ship goes mad, it's spinning, tumbling, throwing you face-first into all those familiar buttons. You feel yourself being broken, pieces of you smashed. But all the time, there is a calm voice inside you. Deep down, you still know *what to do*. It's all in the book.'

'Then it turns out though everything is smashed and broken, including you, the panic is over. You are alive and alone. Alone, Scott, really *alone* ...

'But you make yourself get used to it. The hours pass and you learn to live with it. Your watch tells you that a morning has passed, or a day, or a night: they all look the same up there, you just have to believe your watch. I got very fond of my watch, Scott ...' He showed Scott his wristwatch; there was a curved scar in the metal of the case. 'To me, this watch was humankind. It ticked. It was alive. I used to hold it up to my ear and just listen to it, ticking and ticking.

He paused. Scott suddenly saw a vision, like a photograph appearing in his mind, of the solitary figure in the space capsule. The figure was like a huge, elaborate, insect-like toy. It had a glinting, glassy, bulbous head. Its skin was of metallic silver material. Outside its body were veins – tubes and pipes and wires. But inside the glass-globe head there was a human face, in pain. And from one of the silvery arm-tubes there dangled a human hand, a brown hand with hairs on the back of it, nails on each finger tip and human warmth inside it. The hand moved uneasily and blood dripped from one finger.

'That loneliness . . .' Icarus went on. 'I got used to it. They say you can get used to anything, I don't know. But I got used to my own loneliness after a day or two – or three, I don't know how long. But then, Scott, something came up that I hadn't been expecting. I got used to my own loneliness, but I found there was another sort of loneliness I couldn't get used to. *Its* loneliness! The loneliness of space itself!

'And that's when the nightmare really began. I don't know how to describe this, Scott, but I'll try. They tell you that space is emptiness, nothingness – the void. They suggest that space, empty space, is something negative. I found out that it's not! Space *lives*, Scott. Nothingness, emptiness, has a life all its own.'

They kept walking.

'I found,' said Icarus, 'that space has got its own . . . *atmosphere*. That's a silly word to use! Atmosphere is just what outer space *hasn't* got. But you know what I mean. When I look back and remember space, I can almost smell it, feel it, touch it.'

'What sort of atmosphere had space?' asked Scott.

Icarus replied with one word. 'Alien.'

'Alien?'

'Alone, Apart, Foreign. Unlike anything known to man. Alien.'

'Alien good, or alien bad?'

It took a long time for Blythe to reply. At last he said, 'That's the puzzle. That's the mystery. How can you tell? How can you begin to understand something completely alien? Good, bad, I don't know. All I know is – alien.'

Icarus limped away, fast. Scott was left wondering.

He stayed wondering all day and continued wondering in bed that night.

'We'll never understand, never!' Icarus had said. What had he meant? Could you 'understand' a honey bee? Perhaps he had meant, 'We'll never get through, establish contact, be useful to each other.' Honey bees were useful to humans, so humans made themselves useful to honey bees. Give a hive, take some honey.

The trouble was that Trillions had nothing to offer us and we had nothing to offer them.

And yet, thought Scott, Trillions 'try'. They imitate, make shapes, appear to want to play our game. While all we do is talk about them, write about them, make big newspaper and TV stories about them. Trillions try: we don't.

Scott got into bed and looked around him. There was a dusting of Trillions on the window sill and a powdering of them on the floor. He got out of bed and opened the window. The window ledge was coated inches deep with Trillions. He scooped them up with his hands and put them on the sheet of drawing paper on his table. Soon he had a big heap of Trillions. He sat on the edge of his bed staring at them.

Aliens.

There was a scrawling mark on the paper. Some Trillions were busily beginning to reproduce the mark. Scott watched for a little while, sighed and went back to his bed. The Trillions puzzled him, Icarus puzzled him. He got into bed and turned out the light.

In the darkness, he thought he could just hear the very faint scratch and scrabble of the Trillions as they linked and climbed over each other. Scott turned over in bed and tried to ignore the tiny sounds.

Ah! he thought, I am falling asleep. Gratefully, he allowed the familiar fall-asleep processes of his brain to take over. Colours, picture, snatches of rhyme came into his head from nowhere. He welcomed them. Soon the screen of his brain would go dark and he would sleep.

Charlie Chaplin went to France
To teach the natives how to dance

said his brain. Children skipping. Rope twirls, skinny legs jump.

First he did the rumba
Then he did the kicks
Then he did the turnabout
Then he did the splits

said his brain. But Scott found himself replying, 'No!' He turned over again and his eyes opened. What was wrong?

'Kicks' and 'splits' did not rhyme.

He started another rhyme.

A,B,C,D,E,F,G
That's what teacher said to me

ABC! Teacher! He sat up in bed, wide awake; switched on the light and went to work.

It took him a week to teach the Trillions their ABC. A week that seemed endless. A week that made Scott think that if the Trillions had any intelligence, they were very clever at hiding it.

His method was simple. He wrote an A and the Trillions 'formed' to imitate it. When they were half-way to completing their imitation, he wrote more A's. This confused their purpose. Some Trillions would break away from the A already half-formed to enlist in the armies making new A's. They became so confused that often A's would be formed without the Trillions following a pattern. Eventually, he could write one single small A, watch too many Trillions queueing to form it, scatter the heap and stand back: within minutes, there would be small A's everywhere.

The B's, C's, D's – all the letters of the alphabet. By the end of the week, they could form words. Scott would write WORD once: the Trillions would swarm around the writing: then disperse themselves into groups to make WORD WORD WORD WORD WORD WORD WORD, all over the floor.

At this stage, Scott collected more Trillions from the streets and tried to make them perform the same trick. They could not at first. They had to blend themselves into the mass of trained Trillions. Then they could perform.

'So my trained Trillions are different from just any old Trillions,' thought Scott. 'They can learn. The trouble is, they have no idea of the meaning of what they've learned. They can write WORD without knowing what a Word is. How can I teach them that?'

School routines were broken up. School in the morning: Trillions in the afternoon. Each day Scott's team spent three hours in the noisy streets, where the loud speakers were always pouring out their mixture of soothing music and barked commands and the trucks roared by and the soldiers worked at nothing in particular and the journalists and TV crews went about their mysteries.

This was all wasted time.

More of Scott's hours were taken up with eating, sleeping, being a member of a family. This was wasted time too. All Scott wanted was to get back to his Trillions spelling bee and to the problem of making the Trillions understand what writing was *for*.

He found the answer by accident.

During one 'lesson', he had the radio on. He worked so long and late that by the time the lesson was finished, the station had closed down. All that remained on the air was a single whining note. He turned the radio off. The sound annoyed him.

Immediately, the Trillions slowed down. He tried to get them working again, but it was as if they were on strike.

He turned on the radio. The whistling note sounded. The Trillions busily returned to work.

Excited, Scott got out his xylophone – a good toy instrument he had never wished to throw away. He found the note on the xylophone that corresponded to the note sounding from the radio; turned the radio off; and played the xylophone note instead.

The Trillions were happy with it. They went on working, making R's.

Scott bent down and busily destroyed all the R's with his hands. The Trillions were now just so much dust, all over the floor. Then he sounded the xylophone note and kept sounding it. Slowly at first, then faster and faster, the Trillions began to form R's.

His mother appeared in the doorway, half asleep and wearing her nightdress. 'Scott . . What *are* you doing? For goodness' sake, it's long after midnight . . .'

'Sorry Mother, I was trying something out.'

'Well, try it out tomorrow! Whatever it is, it can't be so important that —'

'It is important, very important —' Scott blurted out. And immediately wished he had not.

She stood looking at him, uncertainly. His face seemed to her suddenly older, and unfamiliar. What *was* he up to?

'You can't carry the whole world on your shoulders, Scott . . .'

'Of course not, Mother. Good night.'

Had anyone been able to carry the world on their shoulders at this time, he would have found it an uncomfortable burden. Trillions fell and 'formed' their strange, often frightening, shapes: the world got in a temper, partly from fear but mostly from habit. Primitive tribes squatted on the ground, made sacrifices and blamed their gods. Grown-up nations sat round tables, made speeches and blamed each other for all kinds of things having nothing to do with Trillions.

In Harbourtown, still more Trillions fell — a great storm shower of them. And the Major announced over the loud-speakers a major offensive against the Trillions, centered on an Exterminator — a machine that was to destroy the Trillions fed into it. Meanwhile, all Trillion truck teams were to report for duty, immediately. So Scott could not start until evening.

He took his sheets of white paper and scattered Trillions over them. Some of the Trillions shifted and moved without purpose.

He sounded the note that meant R on the xylophone. The Trillions formed R's. Scott scattered them before the letters were formed, then sounded the note again.

'It all depends on whether they *like* work,' he murmured to himself. Once again, the Trillions were forming the letter

R. As long as the note sounded, they worked fast and hard. Scott scattered them again. 'R means the note – the note means R. Go on, blast you! R means the note – the note means R.'

There was silence. Scott would not sound the note. The Trillions would not form.

'Go on, go *on* ...!' grated Scott. He sounded the xylophone, then muted the note with his finger. Some Trillions moved, then subsided. It went on like this for an hour, for two hours. Scott found his jaws were aching: he had been clenching his teeth in the effort to force his will on the Trillions – to point a ray from his mind, almost, at the little glittering heaps.

At last they obeyed. Though Scott had sounded the note only in his mind, there was a sudden scurry of movement on one piece of paper. Some Trillions were forming. Scott craned towards them, growling 'Go on, go on, go on! R! R!'

The Trillions formed an R. Scott let out a great shout of 'Whoopee!' Then 'thought' the note harder still.

All the Trillions formed, furiously. There were R's everywhere! Scott tried to reach over his own shoulder to pat himself on the back. He couldn't, and giggled instead. Then he sat down to work out the next steps in the Trillions' education.

'They like work,' he said to himself. 'They want a master – someone to tell them what to do. They've learned. Fine. And now ... what?'

Outside, the Trillion trucks rattled and banged in the streets, the children whooped and hollered.

Scott told his mother that he had something wrong with his stomach – he felt sick. She looked hard at his face. It was white and there were dark patches under his eyes. 'They won't like it,' she said. 'Your being away from the Trillion

Truck, I mean. They're very strict about it. But you do look ill, you really do . . .'

'I feel ill,' Scott said. He did, too. Ill with excitement. Ill with a fever to get back to his room, to his Trillions, to the next step forward.

'Well, I'll see to it,' said his mother. 'Could you eat an omelette, do you think?'

'Oh, yes!' said Scott. 'A big – I mean a bit of one.'

He ate the omelette, drank three glasses of milk, took two apples, a banana and an orange while his mother's back was turned, and made sure that he walked slowly and heavily up the stairs, like someone feeling ill.

Then he closed his bedroom door behind him, took a deep breath and said to the Trillions, 'All right. Back to work!'

Later, he was glad of the fruit. He had not imagined how exhausting it would be – how hard it was to aim his mind as if it was a rifle, to shoot his will at the Trillions like a bullet – and to keep aiming, keep shooting, without ever relaxing, until the Trillions could 'hear' his mind as well as they could hear the note of the xylophone.

By evening, the xylophone had been pushed back under the bed. It was no longer needed: the Trillions had learned to obey the commands 'start', 'stop', 'all', and 'only you'. Scott threw these commands at them with his brain. Now he could make groups of Trillions, or all the Trillions, start to form – or stop forming.

He taught them to use the alphabet. He would think A – form a picture of the letter in his mind, then beam it at the Trillions. Then he would think, 'Start A' – 'Stop A' – 'All start A' – 'Only you start A' – and the Trillions would mesh and climb and gear and build.

'You really don't look well, Scott,' said his mother at dinner that night. 'I've never seen you look so pale. You'd better stay home tomorrow. I'll send word to the Trillion Truck sergeant.'

'All right, mother,' Scott said meekly. To himself, he said, 'And I'll send words to the Trillions. Not just letters. Whole words!'

But then, just as the lessons were reaching the most interesting stage, they had to stop. The General was back: the General was on the warpath. You could tell when the General was on the warpath, simply by watching him march along it. During the past twenty-four hours he had marched up and down, back and forth, to and fro, at enormous speed. The Major had almost to trot to keep up with him. The Lieutenants, non-commissioned officers and mere private soldiers who always attended the General – they formed a small private army – scuttled along behind, looking tough, determined, fearless and baffled.

The townspeople looked baffled too. What were the army people up to?

Mina found out, simply by asking.

She had long since lost her slight fear of the General. He was, after all, only a man, and Mina thought of males as spiders think of flies. Once she had very nearly managed to sit on his lap, but the General escaped by standing up, rather quickly.

You could just detect an air of caution in the attitude of the General now, as Mina approached. The General and his staff happened to be in the Houghton living-room where some local maps had been left. Mr Houghton and Icarus were there. No one else, of course, could have got near the General for he was ringed round by his staff and busily consulting a map held on a clipboard. Mina broke through the circle simply by piping 'Excuse *me*! Excuse *me*!' in a piercingly sweet voice. She attracted the General's attention equally simply: she took hold of his tunic and pulled.

'Aren't your soldiers working *hard*, Mister General?' she said.

The General pretended only just to have noticed her; saluted; and replied, 'Yes, my dear. So am I. Run along, if you please.'

'And the lights are on all night where they're building the Sterminator, aren't they, Mister General?' she continued brightly.

'Exterminator,' the General corrected her. 'And good day to you.'

'But what's the good of the Sterminator, Mister General?' said Mina.

'Gets rid of Trillions.'

'But more and more Trillions keep coming down, don't they, Mister General?' Mina said.

The General said, 'Quite so, highly observant. Now, if you please – '

Then Mina asked the question that everyone in Harbourtown West wanted to ask. 'What's the good of it all, then?' she said sweetly.

'What indeed,' said the General. Then he saluted, turned on his heel and marched away. Mina simply turned to the Major and continued her questions. 'Why don't you blow up all the Trillions, Mister Major?' she said. 'I bet you could! With a great big gun!'

The Major knew even less than the General how to deal with the awful sweetness, the sweet awfulness, of this terrible little girl who asked questions. He swelled and said, 'Ha ha ha.' But Mina had fixed him with her big beautiful eyes: he had to say something more.

'No need for great big guns, little girl! TNW, that's the medicine!'

'TNW?' cried Mina, her voice louder and clearer than any bell – 'TNW? I've never heard of TNW! What's TNW?'

The General had stopped in his tracks. He turned to the Major. Everyone saw that the General's leather face had gone an odd colour, as if the leather had been lightly dusted with talcum powder.

'Major!' he almost shouted. 'Here if you please!'

'TNW?' repeated Mina, knowing full well that the cat had been let out of the bag – and she had opened it. 'What a funny name for medicine! Tee . . . Enn . . . Doubleyew!'

Everyone but Mina seemed frozen. The Major looked as if he had been punctured. The General seemed turned to dusty stone. Scott's father was staring fixedly at the General. Icarus Blythe, who had been almost lying in an armchair, was on his feet.

Then everyone was talking and moving at once.

'Can I have some TNW?' said Mina. 'Can we all have some?'

'We can all have some,' Blythe repeated after her. 'Now run along.' He looked very angry indeed.

Mrs Houghton entered the room and said, 'What is all this?'

Bem answered. 'T for Tactical. N for Nuclear. W for weapons. TNW. That's right, isn't it, Icarus?'

'You mean – nuclear weapons, here – here in Harbourtown West . . .?' asked Mrs Houghton, faintly. 'But that's absurd!'

'Quite absurd,' said Icarus bleakly.

'The Trillions haven't actually *done* anything . . .' Mrs Houghton said. 'They just – just build their silly structures – they don't *mean* anything, do they?'

Icarus shook his head.

'Then why this talk about nuclear weapons? What *for*? What's the good of it? What will happen?'

'Nothing good,' said Mr Houghton, grimly. 'What does happen when you start messing about with these weapons? How will it affect us?'

Icarus, Scott saw, was becoming more than just angry. His movements were jerky and uneasy. His scars were white. His voice was unsteady.

'Nobody knows much about nuclear weapons. Tactical nuclear weapons are small weapons, supposed to have a strictly local effect. A sort of nuclear machine gun, if you like, instead of a nuclear bomb. But poisonous all the same ... because nuclear weapons don't merely burn, blast and break things. They can alter life forms. They distort and twist, change the way things grow, destroy the patterns of nature. Once you start messing about with nuclear devices –'

'Mr Blythe,' the General cut through, 'we face menace. Or rather, fail to face it. I have yet to observe a statesman, or politician or – ' the words came out as an insult – '*man of science* like yourself, offer a positive answer to a definite menace. Wet hens in a thunderstorm. Therefore –'

'Therefore you'll lead us into even worse trouble with nuclear weapons,' said Blythe.

'I shall lead you,' said the General. 'I shall most certainly lead. And you, in your *advisory* capacity, will follow. Be quite clear about that.'

There was a knock on the door and a young Lieutenant entered without waiting for anyone to say 'Come in'. He saluted, yelped 'Sir!' to the General, and said, 'Trouble, sir. They've been forming. In the harbour. Enlarging the fort, sir.'

'Trillions?'

'Yes, sir, Trillions –'

'Then say so.'

The General swept out. 'I think it's about time,' said Mrs Houghton, 'that the General stopped using this house as a sort of unofficial headquarters. At first it was just inconvenient, but now –'

'For that matter, it's about time they stopped using our town as a military HQ for the western world,' said Mr Houghton bitterly.

'Oh, they'll move out of your home,' said Blythe. 'The General has got his soldiers building for him. But leave this town – no, I don't think so. Why? Because Trillions started here. Because Trillions are still happening here. Because Harbourtown is a perfect test area. But above all, because the General is determined to *act* . . . and he can't get the authority.'

'He certainly won't get it from the United Nations,' said Mr Houghton. 'That business on television – nations walking out – hopeless.'

'He won't get it from his own superiors either,' said Blythe. 'They can't make up their minds. So he's forming his own military empire, here in Harbourtown.'

'So we're to be the guinea-pig town,' said Mrs Houghton faintly. 'The General's "test area" . . . The playground for the man of action . . .'

No one could think of anything to say.

There was a mild sun over the harbour, giving the little waves a milky glitter. A great many people crowded the walls. They all looked towards the knot of boats in the widest part of the harbour bowl. The boats bobbed together. In the centre of them was the Harbourmaster's launch, a bigger vessel than the others, which rolled slightly in a dignified way. Standing on its decks were four glistening figures in underwater gear, black rubber with yellow seams. One was reloading an underwater camera.

Scott nodded to Bem and Blythe. Without a word, they

got into Mr Houghton's fibreglass dinghy and quietly rowed out to join the knot of boats. As they splashed through the water, they could observe the young Lieutenant going from one group to another on the shore, obviously asking for a boat to take the General out. No one was being very helpful.

When they reached the boats, everything was quiet and they could hear every word that was being said on the launch . . .

'About two hours, probably sooner,' said the skin-diver with the camera. 'Or I could get down there again and take Polaroids. Then you wouldn't have to wait for the films to be processed. Only I've left the Polaroid back for the camera at home – '

'I don't see why you need panic about photographs,' said another skin-diver. 'Just get a mask on and snorkel, and go and see for yourself. It's all there, only a few feet down. Like a toy fortress rising from the seabed. You know, walls and towers – like we said. About seventy feet high and three hundred feet long. All made of Trillions. It's just like a fortress, a toy fort.'

'A toy fortress, you said?' repeated a reporter, looking up from his notepad.

'For heaven's *sake* – ' said the skin-diver disgustedly. 'How many more times . . .'

There seemed nothing to say or do for the moment. Some people peered over the edge of their boats, trying to glimpse the tops of the towers. The photographers fiddled with their cameras. The hard blonde reporter, who always seemed to be everywhere, put down a portable tape recorder and picked up a lipstick.

Then the General arrived. The Lieutenant had persuaded someone to lend him a little dinghy. A sweating soldier rowed, another carried the General's valise and a walkie-talkie, the Lieutenant knelt to attention in the bows and the

General sat bolt upright in the stern. Heads turned to watch
the approaching boatload. The soldier at the oars, unused to
his work, was digging at the water: the boat came forward
in uncertain spurts and jumps. At each dig of the oars,
another gallon or so of water would spill over the gun-
whales and into the overloaded boat. The General's
magnificent boots were already awash to the ankles. He did
not condescend to notice this, though by moving his feet a
few inches they would have remained dry.

'Halt!' said the General as his dinghy bumped into the
others. Then, 'Radio Operator!' The soldier handed him the
walkie-talkie.

'Clear this area!' barked the General. Voices babbled, but
the General took no notice. Sure enough, the knot of small
boats began to break up and make for the shore.

The General addressed his walkie-talkie. 'TNW section,
report!' he ordered. The walkie-talkie squeaked a response.

'But General –' said Icarus.

'You will kindly leave the area,' said the General, staring
through him and returning his attention to the walkie-talkie.
'TNW section, prepare to receive your orders!' said the General.

Later, only three craft were visible in the harbour waters,
all manned by soldiers. Two of the boats were armed with
small, shining tubular weapons, whose barrels were pointed
downwards into the water.

In the third craft sat the General, like a figure carved from
mahogany.

Icarus, white with fury, either had nothing to say or was
too choked with rage to say it. Scott could get nothing out of
him. Perhaps it was Panda's large black eyes, staring at him
as mournfully as a dog's, that at last made him forget his
own rage and think of things that mattered more. He picked

67

up Panda and sat her on his lap and talked over the top of her head to Scott.

'How far have you got with your Trillions?'

'Much farther. I didn't want to tell anyone until I was quite sure, but –'

'Scott, it's either these – these military morons – or us. Either we can do it the right way, your way, or they'll be blasting off their TNWS ... and to hell with Harbourtown West and everywhere else. Once they've started, there is no telling where it will end –'

He glanced down at Panda and checked himself.

'Scott, you've *got* to succeed. Fast. You've *got* to get in touch with the Trillions – understand them, talk to them, anything you like ... Is there anything that Bem or I can do to help?'

'I don't think so. It's a job for one person and I'm doing very well. If only I could make things go faster!' Scott got up, scratched his head and stared out over the harbour. The shining tubes of the nuclear guns caught the sun.

'I'm going back home,' said Scott. 'I'm going to try –'

But at that moment, the loudspeakers began to blare. 'EVERYONE IS TO RETURN TO THEIR OWN HOMES AND STAY INDOORS UNTIL FURTHER INSTRUCTIONS. STAY INDOORS UNTIL FURTHER INSTRUCTIONS. EVERYONE IS TO RETURN TO THEIR OWN HOMES–'

The loudspeakers were drowned by the roar of military trucks. The trucks stopped at intervals, soldiers jumped down and began to shepherd the people away from the sea wall and back to their homes.

The General still sat bolt upright in his boat and the little figures of the soldiers were busier than ever over the glinting guns.

The explosions, when they came, hardly disturbed Scott.
They were not loud. They barely shook the window panes.
He turned his head towards the window of his bedroom,
half expecting to see smoke arising from the area of water
where the nuclear weapons had been fired, but there was no
smoke. He stared unseeingly for a little while, then shook his
head and returned to what really mattered: his Trillions.

Soon, he knew, they would be able to 'talk'.

The floor of his room was littered with big sheets of
paper, each with a single word written on it with a felt-
nibbed pen: STOP. START. WORK. SCOTT. TRILLIONS.

The discarded sheets were weighted down with Trillions.
A sheet on which was written the word DANCE had attracted a mass of Trillions who had exactly imitated the
word. But the sheet that Scott looked at again and again had
the word WORK written on it in his handwriting – and on
this sheet, the Trillions had written the word START.

Scott thrilled. For he knew now that the Trillions could do
more than merely imitate. They could make a reply, express
a thought. They could tell him, in words, that they wanted
the WORK to START.

The General, too, was happy.

The underwater fortress of Trillions was destroyed – it
had crumbled to nothing under the blasting shock of the
nuclear blast. All that was left, according to the radar echoes,
was a flat surface, a mixture of sand, silt and of course Trillions. Eventually, when any risk of contamination was over,

skin-divers could go down and see for themselves. But in the meantime, the radar waves told a story that everyone could believe – even Icarus.

So now Icarus fell from favour in Harbourtown West, and the townspeople began to speak highly of the General. You had to hand it to him – he got things moving! He got action!

People who supported Icarus replied, 'Action against what? A structure that happened to look like a toy fortress – a fort without weapons or soldiers?' But the supporters of the General shrugged, even when the fish killed by the explosion came to the surface of the harbour waters, floated belly-up against the harbour wall and began to rot and stink. And soon, things happened in Harbourtown that made everyone forget the smell of dead fish; things that made it seem all the more likely that the General was right and that the Trillions were deliberate enemies of mankind. For instance . . .

Mr Binding was a very old man who lived in the old people's home. He loved cherries – they reminded him of summer in the country when he was a boy.

One day, a van called at the home and men delivered baskets of shining cherries – a treat for tomorrow. But Mr Binding wanted cherries today.

Quite late that night, Mr Binding put on his slippers, crept down the stairs in the dark, found his way to the larder and – using his nightclothes as a basket – collected a private feast of cherries.

Still in the dark, he ate them all, one by one. As he ate, his old eyes grew round with greed; his old gums crushed the soft flesh of the fruit (you do not need teeth to eat cherries); and his old, brown-mottled hands trembled with pleasure as they took more cherries to his stained mouth.

At last, he had no cherries left. only a lap full of stones. How could he get rid of them?

He gathered the folds of his clothing around the stones and shuffled to the back door of the home. There was only one bolt to undo and the key was in the lock: soon he was out in the garden. Though it was pitch dark, he knew just where he was and what was around him in the blackness – to his right, there were dense bushes. All he had to do was to take handfuls of the cherry stones and throw them away. They would all be lost in the bushes and no one would ever know how clever he had been in stealing the cherries.

He smiled as he dipped his hand into the mass of cherry stones. He chuckled as he cast the first handful away from him towards the bushes some feet away.

But the stones he threw came back at him, as if someone had caught each one and thrown them at him.

Mr Binding's mouth fell open: it was no longer smiling.

He took another handful of cherry stones and threw them into the blackness – threw them harder this time. But they came rattling back, harder than before.

Mr Binding began to whimper.

He peered into the darkness. and saw – nothing. What was there to see? Only bushes. Only darkness.

So he picked up a third handful of cherry stones and flung them with all his might, high into the darkness. There was a moment's pause, and back they came – a shower of cherry stones, that hit the top of his head! One even lodged, damply sticky, in his trembling, outstretched hand.

Mr Binding stamped his feet and made a queer little sound in his throat.

He began to throw away cherry stones furiously, cursing them as he flung them. But always they came back, as if a thousand black, invisible imps were catching them – throwing them back – mocking, taunting, jeering!

Mr Binding made a still queerer noise. He clutched his throat and sank to his knees. His heart was thumping, pumping, jumping. His eyes were staring, but they could see nothing in the darkness.

And in the darkness, he died.

In the morning, they found Mr Binding. The cause of his death seemed obvious: he was a very old man who had over-strained himself.

But then another old gentleman in the home, Mr Bellamy, met a reporter and told him that there was more to Mr Binding's death than cherry-stealing. The reporter bought Mr Bellamy a pint of beer and said, 'Go on, then! Tell me!'

Mr Bellamy, after many crafty nods and throat-clearings and another pint of beer, told the reporter that he had got up very early in the morning, looked out of the window in the dawn light – and seen a *wall* in the garden! A wall right against the line of bushes! A wall that had glittered in the pale early sun – and had later disappeared!

'Trillions?' said the reporter. 'Trillions!' said Mr Bellamy. '*They* built the wall, you see. A wall of Trillions!'

'But Trillions are always "forming" into things,' said the reporter.

'Ah!' said Mr Bellamy, 'that may be. But it's funny, isn't it, that once that wall of Trillions had killed poor old Binding, all the Trillions just seemed to sneak off and disappear! Almost as if they'd done it deliberately, and then wanted to hide what they'd done . . .!'

The reporter wrote this story for a syndicate of local newspapers and thought no more about it. Other, cleverer reporters thought differently. Mr Binding's strange death became a news item in more than one continent. Mr Bellamy appeared in the most important of the never-ending TV pro-grammes about Trillions – a programme seen in America, Britain and other English-speaking countries. To Har-bourtown viewers, it was strange to see the old chap among so many faces, including the General's. But Mr Bellamy told his story with relish. The audience warmed to him. The programme became almost cosy because of him.

Then the interviewer turned to the General. 'What do you make of this sad business of Mr Binding, General?'

The General said nothing for some seconds. In those seconds, the cosiness evaporated and something as startlingly clear and cold as the General's eyes took possession of the studio.

'This business of Mr Binding,' he said, 'is the business that brings us back to basics.'

'Such as?'

'Such as Purpose. Power. Action. What purpose did the Trillions have? What powers have they got? How do we propose to act?'

'Well, your first point – purpose – do you mean that the Trillions deliberately destroyed this old man? What purpose would they have in doing that? I mean, you don't suggest – '

'I don't suggest, but I have an opinion. Everyone here has an opinion and combined opinions lead to the formation of a purpose.'

'Yes, well . . . What is your opinion?'

'Mr Binding's death was of no importance to the Trillions but of the greatest importance to us as a demonstration of their powers.'

'You mean that from the Trillions' point of view, the death was incidental, just a side effect?'

'The side effect of a tactical exercise. Yes. The purpose of the Trillions was to try out another expression of their powers.'

'By killing an old man?'

'By building a particular form of structure so as to observe its effectiveness in a particular situation. Purpose and power – basics.'

'And if the try-out was satisfactory, you think we may see the Trillions doing the same thing again?'

'I really *cannot* think,' interrupted a scientist who had spoken earlier, 'that the good General asks us to believe that the Trillions are about to start a sort of world campaign directed at old men eating *cherries* . . .!'

There was some laughter.

'What do you answer to that, General?'

'Mr – er – the gentleman opposite me has already given the answer in his own words.'

'I don't understand you –'

'He began by saying, "I really cannot think". I agree.'

This time there was a full-blooded roar of laughter. The cameras held the General's face. He did not so much as blink. Before the laughter had died down, the General resumed speaking. The audience quietened at once.

'I spoke of three basics,' said the General, 'and I have dealt with only two.'

'Your third was action.'

'Quite so.'

'Well, perhaps you will explain to everyone here just what action –'

'There may be others here who have a course of action to propose. The gentleman opposite, for example?'

Unwisely, the scientist answered.

'I can only say that in a situation like this – the Trillions situation – when you're dealing with organisms, if that is the word, whose purposes and powers are so completely un-understood – that is, incomprehensible –'

'Yes?' said the General's voice. The word fell like a chunk of ice.

'Well, in our present state of information, to speak of action is to speak of – of – surely we must *evaluate*, we must *understand*, we must form an *appreciation* of the menace of the Trillions . . .'

'Menace?' barked the General. 'Did you say "menace"?'

'Well, *if* they are a menace – I mean, we cannot tell yet –'

'I see,' said the General. And sat back, stone-faced.

There was a bleak silence until the interviewer said, 'Well, General?'

'I beg your pardon?'

'Have you any more to add, General?'

'Only that I agree completely with the gentleman opposite. He said "menace". I say "menace". We are agreed.'

'But your third basic, General – Action –'

'Ah,' said the General. His face filled the screen. 'Action! I know how unpopular that word is today. Both among the leaders and the led. I have listened to countless discussions such as this one and have learned nothing from them that I did not already know – that we face a mysterious enemy and so forth. A menace . . .'

'We are running short of time, General,' said the interviewer, glancing at his watch.

'We are indeed. The world is running short of time. And I am running short of patience. Patience with men who talk of "understanding" and "evaluating" something we agree to be a menace. Men who would rather talk than act. My background is military; I am by training a man of action –'

'Fascist!' shouted someone in the audience. But a still louder voice answered, 'Throw that moron out!' and the audience was quiet again.

'I tell you that we have the means to take action – to fight a menace of any kind, even coloured dust. We have powers and purposes of our own. And there are men among us who want action. Now. Immediately, I am one of them. I will continue to press for action, effective action, strong action. Such views may be unfashionable, but –'

Voices in the audience cried 'No!' and 'We're with you!'

' – But I stick to them, whatever nonsense I must endure from people in high places who – but enough of that. I say, action. Action of the sort I have already taken. Action with the most powerful and effective weapons at our disposal . . .'

But he could no longer make himself heard. The cheering of the studio audience drowned his voice. Viewers saw, through the credit lines, the interviewer point at his watch, shrug his shoulders, wave an arm to someone offscreen. A man could be seen, indistinctly, as he leapt to the stage and attempted to shake the General's hand. Then it was all over. The announcer's face appeared, apologizing for the fact that the programme had over-run by two and a half minutes.

As the headlines of the world's newspaper showed the next day, no apology had been needed.

At one o'clock that morning, when the rest of the family slept, Scott reached his goal and established the bridge between humankind and the Trillions.

He could write messages in plain English to them. They could reply, in handwriting made of their own 'bodies', to him.

Once established, the process rapidly became easier, quicker and more certain. It was like teaching a little boy to swim. It may take months getting him to enter the water without screaming with fear; weeks to teach him to make a few strokes without choking and panicking; then, quite suddenly, the little boy swims and won't stop swimming.

So it was with the Trillions. Now they could express thoughts in writing, promptly. And Scott, on fire with excitement, began to find out what they were and what they thought.

'Trillions, where from?' he thought and wrote.

The Trillions formed into uncertain shapes. Scott bit his lip. He recognized what was happening. They were 'scribbling' – trying to find a right answer, or words in which to put their answer. But at last their reply came.

'Out there. Sky.'

'From a planet?' Scott wrote.

The Trillions wrote /, which meant Yes. X meant No. ? meant Cannot Reply, or Don't Know. This arrangement saved time.

'Which planet?' wrote Scott.

The Trillions promptly replied, 'Home.'

'Why leave your planet, why come here?' wrote Scott.

'Planet gone,' the Trillions replied. Then they began writing again. 'Planet die. Explod.'

Scott knew that 'explod' meant 'explode' – the Trillions often made spelling mistakes – but had to have a better answer, so he asked, 'Why explode?'

'?'

'Was it a war?'

'X'

'Is the planet gone or is it dead?'

'Dead. Gone. No planet.'

Scott had a vision of a dying planet, too old and weak to hold itself together: a planet that had, after countless centuries crumbled, split asunder and broken like a snowball. But the Trillions were writing again . . .

'X hom for us,' appeared on the sheet of white paper. Scott bit his lips, tried to understand, failed and wrote '???'

The Trillions scribbled, then wrote again.

'No hoem for us. Find new hoem.'

Now Scott thought he understood. The Trillions had been flung from their planet when it died and broke up. Because they were almost indestructible, they had not died as humans would die. Instead, they had travelled or drifted through space seeking a new home – and had found Earth. He longed to know if their search had been a lengthy one and if they had visited other planets. But there were more important questions. What did they do on their own planet? What were they intending to do on Earth?

So he wrote, 'What did Trillions do on home planet?'

'Build,' the Trillions replied.

'Build what?'

'As told.'

Scott felt his excitement rising.

'Who told you what to build?'

'Good masters,' came the answer.

Scott wrote, '?Masters' and the Trillions wrote /.

'Who were your masters?'

The Trillions scribbled for a long time, then wrote 'Good at home. Made home good.'

Scott thought about this. The Trillions found it hard to describe their masters. The best description they could find was, 'good' – a word they had used three times. Probably, then, the Trillions had been simple servants under a 'master' they could not understand but always obeyed faithfully. He decided to try once more for a description of the masters.

'Your masters like us?' he wrote, but got only uneasy scribblings in reply. He decided to try a new tack.

'Where masters now?'

'Dead gone with planet.'

'Who tells you what to do now masters gone?'

There was a great deal of scribbling, then the answer came. 'Build like masters home planet.'

Perhaps, thought Scott, they meant that as they always built on their home planet, they must build still – it is the only thing they know, the only usefulness they have. He tested this idea by writing, 'Why build?'

'Like home planet.'

Ah, Scott said to himself, I was right. The Trillions were like honeybees – working from habit, working skilfully without reason, working for the sake of the work in obedience to a force they did not need to understand. But, no: this was not good enough. The Trillions were showing intelligence. They were answering his questions. They had learned to write. They were more than blind slaves. They had to have a reason for what they did – a purpose in their visit to Earth.

He wrote, '*Who are your masters now?*'

The Trillions scribbled, began to form a word, scribbled again. At last they wrote, '*Good planet.*'

'*Am I your master?*' Scott wrote.

The Trillions formed a /, then an X, then repeated what they had written before – '*Good planet.*'

Scott wrote, '*This planet?*' and the Trillions merely answered with the Yes sign.

Scott sighed. He was more or less back where he had started with the 'honeybee' theory – the idea of the blindly obedient workers. His head ached and his eyes itched with tiredness. He decided to write only two more questions before sleep overtook him.

'*What will you do for this planet?*'

'*Build*' came the answer. Scott smiled to himself. It was what he had expected.

'*What can we do for you?*' he wrote.

The answer came back as quickly, violently and directly as a blow in the face.

'*Hate us.*'

Before he fell into a nightmare sleep, Scott tried everything to change the Trillions' answer. Had they meant 'Heat', not 'Hate'? Their answer came back – X. He put the question into different words, but it made no difference.

At last, he fell asleep knowing that there could be no mistake. Hate us, hate us, *hate us* . . . In the dark, he seemed to see the glittering Trillions form the word. In his sleep, he dreamed of the General's face looming from the television screen, shouting 'FOE!'

When he woke next morning. his eyes ached and his head was agony. He swung his feet out of bed. His legs felt heavy. The floor of his room was a litter of paper, scrawled with his own writing. The daylight streamed in: perhaps what had happened a few hours earlier had been part of a long nightmare? But there on the floor was the same piece of paper bearing the same message.

'*Hate us.*'

He lifted the paper by two corners and flung the Trillions from him, then went to the bathroom to wash. Outside, the usual morning din had already started as the Trillion Trucks and their crews prepared for action. They could do without him today, Scott thought.

Back in his room, he saw the Trillions forming on their sheet of paper. He watched with fascination and disgust to see what they would write.

The words were '*Good home. Work.*'

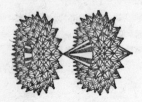

'Plan A,' said the General.

There was a jumbled mumbling of interpreters. A Russian General said 'Da, da, da' impatiently and a German General was having trouble with his earphones. A photographer took a flash photograph and a uniformed man ran up and hissed and flapped at him. The photographer made loud protests, in French. The blonde woman journalist smiled a painted smile, took a tiny miniature camera from her suede jacket and photographed the incident.

'Plan A,' said the General, loudly and firmly. Slowly, the meeting came to order.

'Plan A,' said the General. 'For discussion and I hope approval by all parties present. Representing seventeen nations. Right.'

The Russian General scowled, said 'Da, da, da' again and deliberately broke the lead of his pencil on the clean white pad in front of him.

'First,' continued the General, 'We must establish nature of foe. Know what he is, what he's doing, what he might do.'

This caused the interpreters some trouble to translate. The Russian General shifted his earphones so that only one ear was covered, then took out a penknife and began to sharpen his pencil. The chips of wood flew in all directions. The Chinese General near him made the chips into a little pile.

'Establish nature of foe,' said the General. 'To do this, we will consider implications of film showing Trillions' activities here and abroad. Show film!' A soldier called 'Lights!' Another soldier brushed his hand over switches. Now the big room was almost dark.

It was a dull room – merely a great featureless concrete-coloured hall. The Army had erected it from prefabricated units only two days earlier. But the people in the room were colourful enough. Round the central square of tables sat men of many nations, most of them in military uniform and all of senior rank. There were white, pink, brown, yellow and black skins: blue, brown, buff, grey and white uniforms. The General's soldiers, who acted as attendants, wore white-painted steel helmets, brilliant white belts, webbings and holsters, white anklets and white gloves on their tan uniforms. Not one soldier was less than six feet tall. Their boots shone as if treacle had been poured over them. The splendour of the military men made the civilians look dull and ordinary. Icarus, who had folded himself into an untidy lump on an uncomfortable wooden chair, was lost in the crowd.

The room darkened until only the soldiers' white webbing

stood out. The film began. An American Army Officer commented into his hand microphone: the translators murmured into theirs.

'Harbourtown West,' said the American Army Officer, keeping his voice flat and dry. 'First reports of Trillions. Date, 11 June.' The screen showed the scene – the drifts of Trillions in gutters, a close-up of Trillions, a darker patch in a sunny sky containing more Trillions about to fall.

'Da, da, da' said the Russian General, disgustedly.

But even he sat up a little later when the screen showed the underwater Trillion 'fortress'. And there was complete silence, complete attention, for the film sequences taken during the last few days.

'Paris, France,' announced the American Officer. The screen showed a street crowded with people, all with their heads turned to the dark sky. The cars in the street had stopped. It was raining Trillions. The camera showed a close-up of Trillions bouncing off the shoulders of a man's overcoat. The man constantly brushed at the Trillions in his hair with one hand. The camera pulled back into long focus. Everyone seemed to be brushing themselves while still staring at the sky.

'The heaviest fall of Trillions in Europe,' said the Officer. 'Millions of tons. Now London, England.'

The camera showed the river Thames with Big Ben and the Houses of Parliament in the background. The surface of the water was pocked with the rain of Trillions. A close-up showed the windscreen of a car, wipers going. Trillions formed a thick layer in the angle of screen and body. The camera moved right in on the windscreen and showed a curved pattern of scratches on the glass. The wipers had picked up Trillions: the Trillions had scratched the glass.

'Trillions are almost as hard as diamonds,' said the Officer and added a short description of their physical properties.

'Berlin ... Amsterdam ... Hong Kong ... Moscow ...

Cape Town . . .' There were brief shots of each city. In each, Trillions were falling.

'It is not possible to calculate exactly the total tonnage of Trillions that has descended on this planet,' said the Officer. 'But one authority estimated that sufficient Trillions have fallen to cover the world's land surfaces to a depth of more than one millimetre. This is only an estimation, and not – '

On the table by the Officer, a telephone rang. The Officer picked up the receiver and listened.

'Trillions are at present falling on . . . the south coast of France . . . eastern frontiers of Turkey . . . what was that, Carlsbad? . . . yes, Carlsbad . . . Zürich . . . Black Forest . . . Davos . . . There seems to be a general central-European fall at the moment.' He replaced the receiver.

People were beginning to lose interest. The Chinese General tipped his pile of pencil sharpenings on to the Russian General's pad. The Russian General growled ferociously. The Chinese General smiled and nodded his head as if to say, 'One good turn deserves another.' A British General grumbled, 'We *know* all this stuff, we *know* it all – ' But the dry voice of the American Officer said, 'The forming of Trillions,' and there was complete attention again.

'Trillions forming. Quite a lot of this material is new – some of it only hours old. Much of it has only just been processed. First, Harbourtown West. Underwater. The so-called fortress.'

'We *know* this stuff,' began the British General, but suddenly kept quiet.

'Similar "fortress" in the Black Sea. New material, received this morning,' said the Officer. 'You will notice that this underwater formation is on a very much larger scale. The area covered is some eleven square miles. Maximum depth, 340 feet.'

The cameraman had swung his lens over a great stretch of water. Breaking the surface of the sea, there arose nightmare towers and great haunted turrets, glittering horribly where the light struck them, but dark and secret in the 'windows' and openings.

'These tower-like constructions,' said the Officer flatly, 'rise as high as 200 feet above water. Now, some underwater views of the same constructions.'

Below the water, the Trillion castles seemed even more sinister. The constructions had no meaning – or every meaning. They followed no pattern, suggested no purpose – yet gave an overpowering impression of menace. In every cavern, you could imagine a lurking monster; in every 'window', a grinning devilish face. The Trillions had somehow built palaces of doom and evil.

The screen went white. The telephone rang again. 'Understood,' said the Officer, answering it. He put down the receiver and addressed his audience. 'Film break. The operator is about to splice in important new material. We will continue in about three minutes. Thank you.'

But he was hardly heard. The big hall was buzzing with conversations. Only the General and his soldiers kept quite still and stared straight ahead, expressionless.

From the start, the conference was a world affair. It made headlines in every newspaper throughout the world. Thousands of journalists had tried hundreds of ways to get into the conference hall. Only a few had succeeded.

But Scott was there. And owed it all to Mina.

Her pet soldier, Billy, had been put in charge of the urns supplying the gallons of coffee drunk each day by people attending the conference. It was not a very soldierly or responsible job and Billy had done his best to make it sound more important than it was. Mina pretended to believe him. 'They can't do without you, can they, Billy?' she said, making her eyes big and round.

'You bet they can't, Miss Mina.'

'Not even the General?'

'He's got to have his coffee too. Me and the General,' said Billy, 'are just like *that*!' He clamped two fingers together, and smirked. He felt big. Mina always had this effect on him and she knew it. She also knew that she could be one of the very few people in the whole of Harbourtown West to get into the conference. She did not know what a conference was, or what it was about. But she was determined to go all the same.

She soon found out how to do it. Each morning, a truck delivered groceries including cartons of coffee to the conference. Billy helped unload the truck. He took his cartons of coffee to his little kitchen. One of the cartons said, 'Hello, Billy! Look – I'm wearing my Trillions bracelet. Specially for *you*!'

He pulled open the carton and there was Mina.

When Billy had stopped saying 'But! – but! – but! – ' and was able to speak properly, he begged Mina to go. She would not. 'If anyone comes in,' she explained, 'I'll just hide in my carton.'

'But the General . . .!' implored Billy. 'If the General finds out! – '

'You and the General are just like *that*,' said Mina primly, making the same sign that Billy had made the day before. 'Can I have a cup of coffee, please? Lots and lots and lots of sugar.'

Mina found coffee-making quite amusing to begin with, but she soon grew tired of filling cups and teasing Billy. She was quite glad when, in the late afternoon, she was packed into her carton and driven away from the conference, and she was delighted when, that evening, she met Bem and Scott. They were talking about the conference. Scott was saying, 'I can't see what conclusion they can reach – I mean, I can't see what good they can do. It isn't just a question of blowing up Trillions–'

'I know,' said Mina, grandly.

The boys ignored her. 'Look at the facts,' said Bem. 'More and more Trillions falling all the time – '

'I know,' said Mina.

'Kick her,' said Bem. 'You're nearest.' Scott did not even look at her.

'Look,' he continued, 'the conference is all military. Nearly everyone there is military – '

'I know,' said Mina. 'I was there all day. Ho, hum, the military. They talk and talk and talk.'

Even she was pleased and surprised by Scott's reaction. His face went white. He seized her by the arm. 'What do you mean, you were there?' he said, in a choked-up voice.

Later, it was all arranged. Scott smuggled himself into the conference just as Mina had done. Mina bullied Billy into showing Scott where to hide himself – it was in the second projection booth, used only for film storage. He had a good view from the little square projection window and safe hiding places behind the storage racks. In exchange, he had only to give Mina any really big ruby-red Trillions he found (she was about to make herself yet another and grander bracelet) and let her off her Trillion Truck duties for a week.

Thus it was that Scott saw and heard everything that happened during the conference.

'We will continue in about three minutes,' the Officer had said. And now the new film material he had promised was spliced together – Scott could hear the soldier in charge of the projector moving about in the next room – and the lights were being dimmed in the big hall.

'This material comes from – Moscow,' said the Officer, keeping his voice flat and cold. 'It is described as being of the greatest possible importance because it shows a new phase in the development of Trillions.'

The screen lit up. Russian characters appeared. Scott could not understand them. Then there were moving pictures of enormous weapons – great rockets on multi-wheeled trailers. Although Scott was a considerable distance away, he could see the Russian General's back straighten and his neck become rigid. Obviously he did not like the pictures on the screen to be shown to an international audience.

The screen went blank for a second and more shots of the weapons appeared. They were taken in a vast concrete launching site. The rockets, now in cradles instead of on trailers, pointed almost straight up into the sky. There were many of them, perhaps twenty or thirty; great steel objects, with numbers painted on their flanks.

Among the audience, heads were turning, people were whispering to each other. The Russian General's head was rigidly upright as if with disgust. The translators' voices were sounding over the loudspeakers in the hall. Too many were speaking at once, but Scott was able to pick out an English-speaking voice saying, 'This is highly confidential material and you are asked not to – '

But then the screen showed a slow panning shot. The camera operator had swung away from the rockets and was covering a wide sweep of bleak countryside, only occasionally broken by leafy birch trees. The lens travelled on until it revealed in the distance a rocket site precisely similar to the first. Against the sky, you could see the same pattern of rockets. The camera moved in on these, closer and closer, until the finned base of a rocket filled the screen. The audience was silent. Closer went the cameras until only the bottom of one fin was shown. This shot was held, then brought into still closer focus to show a glittery, glassy texture.

It was then that Scott and everyone else realized what they were looking at: the 'rocket' was made of Trillions! And the imitation was perfect.

Now the camera was exploring the surfaces of more Trillion 'rockets', but no one watched. The hall was loud with voices. Heads bobbed, hands gestured, men left their chairs and dashed across the floor to speak to colleagues.

Scott saw the General stand on his chair and nod to an Officer who shouted an order. The white-helmeted soldiers guarding each door brought their rifles to the ready. The woman journalist had been making for an exit. A soldier barred her way, with his rifle. She said something, angrily, and the soldier made a small, hard thrusting motion with the rifle. She walked slowly back to her place, looking astonished. Then the General walked briskly to the platform and took a microphone. His amplified voice cut through the babble like a blade through undergrowth.

'MEETING WILL COME TO ORDER. RESUME SEATS. TO ORDER. IMMEDIATELY.'

At once, there was silence and people sat down. Scott felt an unwilling admiration for the upright, leathery little man. The General waited, not bothering even to turn his head, until he had complete attention. Then he said, quietly, 'If you please. Resume business in hand. No further delays. All grateful to Russian friends for releasing most important information. All seen film, understand what we have seen. To business, then. Action.'

He left the platform, marched to his seat at the table,

adjusted the microphone in front of him and barked two words into it.

'Plan A.'

He spoke in the tone of one who does not expect to be contradicted and he was not. The new evidence was too strong. At last the nations put their heads together, nodded agreement and decided to act.

The world was prepared for Plan A. Every nation that owned tactical nuclear weapons was instructed to use them. The General was appointed overlord of the operation. It was his voice, and his voice alone, that could give the order to fire. When he spoke, the Trillions would be attacked by explosive powers that made the great bombs of the world war seem like fireworks: by heat so intense that it could turn metal to liquid in a split second.

In Harbourtown West, the loudspeakers had announced that every last Trillion was to be found, collected, delivered and dumped by sundown – General's orders.

'It's mad,' gasped Scott. 'All mad. They've gone mad.'

He gasped because he was running. He was running because he was rushing his Trillion Truck on yet another journey to the Exterminator. The Trillion Trucks were suddenly no longer a joke. Since the conference, everything had changed. At first, the coming of the soldiers had been an annoyance, an excitement, a trial, a scandal – anything you cared to make of it, but nothing really serious. But now, the soldiers were suddenly real and menacing. They were iron men in steel helmets and their guns might fire bullets that actually killed. They had to be obeyed, and obeyed at the double. That was why Scott was running.

Scott, Mina, Panda and Bem reached the Trillion Exterminator plant. They were panting. Ahead of them was a short queue of children and trucks, waiting their turn to tip the Trillions they had collected over the chute. Soldiers holding guns kept the queue moving. The soldiers no longer smiled and joked with the children. They muttered, 'Move along, keep it moving, move along,' and the children sullenly obeyed.

'Where's Billy, mister soldier?' Mina asked the soldier she recognized.

'Move along, keep it moving,' replied the soldier.

'But I want to *talk* to Billy . . .'

'Move along, close up. You lot at the back, get into line.'

The soldier did not even look at her. Yesterday, he had given her a piece of chocolate. Mina's lower lip stuck out and trembled a little.

They tipped out their Trillions, turned the truck round, and started to walk back to collect the next load.

'Double!' said the soldier. 'At the double!'

The teams broke into a jogtrot. Mina ran too, half crying.

When they were nearly back to their area, the fat Major's car swept by and stopped sharply. The driver leapt out, ran to open the door and saluted as the Major got out. As if he were a hunting dog, the Major pointed his sharp nose at the gutter, appeared to sniff, then stood erect.

'You!' he barked, glaring at the children. 'Which one in charge?' His voice was a passable imitation of the General's.

'I am,' said Scott.

'Over here,' said the Major. Scott walked over to him.

'At the double,' growled the soldier who drove the car.

Scott felt his face go hot. He ran to the Major.

'Trillions, lad,' said the Major, pointing at the gutter. 'There. There. And there. Trillions. Sweep up, put in truck, dispose of. NOW.'

'But this isn't even our area,' said Panda.

'At the double,' growled the driver soldier.

Scarlet-faced, the children bent down to pick up the Trillions. There were so few of them that they had to pick them up one by one with their fingers.

'Mad,' said Scott, dully. He was tired and aching.

Bem said, 'I suppose –' then shut up.

'What do you suppose?'

'I suppose they feel they must do something. Anything.'

'But nuclear weapons . . .! Against Trillions!'

'But you yourself said the Trillions were building rockets in Russia. All kinds of warlike things, all over the world. You said that yourself.' Bem took another bite of his lunch-time sandwich and chewed slowly and miserably. 'All the same, it does seem a bit much. Nuclear weapons, I mean, no one really knows what happens *after*.'

'They just make a lot of noise and burn everything up, don't they?' asked Panda, big-eyed and anxious. 'Nothing happened after they blew up the fortress in the harbour, did it?'

'Did it?' repeated Mina. She was miserable and anxious.

'Oh, *you* . . .' said Bem, looking scornfully at Mina. 'What do you know?'

'That soldier was rude,' said Mina. 'I know that.' She began to cry.

Scott put an arm round her and looked angrily at Bem over her head. Bem looked ashamed. He said, 'Mina is right. Sorry, Mina. The soldier was rude and that's really just what we are talking about. It's all got so –'

' – Serious,' said Panda. 'There's a horrible feeling . . . something bad about to happen, something really bad. I don't know . . .'

'Fallout,' said Bem. 'When you let off nuclear weapons, you can get nuclear fallout. The air is poisoned, plants grow all wrong, people get sick –'

Mina looked up, wide-eyed and afraid.

'Not you, you old silly!' said Panda brightly. 'You'll be all right!' And now it was her turn to glare at Bem.

'The Trillions never really did anything to us,' said Panda. 'Those Russian rockets — it isn't as if the Trillions rockets had anything inside them. They can't fly, they can't do anything, they can't blow up ...'

They ate in silence. Scott made himself eat too. But drumming in his head were the words 'Hate us ... Hate us ... Hate us.'

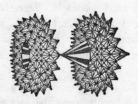

When at last they finished pushing the Trillion Trucks and could go home, the television set showed and talked nothing but Trillions, Trillions, Trillions. Scott switched the dial from one channel to another but it was always the same.

'In this grave crisis of human affairs, the evidence pours in of a world against a common threat —'

He tried another channel.

' — if the existing underwater Trillions barrier were to be extended in this region, the Gulf Stream itself could be diverted and our whole climate changed —'

Try again.

' — scientific age, the ordinary foot-soldier still remains the most sensitive precision weapon we can bring to bear. Only to human hands can we entrust the terrifying power soon to be unleashed against the alien force that —'

He was about to try yet again when Blythe came in.

Scott had almost forgotten about Icarus, yet he had been

with him only yesterday evening. He had told Icarus all about his experiments with the talking Trillions: he had told and showed him everything, saving the message 'Hate us!' until last. Icarus had seemed uninterested and distant. 'Nobody else knows about this,' Scott said, trying to underline what he had been saying. Icarus had answered, 'Good thing. Don't tell anyone else. Oh yes, congratulations. It's amazing what you've done . . .'

He had gone, leaving Scott with a picture of a man who was burnt out, useless and defeated. Scott had had no time to worry about this picture. Now, he could hardly believe it had ever existed. For Icarus seemed to be alight, burning, vibrating with urgency.

'Your room,' said Icarus. 'Finish your soup up there. I'll carry this plate. Come on.'

He ran up the stairs to Scott's bedroom with a plate in one hand and a glass of milk in the other. Scott followed, pushed the door shut with his foot and said, 'What's happened? What – ?'

'You know what Plan A is, don't you, Scott?'

'Of course. International drive to destroy Trillions with tactical nuclear weapons – burn them to nothing. But – '

'Now listen, Scott. It is my opinion that Plan A will do very little to the Trillions – I think they are more or less indestructible. No, don't interrupt me with questions. I and my research team have done a lot of work in the past days. We've tried everything we know to break them, burn them, explode them – Scott, it's incredible the temperatures they can withstand. You can't touch them chemically, of course. And even when you do break them down physically, I have the feeling that they can eventually form again, even below molecular stage . . . But never mind, I'm wasting time . . .

'As I was saying, I think Plan A can do very little to the Trillions. But I am appalled – appalled and terrified, Scott – at the thought of what Plan A can do to *us*. Look at it this way. No one can say definitely what will happen to us – to Earth itself – when the nuclear blasts begin. There are many people – and I am one of them – who see almost every new thing mankind does as a threat. Pesticides, the dust in space left by atomic explosions, chemical waste from factories – '

'I know all this, I know the argument, we're fouling our planet,' began Scott. But Icarus hurried on.

'And now Plan A. Nuclear weapons all over the planet, all to be fired at the same time. Scott, anything can happen – '

'I know, I know. How do we stop it?'

'Ah, how do we stop it. The men who have the power are the Plan A men – the General. Plan A is his toy, his creed and gospel – '

'How do we stop it?'

'Scott, you told me what the Trillions' message was. They said, "Hate us". Just that, "Hate us". When you told me that, I went – sick. I knew, certainly, that nothing could be done. I knew that nothing good could happen – only Plan A. Plan A is as evil as the Trillions: the Trillions are as evil as Plan A. So let the General get on with it, I thought. Either he or the Trillions will finish us all off!'

Watching Icarus, Scott felt infected by his explosive energy. The man was almost raving at him.

'Then something happened, Scott. I was thinking – quite uselessly – about what might happen to us when the nuclear weapons went off. I was thinking of the possible effects on our ecology – ?'

'Ecology – the balance of nature,' said Scott. 'The way any one planet or animal or organism depends on another. Yes, I know what the word means.'

'Good. Well, I was thinking how Plan A might be the last straw for this poor old planet of ours . . . Then I thought of the message, "hate us". What does that mean to you?'

'It's a threat,' said Scott, carefully. 'It's a warning. It

means, "Right – we are going to hurt you. So the only thing left for people on Earth to do is – hate us"!'

'Have the Trillions ever hurt us, Scott?'

'No. Not hurt. Just . . . make themselves look tough. You know, the Russian rockets and the fortress. Things like that.'

'And what did they do in their previous existence – on their own home planet?'

'They built.'

'What did they build?'

'What their masters told them.'

'So the Trillions could be *ecological organizations*, Scott.'

'Ecological – '

'Look. Imagine a planet. Alive, but not like our planet. Not with humans on it – not little units walking about that have their own wills, their own inventiveness, their own ideas of progress. Just a planet. But a planet cannot for ever just roll through space. Things change, things happen. So *jobs need doing, all the time*. Now do you begin to understand?'

'No.'

'But it's simple. The side of a mountain collapses, say. A river is diverted. Things – organisms, plants, even animals – that had lived through the river will die. The water they must have to exist is gone. But then the *servants of the planet* are summoned. They form a dam, or new banks, or repair the mountain – they do whatever is needed to restore the river and make things right again.'

'Bees . . . beavers . . .' said Scott softly.

'Yes – but with a difference. Bees work for the good of the hive, beavers for themselves or their little clan. But Trillions – I believe that Trillions worked for the sake of their whole planet – their whole ecology. I believe their planet somehow told them what to do. Or perhaps it was just one particular life form on the planet that was their "master". It doesn't matter what.'

'They said "good planet",' Scott murmured. 'That could mean a planet where their masters always had work for them to do. So they built on each other and made whatever the planet needed . . .'

Pictures of an alien planet formed in his mind. Fantastic vegetation by a river – the crumbling of a mountain of strangely coloured rock – the Trillions answering their master, the planet itself, and building, forming, repairing . . .

'All right – I agree to your theory!' he said. 'It's wonderful, marvellous, terrific. But what's the good of it? What difference does it make if you're wrong or right? What difference does it make to Plan A and the General and the big bang? They don't want to serve *us*, that's all that matters! They've *told* us so! They told me that they hate us!'

'No, they didn't Scott. They never wrote that,' said Icarus. 'They didn't say *they* hated *us*. They said –'

'They said we should hate *them*,' said Scott; and stopped, baffled.

He could almost feel the answer to the riddle of the Trillions burrowing into his mind. And yet –

'Think, Scott,' said Icarus. 'Suppose my theory is right – then think. I'll go through it again.'

He ticked off his argument point by point on his fingers. 'The Trillions exist only to serve their planet, their master. They lose their planet and become like homeless dogs. They find another planet and wish to do the only thing they know – serve, through building. All right so far?'

Scott nodded.

'Then you manage to get through to them; they "serve" you by learning to write your language. Then comes the important moment. You ask the Trillions what we can do for them – and they answer, "Hate us". Now do you see, Scott?'

'No,' said Scott miserably.

Icarus looked at his watch and jumped to his feet.

'Come downstairs with me, Scott!' he said. 'We'll watch the TV news. Then you'll understand!'

Scott watched but could not concentrate. The room was crowded. His parents were there, and two neighbours. Nothing on the screen seemed to touch on what was in his mind, although most of it was about Trillions. There were pictures of weapon carriers, soldiers, mobilizations in various countries, air-strike missiles. There was a brief shot of the General saying 'No comment' to a group of reporters outside a huge, glassy building. Then brief glimpses of Trillion exterminators in action.

He felt a nudge on his elbow. 'What is it all about, Scott?' said Icarus nodding at the screen.

'Thumping the Trillions, I suppose,' said Scott, with a half smile.

'Fine,' said Icarus. 'Keep watching.'

The news droned on. Student trouble in Tokyo. Police with shields and helmets, bursts of flame from petrol bombs. A man in handcuffs being pushed by the police through a crowd of screeching women, then a shot of the house where the murder had been committed. A girl in a bathing suit holding a huge cup. Troops on the border of somewhere or other. A protest march against something or other. A tennis player making the winning smash, a boxer delivering a knockout. Scott could not concentrate. The riddle of the Trillions was still boring at his mind.

Then came a sequence showing a racing car. 'Grand Prix!' said Scott to himself, suddenly waking up. More cars! a whole bunch sweeping into the grandstand corner! Scott peered at the screen, trying to find his favourite driver's car.

But then another TV camera picked up a single car and the chance was lost. The camera followed the car into a bend. It was catching a tail-ender. The two cars touched, there was a scream of tyres, a mixed-up, lurching, sliding tangle, then a cloud of smoke with bits of metal bursting from it –

Scott jerked to his feet, eyes wide and staring at Icarus.

'You're right!' gasped Scott. 'It must be that! You're right!'

'How else *could* the Trillions serve us?' demanded Icarus.

'I was a fool not to have seen it,' said Scott. 'I mean, we do everything else so well. We can build – anything, anything at all. What could they do for us?'

'So the Trillions couldn't compete. They came to Earth and found what they needed – a planet on which things were *built*. The Moon wouldn't have been any good – it's dead, so nothing needs to be done. It's possible that they tried a hundred planets – a thousand, a million – before they found us. But we seemed right for them, so down they came –'

'And straight away, they did their tricks, their only trick,' interrupted Scott. 'Just like that lost dog you talked about. They sort of wagged their tails to show willing. They "formed". All we had to do was to say, "Yes, good boy, I understand – you're builders, we can set you to work straight away. You can build for us just as you used to build on your own planet. You can form into dams and break-waters and landing strips – " '

'But we thought only of destroying them. And just as bad

– anything they can do, we can do just as well or probably better. Their rockets were only pointed shapes. Their fortress was only a sham. Even Mina's bracelet is only Trillions, not precious stones. You can't say to Trillions, "Form into a reliable wrist-watch!" or "Be a bath sponge!" They could look like it, but not be it. On their home planet, they were part of the life of the place – and part of the soul, too. But here – well, humans are too clever. They had to find a job, a task, a reason for being allowed to continue to live here.'

' "Hate us",' said Scott. 'That's a rotten job, just being hated.'

'Yes, but what else is there for them? That TV news – for heaven's sake, Scott, what else can they do at this very moment? What would you think if you were the Trillions' collective brain or consciousness or whatever it is they have? It's all a fight, Scott – one long battle. Students against police, army against army, nation against nation, boxer hitting another boxer –'

'There was a girl in a bathing costume.'

'And why was she on the news? Because she had won a fight, a beauty contest.'

'Punching bag,' said Scott thoughtfully. 'That's how the Trillions see themselves. As the punching bag for all our fighting instincts. They know that we never stop fighting. They know that we get better and better all the time at doing each other damage. They must sense that the end is near for this planet – unless we can be switched over to hitting something that doesn't matter and can't be hurt. Though I don't see how that can stop people murdering each other, or crashing racing cars, or having riots in the streets.'

'It can't,' said Icarus. 'But don't you see, that's not the part that matters. That's more or less personal stuff. It's the mass fights that can destroy Earth; the big weapons, the big bangs.'

'The General!' exclaimed Scott. 'We've forgotten about him! You talk of the Big Bangs – he's just getting one ready!'

They went to the window. The Army vehicles were rumbling by, making so much noise that they could no longer talk. There were ordinary trucks, filled with soldiers: tanks, with great guns of a strange pattern: little guns on fat rubber tyres, stranger still: control consoles, again on fat tyres, that presumably were used to direct and fire the nuclear guns: electric generators: things like astronomical aerials – great dished fans made of metallic mesh: and, just occasionally, a human soldier.

'Aliens!' shouted Scott, pointing to the last vehicles in the procession. 'There's your aliens! Mine, anyhow . . .'

'Friend or foe?' answered Icarus, grimly. '*I* don't know which. Could be that we're our own enemy. But that's the whole point, isn't it? Who are the Goodies, who the Baddies?'

Scott rubbed his temples with his fists and said,

'Wait, .wait a moment. Where are we? On the one hand, we've got you and me, Bem, Panda, Mina, my parents – oh, nearly everyone we've ever met . . . If you like, the Good People. But then, when you turn on the news, all you seem to see is the work of the Bad People. Killers, vandals, rioters, people hurting and getting hurt . . .'

'Then there's the General.'

'Yes, the General. Is he good or bad? Has he ever done a cruel thing in his life – I mean, has he himself actually used a gun to kill someone? Yet with Plan A –'

'With Plan A, he could condemn half a world to a horrible death for all we know. Good People, Bad People – where do you draw the line? Is that silly soldier of Mina's – you know, Billy – one of the Good people?'

'Of course he is. Old silly Billy.'

'And then the General puts a gun in his hands and gives the order to fire ... And Billy fires, and a man drops dead and Billy gets a medal?'

'All right, leave it at that. I agree. The Good and the Bad People, they're hopelessly mixed up. They can never be sorted out. Agreed. Then along come the Trillions and we both get excited and talk about punching bags – a target for all our bad instincts – '

'Yes, that's it exactly. A *safe* target.'

'But haven't you forgotten something, Icarus?'

'What?'

'Don't you remember telling me about the time you were alone in space – really alone, you said? Don't you remember saying that space was *alien*?'

'Yes, of course I remember.'

'And I asked you, "Alien good, or alien bad?" And you said something like it being impossible to tell, alien meant alien – completely strange, completely mysterious?'

'So – '

'Alien. Alien, *like the Trillions*. That's what you said.'

'Well, I may have said something like that, yes. What are you driving at?'

'This: you have been talking about the Trillions as if they were old friends of ours – jolly dogs wagging their tails and so on. Wanting to make friends and do their tricks for us. Wanting to serve us. Right?'

'I don't see – '

'Yet you also said that the Trillions were aliens. Which do you mean? Are Trillions dogs wagging their tails – or are they strange, alien beings from space – dangerous foreigners? Because that was the feeling they once gave you.'

'I don't remember saying – ' Icarus began, then stopped, staring at Scott. At last he said, 'What are you getting at?'

'We can't tell the difference between the Good People and the Bad People even when we know them – even when they are humans. Billy the soldier can be good one minute, bad the next. We *agreed* that. Yet you seem perfectly willing – so was I at first, I'm not being rude – to say, "Hurrah for Trillions! Trillions must be good, because they told us so!" Yet not so long ago, they were giving you another dose of the most frightening feeling you've ever had –'

'Aliens . . .' breathed Icarus. 'You're right, of course, Scott. What a fool! They're aliens. And for all I know, the best liars in the whole universe . . .'

Icarus got to his feet and began walking back and forth. Scott watched him, miserably. 'The sickening thing about it,' he said, 'is that you might have been right – I mean, perhaps the Trillions really are the Good People, they really do mean to act as targets or punchbags –'

'No. It won't wash. We have to be sure.'

'We never can be sure,' reasoned Scott. 'How do you find out? Go and visit a planet that no longer exists – having first become a Trillion, of course?'

There was silence, then Icarus said, 'Yes.'

'Yes, what?'

'Yes – do what you said! Go and visit that planet that doesn't exist! Become a Trillion!'

'For heaven's sake! – You're joking! –'

'Do I look as if I'm joking, Scott? Do I? Can't you see what I'm getting at? Don't you remember how you taught the Trillions in the first place – by drilling into them with that extraordinary mind of yours?

'Well, Scott – drill deeper! Drill right inside them! Take your mind clean through them and out the other side! Dig into their memory, their history, their past!'

When Scott spoke, his voice trembled. 'What a mad idea!' he said. 'What a terrific idea!'

'Will you *try* it?'

'Of course. Tonight!'

Alone in his room, Scott clenched his jaws, focused his mind and shot it at the Trillions. TELL ME. SHOW ME. TAKE ME BACK WITH YOU. LET ME REMEMBER YOUR MEMORIES ...

Some Trillions grouped: Scott's heart leaped. They began to write. He craned forward to watch.

'?' the Trillions wrote.

Scott cursed and began again. Again. Again. Despairing, he even wrote his questions down on big sheets of paper as well as beaming them with his mind.

TELL ME ABOUT HOME PLANET. TELL ME ABOUT GOOD MASTERS.

GOOD PLANET, the Trillions replied.

TELL ME WHAT WORK YOU DID. WHY? HOW?

GOOD MASTERS said the Trillions. Scott cursed at them.

The Trillions seemed almost to be shuffling their feet. They 'formed' uneasily. The formations would break up for no obvious reason. They would form again and write a shaky '?'. Once, they wrote 'CANOT' – 'can not'. Scott beamed at them the thought, 'You must!' But the Trillions only shuffled and shifted, making tiny meaningless blobs and shapes.

By now, Scott's mind was leaden and stupid. It was telling him, 'No more'. Stubbornly, he resisted. TELL ME ABOUT HOME PLANET, he wrote. Now he needed to write down the words if only to be able to concentrate on them.

The Trillions tumbled, twinkled, made nonsense. Scott mumbled, 'Morons! Idiots!' and kicked at a sheet of paper covered with Trillions. Then he began to undress. Washing his face, his hands seemed to be touching someone else's skin. He looked at his watch: 2.35 in the morning.

'You've had it,' Scott said to his own reflection in the mirror.

He put on his pyjama trousers, fell into bed and turned out the light. 'You won't be able to sleep,' he told himself miserably – and, instantly, fell into the huge, deep, leaden sleep of complete exhaustion.

In the dark, the Trillions formed. They came from every corner of the room, from the fibres of the carpet, from the cracks in the floorboards. They meshed and geared, climbed and rolled, linked and interlinked. Soon there was a pile of Trillions a foot, eighteen inches, high. Still they linked and interlinked. Now they were climbing. They made a dark, dimly glittering patch on the blanket at the foot of Scott's bed. The patch became a wave that travelled towards Scott's head.

Scott groaned and turned in his bed. He lay on his back. A little flow of Trillions fell, like sand, from the sheet on to his neck. They looked like a glittering, moving stain. More Trillions followed. Scott twitched and muttered.

The Trillions formed a spearhead. It crept upward over his neck – over the lobe of his ear – into the ear: then retreated. Three more spearheads formed and probed his nostrils, his mouth, his eyelids. Then a little river crept from his neck, down over his chest and spread into a dark pool over his heart. This too retreated. Now the Trillions were almost still, as if thinking out their next move.

In the dim light from the street that filtered into the room through the curtains, they glittered darkly with each tiny movement. Scott slept on, undisturbed.

There was another wave of movement. Two streams of Trillions crept out from a pool in the hollow of Scott's neck. The streams elongated and climbed the sides of his neck, his jaw, his ears. They reached his temples. Here, the streams thickened, forming two solid pools linked by a thin dark line. More streams stretched out like tentacles: more pools formed at the end of each stream. Now Scott was covered by a crude skeleton – a child's drawing, lines and blobs, of a human body – made of Trillions. There were pools of Trillions in the palms of his hands, on his feet, over his heart and stomach, in the pulses of his neck and wrists. The pools were linked by thin lines of Trillions and this thin line was itself linked to the main mass of Trillions on the floor beside the bed.

Scott slept.
Scott dreamed.

But was it a dream?

He was on the planet of the Trillions. It was a raging, tearing hell.

The wind. The Wind! It screamed and roared and bellowed. It blasted and bored, tunnelled and chiselled. The great red rocks were gouged as if they were potter's clay. The wind had iron fingertips that wiped across them horizontally, tearing furrows and seams into the rocks, sculpting them into nightmare shapes. Spires and spikes swayed and tottered. When they fell, the Wind took the hard dust and fragments and used them to sharpen its claws. Even as you watched, the top of a mountain, savaged by the Wind, would surrender: its throat cut, the gigantic rocky head would be snatched up by the screaming Wind – hurtle, like a stone from a giant sling, across the reeling landscape – smash itself in a fury of fragments and a tearing cloud of dust against another mountain – while the Wind raged and roared in triumph, ready to strike again.

The Wind, Scott somehow knew, never stopped. The sky was a vicious, lurid green, filled with flying clouds. They rolled end over end, like tumbleweed, until they were torn to shreds by the wind. Or until they exploded in a sheet of flame, ignited by the clash and flash of colliding rocks. The sky was gas, the clouds were gas, and the gases were enemies. Their war, Scott knew, never ended.

Scott travelled with the Wind. If he still had a body, it was dust – for no human body could survive for a moment the hideous, never-ending gale. He travelled where it took him, sometimes at unthinkable speeds, sometimes caught in a whirlpool where he spun and spun, dizzied by the whirl of red rocks around him. Once, the Wind took him to an area of calm – a pocket between mountains where the Wind flogged itself into nothingness. Now he could study and observe. But there was nothing to see beneath him, dust – with still finer dust streaming from its surface to follow the Wind. Around him, rock. Above him, the ghastly sky with three of the planet's seven moons visible. Somehow, Scott knew there were seven.

A hundred feet above his area of calm the Wind screamed and raged. Scott saw an enormous boulder, carried by the Wind, smash the mountain peak above him. There was a crashing impact that shivered the sandy dust below him into ripples – a sheet of flame as a cloud exploded in the sky – a spattering dash of wetness from the vanished cloud – then a dreadful note began to sound, organ tones from hell. It grew and grew until even the Wind could not be heard. It grew until the rocky surfaces around him began to shudder and crumble. A few rocks fell, then more, then a landslide. Still the note swelled and grew. Soon Scott knew, the planet would be shaken to death by its vibrations.

Then he saw Trillions.

They were everywhere. They linked, formed, swarmed, crowded and surged up the walls and over the broken tops of the mountain. They filled holes, craters, gaps. As they finished their work, the unbearable note became bearable.

Now still more Trillions began to build. The top of the mountain rose again: it was made of Trillions. The wind, which had invaded the calm area, once more passed over it.

The note was gone.

Beneath him, the Trillions still poured out. Where did they come from? There! – a cleft in the rocks. Scott pointed his mind at it and entered the cleft. His body, if he had one, followed.

He was underground.

How calm!' he thought. Order and calm! Smooth walls, made of Trillions. Geometrical walls, like a maze. To baffle the Wind? He could still hear its roar. Farther on, the sound died. Silence. He went on.

Light! A dim light from the walls or within the walls. The Trillions giittered. Did they make the light, or reflect it?

A sound. A melody, almost. For the sound was many sounds, layers upon layers of sound, like music. It came from somewhere ahead of him.

The walls widened, the light grew brighter, the sound swelled – and he was *there*. In the hall of the Masters!

He was overcome, baffled by a thousand questions. How did he know this cavern was the hall of the Masters? He knew, that was enough. Where are the Masters? What could he say to them, offer them? Why want to give them something? He felt a flood of – reverence, worship? – for these unseen Masters: then a human scorn for himself. Worship! He was being stupid.

'I should have knocked,' he said out loud, cheekily.

In his mind, he heard all the Masters reply. 'There was never a door to keep you from us.' Scott seemed to hear or feel a wave of comfortable laughter. He felt himself smile and thought for a moment that he could see himself standing there, dressed in pyjama trousers and with rumpled hair. Impossible. Concentrate on the Masters. Where are they?'

'Here,' said all the voices.

But Scott could not see them. He saw glittering arches and chambers, vaults and turrets – but even as he looked at them, they seemed to shift and change. Trillions? Trillions constantly forming and reforming?

'Here,' repeated the voices.

A web, floating. Many colours. Or a moving curtain, blown by a breeze? No, a mesh – a circuit, almost. No, a field made of luminous threads –

'Difficult, very difficult,' said the voices sympathetically.

'I can't make my eyes focus properly,' said Scott.

'Close them,' replied the voices. 'Then you will see.' He closed his eyes. Something warm touched him. Far from flinching, he reached out his hand to the welcome presence. He was led forward, then his hand was placed on something of the same warmth.

'Can't I look with my eyes?'

'Now you can.'

And he could see it quite well, though it was very bright and blurred. It was a great three-dimensional, mesh-like structure, infinitely complicated and lovely. He could not see it all. His eyes were playing tricks. It was luminous. It had Trillions in it. It was warm. It was alive.

'Is this – you?' he asked the Masters.

'Is this – you?' echoed the Masters, jokingly – and flashed at him a thousand images of himself in the space of a second – baby, eat, bigger, cut finger, home, circus, sleep, second prize, climb tree, be kind, bully, Sherlock Holmes, Trillion Truck . . .

The images ended: Scott found himself laughing. 'Difficult, very difficult,' he echoed the Masters. 'There's a lot of me. Is there,' he asked seriously, 'even more of you?'

'Close your eyes,' said the voices.

He closed them and saw. The Wind! Tearing, clawing, beating! The green sky, the tumbling clouds! Seven suns, spinning! He let his fingers rest more lightly on the mesh, the veil, the web, that was the Masters. Instantly the pictures in his mind, the sounds in his ears, grew still more clear. He was vibrating in sympathy with their nerves, their eyes, their computer, their brain.

A message! A message of danger, violence, destruction! It rippled urgently through the mesh; centred on one of many points where a thousand glistening, luminous strands interlinked. His mind saw a quick vision of a huge smash of rocks; his ear heard once more the unbearable note made by the victorious Wind; his brain felt the commands tugging the strands of the mesh, flickering through it, darting to and from the Masters' brains. He seemed to hear a command, feel the Trillions link and form in obedience, see them sent, tiny and silent, into battle against the howling Wind yelling its battle cry –

'Yes, all the time,' the Masters answered Scott's unspoken question. 'It grows stronger. Always stronger. All the time, we fight the Wind – build what it tears down – protect what it destroys . . .'

'But why, why?' demanded Scott. Part of his mind could see, under the hideous green sky, the legions of the Trillions swarming into eternal battle. Still the note sounded.

'To save our world.' The note was louder! It made the mesh throb and tremble. It shook the very walls of the Master's cavern.

'But *why*?' pleaded Scott. Trillions built, the Wind destroyed. Yet still they built and still the Masters' will sent them into battle, reformed their broken ranks, planned their assaults, patched the crumbling planet. The Wind howled and stored up vengeance: the Masters made their strange music and healed the wounds. Why?

The note faded. The Trillions had won. The mesh made its soft, gentle, vibrant music again. Peace, for a moment.

'Was there really ever a peace on this planet?' Scott thought.

'Never,' replied the Masters.

'Were there ever trees and plants, animals and . . . a proper life?'

'We understand you. No, never.'

'Was there ever happiness, something to fight for?'

'Never.'

'Then why? Why do you go on?'

There was a pause and Scott, waiting for their reply, heard only the soft music of the mesh. At last they replied.

'We must serve the Master,' said the Masters. 'The Master of everything. The Master of all planets, all lives, all of us, each single Trillion.'

'And the Trillions?'

'Through us, they serve the Master too.'

The mesh hummed gently. The Trillions that made the walls of the cavern shifted, twinkling and changing colour. Now the walls glowed purple, tinged with gold. The mesh vibrated, pleased. A veil of colour rose from it like a mist to thank them.

But the alarm tugged the mesh again, plucking it fiercely and urgently, here – there – in three places. The veil fled from the walls, wove itself in the mesh, became part of it.

The note of the Wind began to sound, louder and louder and LOUDER –

The mesh trembled, slackened, tautened again. Commands crackled from it like sparks flying up a chimney. The note was LOUDER. A wall of Trillions fell, reformed, rebuilt. The note was LOUDER. The wall fell again and struggled to rise. A hole in the mesh! Energy from it poured in burning arcs. The Masters' minds clashed and fumbled, reached out, took hold, linked, clenched – the hole closed. But the note was LOUDER.

Outside, Scott's mind saw a mountain shudder – tilt – split – explode – fly into a million bombs and arrows and hurtling masses that tore ground, burst clouds, smashed more mountains. The Wind screamed and yelled and sounded its war note. The Planet began to shake and thunder. A mountain fell into a monstrous gash that closed like jaws and crushed it to screaming, molten lava that jetted into the sky. Clouds caught fire. Flaming shreds were carried away by the Wind, thundering in the darkening sky. And the note was louder, louder, LOUDER!

Unbearable! Scott clung to the mesh with all his strength. But the lifeline was jerking, tugging, wrenching, writhing. Unbearable! He fell on his knees and let the mesh jerk and throw him anywhere. Only his hand mattered, he must not lose his grip. The mesh shuddered, slackened, tautened and bounded, flinging him across the cavern. The floor tore him. He felt the skin on his knees tearing, shredding.

'Hold on!' cried the mesh. 'Hold on!'

Cliffs shuddered and slid, skies flamed, mountains burst, continents heaved –

A hole in the mesh! Getting bigger !–

A thousand million Trillions, a mountain of them, swallowed by a jagged, smoking, dragon's mouth gaping wider and wider in the ground! –

The sound became a Thing, a pounding triphammer to beat the world to pieces! –

The mesh writhed – snapped – ripped – sundered – gave a mighty cry 'HOLD ON!' – then finally and for all time, was broken.

Scott screamed and let go.

Someone kept asking the same question, so he concentrated and tried to answer it. It was a long fight through the woolliness and greyness and back into the light. It took a long time to find the right answer and speak it, but at last he managed.

'Friend,' said Scott. Then opened his eyes.

It was Icarus bending over him. Good, thought Scott.

Good old Icarus. I'm alive, then. He decided to prove he was alive by sitting up in bed. But moving his knees hurt so much that he gasped and lay back again on the pillows.

'Scott!' said Icarus. 'Well, thank God . . .' His face had an expression on it that Scott had never seen before, but was glad to see now.

'Where's mother?' Scott said.

'At the doctor's.'

'Is she ill?'

'No, you lunatic, *you're* ill. You've been ill for two days. Scott, what happened that night? How the hell did you get your knees in that state?'

'You asked me that before, didn't you?' said Scott.

'I've been asking you that – and other questions, any questions – for the last two days. What *happened* to you?'

'I don't know,' Scott muttered vaguely. He closed his eyes to give himself time to think. He came to a decision. He would tell Icarus.

'You can't get yourself into that condition and not know how – '

Scott opened his eyes, fixed them on Icarus, and said, 'I've been on the planet of the Trillions. That's where my knees got damaged. Right?'

'All right,' said Icarus, after a silence. 'Tell me the easy part first. Exactly *how* did you get your knees damaged on the Trillions' *planet*?'

'I was clutching on to the sort of mesh thing. It's all you can see of the Masters. The planet was shaking itself to pieces. The Masters were fighting to keep it in one piece. They use the Trillions just as we thought – to mend the planet itself. Ecology, remember?'

'Your knees.'

'I think I was shown the planet at the very moment when the last disaster hit it. I think I saw the beginning of the end. The Masters form this mesh, like a complicated street map or spider's web. Brain centre, everything. They radiate commands and the Trillions obey. The mesh began to shake. I was holding on to it and got flung about, on my knees. They got torn up on the floor. That's all.'

Icarus stood up, slowly. 'You've been pretty sick, Scott,' he said. 'And you still sound ill to me.'

'You don't believe me?'

'I must believe you. Your story is as good an explanation as any for the damage you've done yourself. You couldn't have done it just lying in bed – yet you were lying in bed. You haven't been out of bed for two days. So – yes, I believe you.'

'No, you don't,' said Scott. 'How can you? How can anyone?'

'Then make me believe you. Tell me the rest.'

'I will, Icarus. But you will never believe me. You can't. No one can.'

He could see that he had hurt Icarus but did not care. Why? He thought he saw the reason. 'It's all so – important, Icarus,' he went on. 'Nothing matters except the truth. Now I know the truth. I've seen it and touched it and heard it make a colossal noise in my ear. So never mind if you can't believe me. Just listen.'

He told Icarus everything. Then, next day, told his story again to Icarus, Bem, Mina and Panda. 'So you see,' he ended, 'they're friends.'

By now, his mind was completely made up. These four were to be the jury: but he, Scott, was to be the judge. They could listen to the evidence, weigh it up, make a recommendation: but only he, Scott could deliver the verdict – and carry it out.

Plan A was in operation. The world shook with explosions.

A bird fell from a tree. Panda picked it up. She looked up at Scott with her great black eyes and showed the bird to him. 'It's dead,' she whispered.

'Yes, I know. Others will die, thousands of them. But millions and millions will live. It's not the end of the world, Panda.'

'But it's *dead* . . .'

'It's not the end of the world,' he repeated, knowing that what he meant was not what she meant.

'It's the end of *its* world. The poor little thing, it's not fair, it's all wrong –'

'I know, Panda.'

'But you've got to *do* something – your Trillions –'

'I will. I promise you.'

He did.

What he did was almost a joke. It was Bem who suggested it. The four of them – Icarus, Panda, Bem and Scott – had been sitting round the living-room table. The dead bird lay in the centre of it. They had stared at it, thinking and thinking. Somehow Plan A had to be stopped. But how?

Bem suddenly got up and walked from the room. When he came back, he was carrying Scott's father's shotgun. It was a beautiful gun, one of a pair made by the most famous London gunsmith 100 years ago. There were few things Mr Houghton valued more than his shotguns.

'For heaven's *sake!*' shrilled Panda, 'if Mr Houghton finds you with that he'll *murder* you – !'

Bem put the gun down carefully on the sofa and stood in front of Panda. 'All right,' he said, 'let's pretend you are Scott's father. That's right, stand up. You've caught me with the gun. Now murder me!'

'Don't be stupid,' began Panda, weakly.

'I'm deadly serious. Do what I say. Pretend it's all happening. You've found me with the gun, you're angry, you intend to punish me. What do you do?'

'I – hit you, I suppose . . .'

'Then come on and hit me! Stand closer. Closer still. Now, pretend to hit me!'

Panda swung her arm feebly and brushed Bem's face with her hand.

'I said HIT me.'

She hit his shoulder with her fist, quite hard.

'That's better!' said Bem, looking owlish and pleased.

'I don't see much point in this,' Icarus began.

'I wish you'd put that gun *away*,' begged Panda.

'No, wait a moment. Let me go on. I did something wrong. Something to do with weapons. I *attacked* Mr Houghton, or seemed to. So now Mr Houghton can attack me. You've just seen it happen. Right?'

'Oh, all right. But I wish you'd put that *gun* away –'

'Now we are going to do it all over again,' said Bem cheerfully. He picked up the gun. 'Here I come. Priceless weapon. Panda, get ready to hit me again. Well come on! I'm all ready to be hit! What are you waiting for?'

'But I can't, not now,' said Panda.

'Why not?'

'Because you're carrying the gun!'

'Well, I won't hurt you with it, my finger's nowhere near the trigger.'

'It's not *you* I'm worrying about, stupid, it's the *gun*! Suppose I hit you and you *dropped* it . . .!'

She shuddered at the thought. Bem chuckled. 'No, you can't do much when the gun and I are together, can you?' he said. 'Well, there you are, then. I'll put it away now.' He marched out of the room, beaming.

'Wipe it down with the oil rag before you – ' Scott shouted after him – then stopped and whistled. 'He's right, you know!' he said, wonderingly. 'Good old Bem! He's right!'

And he and Icarus began to chuckle, then to roar with laughter.

The plan worked at first.

Next day, when the soldiers were getting ready to obey orders and blast more Trillions, there were serious difficulties. Overnight, the Trillions had formed into great glittering mounds. These mounds appeared only where there were weapons – the very weapons that were to be used against the Trillions.

Even to reach them, the soldiers had to sweep aside billions of Trillions. So there could be no question of using the weapons. How could you fire your TNW Mk III if the target was a mound of Trillions piled against someone else's TNW Mk III? How could a Navy corvette fire on a huge heap of Trillions with another Navy ship in the middle of it? How could aircraft drop bombs if the target area contained other fighting ships or aircraft or soldiers or guns?

For the first time in weeks, the world held its sides and laughed.

The laughter lasted until the General and his staff found the answer. 'In a word,' he said, 'mobility. Constant movement.

'Particularly aerial movement. The Trillions have only limited mobility. They can move as fast as foot soldiers, as fast as road vehicles, as fast as ships. What is more, they never grow tired, blast them. But they cannot move as fast as aircraft. So provided that we are prepared to accept substantial losses of material – of guns, motor vehicles, buildings, ammunition dumps and so forth – we can still attack the Trillions effectively.

'Now, gentlemen, are we prepared to accept such losses? Good. Then let us get to work and find out how best to *outpace* the Trillions – to march faster than them, so to speak. Then we can attack them from the air – and accept losses of our own material on the ground.

'Agreed? Good . . .'

So Bem's plan – Operation Shotgun, he had called it – began to weaken. He strengthened it by asking Scott to send Trillions to military centres – to buildings, war offices, airfields and any big, important centres that could be found. Icarus helped, Scott directed, Trillions travelled the night skies in vast armies. But as time passed, the General found answers. The roar of nuclear weapons began to be heard all over the world.

A bird fell from a tree. And once again Panda picked it up, showed it to Scott and said, 'You've got to *do* something.'

They were back where they had started.

'Plan B,' said the General.

Plan A had, after seven months, failed. Some Trillions, some experts said, had been destroyed by the nuclear blasts. Others said that if any had been destroyed – which they doubted – they were too few to matter. And the price had been too high.

But the Trillions were no longer 'forming', said the first experts. Wasn't that a victory? Too many trees were dying, said the second experts. Too much grassland was turning to mud, too many birds were falling from the trees, too many fish were floating belly-up in the oceans and rivers and lakes. Wasn't that defeat?

'Plan B,' said the General; and set his jaw more firmly. 'We have no alternative. Plan B.'

The world listened and wondered and worried itself sick. Scott judged. He judged the General and found him wanting. The General had changed and was still changing. The leathery skin seemed to be dusted over. The sharp, decisive voice began to bark. The eagle eyes began to glare and the flesh under them seemed puffy. The world was on his back and Scott judged it too heavy. 'There can be no retreat!' the General proclaimed. 'We must press home our attack and increase the pressure constantly. There is no other way.'

'Oh, isn't there?' thought Scott – but said nothing. 'Let my jury give an opinion,' he thought to himself.

'I hate it, all of it,' said Panda. 'The guns, the soldiers, the stupid new exterminators spoiling the town and the poor birds dying – I hate it and loathe it and wish I were dead!'

'I like some of the soldiers,' said Mina. 'I like Billy. But I don't like the Major. And I quite like the General. And I like Trillions.' She looked down contentedly at her latest bracelet.

'It's difficult,' said Bem. 'It's not one thing, it's lots of things, all interfering with each other . . .' Scott listened carefully. 'You remember when we were all asking Friend or Foe? Well, it was the wrong question, really. We should have been asking whether the Trillions were Guilty or Not Guilty. And we know, through Scott, that they're Not Guilty. They're innocent. They're neutrals! So it all comes back to us in the end. Us humans –'

'Bem's right,' said Icarus. 'I couldn't stand the General at first. I hated what he thought and did, what he stood for. He's a sort of walking calamity. Yet he must do what he does, it's all he knows. And now I find myself sorry for him.

But even more sorry for us – all of us, everyone in the world –'

Scott studied Icarus as he spoke, and judged. The mended face, the damaged hands, the nervous mouth, the brilliant, restless, brooding, unhappy brain that lit the eyes ... Scott judged and thought, 'No, not him. He's the other side of the General. He sees white where the General sees black and vice versa. And Icarus, with his singed wings, doesn't even want to fly any more. No, not him.'

Later, they switched on the television. Panda would not watch. She knew, she said, what it would be – Trillions, bombs, soldiers. She was right. The picture came to light and the hearty voice boomed (strange how, these days, the TV announcer's voices were always hearty and booming!) 'A new move of profound importance ... by international agreement, a concentrated drive that promises to rid the world, finally and definitely, of the alien menace of the Trillions ...'

Then there was the General's face. 'Plan B ...' said the General.

'No,' said Scott. 'Not Plan B. But the world must be given something to remember. "Hate me" ...'

He went to his room, closed the door and prepared for a hard night's work.

Two days later, his judgement was carried out; the Trillions began to form.

They formed a mighty tower that enclosed the General's headquarters. They made nightmare forts that rose from the sea and grew, minute by minute, until they soared into the sky. They built strange mazes in the middle of cities that cut the familiar streets into new patterns. They blocked runways and railroads, filled tunnels and motorways. Plan B, like most of the world's aircraft, never left the ground.

Icarus burst into Scott's room. 'What the devil are you doing?' he demanded. 'Have you gone quite mad?'

'Don't interrupt, I'm concentrating.'

'For God's sake – ' began Icarus. Then the boy stared at the man and the man went away.

On the third day, Scott said to his parents and to Icarus, Bem, Panda and Mina. 'Come with me. This is the end. It's going to be worth seeing.'

'I'm making a new bracelet – ' said Mina.

'I'd come if I were you. And Bem, I'd bring your camera.'

Scott led them to the end of the jetty that speared into the waters of Harbourtown West. 'We've got about three minutes before it begins,' he told them.

'But what – ?'

'I'm glad you brought your cine camera, Icarus. I'd use the wide angle lens. And the tripod.'

Nobody spoke for two minutes. A motorboat sped across the harbour and its wake slapped wavelets against the piles of the jetty. There were several sail-boats out at sea.

'Will they be all right when it happens – ' asked Mrs Houghton quietly.

'Oh yes. I'm not the General, mum. No bangs.'

'You're a strange son for any mother to have,' she replied.

Stranger than she knows, thought Scott. From now until the end of my life. It's like holding a pair of scales, water in the pan at one end and weights at the other. And there's a hole in the water pan and someone keeps changing the weights. Yet I've got to keep the balance, always . . .

He looked at his watch. 'Now!' he said. 'It should be now! I'm telling them as hard as I can.'

They obeyed. From the jetty, you could hear a rustling sound. A fizzing. It came from everywhere – from the water, from the town, from the boards beneath their feet. Then, suddenly, the town began to shimmer. The bottoms of the houses became indistinct. The water around them fizzled and puckered.

'Away!' shouted Scott. 'Away, away!'

The houses were veiled in a glittering, shimmering mist. You could not pick out the houses any more, they were hidden –

'It's the Trillions!' screamed Panda. 'They're going up!'

Mina screamed with fright and began to cry.

'Don't, don't cry, it's quite all right!' cried Scott. He turned his face to the sky and shouted 'Away!'

Now Trillions were boiling from the water and leaping for the sky; clouding and crowding from streets and houses and cracks between paving stones; raining upwards, hissing and hurtling. The sky was still bright but the air around them was dark with Trillions. Mina was beating at her clothes, yelling in panic. Scott did not even hear her. He stood as if in a trance, murmuring 'Away, away, away!'

The town was shut off from them now. And in every other town and city in the world, it was the same – the whispering hordes of Trillions, mounting to the skies, clambering over each other to escape when trapped, glinting and turning and linking, then soaring up and up in spiralling corkscrews, constantly building up their acceleration from each other.

Scott was his former self again – a schoolboy with a camera. 'Look! Over there! You can see the church, the base of the Trillions cloud is lifting! The colours! Icarus, I'm giving it 150th at f.11, is that right on your meter? Look at the spire, the spire!'

It was incredible. The Trillions now formed a massive pall over the town – not a cloudy or smoke-like mass, but a glittering, colour-changing, living thing –

'Look up! Look up!' shouted Bem.

Above them, the pall swirled slowly in a huge circle. As they watched, a vast hole formed. The swirling became swifter and a hissing noise filled the air. Then light flooded through the centre of the vortex – the blue of the sky! The hissing became louder, louder – the waves in the harbour ruffled – countless hordes of Trillions were swept into the throat of the vortex and, hissing, were flung upwards and onwards, into the blue.

'They spin each other, that's it! – ' Icarus was shouting. 'That must be it, each one gives the other a nudge and then you get this colossal acceleration in the vortex – '

His voice was drowned by a screeching hiss. Tops of little waves broke off and jumped into the air. Panda was holding her skirt down with both hands and laughing. Mrs Houghton cried,

'The yachts! – those boys in the yachts!'

Then all at once it was over. The sky was dark where the Trillions blotted out the sunshine. The air was still. Harbourtown West, tranquil in the grey light, was itself. Boats bobbed in the harbour and out at sea, the yachts heeled when they caught a breeze. Slowly, it became lighter and lighter. At last the sun shone through and the sky was azure blue, dotted with white clouds.

'Gone!' said Mina. 'They've all gone!' She held up her brown wrist. It was encircled with a strip of glue-y cardboard. Not a Trillion remained.

'All gone!' said Mina.

She was not quite right. Here and there, people still found Trillions. They had been trapped underneath heavy objects, locked in cracks and crevices. People kept them as souvenirs. Mina found enough to make a new bracelet in time.

Plan B was never put into force. The lorries rumbled away. Billy and the Major went with them. When you switched on the television, you no longer saw the General's face. The Exterminator was itself exterminated and Scott returned his Trillion Truck. He and the rest of the gang shouted, 'Hi ho Trillions!' for the last time.

Icarus stayed on at the Houghtons for two weeks of messing about in boats, then he too had to go. He put out his hand to shake Scott's and said, 'I suppose it's all up to you now.' They stood there rather stupidly, hand clasping hand, trying to think of something to say. Eventually, Icarus said, 'There's trouble blowing up in the Far East . . .'

'I know. I've been following it in the papers, on television – '

'There'll always be trouble somewhere, I suppose,' said Icarus. 'Hate. Fighting. Things getting out of balance.'

'Yes.'

'Well, do the best you can, Scott. I mean, you can't do everything, but – '

'I've got friends,' smiled Scott, cocking an eye at the sky. 'I can always call them when I need them.'

Space Hostages

Chapter 1

Billy Bason intended to send down an offbreak. It turned
into a yorker as a single, spiteful ray from the setting sun
shone through the trees right into his eye. Tony Hoskings
made his usual flashy swipe at the ball and as usual connected. The ball hissed away into the long grass, already dew-
drenched, looking for somewhere to hide.

Tony Hoskings yelled, 'Come ON then! RUN!'

He pelted up and down between the wickets – sticks draped
with coats – with his single pad flapping and leaking its
stuffing and his blond mop jigging and his bony legs and
arms pumping. He looked like a puppet gone mad.

'Bung it IN!' yelled Spadger Garrett, at the wicket.

'Can't find it!' shouted Tiddler from the edge of the
meadow. 'LOST BALL!' the other fielders chorused maliciously, not bothering to join the search.

'What do you mean, lost ball? That's my twentieth run,
lost ball or no. I got my twenty!' Tony Hoskings swore,
knocked down a wicket and kicked the coats. No one took
much notice. They were playing so late because they had to,
not because they wanted to. If Tony did not get what he
wanted, there would be trouble.

'It's all right, Tony, you got your twenty,' said Sandra
Rumsey. And then – forgetting all about cricket and fielding
and keeping Tony Hoskings in a good temper – she pointed
to the deepening blue of the evening sky.

'Look at that!' she said. 'I've never seen a star that big!'

'That's the evening star,' someone said.

'It's Polaris,' said Brylo Deniz confidently. He was so sure that he did not bother to look. Brylo was generally right about such things.

This time he was completely wrong.

'Oh no you don't, missy !' said Beauty's mother, Mrs Hopcroft.

'Get off your Dad and up to bed this instant. And you drink your milk, mind !' Her father pulled her hair and said, 'Torment !'

Beauty climbed down off her father's lap. She cupped her pink-white hands round the blue mug of milk and Mrs Hopcroft thought of cyclamens and periwinkles. Beauty shook back her hair and her mother thought of a glass of honey standing in the sun. Beauty smiled and her mother found herself beaming fatuously.

This was not just a mother's doting pride. Beauty's teeth were white and tiny and perfect. Beauty's feet under her nightie were as pretty as sugar mice. It was not her parents that had first called her 'Beauty' instead of her real name, Maureen; perhaps it had been old Mrs Durden, who kept the shop where Beauty spent her Saturday threepence; or Jim Knowles, the landlord of the Ploughshare, who bribed smiles from her with lemonade; or anyone else in Little Mowlesbury barring the Vicar, who called her 'Little One' (he could not remember names) and Tony Hoskings, who called her 'Blondie' or 'Tich'.

Beauty kissed her mother and father and went up the narrow stairs to her bedroom, counting each stair aloud. This was her ritual each night. But tonight, it was broken. Beauty stopped by the little window halfway up the staircase.

'Oh, Mummy, come and look !' she cried. 'There's a big star in the sky !'

Beauty was wrong. It was not a star.

The boy and girl cricketers straggled back from the meadow with bats and pads and stumps. They pushed and hollered round Tony Hoskings, easily the tallest and most powerful of them – half a head taller than Brylo Deniz, though he too was eleven years old.

'I told you I'd get that twenty!' said Tony. 'I got my twenty before you lost the ball!' No one argued. Without interrupting himself, he left the road, squelched into the edge of the foul pond where ducks had once swum and marched over the roof of the half-submerged carcase of an Austin Heavy 12. 'Well, come ON, then! Follow yer leader! That's me!' he yelled, and all the others followed him. Squelch, squelch, thump, scrabble, DOING, DOING, pause, jump, splash, squelch, squelch. The line of figures rose and fell like a caterpillar climbing over a twig. Brylo Deniz hesitated, shrugged and followed the rest. But even then, Tony went for him.

'Heh! Where's Brylo gone, then?' shouted Tony. 'Anyone here seen Brylo?' Some of the boys sniggered. It was best to laugh at Tony's jokes. And this was one of them.

'Oh! Sorry, Brylo boy! Didn't see you!' said Tony. 'Couldn't see you in this light. I mean, how could I?'

More uneasy laughter. For Brylo's skin was dark brown. He was a Jamaican or West Indian or something like that; an orphan adopted by a childless couple in the village. Brylo was clever at school – two forms ahead of Tony. And Tony was leader –

'That's never a star!' piped the Tiddler, eight-year-old Brian Biddle. They all paused and stared at the brilliant dot in the sky. 'There's never been a star that big!'

And it was not a star . . .

'I'm off!' muttered Spadger to Brylo. They had reached his cottage and Spadger could see through the heavy dropping lace curtains that the telly was on. If only Tony didn't see him go. . . .

'I want you, Spadger!' yelled Tony. He had not even bothered to turn his head, thought Spadger, he just knew

I'd try and slide off home. 'All of you!' Tony bellowed. 'We're going to serenade Dirty Durdens.'

'Why can't you leave them alone, they haven't done you any harm,' began Sandra. But Tony just turned on his heel and looked at her, his eyes glinting in the dusky light.

'You *sing*, see?' he said, hoarsely.

They were at the shop now. You could just read the familiar, ancient signs that covered its front. TIZER THE APPETIZER. NOSEGAY. BIRD'S EYE. And Sandra could see in her mind's eye the musty, gaslit back parlour, with old Mr Durden mumbling and dozing in his stiff wooden chair and old Mrs Durden blinking and shuffling and dratting the cat. Sandra was once a Brownie, she had been inside there to clean. It was dark and sad. The rest sounded feeble but Tony's voice was hoarse and piercing as a carrion crow's:

> DIRTY OL' DURDEN
> GIVES SHORT WEIGHT
> EATS DEAD TOM CATS
> OFF A DIRTY PLATE

And sure enough, the backdoor was flung open and old Mr Durden came out as if he'd been thrown out, and he was raving and mumbling and prancing and Tony was braying with laughter and dancing round him, just out of reach.

All the children ran. Not because they were frightened but because they were embarrassed. Even Tony soon gave up and came scarecrowing down the dim road after them.

Behind them, old Mrs Durden scolded old Mr Durden and told him not to fret – come inside and eat your supper *do*. And because he was so old, he forgot the children and stared about him with his watery eyes.

'Never seen a star the like of that!' he said. And so brilliant was the light of the thing that looked like a star that it made his eyes blink even faster.

The group began to break up, bit by bit, as the children reached their homes.

"Night, Tiddler, mind it when you wash – you might slip down the plug'ole!'

'Come inside this instant, Sandra, your supper's spoiling.'

Inside most of the houses and cottages, the telly was on and the places were laid.

'Do switch off the telly, Dad, it makes me sick, the news!'

'Hold on a minute, Mother, I want to hear it . . .'

'Sit up straight and eat your good food properly, my lad . . .'

'It's always the same these days – *they'll* drop a bomb or we'll drop a bomb!'

'Let's hear it, then.'

The man on the telly made it all sound very normal and respectable. 'Mr Tang replied that unless effective guarantees for the unmolested independence of Pian Tuk were offered immediately by the Western Powers, he would have no option but to use nuclear weapons. In the Commons today, the Prime Minister said that Mr Tang's threats were hardly likely to influence the course of action decided upon by Her Majesty's government and supported by the whole free world. We too had nuclear weapons and would not hesitate to –'

'Oh, must we listen to this, it makes me –'

'No, keep quiet a minute –'

'. . . In America, attitudes towards the Pian Tuk situation are hardening. The Defence Secretary, Mr O'Rourke, said today that America wants peace and will fight for it if necessary. Promises had been made and broken. The American nation would not tolerate –'

'Hold your fork properly, do!'

'Threats and bombs and fighting. Haven't we had enough? It makes me sick, I don't know why you listen to it –'

'And now,' said the man on the telly, with a quick smirk, 'cricket!'

'Mum, we saw a whopping great star when we were playing cricket, big as a saucer!'

'Eat up. Your pudding's ready.'

Ashley Mott did not play cricket. He was afraid of Tony Hoskings – and besides, there was his mother. Mother did not like the village boys and girls, they were rude and rough. Mother and Daddy (but especially Mother) were ... *nicer* than the village people. Mother had once known a little boy who had been hit by a cricket ball and they had to take his eye out. His eye OUT!

Earlier, Ashley had heard them playing cricket on the meadow.

'Howzat!' lots of voices shouted. 'OUT!' shouted the umpire. Ashley had shivered then and he shivered now. His eye OUT!

He did not want to play cricket, thank you very much. Mother was right.

He continued undressing, for shortly his mother would call up the stairs, 'Ashley, ready for drinkies?' and he would say 'Yes, Mother! Nearly ready!' and she would say, 'Pop into your 'jamas and Mother will be up!' and she would bring him his warm Ovaltine in the bunny rabbit mug.

A cold, dew-laden draught of air stirred the curtains and Ashley went to close the window. The sky was dark blue overhead, but still pale where the sun had set. He reached forward for the window catch – and there, just behind the peak of the roof, was an enormous star!

'Mummy, Mummy!' he cried, 'Mummy, come and see! A huge star!'

Everyone was home now, but still there was talk of Little Mowlesbury's star.

'Heh! Look at the star! It's got bigger, Dad!' said Tony. 'I'll give you stars...' said his father.

Spadger saw it. 'It can't be a star!' he said to himself.

Brylo saw it. 'It's moved, so it can't be a star,' he reasoned.

The telly was too dull to watch that night with all the

news flashes upsetting the proper programmes. So perhaps half a dozen children in Little Mowlesbury were staring at the 'star' when it went out. It went out like a light. One minute it was there and the next second it was gone.

And now that their eyes were not concentrated on the disc of light, their ears could hear a noise. No, not the transformers of the power substation – they made a lower, steadier hum. This noise was breathier, more whining, more urgent.

'Spaceship!' breathed Spadger to himself. 'I'll bet that's what it is! From Mars!'

'It must have been catching the last rays of the sun,' thought Brylo, 'and then the sun went down – or the star thing came lower and nearer – so it "went out". A spaceship?'

'Poor Mother's quite puffed out!' said Mrs Mott to Ashley.

'What a naughty boy you are! Big star, indeed!'

'But...' said Ashley.

'Give Mother a big kiss and straight off to Dreamland!' said Mrs Mott.

There was the noise of an express train, then twenty express trains – then a tearing shriek of blasting jets mixed with a thunder that shook glass and shifted tiles and stopped your heart beating – and IT landed in the middle of the meadow, burning the grass of the cricket pitch to fine grey powder.

Chapter 2

They poured out of the pub, the church, the British Legion hall, the parish hall and their houses and down to the meadow; the whole village, all 170 souls, even old Mr Durden.

They stopped at the edge of the meadow. They had not known what to expect. The reality was beyond imagination.

It was a vast craft. It would have covered twenty, thirty cricket pitches. It could have sheltered half a dozen great airliners. It was domed on top, slightly concave below (Spadger found himself comparing it to a monstrous hubcap from a car). It was as high off the ground as a house, or two double-decker buses standing on top of each other. It had four gleaming legs like a modern coffee table, with the same disc-like feet. Even in the almost faded light, it gleamed like porcelain containing metal particles.

It was completely silent and showed no lights. But sometimes a tuft of long grass flared briefly for a moment – the smell of burning grass was everywhere – and you could see a glinting reflection magnified in the shining belly of the ship.

People talked as they watched, but their voices were hushed as voices are in church when the service is about to start. A mild breeze blew more grass smoke towards them and some of them coughed. They waited.

They did not have to wait long. A trap in the belly of the craft opened with a slight whine and rumble and a metallic cabin whose floor was the size of the trap descended on a metal shaft. The noise of the descent was exactly that of a lift.

The descent took about ten seconds. The cabin reached the

scorched ground, appeared to sense its presence and stopped. So did the noise.

Suddenly, the whole area covered by the ship and the villagers was flooded with light! The shock drove the villagers back a pace. Someone said, 'Heaven preserve us!' and someone else said, 'Mind my feet!' Then several people said, 'Shush!' It seemed somehow dangerous even to whisper.

But then there was a slight jostling and Mr Gordon, the farmer, and Eric and Fred, his farmhands, were pushing their way to the front. All three had guns. Then, after more shuffling and murmurs of 'Mind out, now!' Jim Knowles joined Mr Gordon. Mr Knowles carried a service rifle. You could hear them muttering to each other.

'You cover it, but leave the accurate stuff to me, you've only got spreadshot in that ...'

'Aye, that's right, you pick 'un off, we'll cover ...'

'But leave it till you're sure, you know what I mean ...'

'Aye, the whites of their eyes.'

'Their tentacles more like!' brayed Fred, and some people laughed.

But only for a short while.

A minute went by and nothing happened.

Then came the Voice: an enormous voice that flooded the meadow and echoed off the belly of the ship.

'YOU WON'T NEED THOSE GUNS!' it roared. Then, 'OH, BLAST!' Then, much more quietly – 'Sorry, didn't mean to deafen you. Look, you won't need the guns, so for heaven's sake put them down. That's better. Now keep quite calm and leave the guns alone. I'm coming out. Right?'

The door of the cabin silently opened. And into the glare of the lights stepped an RAF Flight Lieutenant in his peaked cap and tunic with two rings. He touched a tiny microphone at his throat and said, 'Sorry if I startled you.' Then, 'Gosh, this ground is hot.'

Chapter 3

He was a very ordinary Flight Lieutenant, they discovered; a startling contrast to the ship he flew. They bombarded him with questions. It was surprising how few answers he had. Or was he just handling them very cleverly?

'These flying saucer things,' said Mr Knowles. 'How come we've never even been told about them – never even guessed they existed?'

'Oh, security, old man!' said the Flight Lieutenant.

'But what about all those stories in the papers – you know, unidentified flying objects, all that? Is this one of them?'

'Oh well, you know the newspapers, old man.'

'Well, how many of these things are there? Lots? Just this one?'

'Well, the powers that be don't exactly confide in me, you know. But I think this is the only one.'

'But what's it for? What does it do?'

'Oh, you could call it a multi-purpose craft. Definitely.'

Mr Knowles gave up. Spadger took over.

'Go on, tell us, mister. What'll she do?'

'You mean how fast will she go?'

'Yes, what'll she do?'

'Well over the speed of sound.'

'But lots of ordinary planes do that.'

'So they do. Yes,' said the Flight Lieutenant. Then he added, very vaguely, 'Good show!'

'Now this really won't do, young man!' said the Vicar. 'I'm going to ask you three questions and I want the answers straight from the shoulder, man to man. Question One – why did you land here? Question Two – when will you take off again and leave us in peace? Question Three – who is your chief or superior officer or whatever you call it?'

'Well, let's see, Padre. Why did I land here? Because I jolly well had to. Question two, when will I take off again? – I jolly well can't.'

'You can't?'

'Spot of bother. Had to come down. Question three – never mind, Padre. Call it the R A F and leave it at that. O K?'

'Most certainly not! I'm going to telephone the Ministry of Defence immediately. And the police.'

'No, Padre. Please don't!' The young Flight Lieutenant seemed to pull himself together and become firmer and harder. 'Don't do that. I'll tell you why. I'll tell you all why.' He touched the button on the throat microphone and his voice could be heard by everyone. 'Listen! No telephoning or anything of that sort! I hope no one's telephoned already?'

'They couldn't do that without me!' said Miss Miggs. She was the postmistress. 'I was in such a state when this thing came down out of the sky, I simply flew here, and all the lines...'

'Good. No telephoning, then. Now I'll tell you why. Have you been following the news? The trouble in Pian Tuk and so on?'

There was a low chorus of 'Aaah!' from the villagers.

'Then you can guess what I'm going to say. This craft is secret. That's putting it mildly. It's a British secret – but more than that. You could say that it's part of world affairs. A very important part at this moment. So it's no good telephoning the Ministry of Defence. It's no good ringing up the Income Tax people, even ...' (there was some laughter) '... because what is happening here is bigger than all of them put together. And I'll tell you this: THERE ARE PLENTY OF PEOPLE THROUGHOUT THE WORLD WHO WANT TO KNOW ABOUT THIS CRAFT! Not only where it is, but if it EXISTS, even ! And not all those people are friends of ours. Understood?'

'But surely someone ought to be told? The Government –?'

'The Vicar here says that someone ought to be told,' said the Flight Lieutenant's amplified voice. 'Well, Padre, so they should. But not, I repeat not, by telephone. Surely you've heard of telephones being tapped, listened in to? And surely you can guess what's already happened? No? Well, I'll tell you !' He paused and lit a cigarette. 'Look at this craft !' He flung out an arm and the villagers' heads turned to stare at the vast saucer, black now against the sky. 'Do you honestly think it's got a telephone exchange inside? Dial 999 and ask for Mars? No such luck ! No nice cosy postmistress for us !'

There was a general laugh and heads turned to Miss Miggs.

'No, we don't do things quite that way. Our communications are to do with satellites in space and scrambled codes and security piled on security piled on security ! Now, I can make the ship sit up and beg, even from here – look, I'll show you !'

They watched : and although the Flight Lieutenant seemed to touch nothing, they saw the cabin door open and close, a series of aerials emerge from the belly of the craft and then retract and – as a sort of encore – a single beam of light shoot from a hidden source on to the ground, along which it crawled until it 'found' and spotlit the Flight Lieutenant.

'Down, Fido !' said the Flight Lieutenant and the light went out. 'No, seriously,' continued the Flight Lieutenant, 'I can do a whole lot of things with this ship. But one of the things I can't do is break its communications, its codes, its links with higher authority. That's all built in and programmed and going like mad. Surely you realize that even before I touched down here, the ship had told the whole story to the only people who ought to know !'

'Aaaah !' said the villagers again. They understood.

'Tell you what I'll do !' said the Flight Lieutenant. 'I'll let you hear it talking to our masters ! Come on lad ...' he pulled Ashley, the nearest boy, forward. 'You can press the button and we'll all listen in! Go on, press it!'

He held out what looked like a particularly small transistor radio and indicated the right button. Ashley pressed it. The Flight Lieutenant put the little set to his throat microphone, and they heard a fluttering, whining chatter of electronic sounds – a gibberish that could have come from outer space.

'Well, that's the ship talking!' said the Flight Lieutenant, switching the noise off. 'And if anyone can translate, please let me know. I hope she's saying what I want to hear . . .'

'What's that, Flight Lieutenant?'

'Where I can get another packet of cigarettes. I'm out!' He flung an empty packet away and everyone laughed. Farmer Gordon was the first to succeed in thrusting a pack of cigarettes into the Flight Lieutenant's hand, but several packs were offered. It seemed that their terrifying visitor from the sky was not so terrible after all.

Chapter 4

A quarter of an hour later, the villagers and the Flight Lieutenant were old friends. He had arranged the microphone so that everyone within several yards of him could be heard and he could be heard by everyone. It was almost cosy sitting there in the warm summer night. The whole of the village had not felt such unity since the end of World War II. That had been wonderful. But this was staggering. A flying saucer in Little Mowlesbury!

'No, I just can't answer that sort of question,' said the Flight Lieutenant. 'Please don't ask me too much about the ship. You'll get me shot if I answer!'

'That's right!' said Fred. 'Play fair by the Lieut!'

'Anyhow,' said the Flight Lieutenant, 'even if I gave you a complete answer to the sort of questions your shrewd Vicar has been popping at me, I don't think you would understand me. Even if I showed you over the ship, you wouldn't see a single thing you understood except the chairs and tables.'

'Oh, *mister*!' said the Tiddler. 'You'd never let us see inside?'

'Let's see! Let's see!' the children pleaded. 'Go on, mister! Just a quick look!'

'The Flight Lieutenant has already explained,' began the Vicar, but nothing would quieten the children. 'Do let's see!' they begged.

The Flight Lieutenant shook his head steadily against the torrent of voices. Smiling, he lifted his hand. The chorus died down. 'All you'd get by going aboard is a trip in that cabin-lift and ...' But he had said the wrong thing. Everyone wanted to go up in the lift. This time it was harder to silence the children.

'Sorry, kids!' said the Flight Lieutenant. 'That ship isn't mine. It's not my property.'

'Well, who *does* it belong to, then?' shouted the Tiddler and lots of people laughed.

'Taxpayer's property, sonny!' said the Flight Lieutenant, smiling.

'My dad's a taxpayer!' shouted the Tiddler.

'Aye, all our dads are taxpayers!' yelled the children. The laughter increased.

'Our young friends would rather seem to have established their claim,' the Vicar chuckled. The grown-ups chortled and nodded.

But the Flight Lieutenant suddenly changed the mood. 'What's the time? Half past? For heaven's sake! Give me that radio!' He snatched a transistor set from Tony's hand, tuned it rapidly and listened, his face set hard. It was the news.

'They've gone and done it!' he said, a few moments later. 'They've issued an ultimatum!' He switched the radio off and gave it back to Tony without looking at him. Everyone was silent. The Flight Lieutenant stared straight ahead of himself. The silence lengthened.

'Taxpayers' money! TAXPAYERS' MONEY!' he suddenly shouted.

'My Lord, you're right! You and me – we've all paid our money! Now we take our choice! You want to see inside the craft, sonny?'

'Yes! Yes!' said Tiddler.

'Yes!' cried the others.

'Well, you might as well get some pleasure for all the money you paid!' said the Flight Lieutenant viciously. 'All right, then! All right! All aboard the Skylark! Taxpayers' money! Come on, then! Children first, six at a time! Then the rest of you! All aboard the Skylark!'

Beauty, of course, found her royal way to the front. The others pushed and jostled and shoved. Beauty carefully placed her little slippered foot on the step of the 'lift', and smiled a polite and pearly smile at the Flight Lieutenant and entered. Once inside, she turned and waved to her parents and said, 'Look at me! I'm in!'

'Oh, Beauty, come back!' cried her mother, suddenly afraid. But it was too late. 'AND the next please!' said the Flight Lieutenant, imitating a bus conductor.

Tiddler went next because he was small. His small body and big head, with its 'Mowlesbury Massacre' pudding basin haircut, were brilliantly lit as he went in. He blinked, smiled and blushed.

'AND a lady, IF you please!' said the Flight Lieutenant, still being a bus conductor.

Sandra Rumsey went in. She wore a fawn dressing-gown over her pyjamas and her very long, thick, brown plait swung as she bent down to take Beauty's hand. 'There's our Sandra,' said her mother wonderingly. And you knew what she meant. For Sandra's wide, friendly, homely face and her nice old dressing-gown looked strange in the little metallic room, with its slick brushed-aluminium walls.

Brylo went in, his face solemn and his eyes wide. This was the entry to the world he knew was to be his – the world of the brain, an international world where the colour of your skin meant very much less than the size of your cranium. His parents watched him without expression. They understood. They had reason to: for his parents-by-adoption were 'foreigners' in the village – Mr Deniz, a South American, was an assistant in a biological laboratory. He worked in a nest of concrete buildings some miles from Little Mowlesbury. He knew the villagers had a vague and on the whole kindly contempt for him and for Brylo. He felt just the same distant contempt for them. Nothing ever happened in Little Mowlesbury: but things, real things, happened in the laboratories. He and Brylo talked about these things ...

'Another lovely lady, then!' said the Flight Lieutenant, still jolly. But he looked strangely worn and ill in the light from the lift. A girl called Diana Moyce went forward, then back, then forward, and began to giggle and clutch her friends' arms.

'*Flip!*' said Tony Hoskings, and pushed past her into the lift. He stood there, a head taller than the others, throwing his lank yellow hair back impatiently and daring anyone to challenge him. No one did. He was in.

Diana went in. 'Come back, Di!' 'Go on, Di!' her friends shouted. There was so much screaming and excitement that she had to go in, really, she told herself. And Tony was there. Diana was tall and coltish like Tony. She was twelve and wished she were eighteen. She *felt* eighteen. She rolled her big, dark, bold eyes and smoothed her long black hair nervously and shouted to Tony, 'Hey, Tone! All these flipping kids . . .'

Spadger Garrett and Billy Bason went in together, before anyone could stop them. 'You come out of that, you young limb!' shouted Spadger's father, but Spadger pretended not to understand and shouted back, 'Yes, I'm all right, Dad!' The two boys stood there beaming awkwardly – Billy all freckles and sandiness, Spadger mousy and plump. They did most things together, including ferreting, catapulting, attempting to ride cows, brewing gunpowder that didn't explode and sloe gin that did.

'Better than the fair!' said Spadger.

'That's all for the first trip!' said the Flight Lieutenant.

'Really, these village children,' said Mrs Mott, eyeing Diana. Diana caught the look. 'Why, how simply divine, it's Mrs Mott!' she screeched, 'How-jerdo, my deah!'

Mrs Mott was so shocked by this attack that she let go Ashley's hand and put her own hands to her burning cheeks.

'That's all for the first trip!' said the amplified voice of the Flight Lieutenant.

Disturbed as she was, Mrs Mott saw how ill he looked.

That horrible girl Diana and this horrible spaceship and now this man, this Flight Lieutenant. All of a sudden, she felt sick with fright, she knew there was something amiss, something not nice ...

'Ashley !' she cried. He had slipped away !

'Up we go, then !' said the Flight Lieutenant.

'What about me?'

'And me !'

'Back for another trip round the Skylark later – parents too !' said the Flight Lieutenant.

'Ashley !' screamed Mrs Mott. Her red nails clawed at the throat of her velvet dress. The whining noise of the lift door and the sliding door shifted, and began to slide shut.

And she saw Ashley, clean and pink and white and neat in his warm dressing-gown, slip as cunningly as a stoat through the closing gap and into the lift. She saw the door close. And she knew as certainly as she knew the neatly brushed and parted hair – she could just glimpse it as the door shut – that her Ashley was going to be involved in some sort of dreadful trouble.

'Back in half a minute for the next ...' said the Flight Lieutenant from inside the lift. Then there was a metallic click as if he had disconnected some vital plug. Then the whirring whine as the lift ascended, a little glimmer of light rising up into the belly of the ship. Then the closing of the underbelly doors so that one could no longer see that there had been a lift at all. Then another click, and the voice of the Flight Lieutenant, speaking through a louder, harsher amplifier and in a louder, harsher tone :

'CLEAR THE GROUND. Get away from the ship. Clear the ground. GET WELL AWAY. CLEAR THE GROUND.'

Mrs Mott screamed first. There were more screams, then a roar of voices and a surging of the crowd under the ship. The four guns were raised, but the Flight Lieutenant's voice said, 'None of that !' and the guns wavered and were brought down.

'He must have TV in there,' began Jim Knowles.

'YOU HAVE TEN SECONDS,' said the great metal voice, flatly. 'NINE . . . EIGHT . . . SEVEN   YOU'D BETTER MOVE AND MOVE FAST! – SIX – CLEAR THE GROUND, FIVE . . .'

Some people moved and one or two ran.

'FOUR . . . THREE . . . TWO . . .' A whole crowd ran for the edge of the meadow.

'ONE! ALL RIGHT. I TOLD YOU TO MOVE . . .'

There was a thunderous bellow from the black shape above them – a sound so loud that people screamed from the pain of it and fell to the ground, their hands over their ears. The bellowing stopped. Slowly the figures rose and walked, dazed. The voice spoke again.

'YOU HAVE A MATTER OF SECONDS. HELP EACH OTHER OFF THE GROUND. CLEAR THE GROUND. I AM GOING TO TAKE OFF.'

The Vicar looked up at the glinting metallic blackness, and whispered, 'But you said you couldn't! You lied!' Next to him old Durden fell down and lay gasping.

'CLEAR THE GROUND. CLEAR THE GROUND. YOU PEOPLE THERE AROUND THE OLD MAN – LIFT HIM UP AND GET HIM AWAY. DO IT NOW. CLEAR THE GROUND. I AM GOING TO TAKE OFF.'

'Ashley!' screamed Mrs Mott. She ran to one of the great legs of the ship and hit it with her fists.

'CLEAR THE GROUND. GET THAT WOMAN AWAY. YOU TWO MEN, TAKE THAT WOMAN AWAY. CLEAR THE GROUND, YOU HAVE VERY LITTLE TIME.'

A new noise, a thin electronic scream, came from the ship. The scream rose higher and higher and settled to a single steady note. 'THAT'S RIGHT, CLEAR THE GROUND. THAT'S GOOD. NOW KEEP WALKING. WALK AWAY. GET WELL CLEAR. KEEP WALKING. GET WELL CLEAR. YOU HAVE ONLY SECONDS LEFT!'

Women were crying and stumbling. Knowles fired six shots from his rifle in quick succession. You could see the spark and glitter where the bullets hit the ship. The Flight Lieutenant's voice, suddenly quiet and tired, said, 'Don't be a silly man.' Then the voice came back, not so loud.

'Now, listen. Your children are coming with me. As long as I last. They will find a way, somewhere, somehow. Away from this world.' The voice faltered.

'He's ill,' whispered the Vicar.

'He's mad,' said Mr Knowles.

Almost as if he had heard him, the Flight Lieutenant said, 'Perhaps you think I am mad. I think you are mad. Yes, all of you. The news — surely you must realize by now what is going to happen. War, destruction, everywhere. The whole world. And you do nothing, nothing. Someone must do ...' They could hear him coughing.

Then, 'Hostages to fortune, that's the sort of nonsense you understand. Your children are hostages to fortune. They can start again when you lot have destroyed yourself and your world. You should thank me. You should ...'

Silence for a few seconds. Then the voice spoke for the last time:

'GET CLEAR. TURN YOUR HEADS. DO NOT WATCH. LIE DOWN. I AM GOING TO TAKE OFF NOW. I AM GOING TO TAKE OFF NOW. COVER YOUR HEADS AND GUARD YOUR EYES. THE CHILDREN ARE ...'

There was the noise of an express train, then twenty express trains, then a tearing shriek of blasting jets. The great craft seemed bathed in fire. It rose slowly, slowly, and the legs entered the body. The fury of the noise increased. The people clutched their heads. Their mouths were O's, but their screaming could not be heard above the huge outcry of the ship. It rose, still slowly, then faster. Then much faster.

People raised their heads and looked. They saw a dwindling point of fire in the sky, heard the rumbling express-train noise booming and re-echoing among their familiar little hills.

It was gone.

Chapter 5

The Flight Lieutenant hadn't moved. He lay at full length on the floor, his head in Sandra's lap. His face was glazed with sweat. His colour was red, yet bloodless.

'You're ill,' said Sandra softly. She touched his forehead. It was moist and burning. She removed her finger quickly. She disliked the feeling of his skin. She could not help staring at the spots on his face: spots like tiny water blisters. She had never seen anything like them before.

He moved and spoke. 'Stand clear! Get well clear!' he said, in the harsh, loud tone he had used only minutes before when they were still on Earth, still in Little Mowlesbury.

'Get that old man away!' said the Flight Lieutenant, loudly.

Tony came to. He blinked, shook his head, and got to his feet, staring. 'What happened?' he said. 'Where – Oh! That Flight Lieutenant! He done it to us then!' He said all this quite calmly, then looked dully at Sandra with his mouth open. He was still dazed.

The other children stirred, and one by one awakened. Spadger was quickly and tidily sick in a newspaper. The rest were silent and wide-eyed. They formed a ring round Sandra and the Flight Lieutenant. They stood silent, some of them pressing their hands against their ears.

'If your ears hurt, open your mouth wide,' said Brylo. 'As if you were yawning. It's the change of pressure.' Some of them did, and Sandra thought to herself that their gaping faces above her made the whole thing even more mad and unbelievable and terrifying. They were in the sky, in space, rocketing further and further away from home. Yet all around her were the untidy, familiar faces of Tiddler and Spadger and Di and Tony and Brylo, all of them framed in the tidy, unfamiliar cabin of the spaceship or flying saucer – what *was* its proper name? What *were* they doing in it? Why? How long?

Violently, the Flight Lieutenant jerked upright, pressed his hands to his ears, opened his mouth and appeared to scream silently. His eyes lost their vacant look. He shook his head once and spoke – this time in his ordinary voice.

'That was a shocking take-off. I'm sorry. I flaked out early on, I think – passed out cold. I don't know how many g's we hit – what I mean is, we came up too fast – I'm sorry! Help me up.'

They did so. And Sandra thought, why does he need help to get up? What's wrong with him?

They put the Flight Lieutenant in an aluminium-framed, padded chair in front of a console of instruments. On all four sides of the crowded space around him were more instruments, more dials, more screens, more gauges, meters, warning lights, counters, knobs, pointers, handles, displays.

'I want to go home now,' said Beauty, bravely. But her eyes were swimming.

'Oh, Beauty!' cried Sandra, hugging her. 'And I don't understand *any* of it!' She burst into tears.

Suddenly all the children were talking at once, shouting questions and threats and demands and more questions . . .

'SHUT UP!' yelled the Flight Lieutenant. 'SHUT UP, SHUT UP, SHUT UP!'

They stared at him, silent. His face was scarlet except for his nostrils, which were bone-white. They could see the pulses pounding in his temples and the tiny things like water blisters standing out on his face.

'I'm sorry,' said the Flight Lieutenant. 'Or have I said that before? Yes, I have. But I'm not. Not sorry, I mean. I mean, I'm sorry to drag you away from your homes like this – well, that's putting it mildly – but it had to be done. That should be obvious enough even to a child.'

He mopped his forehead with a handkerchief.

'No offence. You're all children, I know. That's the whole point, you see. It's *because* you're children – can't you understand?'

He faltered and stopped. 'Say something, someone!' prayed Sandra. 'Say something, do something, make him take us back home!'

It was Tony who spoke. His crow's voice hit at the Flight Lieutenant.

'You're off your flippin' nut, mister airman,' he said, his voice hard and jeering. 'You made a mess of getting us up here and you're making a mess of telling us *why* we're up here. But there's one thing you mustn't make a mess of, and that's getting us down. DOWN. See?'

He poked his head forward so that it almost touched the Flight Lieutenant's face. 'DOWN. Now you're taking us DOWN. See?'

'That's right, you tell him, Tone!' said Di in a nervous scream.

The Flight Lieutenant did not move. Tony put a hand on his shoulder and shook him.

'Hey, MISTER AIRMAN! I want to go DOWN! Get the message? DOWN!'

The Flight Lieutenant's elbows slid forward lazily and his head fell forward with a soft bump on to his arms. Brylo was at his side quickly. He looked hard at the Flight Lieutenant's face, then lifted an eyelid with his finger. 'It's no good, Tony,' he said. 'He's passed out again.'

'Is he dead?' screamed Di.

Chapter 6

They knew from the clock – the only dial they could understand – that two hours had passed since the Flight Lieutenant had lost consciousness. During that time, they had explored most of the ship.

It was huge. The control cabin where the Flight Lieutenant lay – white faced, but breathing regularly and cocooned with blankets – was only a small and still mysterious part of the whole. A dove-grey corridor from Control led to what Brylo thought was a navigation room with a single bunk. Facing it was what appeared to be a Communications or Radio Room, also with a bunk.

From there on, dove-grey corridors led to rooms that were increasingly to do with humans and less to do with the ship. There were, for example, two separate shower rooms, one with equipment of a sort that Brylo guessed to be connected with decontamination: if you suffered some sort of injury, obviously this was the shower you used. Brylo kept this conclusion to himself. He thought he could guess the sort of injury and he did not like his thoughts.

There were also a very small library (the books and magazines, Brylo noted, were all non-technical); a cinema with twenty seats and a large television screen; a music room with an excellent record player but no records in the shelves; a very small gymnasium only partly equipped; a small dormitory and a number of separate cabins with beds; a canteen seating twenty, a small and well furnished dining-room seating six and a gleaming, elaborate kitchen.

'Do themselves well, whoever they are,' sniffed Di.

'Let's find out how well,' said Tony. 'We got to eat . . .'

Brylo began to prod knobs one by one in a methodical fashion. Tony said, 'Oh, for flip's sake!' and pressed all the knobs at once. It worked. Pilot lights lit, electricity hummed. Tony kept pressing the knobs. A hatch opened and an egg salad on a plate appeared. Then another and another.

'Dish 'em out,' said Tony grandly.

'I haven't got a fork or a knife,' Beauty complained.

'Look till you flippin' find one,' said Tony. Beauty opened the drawer nearest her. It was filled with knives and forks.

'Oh, thank you, Tony!' she said. She looked at him wonderingly and he could not help grinning. She smiled back and decided that Tony was very nice.

'You are clever, Tony,' she said. As she ate, she kept her eyes on him, admiring him.

The girls were busy. 'This hotplate's hot,' said Di.

'Find out which switch,' said Tony.

'The water boiler's full and the water's getting hot . . .'

'Find some tea or cocoa and bung it in and brew up, then.'

'Look, this knob makes cornflakes come out . . .'

'Well, don't stand there. Find flippin' BOWLS.'

They ate, left the dishes, and went on exploring.

They found a wine cupboard full of wine bottles, all full.

They found, low down in the ship, a whole gallery of corridors and doors, all marked DANGER. Behind most of the doors, they could hear the sounds of power – the hum and whine and roar of the things that drove the ship.

'I'll take a look,' said Tony, still chewing at a hard-boiled egg.

'Don't, Tony,' said Brylo, very seriously.

Tony stopped, turned and faced Brylo. He finished chewing his egg and then asked, 'Who's the boss here, Brylo boy? You or me?'

'Don't go in there, Tony, you've no idea what . . .'

'I said, who's boss?'

The rest watched silently. Di sidled up to stand by Tony. He stared at Brylo.

'It's nothing to do with who's boss,' said Brylo. 'I don't care who's boss . . .'

'Well, I do and it's me. I'm boss. All right, Brylo boy?'

'Just don't go messing about behind those doors . . .'

'You never know with old Brylo boy,' said Tony to Di, turning away from Brylo. 'Never know whether he's all brown, or brown with a yellow streak.'

Di gave a scream of laughter. Some of the others sniggered weakly. Brylo swallowed, blinked, racked his brains for a reply and found none. It did not help when Beauty slipped her hand into his and confided, 'I'm glad Tony is the boss, aren't you?'

But at least Tony did not open any of the doors marked DANGER.

Chapter 7

The Tiddler came running up the corridor. 'He's still asleep, Tony,' he said. 'I took a good look at him and he's no worse.'

'Did you make sure his blankets were still on him?'

'He'd hardly moved, Tony . . .'

'I didn't ask if he'd moved, did I? I asked about his flippin' *blankets*. You want to wash your ears out. And there's something else you can do. You can stop calling me Tony. You can call me Captain. That goes for all of you. Right?'

'Aye, aye, Cap'n,' said Tiddler, giving a nautical salute and rolling his eyes. There was some friendly laughter.

Tony walked over to Tiddler and hit him twice almost in the same movement, once with the back of his hand and once with the front. Tiddler's eyes popped with surprise, then his face puckered and he began to cry. 'You hurt my *ear*, you rotten idiot!' he yelled and ran at Tony. Spadger caught Tiddler's arm and pulled him aside.

It was just as well. Tony's face was set in hard fury. His fists were clenched, his mouth twisted. They were used to his rages and his outbursts, but they had never seen him like this.

'IT'S NOT FLIPPIN' FUNNY!' he shouted.

'We weren't laughing, Tony, honest,' said Billy Bason.

'You laughed when I said call me Captain! You did, I saw you!' shouted Tony. 'And *you* laughed! And *you*!' He jabbed his finger at Sandra and Spadger. They turned to Brylo for support, but he was looking down at the ground.

Brylo was thinking. The Flight Lieutenant sick, with an illness Brylo could not place; themselves in a flying saucer, which might be heading for an infinity of space or for a head-on smash against the Earth, the Moon – anywhere; and Tony – Tony already beginning to act like a little Adolf Hitler. He wondered miserably if Tony had ever heard of Adolf Hitler and then pulled himself together and tried to think of something more to the point. But once again, Tony got there first; suddenly he was all smiles and friendliness.

'All right! Come on Tiddler, turn it up – you'll frighten Tich here!'

Beauty smiled at him uncertainly.

'All I ask is, just remember one thing. All of you. Someone's got to be boss. It better be me. So just you call me, Captain. Captain. OK? Captain! Simple enough, isn't it? I'm your Captain. I'll see you through so long as no one interferes. OK, Brylo?' Brylo did not look up. 'Good boy, that's my Brylo! Now, where were we? Exploring the ship, that's where. All right, follow me!'

They found the biggest room of all.

It was positioned right away from the 'Danger' parts and well away from Control. It was a beautifully equipped lounge, with a conference table in an annexe and a number of softly upholstered easy chairs. There was a drinks cabinet, a TV screen with a small console of controls in front of it and a hatch to serve food. There were two antique globes, one of the stars and the other, of Earth, beautifully restored to bring the map up to date. There were provisions for wall displays, a little square window denoting a cinema projection booth and everything else needed for comfort, discussion, work or relaxation.

'It's like those great Board Rooms you see in the films!' said Billy Bason. 'You know, Big Tycoon!'

'Number 10 Downing Street, Space version!' said Di, throwing her legs in the air from one of the deepest chairs.

'What do you make of it, Brylo boy?' said Tony, being consciously affable.

'Di's right – that's what I think,' said Brylo shortly.

'What do you mean? Do you mean that . . .'

'Be all right for that perishing little Ashley. Just his style !' said Di maliciously.

'Where is Ashley?' said Sandra.

'Heh ! That's right, he came aboard with us ! Where is he?' said Tony.

'Anyone seen him?'

'He didn't come exploring with us, I don't remember seeing him after we left the Flight Lieutenant . . .'

'And he's not with the Flight Lieutenant or I'd have seen him,' said Tiddler.

'You, you and you – go and find him !' said Tony pointing at Spadger, Billy and Sandra. He stretched himself out in a chair and added, 'Go on ! Get moving !'

Spadger and Billy looked at each other and shrugged. 'All right, Tony,' said Spadger.

'Not Tony,' said Tony. 'It's *Captain*. You say, "All right, *Captain* !" Remember?'

When they came back from the search, Billy and Spadger were laughing and even Sandra could not help smiling.

'You'll never guess where we found him, Ton . . . Captain !' said Billy.

'He was in that little room where all the radio bits are, you know . . .'

'The Communications room . . .' said Sandra.

'And he'd got himself some blankets and he'd made them up all very tidily into a proper bed . . .'

'Like a nest !' said Spadger.

'. . . And he'd got himself all burrowed in among the gear in there, with his dressing-gown hung up on the wall all tidy and his slippers . . .'

'. . . Bunny-rabbit slippers !'

'. . . His slippers on the floor side by side, and we came in and he half woke up and you'll never guess what he said, Tony !'

'*Captain*. Well, go on, tell us, then.'

'He said, "*I'm ready for my drinkie, Mummy*"!'

Billy and Spadger clutched each other and roared. Everyone laughed except Tony. He said, 'My drinkie, Mummy. It makes you sick. Flippin' *sick*!'

And everyone stopped laughing.

Chapter 8

The Flight Lieutenant regained consciousness at five o'clock in the morning. Sandra was awakened by his murmurings and got up from her improvised bed beside him. He opened his eyes. Sandra said, 'Are you all right? Can you hear me? Do you want something?'

He looked at her in a dull, tired way, and replied, 'I think I'm all right. Help me to sit up. That's better. I've got to talk to you, all of you.'

'I'd better get Tony, he's the Captain.'

'Is he all right?' said Spadger, waking up. He, too, had made his bed in Control.

'Go and get Tony. You know where he is,' said Sandra.

'I know where Tony is – pardon, *Captain* Tony,' said Spadger bitterly, disentangling himself from his blankets. 'He's in the Captain's Cabin. The Executive Suite. Big Tycoon. Oh well, I'll go and get him. Are you really better?' he asked the Flight Lieutenant. 'You look a bit better anyhow. I'll go and get Tony.'

'I must look like hell,' said the Flight Lieutenant miserably.

Brylo came in and, without speaking, put his hand on the Flight Lieutenant's forehead and took his pulse. 'I think you're a bit better than you were, but you don't look too good.'

'Don't want the rest to see me like this,' mumbled the Flight Lieutenant. He got a comb out and began to use it.

As he combed his hair, great tufts of it came out.

Sandra gave a strangled 'Oh!' and began to cry quietly. Brylo put a hand to her shoulder and said to the Flight Lieutenant, 'Listen! Talk quickly before the others come – Sandra here will be all right, she's got sense. What's wrong with you? What have you got?'

'Do you know what radiation means?' said the Flight Lieutenant. His voice shook.

'Yes. You mean atomic radiation. Radiation sickness? Yes, I know.'

'Well, I know too. I've learned the hard way. Pretty, isn't it?' There was a pause. 'You seem a pretty sensible kid. And you too, Sandra. I don't know so much about the others. That boy with all the blond hair, there's something wrong there, you'll have to watch him ...'

'Your sickness,' said Sandra.

'Oh, yes. It's radiation sickness all right. What the service calls a self-inflicted injury in my case. I asked for it, I got it. Over-gunned the nuclear motor when I took the ship. Too much for the shielding to take ...' Once again, the Flight Lieutenant seemed to come to a full stop, as if he had been run down.

'But how? When?' Brylo pressed him.

'Here. In this ship. And recently. A matter of days.'

Tony came in, wide awake and there were sounds of the approach of the others. The Flight Lieutenant hid the comb under his blankets.

'What's going on?' Tony demanded. 'You got up, Flight Lieutenant. Why did you do that? Are you better or what?'

The Flight Lieutenant looked at Brylo and gave a twisted smile. 'Get all the children in here, Tony,' he said. 'I've got to talk to all of you. Immediately. There isn't much time. Oh, Lord, I think I'm going to be sick again.'

'Sandra, get the kids. All of them. Even flippin' Ashley.'

At least, thought Brylo, Tony has got sense. He knows when to act fast. I wish I did.

By the time the children had assembled, the Flight Lieutenant was back from the bathroom. He looked very ill indeed. He kept putting his hand to his face as if to make sure it was there. He would speak, and then touch himself experimentally, almost as if he were trying to assure himself of his own existence.

'All right,' he began, 'First of all, why you're here. You're here because I brought you here. No one else is involved. Only me and you. I brought you here because I think there's going to be another war, one heck of a blow-up – the final war. A complete mess. Nothing left of anything. Of course, I could be wrong . . .'

'He could be wrong!' jeered Tony.

'Wait a minute!' said Brylo. 'What about that news flash? You remember, when we were all under the ship on the meadow. You borrowed a transistor set and . . .'

'Oh, *that*!' said the Flight Lieutenant wearily. 'Bit of play-acting, that's all, to persuade your parents to let you come aboard. There wasn't any more news, still the same old nonsense about what *we* said and what *they* said. Threats and counter-threats, the same old rigmarole . . .'

He lost concentration and touched his face. Then he seemed to gain a spurt of energy.

'But you can't blot out a whole world!' he cried. 'Or even if you can, something must be saved. You, *you* must be saved! You can start again, your children could rebuild life on Earth. Or perhaps they couldn't I don't know.'

'Rebuild it?' said Brylo. 'But you've just said that the world might be destroyed! You can't rebuild a lump of radioactive clinker!'

'Did I say Earth?' said the Flight Lieutenant. 'I suppose I did. Habit. What I mean is you could rebuild human civilization . . .'

'On this ship? But . . .'

'No, not on this ship, this is only a means of transport.'

'Then where?' Brylo demanded.

'Oh,' said the Flight Lieutenant, touching his face, 'on the moon, I suppose . . .'

The children gasped.

'He supposes!' said Tony, bitterly.

Brylo interrupted him. 'You mean on the Moon Station? But they've only been up there just under a year, they've only just started!'

'Oh, they'd make room for you!' said the Flight Lieutenant. 'That's the whole point! You're all kids – children. Everyone loves children, even that shower of politicians and generals and lunatics on Earth! Don't you see, the whole world will be made to see reason now you're up here! You're hostages! Hostages to the whole world – to world peace! They'll kill a thousand soldiers here and ten thousand civilians there and not even notice. But children! That's different. Oh, they'll take notice of you all right!'

'Get him!' said Tony wryly, biting his thumbnail. 'Just the right bloke to be cast adrift in space with! And all because he thinks there might be a war . . .'

'Are we really going to the moon?' said Beauty, huge-eyed.

'We'll be lucky if we get to Southend with *him*,' said Tony.

'Never mind that, there are far more important things,' said Brylo. 'Listen, Flight Lieutenant. Are you listening? Tell us what we've got to *do*! Tell us how long the engines will run, how much food there is, how much oxygen if that's what we're breathing, how to navigate, how to get in touch with Earth!'

'He's not hearing,' said Sandra quietly. Gently, she tugged at the Flight Lieutenant's sleeve. He just sat slumped, his hand to his face.

'Get something wet and cold and put it on his head,' said Tony.

'Look!' said Brylo. 'Let's see what we *do* know. We know that almost everything he told us when he landed was lies. He could take off and he did. There hasn't been an ultimatum about peace and war, they're still arguing. He's only a Flight Lieutenant, yet he was alone in this ship – so he must have kidnapped it, just as he kidnapped us.'

'He didn't tell us what the ship is for,' said Spadger.

'Well, that's obvious, isn't it? It's a special ship, probably a one-off thing, for important people ...'

'It's a VIP funk-hole, if you want to know!' said the Flight Lieutenant, without raising his head. 'It was built to get the government big-wigs and the top brass away from the bombs they're preparing to drop! It's a technological marvel, furnished in the best possible taste throughout with soft seats for a limited number of distinguished backsides! It's the cleverest, stinkingest, most highly advanced funk-hole the world has ever seen – although I suppose they've got just the same things in Russia and America and ...'

'Never mind all that!' yelled Tony. 'Just tell us how long it will run, how to make it go, how it all *works*!'

The Flight Lieutenant lifted his flushed, perspiring head and stared at Tony.

'Me tell you?' he gasped. 'Me? The humble dogsbody Flight Lieutenant?' He broke into a coughing laugh. 'Me tell you how the thing works? Look, sonny, I got radiation burns that will kill me in a week learning what I learned, and I don't know *anything*!'

Chapter 9

In fact, the Flight Lieutenant knew quite a lot.

For the next two days, Sandra nursed him and Brylo patiently cross-questioned him, noting down everything that seemed significant. He did this for his own benefit and also for the others in case anything happened to him.

Water, Food, he wrote. More than enough packaged and prepared meals for a month. Plenty of food in tins and cold store. Plenty of water and apparently a regenerating unit to make more.

Oxygen: uncertain, but probably enough. All oxygen cylinders believed full (check by tapping, full cylinders gave different note from empty). Ships own Carbon monoxide recycling unit – performance not known. In operation now? How is Oxygen content read and stabilized? Instrument somewhere? ?

Lighting: electric power: available indefinitely.

Power: ship has three motors, one more or less a rocket drive for maximum take-off and counter-thrust when landing, the others 'space' drives to propel ship. These two nuclear.

FLIGHT LIEUTENANT GOT HIS RADIATION DOSE FROM ENTERING 'DANGER' ROOM CONTAINING NUCLEAR-DRIVE MOTOR: ALSO FROM RUNNING THESE ENGINES ABOVE THE SAFETY LIMIT INDICATED ON THE DRAWING ATTACHED. READINGS ON THESE DIALS MUST NOT EXCEED LIMITS MARKED – FLIGHT LIEUTENANT DID NOT UNDERSTAND AND EXCEEDED LIMITS. RADIATION SHIELDS INEFFECTIVE WHEN LIMITS EXCEEDED BEWARE OF THIS.

Take-off procedure: Flight Lieutenant gave maximum 'boost' from rocket-type motors (probably unnecessary to use maximum) and also nuclear space drive early on. Thus violent take-off? Less power needed?

Landing: same as above, but Flight Lieutenant says easier to judge power for landing, you can watch ground coming up. OBVIOUSLY ROCKET DRIVE IS THE ONE THAT MATTERS WHEN YOU ARE ANYWHERE NEAR EARTH. CONTROLS: SEE DIAGRAM.

Navigation: not understood. Flight Lieutenant believes craft can be navigated only from inside, not from Earth (because craft used to escape from destroyed Earth??).

Vision: Flight Lieutenant has shown me how to work Near Vision, but cannot understand long-distance apparatus. Does it exist? YOU CAN SEE IMMEDIATELY AROUND YOU FROM SHIP, BUT NOT OVER LONG DISTANCES. NO WINDOWS IN SHIP.

Controls: SEE DIAGRAM.

Communications: Flight Lieutenant says ship capable of receiving and sending radio, and able to receive TV but cannot work the sets, which seem dead??????

State of ship: the ship was kept in almost 100 per cent readiness always. When the Flight Lieutenant stole it, it was fully fitted out except Communications equipment not working???? Flight Lieutenant thinks missing items, if any, would most likely be very minor – e.g., luxuries, toilet items. (Thus no records for music room??)

First Aid: Medical Room with Red Cross on door. DO NOT TOUCH CONTENTS OF SMALL TIN BOX WITH PADLOCK – DANGEROUS DRUGS.

Showers – the medical showers are for people who have got a dose of radiation or think they have. HAVE TAPED INSTRUCTIONS FOR USE TO DOOR. DO NOT REMOVE.

As Brylo made his notes, he acted on them methodically, putting first things first – oxygen, because that was the very air they breathed; water, because he knew that they could live longer without food than without water; and so on. He soon discovered the oxygen instruments, for example, and noted that both his reserves and the oxygen balance inside the ship were completely satisfactory; apparently the balance was maintained automatically, for the dial needles barely shifted.

He inspected the food stores with Sandra and discovered the secrets of the egg salads. There were considerable stores of ready prepared foods delivered from a deep-freeze electric conveyor belt with a push-button programming and actuating system. To Brylo, this seemed unnecessarily elaborate. So did the electric and electronic trickeries and gimmicks of the great lounge. He began to understand the resentment that had invaded the Flight Lieutenant's mind. The ship was indeed a sort of scientific jewel-case, far too generously filled with jewels.

He worked with increasing urgency at his notes, for the Flight Lieutenant was weakening. He was constantly vomiting. His temperature was 104. The water blisters multiplied, joined, made islands, countries and continents on his face. Brylo preferred not to think about his hair, and what happened when he combed it, or even tossed his head on his pillow.

Brylo made another note:

Waste matter: human and kitchen waste products automatically voided from ship via toilets, waste-disposal units etc, with very slight and unimportant loss of air. IF SOMETHING BIG MUST BE EJECTED FROM SHIP, USE AIRLOCK IN EXIT COMPARTMENT.

He finished writing this and looked at the Flight Lieutenant for a long time, pitying him. Then he picked up his ballpoint and added a footnote to what he had written:

HOW MUCH AIR IS LOST WHEN AIRLOCK IS USED?

Chapter 10

It was night again (or was it? Only the clocks told them when it was night and when it was day). The children prepared to go to their beds.

Sandra combed out her long, heavy brown plait; plaited it again; looked in the mirror and wished yet again that her face was not so broad, not so 'jolly'. She thought of her favourite pop star, Cindy Sue, and wished for the millionth time that she, Sandra, could have that almond-shaped face, the long-lashed dark eyes, the curling mouth with huge dimples at each corner, the glinting, sweeping wave of hair . . .

'You wouldn't want to sound like her, anyhow!' she consoled herself. And she began to imitate Cindy Sue's hiccoughing whine when she sang 'Don't Mean It, Baby'.

'You are making a funny noise!' said Beauty.

'Come here and I'll do your hair and make you look smashing,' Sandra replied. She took a firm hold of the thick, honey-coloured, silken waves and parted them down the middle to reveal Beauty's tender, slender neck. She touched the gold down on it with a fingertip and said, 'Your neck's too thin to hold your head up, did you know that?'

'My head will go all wobbly, won't it?' gurgled Beauty, delighted with the idea. She began to murmur 'wibble . . . wobble . . .' in time with the strokes as Sandra put aside the brush and took up a comb. Sandra thought of home.

She thought of the hundreds, thousands of times that her mother had combed her hair for her just as she was combing Beauty's. She remembered how she had sometimes tugged and complained – 'Oh, Mum-mee!' –and how her mother used to say. 'Eh, be quiet! Eh, be still!' She remembered learning to make her own plait – practising for hours in the kitchen, with the sun streaming through the little green-painted window with its red and white check curtain. She remembered the dishmop and the lazy buzzing of a fly and the hollyhocks outside and the enormous box of matches with a ship on it that was cheaper than buying lots of little boxes. She remembered her father smacking her hand when he found her playing with the matches and how she shouted, 'I hate you! I hate you!'

'It's this ship I hate,' thought Sandra. 'I didn't even know what hate meant when I was a little girl. I know now. It's this ship.'

'Am I done now?' said Beauty. 'Am I smashing?'

'You look like a bunch of flowers in a red ribbon!' said Sandra, using the old Mowlesbury words that her mother had used to her.

Beauty ran from her and dived straight on to her bed, flailing her legs. 'Smashing, smashing, smashing!' she yelled.

'Don't say that word any more, lovie, I'm sick of it,' said Sandra.

'Why, what does it mean?'

I could give her more than one answer, thought Sandra, and shivered suddenly as she tucked Beauty in.

Spadger, Billy Bason and the Tiddler shared a room. It wasn't a bad sort of room. The bunks were alloy, the walls light grey, and there were pipes and cables running over their heads across the ceiling. Set into one wall was a metal plate with a grille at the top from which came clicking noises at regular intervals. They had made these noises into part of their play. They called themselves 'The Three From Outer Space'.

'Check the airlock,' said Spadger. Billy Bason and the Tiddler seized the door and, grunting with pretended exertion, forced it closed. They waited for a few seconds, and sure enough – *Click!* went the thing behind the panel in the wall.

'Airlock closed !' said Tiddler.

'Proceed to count-down !' said Billy Bason.

'All right men ... awaiting synchronization ...' said Spadger, examining an imaginary wrist watch.

Click! went the thing behind the panel.

'Ten ... Nine ... Eight ... Seven ... Six ... Five ... Four ... Three ... Two ... One ... BLAST OFF !'

They flung themselves on their bunks and covered their heads with their hands. They made jet howls that got louder and louder and higher and higher, until ...

Click!

'Cut all jets! Switch to Spacedrive! Bring in Anti-grav when you hear the signal ! ...'

Click!

'Antigrav operational ! All right, men, we're on our own. Us against *Them* !'

'Can you hear anything, Brains?'

'I – thought – I – heard ...' said Tiddler, in his metallic 'Brains' voice.

'Herr Oberschnitz?'

'Nein. I am hearing not one thing. Should we the light turn out?' said Spadger.

'Sure thing, men,' said Billy Bason in his voice of Captain Freedom. He switched out the light. 'Reckon if they're going to show, we'll be hearing from them real soon. ...'

Click!

'I wish you'd get another name for yourself, Billy,' said Spadger in his own voice. 'All this "Captain" stuff makes me sick. We've got enough Captains ...'

'One's enough. More than enough.'

'*Captain* Tony. Captain Tony Hoskings. Makes me sick.'

'He's gone off his nut with this Captain lark.'

'He was off his nut before ...'

Click!

'Vot was dot, mein kamerads?' whispered Herr Ober-schnitz.

'Get – your – Ray-guns – ready – for – immediate – action –' said Brains.

'Cool it fellers! Play it real cool . . . !' murmured Captain Freedom.

Click!

Tony pressed a button and an egg salad came out. He ate the egg, dipping it in the blob of mayonnaise, then threw the rest down a disposal chute. Then he made his way back to the biggest room of all – the beautifully equipped lounge. The Captain's room. His room.

It was time for bed and he felt sleepy. Good and sleepy, sleepy and good. Not sick at all – yet the bottle of wine on the table was almost half empty. Tony decided he must have a pretty strong head. He could drink like a man. A man among boys. He was the only real man on the ship: you couldn't count the Flight Lieutenant any more . . .

'You're on the way out, Lieut!' he murmured. 'Ya know that? Finished! Washed up! Believe me, man, you're on the way out!'

He let himself fall into a big armchair and hardly felt the pain as one of the arms thumped into his ribs. 'Not a good landing, man!' he said to himself, and caught himself chuckling.

This surprised him. He sat bolt upright in the chair and thought hard. Why had the chair hit him? Because he had fallen into it untidily. Why had he fallen into it untidily? Because he had drunk nearly half a bottle of wine.

'Moron!' he said. 'You're the Captain, remember?'

He poured the rest of the wine down a disposal chute and let the bottle go too.

'You're in command,' he reminded himself.

In command of what? He sat down carefully, and began to work it out. 'Take a roll call,' he instructed himself.

Flight Lieutenant? Dying. No action until he actually died. Brylo? Well under control. Brylo knew when he was licked and Tony had him licked. Sandra? Good girl. She takes care of Beauty and the Lieut. Spadger, Billy Bason, the Tiddler? Like kids at a carnival. No sense, not an idea among the three of them. Kids playing kids' games. Forget them. Ashley? Flippin' mummy's darling. Get Sandra to take care of him, make sure he eats, clean his toofy-woofies.

'What a mob!' he thought. 'What a shower! But they'll do what I tell them. They'll call me Captain or get their heads punched. They admire me, because I know what to do. . . .'

Something was wrong, though. Tony got up from the chair and stood by a table, kicking it gently with his big toe. What exactly *were* they doing? Heading for the moon, or for outer space, or back to earth, or what? And did it matter? As long as he was boss, everything was all right. It was being boss, being Captain, that mattered. They never let him be boss at home. The teachers were always picking on him at school, he was never boss there. Now he was boss. It wasn't *his* fault if he couldn't make the ship go where it should go, wherever that was. It wasn't *his* fault that he couldn't work the controls – if the Flight Lieutenant couldn't, and brainy Brylo couldn't, why expect him to be able to? Why pick on him? Why blame him?

Suddenly, he felt a little sick. The wine! Better go to bed, it was nearly twelve. He lay down on the long couch and pulled a blanket over him, then realized that he would have to get up again to turn out the lights. Flippin' lights! He closed his eyes to see if he could go to sleep with them on, but the room seemed to lurch and swing. He sat up.

'Where was I?' he said out loud. That's right, he was taking a roll call – ticking off everybody on board. He started to go through it again. Had he remembered everyone?

'Remember me?' said the piercing voice of Di.

She stood in the doorway looking at him with her head on one side.

'You keep out of here,' said Tony. 'My room. Captain's cabin.'

Di ignored him. 'You've gone white!' she said. 'Your face is all *white*! What have you been at?'

'Flippin' – clear – OUT!' said Tony. But the effort brought a wave of sickness to his throat and he gasped, disgustedly.

'I'll get a cold cloth . . .'

'Don't bother yourself. Flippin' clear out.'

'You've been at that wine, that's what it is!' said Di, bustling out.

Tony could have killed her for knowing. He propped himself up on one arm and was about to shout at her when the wave of sickness came back, worse than ever.

Di flounced back into the room with a wet cloth. She sat down beside him on the couch and put it on his forehead. 'You've been a soppy old Captain, haven't you?' she said. Tony writhed, but the cold cloth felt wonderful.

'Can't say I blame you,' she went on. 'I mean, it's a big responsibility, isn't it? Being Captain, I mean . . .'

She turned the cloth. It felt even better.

'You take care of them,' said Di, speaking softly for once, 'and I'll take care of you. Right?'

Tony didn't answer. But he let her stay.

Chapter 11

Brylo put down his ballpoint and rubbed his forehead with both hands. He looked again at the clock: almost midnight. No, he thought, almost twelve. There is no night, no day, up here. But day or night, I should go to sleep. I cannot work any more.

He lay down on a bunk in an annexe of Control. The bunk was of alloy and pulled from the wall. It had a plastic foam mattress with a pillow shaped in it. He wondered how much the whole thing weighed. Very little. Probably a pound or so. Ingenious . . .

And comfortable. Tomorrow, he would look more carefully at the radio console in Control. Obviously their immediate needs were taken care of – food, water, air. If only they could communicate! If only they could get in touch with Earth! But the Flight Lieutenant was delirious. And when he had been fairly normal and able to speak rationally, he had made it quite clear that he understood very little of the functions of the apparatus in Control.

Brylo decided that he must yet again go right over every item in Control, concentrating on its radio and television equipment – the possible links with Earth. But should he also take a look at the Communications room? No, don't bother. If you were designing a craft like this, he told himself, you would put everything you needed in one place, in one room. So Control was like a ship's bridge. Everything the Captain and the senior officers might need was controllable from the bridge. The Communications room was merely a specialist department – like, say, a telephone exchange. To use a telephone, you don't go to the telephone exchange: you merely lift up your receiver and dial. So what he had to do was to master the dialling system, so as to speak. And that should operate from Control . . .

The bed was very comfortable. Brylo realized, with a dim pleasure, that he was falling asleep. He encouraged his mind to form pictures. Obligingly, it came up with an old cigarette card – a slightly blurred picture of the bridge of the Queen Mary, with a beef-faced portly Captain standing in front of a shining brass binnacle, a sailor at the wheel and two officers in the background. What were the other cards in the series? Were they all to do with Captains?

His half-asleep mind presented him with another cigarette card – Captain George Eyston, holder of the World Land Speed Record in . . . in . . . When? And had George Eyston been a Captain, or had he got it all wrong? He mused, drowsily and pleasantly.

Suddenly his mind switched tracks and Tony's face was right in front of him, jeering. Captain Tony!

Brylo jerked and sat half upright. Then he forced himself to lie down and clear his mind.

But his mind would not clear itself. Tony appeared again and Brylo resolutely switched him off by thinking of home. What was on his bedside table the night the ship landed? Think of that, he told himself. Memory training. Pelmanism. Remember each item . . .

There were, almost certainly, his green fountain pen and his maths homework because he had been getting ready to work in bed. Also a glass of water – the fluted tumbler. Also a stick of chewing gum. Also *The Adventures of Sherlock Holmes*, which he had been saving for later. He could now picture the top of his bedside table with complete accuracy. Good!

But his tired brain would not hold the picture: it slipped. It fell away, downwards, and became smaller as if he were looking at it down a chimney through a telescope. The table was tiny now, a long way below him. And now it was slipping away and away (or was he rising faster and faster above it?) and he could see the house and the garden and the trees and then the whole village, dimly in the dusk.

Faster still! Now it was like looking down a well at a miniature village, a miniature world – a world in a fish-bowl! He saw that, connecting him and the world, was a gossamer-fine filament like a spider's web, a filament that must not be broken.

He was in space, infinite space, and there was blue-blackness all about him. A million miles down, the tiny world slowly twisted and spun at the end of his filament. As long as the filament held! . . .

Then almost total darkness. The world had dwindled to nothing, it was gone. He peered into the darkness, seeking it, following the still-taut line of the glinting filament that connected him to it.

Then the filament loosened, rippled, floated aimlessly in the void.

Uneasily, Brylo slept.

Chapter 12

Ashley had long since crawled into his solitary nest in the Radio Communications room and gone to bed. But he was not asleep.

He lay in the neat bed he had made for himself of three blankets and his woolly dressing-gown. His bunny-rabbit slippers were neatly placed side by side within reach. His comb lay by a folded handkerchief (which he was trying not to use, so that it would keep clean) on the ledge of an insanely complicated console of communications equipment under which he had burrowed to make his bed. His hair was combed and he lay on his back with his hands folded outside the coverlets. He was ready.

'I'm in bed, Mummy!' he called softly.

He waited for a few moments, then said, 'Yes, I *am* in bed. And everything's put away tidily.'

He waited again.

'Can I have my hot drinkie now, Mummy?'

He waited and waited. If he kept still enough, surely something would happen? Something nice? Surely Mummy would come up the stairs, step by step, carefully and surely, bearing his nice hot drink? He waited.

Mummy didn't come.

Ashley rolled over in bed and buried his face in his pillow. He clenched his plump, clean fists and tried not to cry. He succeeded and felt proud of himself. He sat up in bed.

By the dim blue glow from two little lights on the console, he could distinguish a shape that puzzled him for a moment until he remembered what it was: earphones. They lay on a shelf. He got out of bed and picked them up, turning them over in his hands. The earpieces were heavily padded with foam-plastic mouldings. He wondered if they would be comfortable and if wearing them would help him sleep. He tried them on. They felt very nice.

Then he had a better idea. At home, they had a radio set and Daddy understood all about radios. Perhaps – he was not very clear about this – perhaps if he plugged the earphones in somewhere, he would hear Mummy?

He got out of bed and switched on a little light that illuminated the console and a desk in front of it. He examined the jack-plug at the end of the earphones' cable and looked for a hole it would fit. The trouble was, that there were so many holes. And Ashley knew how dangerous electricity is – Mummy was always telling him. 'Don't touch the vacuum cleaner, Ashley !' she would cry, 'It could give you a nasty, nasty, shock !' Ashley didn't want a nasty shock.

But then he remembered Daddy saying that if you touched a 'live' electrical mechanism with the back of your fingers and *did* get a shock, your fingers would curl up into a fist *away* from the shock and you would be safe. Whereas if you touched the dangerous thing in the usual way and got a shock, the shock would make your hand clench the thing and you would go on and on getting the shock until there was smoke curling from your hair and –

Ashley shivered and decided to be very, very careful.

He put the earphones on the shelf, picked up the jack-plug and put it in a hole marked CH 3. He then touched the earphones with the back of his fingers. No shock. Gingerly he put the earphones on.

Nothing. Not a sound except the dull plunging of his own pulse.

He took the earphones off, and went through the procedure again and again. CH 1, CH 2, CH 4, PA 1, PA 1 ex, PA 2, PA 2 ex . . .

Nothing.

Then he noticed that all these holes were in a console that did not have a blue light burning. He moved to another console beside it that did have a blue light, and tried again. He plugged into a socket marked COMM 1.

He was successful immediately. As he put the earphones on, he heard the frizzling, crackling, frying sound of 'live' radio.

But only that. After a time, he reached out a trembling hand and began to turn dials. The first dial made no difference to the sound he heard in the earphones. He tried another, then another.

Suddenly his head was almost burst open by a horrifying scream ! – a scream that went on and on. Screaming himself, Ashley tore at the headphones and scrabbled them from his head – then flung himself into bed and drew the blankets over his head.

The earphones lay on the floor, their metal parts glimmering with reflections of blue light. From them came a continuous, unvarying whistle. . . .

Many minutes later, Ashley slowly uncovered his head. His eyes flickered with panic at first, then fixed themselves on the devilish, whistling, blue-glinting thing on the floor.

Chapter 13

The Flight Lieutenant was sitting bolt upright in his dis-ordered bed when Sandra visited him at two o'clock that night.

'Glad you could come, I'm feeling a bit depressed,' he an-nounced cheerfully. His voice was as she had first heard it – confident and racy.

'What's the matter?' Sandra asked him, smiling. It was wonderful to know that he was better – almost back to nor-mal.

'It's the kids I'm worried about,' said the Flight Lieutenant. 'I mean, suppose there *were* another war! Everyone would cop it! Not just the soldiers and fighting men, but even the ordinary men and women. And the kids. Even the politicians might find things a bit umpty,' he said, knowingly. 'But of course, they've always got a way out. Confidentially –' he paused dramatically – 'I happen to know something that very few other men know. It's about the politicians and the top brass. They've got a funk-hole!'

Something cold seemed to crawl up Sandra's back. He's delirious, she thought. He's worse than ever.

'It's a funk-hole in the sky,' said the Flight Lieutenant. 'Right up high! Higher than a kite! Right up there with the Man in the Moon! I say, that's funny! – because it's true, you know!' He laughed, then said, very seriously, 'I say, I'm glad I never married. Aren't you?'

'I'm a bit young,' said Sandra dully.

'Never too young!' cried the Flight Lieutenant, gaily. 'Never too old! I had to make a speech when I was best man at Toby's wedding. Wish 'em all the best and all that rot. You know Toby, don't you?'

'Oh, yes,' lied Sandra.

'The speech was a bit of a flop, really,' continued the Flight Lieutenant. 'Never could do that sort of thing really well – speaking in public and so on. Not the right type, I suppose. Never make a politician, eh? Blasted politicians. All scum! ...' He picked at the blanket gloomily. Sandra wished only that he would stop – that she could go, could escape. But she knew that she must stay with him.

'Old Toby!' said the Flight Lieutenant, raising his head and grinning delightedly. 'He was a case! He really was a boy! You know Toby, don't you?'

'Oh, yes,' said Sandra. 'I know Toby.'

'What a boyo!' said the Flight Lieutenant. 'Do you remember the time when we were all in Flight B at Nestlington, and he got all the fire extinguishers going at once and we all stood round him playing them on him ... And he wrapped a towel round his head and sat in the middle, like a sultan, singing that song ...'

'I remember,' said Sandra.

'What *was* that song?' said the Flight Lieutenant, earnestly.

'Roll out the Barrel?' said Sandra.

'No, not Roll out the Barrel. Not *that*. Oh come on, you remember . . . Was it Roll on, Roll on Harvest Moon?'

'That was it,' said Sandra.

'What a boyo, old Toby!' said the Flight Lieutenant. '"Roll on Harvest Moon!"' He hugged his knees ecstatically. 'One of the boys, old Toby. He'd never have made a politician! Not old Toby! Nothing brass-hat about good old Toby!' He began to sing 'Roll on Harvest Moon' in an unmusical voice. He seemed quite happy.

You poor man, thought Sandra. But really, you're not a man at all. Only a little boy trying to escape it all. Blaming the politicians, the brass-hats. Anyone. If only you could *help* us.

'You were talking about the moon,' she began. 'Harvest Moon!' said the Flight Lieutenant, grinning. 'No, the real moon,' said Sandra, leaning forward. 'We're going to the moon, aren't we? In this ship?'

'A flight to the moon on gossamer wings,' sang the Flight Lieutenant. 'Just one of those things.'

'Look, you must concentrate!' said Sandra. 'Listen to me. You brought us out here in this ship. The ship you stole. The funk-hole ship. We're in it now, at this moment, flying in space. We don't know where we're going. We don't know what might happen to us. Try and help us. Tell me what to do to steer the ship.'

'Oh, that!' said the Flight Lieutenant. 'Well, that's a bit of a teaser. A bit of a teaser. Rather top secret, you see. Just the least bit teasing, *vous comprenez?*' He gave an easy laugh, a grown-up, sophisticated laugh. He's trying to escape anything difficult, thought Sandra. I'll never get to him.

She moved closer to him and turned a swivelling lamp so that it lit his face better. He looked awful. Most of his hair was gone. His face was a mass of small blisters and all the skin glistened fiercely. His eyes were red rimmed and brilliant. She nerved herself to put her hand on his forehead: it was burning, burning hotter than ever before. She got up.

'Don't go away!' said the Flight Lieutenant cheerily. 'Sit down and have another! Old Toby will be along in a jiffy.'

'I'm going to fetch him,' said Sandra.

She left the room, and felt tears welling up in her eyes and her throat choking. 'Oh, come *on*!' she said to herself. 'None of that!' She went into Brylo's cabin, switched on the light and woke him up. 'The Flight Lieutenant,' she said, 'he's delirious. And getting worse. Brylo, I think he's going to die quite soon.'

Brylo got out of bed quickly, then slowed himself down and stood thinking. 'My notes,' he said.

'But don't you see, we've got to hurry . . .'

'If he's delirious and getting worse, we probably haven't got him for much longer. And he's the only one that can help us. I've got to make him answer at least one question sensibly and I've got to make sure that I ask him the right question . . .'

'Oh, Brylo, you're hopeless!' shouted Sandra, and ran from him. She would have to get Tony. At least Tony would do something.

Brylo looked at his notes for less than thirty seconds. At the end of that time, he knew what he wanted to know. He left the cabin, shut the door, and walked quickly to the Flight Lieutenant's bedside.

'It's me, Brylo,' he said.

'Hi-ho!' said the Flight Lieutenant. 'I thought you were bringing the boyo himself – old Toby! Where's old Toby?'

'Don't you mean Tony?' said Brylo, uncertainly.

'Don't know any Tony. Toby's the boy we want! He's the lad to make the party go . . .'

'Flight Lieutenant, listen!' began Brylo. 'You've got to think. You've got to listen and answer my questions. We're on a ship, remember? Like a space ship. You got us all on to it. But we don't know where we're going or how to work the thing . . .'

'Very, ve-e-e-ry confidential,' said the Flight Lieutenant. 'Funk-hole. Where's old Toby? They'd never make a politician out of old Toby!'

Chapter 14

During the whole five minutes that it took Sandra to waken Tony, wash his face with cold water and get him free of the effects of the wine, Brylo fought a losing battle with the Flight Lieutenant. He understood Brylo's questions, but seemed to slide away from them. It was almost as if he were living in two worlds at once: a world of memory and parties and jokes with good old Toby, and the dimmer world of the ship – a world that was nothing like so attractive.

'All right now, Cap?' said Di, who had been helping Sandra.

'Leave me *alone*, you nit,' said Tony, furious and dishevelled.

'Please hurry, Tony . . .' said Sandra.

'All right, all right! Now, tell me again exactly what that flippin' Flight Lieutenant has been saying. And give me that comb.'

Sandra told him again, watching his eyes in the mirror as he combed his mop of strawlike hair. This time, he was taking it all in. She could see the quick, animal intelligence in his eyes. She could see too that he was planning.

'And Brylo the Brains is with him now?' he interrupted her.

'That's right, he's trying to get him to answer just one question – the question he thinks most important.'

'What question?'

'I don't know, how should I know?'

'Where's the Flight Lieutenant's uniform?' said Tony, cutting across her.

'It's in a cupboard in Control, I put it away when . . .'

'Go and get it. Don't let him see you. Go and get it and bring it here. Move!'

Sandra opened her mouth to say, 'But ...' then thought better of it and ran off. She came back immediately with the uniform.

'Out of my way,' said Tony, by way of thanks. He pulled on the trousers, then the tunic. They were much too big for him. 'Doesn't matter,' he murmured, and put on the peaked cap. It fell over his eyes. 'Get some toilet paper,' he ordered. Di brought him several sheets. He folded them into pads and stuffed them into the lining of the cap until it more or less fitted.

'Get that flippin' shaving cream in the aerosol,' he said. Di brought it.

'All right, you know what Scrambled Eggs is? You don't. Flippin' 'eck, you're dumb as they come. Here, give it us ...' He took off the peaked cap, uncapped the aerosol, made a practice line of foam on the table, then very carefully drew a blobby line of foam right round the curved edge of the cap's peak.

'Scrambled egg,' he muttered.

'Tony, please! We've got to ...'

'Belt up!' roared Tony. Then, recovering his temper, he said: 'Look, you told me that Boy Blue – the Flight Lieu-tenant – is going off his nut; he's gone all jolly and la-di-da, romps with dear old Toby and all that. And you can't snap him out of it. And you told me that Brainy Brylo is down there with him taking notes and doing his sums. And a fat lot of good that'll do. All right, now I'm going to try a dose of scrambled egg. Come on, let's get cracking.'

He walked to the door. Di flew after him cawing, 'What's all this about scrambled egg, what do you mean, scrambled egg?'

Tony merely replied, 'Top Brass. Air Commodore. Big deal. Come *on*!'

Sandra and Di followed him.

Chapter 15

In the dark corridor, they could hear Brylo's voice and the Flight Lieutenant's. They heard Brylo say, 'But listen, you must ...' and the Flight Lieutenant's reply by beginning a story about what old Toby did in the Mess on Boxing Day.

'Wait!' said Tony, stretching out a uniformed arm to halt the two girls. 'I want to hear more!'

'Please!' said Brylo. 'Please, Flight Lieutenant, just answer me one question. Look, I've got to know about the radio. The radio! Communications! Tell me how to work the radio ...'

'So that's it!' whispered Tony. 'Good question. Old Brylo's dead right. Question number one – radio. OK! Now listen ...

'Di, stay here. Don't follow me. Don't show yourself. Don't make a sound. Just stay here.

'Sandra, you're to go in there,' he whispered in her ear, 'and you're going to turn the light down or arrange it so that it won't fall on me when I walk in ... and if he asks you any stupid questions, just say "Toby is coming". Got that?'

'Toby is coming,' repeated Sandra, and began to move away.

'Wait a minute, you nit!' whispered Tony, grabbing her arm. 'When you've said that, you've got to say "But he's got someone with him. Scrambled eggs!" Got that? Right, say it!'

' "Toby is coming," ' whispered Sandra, ' "But he's got someone with him. Scrambled eggs!" '

'Sound more frightened about the last bit,' said Tony, pinching her arm.

' "But he's got someone with him ..." ' said Sandra in a frightened whisper.

'Good. Lovely. Now wait until I give you a shove and get in there and do it ... NOW!'

Just as Brylo began speaking again, Tony pushed Sandra. She walked into the cabin. Tony and Di listened.

'Pardon me, old chap!' said the Flight Lieutenant, turning from Brylo to grin at Sandra. '*Que volez-vous, ma chère Mademoiselle?*'

'Hallo,' began Sandra nervously. She walked casually to the single lamp, and turned it so that its reflector faced the wall.

'Just been telling the laddie here about the old days,' said the Flight Lieutenant. 'You ought to hear. Old Toby and I ...'

'Toby is coming!' said Sandra.

'Oh, good show!' said the Flight Lieutenant, delightedly.

'But he's got someone with him,' said Sandra in a significant voice. 'Scrambled eggs!'

The Flight Lieutenant's face showed bewilderment mixed with apprehension. 'Who ...' he began. But at this moment, Tony made his entrance.

By the dim light from the single lamp, even Sandra could have been deceived. Tony's old-young face, with its angular nose linked to a determined mouth by sharp lines, was made ten, twenty, any number of years older, by the peaked cap with its rim of 'scrambled egg' – gold braid – denoting senior rank. The Flight Lieutenant was completely taken in. He struggled uncertainly to his feet and tried to stand to attention.

'Sir ...' he gasped.

Tony stood stock still in the doorway with his chin jutted forward and his hands behind his back, to conceal the tell-tale two rings on the sleeves of the Flight Lieutenant's jacket and also to give himself a still more aggressive, authoritative pose.

'Stand at ease!' he barked, in his hoarse voice. The Flight Lieutenant, swaying, relaxed slightly. Sandra, watching his pitiful face and his weak figure, thought to herself, 'I don't know whether to laugh or cry . . .'

'Your orders are,' said Tony, 'to keep Control in a state of readiness. It's not in that state. It's in the state of a pig-sty.'

'Sir . . .' said the Flight Lieutenant.

'Radio!' barked Tony. 'I want radio contact with Earth. I want it now. Do it!'

The Flight Lieutenant tottered, put his hand to his head and drew it away, dazedly. Then he inspected the moisture on his fingertips.

'Radio!' barked Tony. 'Come on, man, radio!'

The Flight Lieutenant woke up, and staggered towards Control. Brylo slid from the gloom like a shadow and took his elbow to help him. Together they entered Control. Brylo switched on a light. It was brilliant in there after the gloom of the place where the Flight Lieutenant slept. Tony remained in the gloom.

'Radio!' said Tony's hard voice.

The Flight Lieutenant half walked, half staggered, to a console of radio equipment and stretched out a hand to it. The hand wavered.

'But I don't . . .' he began.

'Come on, man!' said the grating voice of Tony.

'You see, sir, I'm General Duties –' said the Flight Lieutenant, turning his head to the voice from the gloom. 'I never really . . .'

'RADIO EARTH,' said Tony, in a voice as cold as a steel hatchet.

'But I shouldn't . . .'

'You're not fooling me!' said Tony. 'You know. I know you know. Do it!'

Again, the Flight Lieutenant touched his head. Then, with growing certainty, he began to flick switches and turn dials. As he worked, he almost sobbed out excuses and denials.

'I'm not a Tech. man,' he said. 'I've only watched them. It was confidential, secret – I shouldn't!' But his hands continued to obey the threat of Tony's presence.

There was a hum from a loudspeaker, then an oscillating whine, then a continuous crackling whine that changed pitch as the Flight Lieutenant made fine adjustments. Once, there was an ear-filling howl that made the Flight Lieutenant turn apologetically and shamefacedly to Tony. Then he turned back again to his work.

'You – boy – come over here,' said Tony to Brylo.

Brylo went to Tony. 'Is he getting anywhere, the great nit?' muttered Tony. 'Can you understand what he's doing?'

'Keep him at it!' whispered Brylo. 'I've memorized every move he's made. You're doing fine! Keep him trying!'

But Tony didn't have to. Suddenly a French voice filled the room! It rattled on, obviously announcing something, and then there was the undulating whine of Moroccan music!

'Get London!' said Tony, his eyes glittering with excitement.

'Yes, sir! London!' said the Flight Lieutenant. Now he was breathing in gasps and sobs. The sweat from his forehead fell, drop by drop, on the dials and meters, on the controls, on his own hands. Suddenly he swung round towards Tony. His face was agonized.

'I can't get it, sir!' he said. 'Not London! Please, sir, I can't get it! There's a whole frequency band missing . . .'

He fell. Brylo and Sandra rushed to him. Tony flung his cap on the ground and stamped with rage. 'Get the perishing nit on his FEET!' he screamed. 'Get him back on that board!'

'Shut up, Tony!' shouted Sandra. 'Can't you see, he's dying. Dying!' She began to cry bitterly.

The Flight Lieutenant moved. 'Frequency band missing,' he said, in a quiet, normal voice. 'Sorry, sir. Not my fault, sir. Slight fault – jack-plug out in Communications room. Not *my* fault, sir. Not me. Don't blame *me*, sir. It's them. The politicians . . .'

He sank back. His breathing became very noisy.

'He's dying,' sobbed Sandra.

Violently, the Flight Lieutenant jerked upright, with his eyes staring.

'Always me!' he yelled. 'Always me! Always the flaming, dogsbody, Flight Lieutenant!' He choked and fought for breath.

'I'M AS GOOD AS YOU ARE!' he screamed. 'GOOD AS ANY OF YOU! GOOD AS THAT STUPID SWINE TOBY! GOOD AS YOU ROTTEN TOP BRASS! GOOD AS YOU FILTHY POLITICIANS!'

He fell back, heavily.

'He's gone,' said Brylo, a minute later.

Chapter 16

Even Tony was shocked, not only by the Flight Lieutenant's death, but by the hysterical attack from Sandra. She beat at him with her fists. She kept repeating that Tony had killed him, murdered him. Tony backed away from her. Brylo tried to comfort her. But it was not until he said, 'You *must* be quiet. Beauty will hear you !' that she was still.

'Listen, Sandra,' said Brylo, 'you are wrong. Tony was right. He did the right thing. The Flight Lieutenant was going to die anyway. But we, all the rest of us, we want to live. And we can live perhaps if we get the radio working. Tony was right ! I wish I'd thought of doing what he did....'

'Flippin' right you wish you had !' jeered Tony.

Brylo turned to him and said, very seriously, 'What you did was absolutely right and you were jolly clever to think of it. But there's no need to ...'

'Who's that?' said Sandra, tensely. 'Footsteps !'

The footsteps came nearer. 'Who's jolly clever?' said Billy Bason's voice, sleepily, from the corridor.

'Who was yelling and crying?' said Spadger.

Tony leapt to his feet. 'It was me that was jolly clever and it's you lot that's staying outside. Git !' And he slammed the door of Control in their faces.

'What about *him*?' said Tony, his back against the door. He flicked a finger towards the body of the Flight Lieutenant. 'Got anything to cover *that* in your notes, eh, Brylo boy?'

'Don't speak like that about him ...' said Sandra.

'Yes, it's all in my notes,' said Brylo, staring hard at Tony. 'I know what to do. Do you? And did you know that it's the

188

Captain that reads the burial service? Are you ready for that?'

'I know just what to say about that flippin' ...' Tony began, when Sandra jumped up and hit him across the face. At that moment Di came in – her face was white and her eyes red. But she wasted no time.

'Shut up,' she said to Tony, flatly. 'And you shut up too, you soppy little piece,' she remarked to Sandra.

'Brylo, what were you saying? We've got to work fast, the rest are waking and they'll come barging in here ...'

'You, Di; and me; and Sandra. We'll do what's necessary,' said Brylo.

'I happen to be Captain!' shouted Tony.

But Di turned to him and said, 'Look, Captain Marvel, the whole lot of them are bunging up the corridor already. Get them back into their rooms. Get rid of them. And we'll get rid of – we'll see to the Flight Lieutenant. What do we do, Brylo?'

'There's a big chute with air-locks,' said Brylo.

'When Tony has cleared the corridors, we'll get going. And Sandra can say something ...'

'Yes,' said Sandra. 'I'll think of something.'

Together, Sandra, Brylo and Di committed the Flight Lieutenant's body to the invisible and boundless void surrounding the ship. Sandra thought hard to remember the words of the burial services; she could remember only the phrase, 'Ashes to ashes, dust to dust.' She thought of the nothingness around them and knew the words were wrong. This was not even a burial, she thought.

In the end, she said, over the blanket-wrapped body resting in the air-lock, these words:

'We know that you meant to help us. We know you meant it for the best. We understand. God will understand. May you find peace with God. God bless you.'

Brylo turned a switch. A door came down so that they

could not see the Flight Lieutenant any more. There was a noise of rushing wind that was cut off by the dull thud of another door closing and a door outside opening. They felt a slight and sudden draught. Brylo kept his hand on the switch. They heard the same sound of opening and closing doors. The door nearest them slid upwards. The space beyond it was empty.

They stood there, looking at the empty space. Sandra said, 'I don't know if I did it right.'

Brylo put a hand on her shoulder and told her, 'You said the right words, Sandra.'

Di said, 'It was all right, what you said, Sandra. I'm sure it was. And don't worry about him any more. It had to happen, and it's over now. I'm glad it's over.'

Sandra thought, I am too. Although he was a grown man, he had been only a boy. Why, if you compared him and Tony, she thought, he was younger than Tony in many ways. She was glad that she had said no more than she had, for all that she had said had been the truth and God wanted to hear only the truth. But had He heard? Suddenly, she had a strong feeling, a certain knowledge, that He had. She knew, quite certainly, that the Flight Lieutenant really would rest in peace and that God really would bless him. She felt as if she had been on trial for her life, and found Not Guilty.

'Let's go and find out what the others are doing,' she said.

Chapter 17

They went back to Control, but no one was there. Brylo discreetly picked up the few things that had belonged to the Flight Lieutenant and put them down a disposal chute.

Then Spadger rushed by in the corridor.

'Where are they all?' shouted Di.

'Meeting in the Captain's cabin!' shouted Spadger, and ran on.

Brylo and Sandra looked at each other wryly. 'We'd better go and see what he's up to now,' said Sandra.

'Captain's cabin! La-di-da!' said Di.

When they got to the big lounge, they found all the children sitting in a circle round Tony, who sat on a raised leather armchair. He was in full spate.

'And there's another thing,' he was saying. 'When you come in here, I don't want you lot making a noise and messing about and sitting in any flippin' chair that takes your fancy – oh, you're here, are you?' he broke off, as Sandra, Brylo and Di came in. 'Di, you can sit on that chair. Brylo, come up here. Sandra, sit with the others.'

'Bossy,' said Di. But Tony had spoken so positively that they obeyed him.

'All right, down to business,' said Tony. 'You probably don't know what's been happening, and I'm going to tell you. The Flight Lieutenant's dead and these three have just come back from burying him. Right? All right. And there's no need for any of you to start talking about it or crying about it or anything else, because it's done and over and that's all there is to it. So *keep quiet.*'

They kept quiet.

'All right, next item,' continued Tony. 'As you all know, we're stuck up here in the middle of nowhere and we've got just as much idea of what to do with ourselves as old Durden has about keeping shop.'

Spadger, Billy and one or two others giggled and Sandra wished they hadn't. She could see trouble coming.

'So I had a think and I thought to myself, "What we've got to do is — do something. It's no good drifting about not knowing where we're going or why or how long. We've got to find out!"'

Tony paused dramatically, then went on.

'And how do you find out? If you'll kindly stop pushing and fidgeting — yes, you, Tiddler! — I'll tell you how you find out. You *ask*. And who do you ask? You ask the people who matter back on Earth. And how do you ask? You ask by radio. Radio! That's the conclusion *I* came to. Perhaps I was wrong, but that's what *I* thought. Use your loaf and use the radio, then you'll be ALL RIGHT! OK?'

Sandra's heart sank. He believes every word he's saying, she thought. He's quite forgotten that it was Brylo's idea.

'Of course, on a ship like this, the radio's bound to be a bit complicated. You don't just twiddle a knob on your transistor and get the Beatles. Oh, no! It's not like that at all. Quite frankly, I don't know how to work the radio on this ship. Didn't know then, don't know now. But I knew someone who *did*. . . . No, not you, Brylo boy!'

This got a laugh. Brylo had been staring ahead of himself and biting a thumbnail. He was worried. Tony startled him. Several laughed at his surprise. But Tony wanted more than this.

'The Flight Lieutenant! He's the one, I thought. He'd know about the radio. But he was acting funny. A bit off his rocker. Couldn't get any sense out of him. So I got hold of old Brylo, here, and set him to work on the problem. Brylo the boy with the brains, I thought . . .' (again, there w some laughter) . . . 'Let *him* fix it. Tell them about it, Brylo !'

Once again, he had Brylo completely off guard. And while Brylo, too surprised to protest, told a limping story about his attempt to make the Flight Lieutenant explain the radio, Tony made faces, picked his nose, crossed and re-crossed his legs and pulled Di's hair. And Sandra thought to herself: 'Why must Tony do this? Why can't he be content?'

Brylo had almost finished his story, when Tony interrupted him.

'Well, thank you for your report, Brylo boy,' said Tony. 'Goes on a bit does our Brylo, but it's all clever stuff. *Brains*, you see !' He twiddled a finger against his forehead and raised a laugh.

'But you didn't tell us one thing, Brylo. You didn't tell us if you got anything out of the Flight Lieutenant with your questions. Did you?'

'You know I didn't,' said Brylo, flustered. 'You know I didn't, because after that, you . . .'

'I took over,' said Tony. 'Yes, I took over. I got to work on the Flight Lieutenant. I thought to myself, if brains won't do it – even Brylo's brains – we'll have to try something a bit different. So I'll tell you what I did. Come a bit closer . . .'

They shuffled forward to make a closer ring and Tony began his story. Sandra watched their faces. Brylo, sullen and humiliated. Di, stroking the leather of the chair she sat on, then stroking her own hair. Beauty, her eyes fixed worshipfully on Tony's face.

The rest of them, completely accepting Tony's leadership.

Then she looked at Tony, telling the story of his triumph with the 'scrambled eggs'. And it had been a triumph, thought Sandra. He had been brilliant to think of it. And Brylo didn't think of it, Tony did. If only, if only, if only, if only Tony would stop puffing himself up and ramming his cleverness down everyone's throat !

Tony came to the end of his story. 'So there it is,' he said, waving a hand in a large gesture. 'You're going to be all right. You're not home and dry yet, mind you – I never said you were – but at least we've got some hope. We've got the radio. We can get in touch with Earth and home. We've got – the – radio!'

They actually applauded! And Tony, flushed and victorious, could not resist a last jab at Brylo. 'Yes, we've got the radio, thanks to your friend and my friend, Captain Tony. Right, Brylo?'

Several of the children laughed. And Beauty laughed too.

Brylo's dark face did not change expression. He was waiting for that last little jeer, thought Sandra: I wonder what he'll say . . .

'Not quite right, Tony,' said Brylo. 'You've forgotten one thing. We've got the radio, yes. We know how to turn it off and on. We can work it on several frequencies. But we haven't got it on the right frequency, remember?'

Tony's mouth fell open. He *had* forgotten, thought Sandra. He was so pleased with himself that he's forgotten that we never actually got through to anyone.

Tony rose to his feet, trying to take hold of himself.

'Well, for flip's sake! –' he shouted, furiously, 'I did all the real work – getting the Flight Lieutenant to talk and all that – and all you do is talk about frequencies! Who cares about flippin' frequencies, the radio's working, isn't it?'

He came towards Brylo – and tripped on the edge of the carpet. Once again, he raised a laugh. But this time, the laugh was against him. And Beauty, quite innocently, laughed too.

'Funny Tony!' she said, delightedly.

Tony turned and hit her across the face, hard.

There was complete silence. Beauty fell on her side, then propped herself up again on one plump little hand. The other explored her face. There was a vivid red print of Tony's finger on it. Big tears filled her eyes and ran down her cheeks. At last, she gave a wail and began to cry.

Sandra ran to her and put her arms round her. The rest stood up, uneasily. But their eyes never left Tony's face.

Billy Bason moved towards Tony and stood in front of him, staring hard at him. He pulled Tiddler forward in front of Tony, and said, mildly, 'Here, Tony – sorry, *Captain* Tony – why don't you have a smash at the Tiddler? He's nice and small, too.'

'That's right, Captain, have a bash at Tiddler . . .'

'You like 'em small don't you, Captain?'

'Go on, Tony, you're much bigger than him. Hit him!'

'I'll smash the lot of you, see if I don't!' muttered Tony, scarlet-faced.

'He could, too!' said Di coming to Tony's side. Her eyes were blazing.

Tony had not moved. But now, he flung off Di's hand and walked to his big leather chair. He sat down in it slowly, folded his arms, and stared straight ahead.

'I'm still Captain!' he said. 'You lot get out. Get out of my cabin! GET OUT!'

Without looking at him, they left.

Only Di remained with Tony.

She remained sitting in the same big armchair and continued to stroke the leather with her finger. She noticed that her nails were growing to a nice shape. She wondered how much longer they would grow before they got back to Earth.

'You stupid fool,' she said. Tony did not answer.

'What did you want to go and hit her for?' she said. 'They'll hate you for that . . .'

'That's right, now *you* start,' said Tony.

'It was all right before. You'd got what you wanted. You got this room, and you were the Captain.'

'I hadn't got the radio, but I'm still the Captain,' said Tony. 'Remember that.'

Di got up from her armchair and walked over to Tony. She put her hand on his forearm and said, quietly, 'Tony, what's the matter with you? Just when you'd done something really clever, just when you'd got them all on your side, you have to go and ruin it all. Showing off! Then hitting Beauty! And before that, they were eating out of your hand . . .'

'They hate me,' said Tony. 'Everyone hates me. They always have . . .'

Di could think of nothing to say.

'I'll *show them*,' said Tony. He spoke in a low, ferocious voice. The sound of it frightened Di. What does it matter, she thought, whether they hate you or not? I know what they think of me, back at Little Mowlesbury. But what did it matter? She wouldn't stay there a minute longer than she needed. When she was fifteen or sixteen, she'd shake the dust of the place off her feet. She'd go to London. She'd be part of the swinging scene!

'Little Mowlesbury!' she sneered. 'What's it matter what Little Mowlesbury thinks. Dead square . . .'

'I'll show them,' said Tony, venomously.

Di shrugged and pressed a button for an egg salad. Nothing happened.

'Press it again,' said Tony.

She did, but no egg salad came out. Tony strode over and jabbed the button again and again. It was useless. He swore, kicked at a chair, and shouted to Di, 'Well at least there's plenty of wine left!' And he strode out to get a bottle.

Chapter 18

No one noticed that one person had been absent from the meeting in the Captain's cabin. That person was Ashley.

He lay in his seat among the radio-communication apparatus. The shelves above his head were filled with neat lines of plates each filled with an egg salad. He had crept out and stolen them from the Captain's cabin, brought them back two at a time, and arranged the salads so that each egg was on the left of its plate. It was tidier that way, and Mummy loved tidiness.

The earphones were still on the floor, whistling faintly but shrilly. He had forgotten his fear of them. He picked them up and turned them over in his hands idly. Then he put them on his chest, reached up and turned the first knob his fingers touched. The whistling warbled and fluctuated, then stopped.

This interested him slightly – enough to make him stand up and put the earphones on. He arranged them so that they did not cover his ears: he did not want that nasty screaming in his ears again. 'Never put things in your ears,' Mummy had told him.

He extended a hand to the knobs and dials. One of his finger-nails had a black rim of dirt. He said, 'Tch! Tch! Dirty!' and looked for his comb. He broke off one of the teeth and cleaned the dirty fingernail. But perhaps he should not have broken the comb, he told himself. It looked untidy with a tooth missing. What would Mummy say?

He thought about this for some time, then tried to put the tooth back in the comb. It went into position perfectly, but then fell on the floor. Mummy used to tell him a story about a lady who was going to be married; the lady was untidy and had let a pin fall on the floor and not bothered to pick it up. On her wedding day, she had needed a pin dreadfully badly, because her wedding dress was torn. The guests were all at the church, the organ was playing, the bridegroom was standing ready at the altar – but where was the bride? (Mummy used to make her eyes round and hold her hands up when she came to this part of the story.) Why, the bride was on her hands and knees, still looking for the pin! And in the end, because of her untidiness, the lady never did get to the church to get married. All because she had left a pin on the floor.

Ashley bent down to pick up the tooth from the comb. Ah, there it was, near the corner! He supported himself with his left hand and reached for the tooth with the right. His left hand slipped slightly and brushed over a number of keys and switches on the radio console. And suddenly! –

'WELL, LATEBIRDS,' said the earphones, loud and clear, 'SEEMS THAT A LOT OF YOU HAVE BEEN DIGGING THAT FAST-RISING GROUP, THE LITTLE DARLINS! AND CONFIDENTIALLY, FOLKS, YOURS TRULY KINDA DIGS THEM TOO! SO LET'S DIG THAT LITTLE BIT DEEPER, SHALL US? – RIGHT BACK INTO THE ROOTS OF A GROUP THAT COULD BE MAKING POP HISTORY . . . RIGHT BACK TO ONE OF THEIR FIRST RELEASES . . .'

Ashley stared unseeingly ahead of himself, holding the tooth of the comb in his fingers.

'. . . ONE THAT NEVER MADE THE CHARTS, BUT IT'S A VERY SWINGING, VERY PRETTY LITTLE DITTY FOR ALL THAT. SEE IF YOU AGREE AS THE LITTLE DARLINS PLAY IT SWEET AND TENDER WITH . . . "DOLLY MOMMA"!'

Ashley did not move. He stared unblinkingly ahead.

'DOLLY MOMMA . . .' sang the four voices, lovingly, 'YOU'RE SO LITTLE AND CUTE . . . IN MY HEART . . . YOU HAVE JUST TAKEN ROOT . . . IN MY DREAMS . . . YOU'LL

ALWAYS BE THERE ... I KNEW JUST WHERE ... I COULD FIND YOU MY DEAR ...'

Ashley did not move.

'BUT YOU'VE CH-AY-AY-AY-ANGED!' howled the singers. 'WHY DID YOU GO AWAY, DOLLY MOMMA! ... WHEN I BEGGED YOU TO STAY ... IN MY ARMS! ... WHERE YOU BELONG! ... IT'S SO WRONG! ... YOU NEVER SHOULD GO! ... I'VE BEEN MISSING YOU SO!'

A female voice of piercing sweetness took over the melody. Ashley did not move.

'I'LL RETURN ...' promised the voice, in a catchy, fluttering soprano, 'I'LL BE DRYING EACH TEAR ... HELD SO TIGHT! ... HOLD ME CLOSER, MY DEAR! ... ETERNALLY ... MINE'S THE VOICE THAT YOU'LL HEAR — YOUR DOLLY MOMMA ...'

'DOLLY MOMMA ...' echoed the Little Darlins.

'DOLLY MOMMA ...'

'DOLLY MOMMA ...'

Ashley took the earphones from his head and blinked his eyes. He seemed to be considering. He flung the earphones with all his strength into the corner. The jack-plug jerked from the console as they disconnected. Ashley's lower lip trembled.

'I want my Mummy,' he said. '*You're* not my Mummy.'

Chapter 19

Brylo walked away from the meeting in the Captain's cabin almost blind with anger. He could feel his own fury pounding in the sides of his head; could feel a headache tightening a red band round his brow.

He strode down the corridor and blundered into Sandra, who was carrying a tear-stained Beauty in her arms.

'Oh, Brylo!' began Sandra, 'Wasn't it awful, hitting Beauty. . . .' But Brylo went on, hardly hearing.

'Brylo is cruel too!' cried Beauty after him, and more tears came.

'Wrong again!' said Brylo to himself. 'Wrong again! Idiot! Why didn't you say something to Beauty? Why didn't you make her smile, make her like you? Why didn't you capture her now that she hates her old hero, Tony? Why didn't you say something to Sandra? Why don't you get Beauty and Sandra and all the rest of them to follow *you*, to make you their leader?'

He reached his cabin, shut the door and flung himself down. Think! he told himself. It never seems to get you anywhere, but think! Pretend you are writing it all down on a sheet of paper . . .

Why do you want to be the leader?

Because very soon there must be a leader – a real leader. Not Tony.

Why not Tony? Because you envy him? Because you're half afraid of him?

No, because we cannot go on like this. I do often envy Tony and I am afraid of him.

Why?

Because he can always . . . get at me. Through my colour.

But that isn't all. If I were the same colour as he, it would make no difference. He would still find some weakness and make use of it – he would still think and act faster than me. He would do something flashier, 'cleverer' . . . Like his trick with the 'scrambled eggs'.

So why should you be the leader?

Ah, thought Brylo, stirring on his bed. That is the real question. Answer that one! He lay back and imagined the sheet of paper again . . .

Why? Because so far we have just been a lot of silly kids stuck in space. But now, things must change.

Either they will get slowly worse or violently different.

Take 'slowly worse' first . . .

Well, suppose that we do *not* manage to get in touch with Earth. Suppose that we are entirely forgotten and adrift in space for ever. Suppose that we run out of food and air and water . . . Someone must take charge. It will be awful, but someone must do it.

But why?

Because it would not be . . . dignified . . . to come to the end and die in Tony's way. Everything would be in a mess . . .

But how would your leadership make it better? Never mind . . . What if things become 'violently different'?

It's obvious : everything will be different once we get in touch with Earth. Then, we will not be just a lot of bodies, adrift in space; we will have things to learn, things to do, to help ourselves get back to Earth. And the sorts of things that we will have to learn and do are the sorts of things that I can do and Tony cannot.

Why?

Because they will be technical things. Understanding instructions, for example. Learning to use all the instruments in Control. Learning to navigate and direct the ship. Tony could never learn things of that kind. I could.

But you are not yet in touch with Earth. The radio is not yet working.

No.

Then why are you lying in bed?

Brylo jerked himself out of bed, washed his face with cold water, picked up the notes marked 'Radio', and made purposefully for Control. He did not even notice that his headache was gone.

Chapter 20

Control was deserted. Brylo snapped on the lights and went to work. With the help of his notes, he repeated the whole sequence of operations that he had watched the Flight Lieutenant carry out. As he worked, he made more notes. So much of what the Flight Lieutenant had done was unnecessary, or repetitive, or even meaningless.

A steady hum grew in the loudspeakers. Brylo paused. 'Recap,' he muttered. He began to realize that despite its seeming complexity, this was a fairly ordinary radio. It's a pity, he thought, that radio is not really my subject. . . . But on the other hand, it is obvious that I do not have to understand radio to work it. After all, there's nothing wrong with this equipment. It's only the missing frequency band that I must sort out . . .

He worked on. The hum remained constant. The excitement that had possessed him at the beginning began to wear off: worry took its place. Why, he wondered, am I getting *nothing*? Why aren't any stations coming through – even if they are the wrong ones? Then suddenly he noticed that he had failed to readjust a 'Gain' knob that he had turned down – he had not wanted to produce any of the howls and shrieks that had happened before. He turned the knob.

'SO LET'S DIG THAT LITTLE BIT DEEPER, SHALL US?' said the loudspeaker. 'RIGHT BACK INTO THE ROOTS OF A GROUP THAT COULD BE MAKING POP HISTORY –'

Brylo's heart leapt! So did his hands. He lowered the volume. At all costs, he wanted to avoid interruption. Particularly from Tony.

The voice from the loudspeaker burbled on, quietly now. 'See if you agree, as the Little Darlins play it sweet and tender with ... Dolly Momma!' it said. The sugar-sweet smile in the voice was vaguely familiar to Brylo. He knew he had heard it before. Where? That's right – at home! It was one of those continental stations that put out pop most of the night and day. Which means, thought Brylo, that I am on the right frequency after all!

He was about to explore the tuning dials to see what other stations he could get, when caution stopped him. First, he thought, I will note the position of all the dials. It would be terrible to lose this station and not be able to find it again ...

He began jotting down notes. Now the group was singing. Something about Dolly Momma going away, and missing her so, and holding you tight. The usual nonsense. Yet to me, thought Brylo, it's the most wonderful and exciting song I will ever hear. It means that Earth remains: that there hasn't been a war, that people are still doing the same things they always did. ... It means that we might possibly get home – and that there is a home to go to.

They were coming to the end of the song. Brylo put down his ballpoint to listen. I must remember this, he thought – must remember the very words they sing. 'Dolly Momma! ...' crooned the singers. 'Dolly Momma ... Dolly Momma! ...' It was the end of the song.

But Brylo still waited, his head cocked and his ballpoint idle. What would they play next? And would there be a station identification? He waited – and actually heard the announcer draw breath to speak as the station went dead! All that was left was the slight 'live' hum of the loudspeaker.

Brylo felt a sick wave of panic: he checked it. Don't touch anything, he told himself. Just *think* ...

But all he could think of was the terrible loss. That had been Earth – and now it was gone. It had been the promise of home – and now the promise was broken.

'Think!' he said, out loud.

A fault in the radio? If that was the trouble, then things were really serious. He would be able neither to find the fault nor correct it. Best to assume that it was something else . . .

He buried his head in his hands and tried to think. A voice very close to him said, 'Don't want to fall asleep on the job, Brylo boy!'

It was Tony.

When Brylo, unwillingly, had explained what had happened, it was Tony who guessed the answer.

'Seen anything of dear little Ashley?' Tony said musingly. 'I haven't. Wasn't at my meeting, come to think of it. And he lives in his cosy little nest in . . .'

'The Communications room!' Brylo finished for him. 'That could be it! It's just possible that Ashley is the one who . . .'

'Let's get going,' said Tony tightly, and led Brylo down the corridor to Communications. As they reached it, they heard the soft click of a lock.

Tony seized the knob on the door and twisted it. It would not open. He shook it and rattled it and tore at it. He was about to shout something when Brylo silenced him with a look and whispered, 'Don't frighten him! Quietly!'

'Ashley!' said Tony, in a reasonable voice. 'This is Captain Tony. Be a good boy and open the door!'

Silence.

'I'll try!' muttered Brylo. 'Come on, Ashley!' he said, 'you want to go home, don't you? You want to see your Mummy? Well, if you open this door, we can all get home! Come on, Ashley . . . open it!'

Silence.

'That's right, Ashley, your mummy's waiting!' said Tony, hoarsely. 'You want to see your mummy, don't you?'

They heard Ashley move inside the Communications room! And then his babyish voice, on the edge of tears, shouted, 'I won't! I won't! That lady on the wireless – she wasn't my mummy!'

Tony, Brylo, Di and Sandra held a council of war in Control.

'Look, if you woke me up and got me in here simply to help you drive the poor little thing mad ...' Sandra was saying.

'We flippin' got to get in there,' said Tony savagely.

'Not by breaking down the door! Can't you see, he's hysterical already! He's going all ... peculiar! And if you break down the door, you'll finish him! He'll go really hysterical! And we just won't be able to cope, not with all the others as well ...'

'If you break down the door,' Di said, 'the others will come tearing down the corridor to see what the noise is. They're asleep at the moment. But if you get the whole mob down here ...'

'I need a flippin' drink ...' said Tony, gloomily. Di rounded on him.

'That's just what you don't need, Master Captain Tony!' she stormed. 'You're Captain, remember that, and this is serious, so you can jolly well behave properly just this once and not make an exhibition of yourself.'

They were staggered by her outburst. They were almost as much surprised by Tony's response.

'All right, keep your hair on,' he said, mildly.

There was an awkward pause. Then Sandra jumped up and said, 'Tony's right, we do need a drink! I'll go and make something ...'

She ran out. The rest sat in Control, exhausted. Sandra, in the kitchen, thought, 'Tea? Can't be bothered. Coffee? Just as much trouble as tea.' She cast her eye over the tins and jars. 'Oh, well,' she said, 'even if we're never, ever, going to get any sleep, we might as well have a night-cap ...'

And she made four cups of hot Ovaltine.

She put the steaming cups on the tray and walked up the corridor, treading softly. She noticed as she passed it that there was a very slight sound from behind the door of the Communications room. In Control, she handed round the cups. The smell was delicious.

'This flippin' muck,' said Tony, dismally. But he drank his with the rest.

'We've got to find a way,' continued Tony, sipping his Ovaltine. 'Can't we think of some bait, some reward, to...'

Di held up a warning hand and pursed her lips to imitate the sound 'Shh!' For standing at the door, rubbing his sleepy eyes with the back of his hand, was Ashley!

'Mummy's here!' he said. 'She's bringing my drinkie! I can smell it!'

'That's all right, love,' said Sandra, managing to keep her voice even. 'Come over here and share mine!'

Ten minutes later, Ashley was happily asleep in bed, tucked in by Sandra; and coming through the loudspeakers in Control was the sound of the Home Service from London.

Chapter 21

'...and now, the news,' said the BBC voice.

Sandra and Di reached for each other's hands and held tight. Brylo and Tony exchanged a glance.

'The Pian Tuk talks, now in their third day, will shortly end. Although no official announcements will be made until the conclusion of the talks, Mr Tang, at a news conference, expressed himself as more than satisfied with the western powers' proposals. And when our spokesman at the talks, Mr Trueman, left the conference chamber at the end of to-day's session, he was seen to be...' here the announcer made his voice respectably winsome... 'smiling broadly. Tomorrow, the agenda will include the disputed issue of the...'

'I don't like this programme,' said Ashley, petulantly.

'Drink your flippin' drink,' said Tony, quietly and venomously. Ashley shut up.

The news continued. It spoke of rain stopping play, of sterling balances, of disagreement over the proposals for the Channel Tunnel.

'Same old guff,' commented Tony. 'What price the Flight Lieutenant now? Stupid nit....'

'The children in space,' said the announcer. The children tensed. 'Today, the third day, renewed efforts were made to establish communication with the missing space craft; but again, without success. The automatic sender on the craft indicates that it is moving steadily away from Earth towards the sun. In reply to a question in the House of Commons, the Minister of Defence said that despite protracted consultation with scientists of seven countries, including Russia and America, no suggestions had been forthcoming as to possible interception of the children's craft by another. The craft was by now well outside the limits reached by any space craft, manned or unmanned, sent from Earth. Messages of sympathy and condolence have been pouring into Little Mowlesbury, home of the missing children, from all corners of the globe. At Downing Street, the parents of the children were received by . . .'

'Can I go to bed now?' said Ashley. Once again, he was viciously silenced by Tony. They missed several sentences.

'The Minister of Defence reiterated that there was no reason to suppose that the children are not alive. The craft was generously provisioned with ample supplies of air, food and water. The Minister once again declined to comment on the rôle of Flight Lieutenant Barclay. He merely repeated that the flight was unauthorized. Asked for further details of the space craft, the Minister refused to reply, saying that it was not in the public interest to release any information at the present time.'

They heard the announcer shuffle his papers. Then – 'By international agreement a continuous radio signal consisting of the word Earth in morse is being beamed at the craft on the following frequencies: 15.9, 200 and 1300 metres. I will repeat those frequencies: 15.9, 200, 1300. The signal is continuous except for transmissions in spoken words every hour on the hour . . .'

Four heads turned to the clock on the wall. They had forty-three minutes before the next spoken transmission . . .

Brylo went to work. 'I'm going to try and pick up the steady transmission – the morse transmission,' he said, 'What's "Earth" in morse code? . . .'

His hands shook as he wrote:

E .
A . _
R . _ .
T _
H . . . .

'Dit, dit da, dit da dit, da, dit dit dit dit . . .' he repeated to himself – and almost flung himself at the radio console.

'Dead,' he muttered to himself, then rushed from the room into Ashley's cabin. They followed him and lived with him through the agonizing pauses when he clutched his hair with one hand and his notes with the other – then sprang to his feet to try another combination of setting on the Communications Room radio console. For once, Tony was completely silent. He spoke no word, made no unnecessary movement, showed not a trace of expression.

'All right, that should be it,' mumbled Brylo. 'We should be able to hear it in here on the monitor – no, let's go back to Control, where the big speakers are . . .'

They trooped back. The clock said three minutes to the hour. 'Nicely timed,' said Tony – the first words he had spoken.

Brylo's brown hands scrabbled over the controls of the radio console. There was a brief shriek from the loudspeakers which Brylo cut with a flick of a dial – then, to a fluctuating background of howls and flutings and whistles, the sound they had been waiting for. *Da. Dit da. Dit da dit. Da. Dit dit dit dit.*

They cheered, but Brylo stopped them by pointing to the clock. One and a half minutes to go . . .

The second hand silently and greasily slid its way round the slickly-styled clock face. Brylo caught himself wondering why the hands did not show fractions of sections, then remembered the array of 'precision' time pieces and stopwatches built into what looked like a navigation console nearby. Thank heavens, he thought, that we may soon be finished with loose time, endless time, time on our hands. Soon we may be talking in split seconds, milliseconds – the precisely calculated fragments of time and distance that will mark our journey home . . .

At that moment, the morse code cut out: a different sound filled the loudspeakers: and a voice spoke !

Chapter 22

'This is Earth calling!' began the voice. 'This is Earth calling the children in the space craft, the children from Little Mowlesbury. And Flight Lieutenant Barclay. This is Earth calling you . . .'

The voice fell on them like a soft blow. It was a surprising voice – kindly, informal, a little tired, dutiful, matter-of-fact. But most of all, it was a voice that seemed amazingly close at hand. None of the children would have been surprised if its owner had walked in at the door. And each would have expected to see much the same man – a man in late middle age, probably in uniform, with a disciplined but pleasant face. The sort of man that, if you fell off your bike and gave yourself a really nasty knock, would pick you up and dust you down and see you home. Without fuss.

'He seems so near . . .' said Sandra. 'I'll get the others!' She ran out. And later, as the voice continued speaking, there came a ring of faces at the door of Control, all intently listening.

'This is another of the regular hourly broadcasts,' said the voice. 'I wonder if you've heard any of them? Of course, we quite understand that you may have heard all of them, but cannot reply. That is why, at the end of this broadcast, in five minutes time, I am going to repeat exact instructions for using all the communications apparatus on board your craft – the radio. But first, messages from home – incidentally, the whole world has been sending you messages . . . we had a post of four thousand letters today, including several from Pian Tuk, where the peace talks are going on. And going well. In fact, the President wrote . . .'

'So the Flight Lieutenant wasn't so mad after all!' whispered Sandra to Brylo, as the voice read the message.

'But you'll be wanting to hear from your parents,' continued the voice. 'Let's start with the youngest. Here's a message for you, Beauty! Your mother says she loves you very much and she knows you're being a good girl because you always are, and are you saying your prayers every night? Ask Sandra to help you with them if you forget them. And your dad sends you a big kiss and says he'll soon have you sitting on his lap again ...'

Sandra saw Beauty's face, smiling uncertainly when her name was first mentioned, then beaming as the voice spoke of sitting on her dad's lap. 'I did say my prayers ...' said Beauty loudly. 'Tell Mummy!'

The voice went on. There were messages for each of the children and also for the Flight Lieutenant. As each message came through, a face within Control room would become fixed in concentration. At the end, a head would be lifted and there would be a slow and private smile.

'He's all right, that bloke,' said Tony, nonchalantly. But you could see that he too was strongly stirred by the voice from home.

'That's the end of the messages,' said the voice. 'I will repeat them – and perhaps some new ones – in an hour's time. Now I am going to break off for seven seconds to repeat the call sign, EARTH, in morse code. Listen to it. Tune to it ...'

They heard the already familiar pattern of the morse code. Then, the voice repeated the frequencies they should tune to, and said good night.

Immediately, another voice took over. 'Communications,' it stated baldly. 'This is what you do to get in touch with Earth by radio. Write down what I am going to tell you. This is what you do. This is how you operate your radio. Listen and write it down. Are you ready? Write it down ...'

'Must think we're barmy!' said Tony – then suddenly realized that this was just what the people on Earth might be taking into account. How could they know what was going on in the space craft?

'Sit in the seat facing the radio console in Control,' began the voice (Brylo was already sitting there). 'You will recognize this console by . . .'

Brylo listened. The rest were whispering to each other. Brylo wrote. Tony stared ahead, seeing nothing. Was he listening too?

The voice, cold and clear, went on. Brylo stretched out a hand now and then to touch a control the voice had mentioned, then wrote again. The children's whispering grew into a babble.

'Shut up,' said Tony. The babble died.

'I will now recap,' said the voice. 'First, ensure that each control facing you is set as I have told you. Then take the instructions you have written down at my dictation to the communications room and set the console there according to those instructions. You are then free to send – free to transmit in plain speech through the microphone – to Earth. Remember the four seconds interval between sending and receiving. Remember to say "over" when you have finished speaking. Transmit at any time. Do it soon. Do it *now*.'

Brylo swept his hands over a row of switches. The loudspeakers were instantly silent. So were the children. He swung round in the swivel chair to face them. Everything was utterly still and silent.

'All right, then?' said Tony, hoarsely.

'Yes. We can send.'

'Let's get weaving,' said Tony.

'Calling Earth!' said Brylo. He cleared his throat and said it again, this time clearly. 'Calling *Earth*!'

'Say "Over"!' hissed Tony.

'Calling Earth! Over!' said Brylo.

'Flick the flippin' *switch*!' said Tony. Brylo started, then flicked a tiny switch on the hand microphone. The loud-speaker filled the room with sound – with a cosmic litter of echoing trills that sounded like laughter, with the hiss and sputter of frying food, with a hollow, endless note like the dying call of an operatic soprano.

'They're not . . .' began Tony.

'Wait – time lag!' replied Brylo, urgently.

Then they heard it – a voice that distinctly said, 'My God! It's them!. . . Come in, space craft! Come in!' said the voice, recovering itself. 'Come in! Keep talking! Over!'

'It's *us* . . .' began Brylo weakly. Tony leaned over and with furious impatience, clicked the switch on the micro-phone. 'Now *speak*!' he shouted.

'Hallo, Earth, this is the space ship – the one from Little Mowlesbury. It's *us*! Over!'

Another four seconds of silence. Then: 'I hear you, I hear you!' cried the voice. 'Reception fair! Your signal coming through OK! OK! Keep talking! Over!'

Brylo's face was working. Tony snatched the microphone handset from him and almost spat words into the microphone.

'Hallo Earth, it's the Little Mowlesbury space ship! This is Tony Hoskings, Captain Tony Hoskings, I'm running this ship and we're all all right! All all right except the Flight Lieutenant, he's dead! All the children well, got that? – all well. Did you get that? Over!'

Again the pause, and then: 'Message received and under-stood, you are all well, Flight Lieutenant dead. Have you dis-posed of body?' Again, they caught an aside: 'Poor little devils!' the voice said. 'Have you disposed of body? Over!'

'Yes, through the big air-lock, but never mind that, what do we do to get back to Earth? *Can we get back to Earth?*'

They listened through the never-ending four-second pause. Then the voice from Earth spoke again.

'We'll get you back. Somehow. We'll get you back. But

you will have a lot to learn and you will have to learn fast. We will start immediately. Which one of you is best at school? Which one is best at mathematics – the best at school subjects? Is it you, Tony? Over.'

During the next four seconds they watched Tony's face and saw written on it the fight that was going on inside him. They watched as he pressed the button on the handset and saw his lips twist as he spoke.

'Hallo, Earth. You want brains, you want Brylo. He's the clever boy. I'm only the Captain. Here you are, Brylo boy . . .'

He handed over the microphone and walked out of Control without a glance at any of them.

Chapter 23

But very soon, Tony came back. By then Brylo had already covered several sheets of paper. He seldom spoke unless to say, 'Yes, receiving you. Over.' Tony quietly cleared the rest of the children from the room and made them go to their beds. Then he looked closely at Brylo's face. The brown skin was pasty, the eyes red-rimmed. He took the handset from Brylo and spoke.

'This is Captain Tony Hoskings speaking. He's had enough, Brylo has – the one you've been speaking to. He's gone a long time without sleep. We all of us have. He ought to rest. What say? Over.'

The pause, then : 'All right, let him rest. He's done well, he's very quick. Make him go to bed. You hear that, Brylo? Go to bed, you've done a good job so far. Tell you what – leave the set on, we'll give you an alarm call in three hours. We'll clear the air now, and alert you in three hours. Understood? Over.'

'Wait a minute !' said Tony, after the pause. 'He'll need longer than that – he's flaked out, I tell you ! Can't you give him six hours? Over.'

The pause. Then 'Six hours? Not a chance. We've got to act fast and so have you. Didn't you know? You're heading for the sun !'

Tony gasped and turned white. 'We'll be fried !' he said to Brylo.

'No, it's not as bad as that,' Brylo replied. 'It's a long way to the sun. A very long way. What they're worried about is communications. The further away we get, the nearer we get to the sun, the worse radio contact gets. They're worried about interference – about our radio reception. It isn't all that good some of the time – an awful lot of background noise, great waves of it. It gets tiring.... And it could get worse.'

'Three hours, then,' said Tony into the microphone. 'Brylo's going to bed now – off you go, Brylo – and I'll stand by here in case there's anything you want to tell me. Good night. Over.'

'Good night. God bless you all. Over,' replied the voice from Earth. The loudspeakers suddenly became silent but for the morse. *Dit, dit da, dit da dit, da, dit dit dit dit* it went, endlessly.

Tony didn't even notice. Pausing only to make sure that he was alone, he closed the door to Control, sat down in the seat that Brylo had left, clutched his temples in either hand and began to read Brylo's notes.

As he read, his eyes darted from the papers to the controls they described. Sometimes he got up and looked carefully at a particular control set-up. As he looked, his lips moved, repeating the words he had read. Sometimes, his concentration was broken by a fit of impatience or despair. He would mutter in puzzlement or disgust. But he worked steadily on as the minutes and the hours passed unnoticed.

Just before the loudspeaker came to life again and the voice from Earth called for Brylo, Tony thrust the papers away from him and muttered the words he had spoken earlier.

'*I'll show them!*' he said.

Chapter 24

Four hours later.

'All right, we've got to try it some time. Let's try it now!' said the voice from Earth. 'All right Brylo? Over.'

'All right,' said Brylo dully. 'Over. No, come back – let's get it right. I'm to operate directional drives only, check? Over.'

'Directional drives only, check. In other words, Brylo, you're going to give the ship a mild nudge employing ONLY the main drive motors you're using now to stabilize your flight. No atomic drive, no rockets. So don't sound so worried, it's not much different from turning up the gas! Anyhow, it isn't the motors we're interested in: what we want you to do is to check the change in course from the instruments once you've *used* the drive deflection. All right, let's do it! Over!'

Brylo, closely watched by Tony, left his chair and walked over to another console. He hesitated, then took hold of two hammer-shaped levers by their heads.

'Am about to operate Left 1 and Left 2, now both at ...' he quickly checked the position of the levers' shafts on the graduated scales ... '0.5. Am now moving them to 0.6 ... 0.7 ... 0.8. Left 1 and Left 2 at 0.8! Over.'

'Big deal,' muttered Tony, during the pause.

'Well done, Brylo!' said the voice from Earth. 'You got the drill right! Always get the drill right! Always report to us like that, it matters more than anything else! Now ... do you feel any difference in the ship? Over.'

'Nothing to report. No change. Over.'

'Fine. As I told you, what you've done is to very gently nudge the ship to port – to the left. In another few hours, you'll have changed course a bit and that's all to the good. Sure there are no changes? No difference in the note from the ship for instance? Over.'

'Nothing to report. Over.'

'All right, now give me a series of course readings taken at ten second intervals. Can you manage them that fast? Over.'

'I could manage them faster than that – never mind, I'll stick to ten seconds. Stand by, do not contact me until you have received six readings. Over!'

Brylo swivelled in his chair with a movement that was soon to become second nature to him, and fastened his eyes on a display with three crossed pointers. Simultaneously he adjusted a switch on a clock which zeroed itself and began to tick off seconds.

'Brainy Brylo!' Tony whispered to himself. But he watched every move.

'Oh four, seven oh,' said Brylo. 'Oh four, seven one ... Oh four, seven one ... Oh four, seven two ...' Tony stood by his shoulder watching the hairline hand of the clock. He felt a savage thrust of impatience, but held it back.

'Oh four, seven four. That is all. Over.' He waited.

'That flippin' pause,' said Tony, and endured it. Then the Earth voice spoke.

'Excellent, Brylo! You're a bright lad! We were afraid the nonsequential co-ordinates might throw you. You see the whole thing is based on a progression of – well, never mind, you're doing fine. Rest for five minutes, you've earned it! For five minutes, over and out.'

The loudspeaker hushed. Brylo sat back in the chair and whistled his breath out. He smiled slightly with relief, then turned to Tony and said, 'Wow! ... Do you think you could get me something to drink, Tony?'

'*Captain* Tony!' shouted Tony.

But he stumped out and came back within the five minutes with hot cocoa.

Chapter 25

It went on for two days. They were days in which Brylo learned and listened and made notes and calculations and trial runs and performed simulated operations as dress rehearsals for the real thing: days in which Tony sulked and muttered and exploded in sudden furies – but watched and listened constantly.

'What's it all in aid of?' Tony demanded during a rest period on the second day. 'What's it flippin' for?'

'It's to teach me to operate the ship,' said Brylo, his voice high with exasperation and tiredness. 'You know that as well as I do! It's to teach us how to get home...'

'What do you mean, home? Why was that bloke raving on about the Moon Station? What's that got to do with home?'

Earlier, the voice from Earth had told Brylo that no one yet knew where the ship was to be landed. Some experts wanted a desert landing, some a sea landing – and some, a landing on the moon. Tony had missed the real point of the arguments. Brylo had not...

'The Moon Station? Well, they've got to land us somewhere,' said Brylo, 'And the moon has a nice soft surface and a whole lot of specialized, concentrated equipment all ready to deal with us. After that, they'd ferry us to Earth...'

'In a pig's eye!' said Tony. 'We're landing on Earth if I have anything to do with it!'

'But Tony,' said Brylo, rubbing his tired eyes. 'You haven't anything to do with it. So shut up.' He stopped rubbing his eyes and stared hard and unblinkingly at Tony.

Tony felt something swell in his head and threaten to burst. He felt himself choke with fury. Yet he held back.

'Brylo the Brains,' he said softly. 'Not Brylo the Brawn. Talking flippin' tough, aren't you, Brylo? Proper Cassius Clay. Big mouth and all!'

'And all?' said Brylo. 'Go on . . .'

'Why can't we land on Earth?' yelled Tony.

'Go on about me and Cassius Clay,' said Brylo. 'Me and Cassius Clay – and all?'

'WHY NOT EARTH?' screamed Tony.

'Shut up, and I'll tell you!' shouted Brylo. All right, he thought, I'll leave the Cassius Clay thing until later. But later, I'll . . .

'All right, tell me,' said Tony, very mildly. And he thought, that one got home. That's the thing old Brylo boy can't stand. I'll stick the old needle in his brown skin again later . . .

'All right, *Captain* Tony, try and get your thick head to understand this!' began Brylo, forcing himself to keep his voice low. 'This ship is a sort of bomb. An atomic bomb. The radiation from the nuclear motor killed the Flight Lieutenant, you remember? So it's a sort of bomb that doesn't even have to go off to kill people. Now, if it did go off, it could wipe out half England for all I know. . . .'

'For all you know!' jeered Tony. But he listened.

'My guess is,' continued Brylo, taking no notice of Tony, 'that they're terrified of us on Earth. Terrified of us landing! Think of it from their point of view. The only people they've talked to – the only people they can talk to – are a couple of schoolkids. You and me. One of the schoolkids is being made to learn how to fly a space ship. I've got to learn it in days and learn it by radio. No blackboard, even . . .'

'I thought we'd got telly,' said Tony, shaken.

'What you call "telly" is just an old lady's reading glasses. This ship's telly is just its eyes. And they're short-sighted. They can only see the empty space around us. Nothing to do with Earth telly. Get it?'

'All right, I only thought . . .'

'As I was saying, they're terrified of us landing on Earth. If I get the landing wrong – BARRROOM! Even a sea landing doesn't cut out the risk very much. And if we made a good landing, this ship might sink. But that's another story. The real thing – or this is what I guess – they want us to land near the Moon Station because it's got a good surface, because it's got every sort of gadget to help us and them . . . and most important of all, because if the whole thing blows up, it will only black the eye of the Man in the Moon instead of wiping out London or New York or something . . . And I'll tell you what else I think. I think they're quite right, and I think that you're mad to make such a fuss about it. You'll end up at home either way – IF we get home at all. So what does it matter to you, Earth or Moon, what's the difference?'

'Yeah, what's it matter?' said Tony, quietly. 'What's the difference, eh, Brylo?' He walked away and began to whistle, repetitively and annoyingly. He seemed entirely to have forgotten the argument.

Brylo felt the old, familiar feeling of useless, churning resentment – the feeling of defeat in a battle that did not matter and had no meaning yet was somehow important. He turned on the ship's TV. 'Look, Tony,' he said, as the screen became luminous. Tony came over to look but did not stop whistling.

They stood side by side as the screen filled with a black glow of nothingness. Once, a tiny particle of light shot across the blackness. 'Shooting star,' said Tony.

'No, just the TV tube,' said Brylo. 'There's nothing there to see. Nothing.'

'Turn it through 360 degrees,' said Tony. Brylo, mildly surprised that Tony used the phrase '360 degrees' for 'full circle' – and equally surprised to find that Tony had picked up something of the working of the TV – operated a knob like a gear lever. 'It swings the viewing system,' he began.

'Yes, I know,' said Tony. 'Angle of acceptance, forty-five

degrees. Push this knob here and you get it sort of telephoto. Zoom lens sort of thing. I'm not dim, you know . . .'

No, you're not, thought Brylo. When was it, he thought, that Earth and I talked about this TV set-up? Yesterday? And then only for a minute or two. Yet Tony has remembered it all.

The screen became brighter. 'What's that?' said Tony, interested.

'The enemy. The sun,' Brylo replied.

'What's the threat from the sun?'

'Communications, nothing else. But I don't like it, you can't predict it. They said that communication conditions aren't all that good – you must have heard those bursts of noise . . .'

'That's the sun?'

'Yes, and it's unpredictable. Good one minute, bad the next.'

'But you've already changed course, we're already heading away from the sun,' said Tony.

'It doesn't make much difference. Look, imagine that we're a grain of birdseed on the carpet of a big living-room. At the moment, we're somewhere in the middle of the room and it's taken us quite a time to get there. Meanwhile, there's a canary at the other end of the room and the cage door is open.'

'For flip's sake, why don't you just say what you mean?' began Tony. Brylo took no notice.

'The canary might notice us and it might not; we decide to retreat and get out of the way. We turn, and move away. Perhaps we move a whole six inches, even a foot. But what difference does that make to the canary?'

'The canary being the sun,' said Tony. 'Well, just for your information, the sun doesn't hop about like a canary.'

'No, but the stuff it sends out – the things that disturb our radio contact – they do hop about. Or so it seems. And you can't predict how far they jump.'

'I thought you scientific blokes had it all organized. Even

the sun. I thought you knew it all, solar radiation, sunspots, the lot . . .'

Once again, Brylo was surprised by Tony's choice of words. Solar radiation. Sunspots. Tony was quick . . .

'Look, think of the single canary seed on the carpet again,' Brylo said. 'If you don't *mind*, that is. Canary at one end of the room, right? Earth at the other. And somewhere in the middle, the grain of seed. Can't you see that nobody *can* know anything about the carpet – that nobody has ever explored the carpet before?' he paused, then said : 'You're right, Tony. I never should have brought in the carpet. We're not just a seed on a carpet, we're a seed on the whole of Greater London, or something like that. We're *tiny* ! And we're exploring, for the very first time, *this* !'

He pointed at the radar screen and pushed the lever. The black yet luminous carpet of nothingness traversed the screen, its movement suggested only by the minute traces left by the TV scanner itself. Once again, they saw a slight brightening of the glow as they passed the direction in which the sun lay, millions upon millions of miles away. Then the bright blackness again.

They stared silently for a long time, until Brylo whispered, 'Nothing. That's what we're looking at. Nothing at all. *Absolutely nothing!* No wind, no air, no life, no death. Absolutely nothing at all . . .'

As he spoke, what looked like a spark flashed a line across the screen and was gone.

'Nothing?' said Tony, in a low voice. 'You're sure?'

'I told you,' said Brylo, speaking like a sleepwalker from his dream of infinite space. 'It's only the TV. Even the light of the screen. . . . Only the TV itself. Nothing.'

Again a sudden, darting spark ! – so fast, that Tony had to close his eyes to 'photograph' it on his mind. 'It went the same way as the others,' he said. 'Right to left across the screen.'

Brylo came out of his trance, and looked at Tony. The

radio loudspeaker still said 'Dit, dit da, dit da dit, da, dit dit dit dit . . .' again and again. Brylo's eyes wandered. The neatly shaded lamps cast demure, correctly positioned pools of light on the consoles and desks and chairs of Control. There were his papers and his ballpoints, the only untidy things in the room . . .

'It's funny,' said Brylo, 'how, when you're tired, everything seems to freeze in position. Do you know what I mean? Everything seems to stand still, absolutely still . . .'

Although neither was looking at the TV, both saw out of the corners of their eyes the shower of sparks that fleetingly lit the screen. Both heard the quick, light, finger-tapping drumming of something small touching the side of the ship, as if a cat had made a lightning dab with its claws.

They saw the pools of light from the lamps shift and swim ever so slightly; and a single sheet of Brylo's papers detach itself from the pile and float, back and forth, to the floor.

'Nothing out there?' said Tony. 'I'm not so flippin' sure!'

Chapter 26

They contacted Earth.

'This is Harry Baines,' said the familiar voice. Somehow, the mere sound of it made them feel better, but the four-second pauses were agony. They explained what had happened.

'What is the screen showing now? Anything? Over,' said Harry Baines.

'Nothing at the moment,' said Brylo. 'No sparks. Nothing. Over.'

'Where was your TV scanner pointing when you saw the sparks? Over.'

'I don't know – Oh, yes I do, we haven't moved it ... I will take a reading. Hold on ... seventy-three degrees to left of ship. Seventy-three degrees to left of ship. Over.'

'Seventy-three degrees to left of ship, understood. That accounts for the apparent movement across the screen ...' They heard another voice talking to Harry Baines. Then, 'Yes, it seems clear enough. What has happened is this. You have run into some cosmic dust – some tiny particles of matter, the litter of space. It's a matter of chance – quite literally, infinite chance. Over.'

'Why did they give a trace like sparks on the screen? Over.'

'Because the scanner is situated amidships at the bottom of the spacecraft, and when the rim of the ship hit the particles, they broke up, leaving a radiation trace. As if they had been burning. Because your scanner was pointing sideways, the particles appeared to move sideways. Really you must have hit them straight ahead. Is that clear? Over.'

'Yes, I understand. What action do we take? Over . . .'

'First, you have red button-lights all over the ship to warn you if the skin of the ship is damaged. There are four or five in Control, near the ceiling. Have they lit up? Over.'

'No. Over.'

Tony grabbed the handset.

'This is Captain Tony speaking. What happens if we run into more of these flippin' particles? What happens if we hit a big one? What do we *do*? Over !'

'You have a number of self-sealing bulkheads in the ship, dividing it into . . .'

A storm of noise swamped the voice from Earth. And suddenly the screen was streaming with sparks !

Brylo leaped for the lever and traversed the TV scanner to the straight-ahead position. Now the sparks were like continuously exploding rocket burst, coming from the top of the screen and flowing past in a fan of slightly curved lines. It was like driving along a brilliantly lit road at a crazy speed. Sometimes, the stream would be interrupted as if the lights had all been switched off simultaneously. Brylo watched in a sort of ecstatic horror, his left hand fixed to the lever like a claw.

'The lights !' screamed Tony. 'For God's sake, the red lights have gone on !' He danced in a sort of writhing agony of urgency, stabbing his finger at the tiny red lights high on the walls. They gleamed on, off, on, off, in a regular pattern.

'We're holed !' gasped Brylo.

The loudspeaker spat out its crazy stream of howls and sputters and sharp explosions. More of Brylo's papers slipped off the desk and fluttered lazily to the floor. The pools of lamplight jigged and shimmered.

'The screen's gone black, we're through . . .'

'Or the flippin' scanner's bust . . .'

'No, there's another spark, the TV's working . . .'

'The air ! I'll check the air meters !'

Tony grabbed Brylo as he ran for the door. 'No, wait a sec. You check the air so that we know what we're losing.

right? I'll switch on the ship's lights and use the TV ...'

'You can't! We don't know how to work the lights, we've never used them ...'

'Flippin' hell, that's right. OK, I'll check each room in the ship and see if the kids are all right ...'

'Get someone sensible to stand by the radio in here, we must get back in touch with Earth ...'

'Billy Bason. Now listen, be back here quickly as you can. Mustn't lose touch. Get back here pronto. OK?'

'OK! OK!'

Brylo dashed out. The loudspeaker said, '... on the left of the PPI display, just to the left of ...' Tony hesitated, cursed as the voice dissolved once again into madness, and hurtled after him.

Chapter 27

From Ashley's room there came a scream so intense and horrible that it seemed to wrap itself round Tony's ribs and squeeze them so that he could not breathe or move or think.

His terror of the scream held him for perhaps two seconds. Then, with a huge effort, he forced himself to move. He made himself breathe in a shuddering gulp of air; made himself relax his mouth from the contorted grimace in which it was set; made his brain obey his will.

But the scream! Still it went on and on! Still it pierced his very skull! It was horrible, indecent, inhuman ... Suddenly Tony realized that it must truly be inhuman. And at the same instant he felt a strong draught around his ankles and noticed a chink of light under the door. The draught was blowing *into* there ...

He nerved himself, and flung open the door.

As he did so, he saw Ashley's folded handkerchief rise from a shelf, unfold itself in mid-air, fling itself across the room to the wall facing him, then disappear into the wall.

Tony yelled with terror and stepped backwards, blundering into a shelf. A notebook on the shelf rapidly turned the pages over one by one and stopped at a page with the words 'Dearest Mummy' written on it with a ballpoint. This page detached itself from the book, flew across the room in a straight line to the opposite wall, then disappeared into it. A sheet from the bed stood on end, climbed the wall and, bit by bit, fed itself into the wall until nothing was left.

The screaming stopped. Now there was a roar.

Tony swore ferociously, using every evil word he knew.

It did him good. Now he could feel himself trembling and despise himself. Now he could not only look, but see.

He saw that every loose object in the room was directed to the opposite wall. Jackplug cables on the Communications console idly raised themselves to a near-horizontal position, pointed to the opposite wall, then fell again. A dressing-gown cord lazily pointed itself, like an arm with a wagging finger, at the wall. Three pieces of paper scribbled with notes left Tony's pocket and, one after the other, crossed the room, entered the wall and disappeared into it.

Tony shuddered with fear and hate. '. . . you too !' he screamed. He picked up the earphones and flung them at the wall. They bounced off and fell on Ashley's bed.

Where was Ashley? His bed was a humped pile of sheets and blankets and pillows. Perhaps underneath that pile, Tony would find what remained of Ashley. . . . But he was past fear now. 'It's all a flippin' nightmare . . .' he muttered, and went over to the bed, the draught making his trousers flap like a ship's sail around his legs.

He fought the draught and tore at the bedclothes. He knew almost immediately that Ashley was not there and found himself shouting with laughter at the relief. As he bent over, he felt his hair pulling at his scalp. The draught was pulling it out straight towards the wall.

Suddenly, Brylo was beside him. 'You didn't go back to Control . . .' shouted Brylo above the roaring, but then stopped and stared at the wall. Where two panels should have joined in a neat, almost invisible line, there was a slit-like gap eighteen inches long and one inch wide. Brylo picked up a piece of notepaper from the pad and offered it to the slit. It was snatched from his fingers and disappeared.

'Ashley's not in beddy-byes !' yelled Tony, and began to laugh again, hysterically. Brylo tore at the wall panels and ripped off a whole section of wall. Beneath the panels, there were dully-gleaming alloy structural members and beyond them, a skin of metal. In the skin there was a small tear that nad rolled a strip of the metal skin into a neat spiral coil. A fragment of a sheet was gripped in the tear. The sheet was folded into incredibly tight creases, indicating the enormous suction pressure. Brylo pulled at a loose end of sheeting: instantly, the sheeting disappeared into the hole and the screaming started again.

Tony was doubled up. His eyes were filled with tears, his mouth was wide open and the laughter shook him so that the tears were jerked from his cheeks and sucked into the hole. Brylo slapped his face hard and he stopped laughing. Brylo fed a blanket into the hole. The screaming stopped and even the roaring quietened as more and more of the blanket squeezed itself into fold upon fold and locked into the mouth of the hole.

'I thought it was ghosts!' said Tony, feebly. He remembered the sheet. 'Ghosts wear sheets!' he said, and began laughing again. 'Ghosts! ... Sheets! ...' he choked. Brylo slapped him again and he stopped immediately. 'Cripes,' he said after some time. 'It was like a nightmare. You know, Brylo, when you wake up screaming ...'

'I believe you,' said Brylo. 'Ashley's with Tiddler and the others,' added Brylo. 'He's all right.'

Tony rubbed his face with his hands. 'What about the air? Vacuum outside, our air inside rushing out of the ship – that's what all this is about, right?' He pointed to the hole.

'Yes, that's it. Our air escaping. We've lost about a fifth of all we've got. That still leaves us ... enough,' said Brylo.

'How do you know?'

'Well, I'm assuming that we won't be up here for more than a couple of weeks. We ought to have plenty. Unless that hole can't be filled. Listen to it roaring ...'

Tony jumped up. He was very pale. 'Suppose it's not the only hole?'

'It is,' said Brylo. 'I've been right round. I didn't hear anything like this one anywhere else.' He kept to himself the thought that there might be further damage to the ship ...

damage that would reveal itself later on. And he refused to think of any further encounters with cosmic dust, let alone bigger fragments.

'And all the kids are all right?'

'Yes, Tony, they're fine. Really. I think you'd better get some sleep. You must have had it pretty bad in here.'

'It was flippin' horrible,' admitted Tony. 'Think I'll turn in for a couple of hours. You'll be back in Control?'

'Yes. All the warning lights have gone out, so we're not leaking badly any more.'

'Even then, I'd get someone to sleep outside this door, Brylo. You can't trust lights . . .'

Tony went. Brylo looked long and earnestly at the hole. There was still a huge surplus of blanket left on the inside. He tied it into a knot. If more of the blanket gets sucked through, he thought, the hole will still have to swallow the knot. And instead of swallowing it, it will tighten it.

Finally, he packed bits of blanket into every aperture he could find around the edges of the hole, until the roar was almost inaudible. Then he picked up the mattress, and laid it against the wall so that it covered the hole.

'So this is what it's like in the Space Age,' he murmured to himself wryly. Then he headed for Control.

Chapter 28

Communications were noisy but usable.

'Brylo, we're going to have to speed everything up,' said Harry Baines. Brylo thought that he knew Harry Baines well enough by now to detect a sharp edge of anxiety in his voice. 'And that means that you have got to work even harder, Brylo. I'll tell you the syllabus. Write it down. Acknowledge and over.'

'OK, am ready. But first tell me what you are worried about. I might as well know. Over.'

The pause, Brylo noticed, was still much the same duration. At least they were no further from Earth . . .

'We are anxious – not worried, Brylo – about the condition of the ship. There could be other damage to the skin. You might run into more particles, even, but that is not very likely. You can work out the odds for yourself – so many hours before you did actually hit something related to the number of hours it takes you to get back to Earth. And communications. They are not getting better, Brylo. From what we hear, we may be in for a spot of bother from the sun. Anyhow, we've decided to get you back here as fast as we possibly can. Which means that you've got an enormous amount of learning to do. Are you getting all this loud and clear? Over.'

'Loud and clear. Over.'

'All right. The first thing we will tackle is the "space drive". The nuclear motors. Now, these are strictly Model T – you know, Brylo, like a very early car engine. In other words, they are perfectly all right as long as you know all the tricks. The Flight Lieutenant didn't and that is why he died. Now, Brylo, I do not intend to tell you how the motors work because it doesn't matter to you. But I am going to take you a stage further in operating them.

'And particularly, I am going to explain to you how to use the displays on the consoles in front of you ...'

It took hours. Then hours again as Harry Baines went over it all once more. When 'Over and out' was finally said, Brylo was too exhausted to notice more than two things: first, that he had drunk four cups of cocoa and eaten two plates of food; and second, that it was Tony who had brought him the food and drink – and that Tony had been there all the time and was still beside him now, his hands filled with pages of laborious, ill-written notes and his face set in a peculiarly determined expression that made Brylo uneasy.

An hour later Brylo was instructed by Earth to cut in the atomic motors. He did what he had been taught without any difficulties whatsoever and with surprisingly little difference to the sound and feel of the ship. Everyone was conscious now of a constant but distant sound of thunder. It was the motors. But not a tremor disturbed the ship. Nor had there been any feeling of acceleration. The motors, as Tony correctly explained to the others later, were brought in at quite high power – they were not 'slipped in' like starting a car from rest – but their power output was meaningless until translated into thrust. The power of the motors had to be given something to push against. This something was the ship itself. To begin with, the motors vented their power into space, where it had no effect. Later, and very gradually, 'vents' in the ship were closed: now, the motors' thrust pushed against the ship in one direction, and escaped through a sort of exhaust in the other.

'But ... what's it all look like?' said Spadger. Tony turned to Brylo for an answer and Brylo turned to Tony. Neither knew. They laughed at the absurdity of it. 'Haven't the faintest flippin' idea!' said Tony.

'How fast are we going, then?' said Spadger.

'It isn't a matter of miles per hour at all,' said Brylo. 'Even if I could work it out – it wouldn't help us in any way. So I haven't the faintest flippin' idea!'

Everyone laughed.

Later that night, the time lag on the radio was down to three and a half seconds. They were heading for Earth and moving there fast.

'The rocket motors are something else again,' said Harry Baines. 'The atomic motors are your long-range, cruising motors so to speak. They take you from where you are now to within striking distance of making your landing on the moon . . .'

So it is the moon, thought Brylo. Oh, well . . .

'The rocket motors, on the other hand,' continued Harry Baines, 'are only used on two occasions: on take-off and landing. You've heard the term "Blast-off"? Well, the rocket motors do just that. They blast you off. Violently. You know what it's like, you experienced it when you left Little Mowlesbury . . .'

In fact, Brylo did not know. He had been made unconscious from the appalling acceleration. He shuddered at the memory, and let the point pass.

'Landing is just the same, but in reverse. You approach the moon, still under atomic drive, at an enormous speed – thousands of miles an hour. Hitting the atmosphere around the moon slows you down quite considerably – but you will still be going at an enormous rate. You therefore use the blast from the rockets as decelerators. You fire the rockets, the ship slows. You literally hold yourself off the surface you want to land on with rocket thrust. Are you hearing this loud and clear? Over.'

'Loud and clear. Why must we make the landing at all? Why can't we be transferred to another space craft, actually in space? Over.'

'Because you can't. Even if we could be sure of making the rendezvous successfully, there's no way of getting all of you from one ship to the other. Forget it. Right, we hold off with the rocket thrust. This is a very delicately balanced business – it was a miracle that the Flight Lieutenant ever made a landing at all ... in fact, he was able to land only because the whole business is more or less computerized. You do not have to decide the next stage, either, when you are very much closer to the surface you wish to land on – although you can override the computers if you think that your approach is going wrong. To make this clearer : the first stage is when you are approaching the moon, and if you looked out of a port-hole you would have a view of part of the moon; the second stage, the nearest stage is when you are so close to the place where you want to land that if you looked out of the porthole, you could see most of an area the size of, say, Sussex. Is that clear? Over.'

'Loud and clear and understood. Over.'

'The final stage, like the other two, is computerized and automatic – BUT there is and must be a very considerable degree of human judgement. Your judgement, Brylo. At this final stage the village you came from – Little Mowlesbury – would be recognizable to you. You would be able to pick out the cricket pitch. Later, you would see people on it. Eventually, you would land on it. Whether you ploughed into it with an almighty thump or flopped on to it like a ton of bricks would depend on your ability to use the rockets to hold the craft off it for just the right length of time. The computers help, but you do it. Over.'

'Loud and clear and understood. Over.'

'Little Mowlesbury ...' said Tony, during the three-second pause that followed. 'The old cricket pitch, eh?' And once again, Brylo noticed the mask-like expression of determination that had frightened him before. He had little time to brood on it. Once the generalizations were over, his lessons on rocket drives, instrumentation and control techniques began. They lasted for four hours. At the end of them, he thought of nothing but sleep.

Chapter 29

The next day, communications got worse.

'Billy, have you seen anything on the TV screen? Any sparks or fireworks?' Tony asked.

'Not a thing,' said Billy, rather guiltily. He, Spadger and the Tiddler had been forced to give up their private world and to stand eight-hour watches in front of the TV screen. They disliked the new regime. But if there were to be further encounters with cosmic dust and debris, Tony intended to know about it in good time.

' "Not a thing, *Captain Tony*",' said Tony, eyeing Billy.

'Oh, all right – Captain Tony.'

'Brylo, what's the time lag?' asked Tony.

'Just under two seconds. We're more than half-way home – in terms of distance and time, anyhow.'

'What do you mean?'

'Well, the last bit is the tricky bit ... You know, the landing.'

'Nothing to it, Brylo boy!'

'Well, you haven't got to do it, have you?' Brylo replied.

'Ah yes, that's right. I haven't got to do it, have I?'

He left Control, whistling. He seems very cheerful, thought Brylo. And apart from his idiocy about making people call him 'Captain' (not that he ever tries that one on me), he is doing a wonderful job. Everyone has something to do, they all seem quite happy ...

At that moment, Sandra came in with his lunch. 'We've struck gold, Brylo!' she said grinning. 'We ran out of all those prepared dishes on plates and now we're on to the stuff I found in the deep freeze. Look!'

She put down the tray on Brylo's desk.

'Steak!' said Beauty. 'Oh, yummy, yummy!' She began to prance round Control. The gold and glitter of her was almost dazzling to Brylo, after his hours of dictation and learning and trial runs on the consoles. She seemed to beam light at him. Brylo beamed back at her.

'You didn't mind me bringing her?' said Sandra. 'She's being so good. She follows me everywhere, helping. That's what she calls it, helping. Fat help!' she ended loudly and managed to land a smack on Beauty's behind as she pranced by.

Beauty squeaked delightedly and began to call: 'You can't catch me! You can't catch me!'

Tony came in. 'What the flippin' heck . . .' he began, quite jovially. And he reached out his arms to catch Beauty. She stopped short and shrank back.

'Come on, Beauty!' said Tony, 'I'll catch you!'

Beauty went behind Sandra and clutched her legs. To Tony, she said, 'I don't like you. You hit me. And you haven't got nice white teeth like Brylo, yours are yellow.'

'Oh, they aren't yellow!' said Sandra, straining to keep her voice cheerful and easy. 'It's just that Brylo is so brown – Oh! . . .'

The five of them stood there. Brylo looked at Tony. He was white with rage. Everyone, he noticed, was looking at Tony.

'Yellow teeth, have I?' said Tony. 'Well, that's better than being a flippin' blackamoor, isn't it, Brylo?'

'I've been in the sun,' said Brylo and forced a laugh. It was a failure.

'Get her out of here,' said Tony, in a dead voice, pointing at Beauty.

Sandra and Beauty left. Billy stared hard at the TV screen, which showed nothing. And Brylo stared at his notes without seeing them. The whole thing is ridiculous, he thought –

but important. Very important. And yet he still could think of no reason why it should be. After all, what could *Tony* do?

'I'll show them . . .' muttered Tony, very quietly.

Chapter 30

Sometimes, the training sessions would go on so long that Brylo thought his head would split, and whatever fell out would lie pulsing on the table beside him. Brylo's Brains: pulse, pulse, pulse. He forced himself to smile at the thought, then wondered why he had bothered. It was not a particularly amusing thought. But then, he had always been a bit apologetic. The very opposite of Tony . . .

He looked at Tony. As usual, Tony sat a few feet from him, overhearing – no, listening to – every word. As usual, his notes were strewn around him. He was still writing. His large knobbly, efficient fist covered a lot of paper, creating a chaos of words. Yet again, Brylo asked himself, why does he bother? Why does he want to learn how the ship works? How can it benefit him?

Tony, aware that he was being stared at, suddenly looked up. His eyes and Brylo's locked in embarrassed surprise. They had hardly spoken to each other since the last quarrel. 'I won't be the first to drop my eyes,' thought Brylo.

Tony, still staring, said, 'You wonder why, don't you, Brylo boy?' and laughed. His eyes glittered with malice and amusement. Brylo could think of nothing to say in reply.

'I wonder why myself,' said Tony. He dropped his eyes and Brylo knew that he was lying, or about to lie. But why?

'I want to be the bright boy at school, that's what it is,' Tony continued. 'Bright like Brainy Brylo. There is Brylo the Brains, and there's Tony the Terrible Turk. That's it, isn't it Brylo boy?' He laughed.

'I've heard it all before,' said Brylo, flatly. 'Why don't you just shut up?'

Tea time for Teddy Bears,' said Tony, in a completely different voice. 'Time to listen with mother. Eight o'clock, get it?'

He nodded at the clock on the wall. There were footsteps outside, then all the children crowded into Control. At eight in the morning and at eight in the evening, the children spoke to their parents at home, on Earth. Brylo found it difficult to find words. So did Billy Bason and Spadger. The rest, though, just rattled on, talking about the food they had just eaten, or not forgetting to feed the rabbits and has the tortoise come home yet?

Di, however, spoke as if she were appearing in a very up-to-date documentary play about Parents and Teenagers and the gap separating them. She made her voice sound as if it were perpetually shrugging its shoulders. 'Are you *really* all right, Di darling?' said her mother with more than a hint of tears in her voice.

'Yeah, I'm all right, why shouldn't I be?' Di answered, shrugging off the question.

'We pray for you every night, your dad and me ...' said the voice, the tears very close.

'That's nice,' said Di, deliberately leaving a vacuum at the end of her words. And so it went on.

Tony either refused to speak to his parents at all, or used the talk as a way of advertising himself to the world.

'Are you all right, Tony?' said his mother (all the mothers began with that question).

'Everything's well under control on the ship,' replied Tony, 'I've got nothing to report that need cause any anxiety ...'

'But are *you* all right, you yourself, Tony?' said his father.

'Well,' answered Tony. 'The ship takes a lot of running. But we're all in good spirits and looking forward to a safe return.' He looked around the other children in Control as if expecting them to murmur agreement. Some of them actually did. 'Love to all of you from all of us,' he said finally; and Brylo was interested to see his cheeks flush slightly. He knew

241

that was the wrong note to strike, thought Brylo. It was too slick. It sounded too like a commercial . . .

They left Ashley until last because they did not like to watch him and could not bear the sound of his mother's voice. As it mounted towards tears, then hysteria, they silently left Control without looking back at the stricken figure of Ashley, hypnotized by his mother's moanings and sobbings and endearments and beseechings. Generally, she was cut off when the time ran out at the very peak of her hysteria.

'It must be flippin' lovely in the studio, dealing with her,' said Tony. 'You know what? We're safer out here!'

Eventually, Sandra would go and get Ashley and lead him, tear-stained and shaking, back to his nest among the consoles in Communications. She hated this beyond all the many jobs she did.

'You're tired out, aren't you, Brylo?' said the voice of Harry Baines from Earth. 'Well, you've had a pretty gruelling time of it over the last day or so. But do you realize that you're nearly there? It's a fantastic operation they've got going on the Moon Station in your honour. . . . Look, I'll tell you what, you get yourself something to eat and drink and then sit back in a comfortable chair and listen to some of the tapes I've got. It's all stuff that you ought to know about, but on the other hand you don't have to understand it and work it yourself. Not like the extrapolaters, eh, Brylo?'

No, not like the extrapolaters, thought Brylo. Not like them, thank goodness. They had been an endless solid grind, repetition after repetition, dummy run after dummy run . . . He asked Sandra to send him in some food and drink, and settled down in the biggest chair.

'All right, here we are again,' said Harry keeping his voice bright and breezy. 'Now, I promised you these tapes about Moon Station and I think you'll find them fascinating, Brylo, fascinating ! For instance, I've a few feet of tape here – not too much, Brylo, just the guts of the thing — from the men who started the Station. Karmesin, Strauss, Professors Desbrosses and Lutter from France and Germany ... and our own Professor Highan, of course, and the Japanese professor who helped so much with the environmental side. None of us could pronounce his name but it sounded something like "Eyespecs". So we called him that. Are you receiving? Over.'

'It's all right, Harry, you don't have to dress it up for me,' Brylo replied. 'Let's get on with it. I'll bet you are as tired as I am. Over.'

'All right, Brylo,' said Harry Baines, in his usual pleasant but decisive voice. 'As you say — let's get on with it. Now, about the conditions you may expect approaching the moon. You'll be able to use your TV of course, and you'll have no trouble at all with visibility. No fogs or clouds or anything like that. The gravitational pull of the moon is nothing like so strong as Earth's, so you will select the computer settings we have already discussed. We needn't do all that again, thank heaven. We'll skip all the procedures for landing the ship — you must know them better than I do by now — and talk instead of the conditions you will meet on landing. First, the surface. It really is ideal, Brylo. Very few areas on Earth offer anything to approach it, for two reasons. First, it doesn't matter if you miss by a hundred miles or so — no cities, no worries about hitting anything ...'

So I was right, thought Brylo. They are afraid of what might happen if we made a duff landing on Earth.

'... in fact, you can't very well miss the target area we have selected, it is several hundred miles wide in one direction. And it will be a soft landing. Better even than water ...'

Brylo's attention wandered. He looked across to where Tony sat. But Tony was not there!

Brylo interrupted Earth with the Call button and said, 'I'm sorry, Harry, I'm going over and out for ten minutes. There is something that I want to attend to here. Over.'

He switched off, got up and stared at Tony's vacant chair.

This was the first time, the very first time, that Tony had ever failed to listen to every word of Harry Baines' instruction. He had to find out why.

He found Tony in the 'VIP lounge'. Tony was sitting in a big leather armchair with a bottle of wine perched on one of its arms. Di sat on the other arm with a wineglass in her hand. When she saw Brylo, she gave Tony a drink from her glass and giggled. Tony felt embarrassed.

'Don't say old Brylo the Brain is going on the vino!' said Tony.

'Here, have some out of my glass!' said Di. She flapped her eyelashes at Brylo with mock sauciness and offered him the glass.

'Watch it, Brylo! She's after you!' Tony yelled. He was not drunk. Brylo could see the solid, unflinching malice in his eyes as he clowned.

Brylo took no notice of the glass and said, 'You weren't there.'

'Where, Brylo boy?'

'In Control.'

'He missed you!' squawked Di, hooting with laughter. 'He's a case!'

'Why should I be in Control, Brylo boy?' said Tony. 'Control with a capital C, that is. I'm in control anyhow. Get it?'

'He's a wizard with words,' said Di, nuzzling Tony.

'You weren't there. I thought something might have happened to you,' said Brylo. He was beginning to feel foolish.

'Oo, that would have been a worry, wouldn't it?' said Di. 'Tony die, Brylo cry. Inky, pinky, ponky!'

'Something come up, then?' said Tony innocently. 'Something the Captain ought to know about? We haven't run into a tram, or something, have we?'

'I didn't feel a shock,' said Di. 'But that's because I'm a shocker! Aren't I a shocker, Tony? Aren't I?' She poured herself more wine and spilt a dark patch on the leather

'No, seriously Brylo boy,' said Tony, taking no notice of Di. 'What were they on about? Was it the moon? Was it about landing on the moon?'

'Yes,' began Brylo – then realized that Tony was playing with him. For how could Tony have known?

'Good place to land, the moon,' said Tony. 'Old Harry Baines said so. The great git.'

'How did you know?' said Brylo, trying to keep his voice steady.

'Miracle of electronics,' said Tony. 'Bet you couldn't say that, Di. Go on, try: Miracle of electronics!'

'Mirrick – mickle of . . .'

'What miracle of electronics?' said Brylo through his teeth.

'Oh, this,' said Tony. He lifted up a transistor radio, hidden by the arm of the chair. 'Good radio, this. Best transistor I've ever seen. Must be a new model. Gets Earth just like that, even on the frequency you and Harry Baines use. Of course, it works only one way, I can hear either you or Harry. I prefer old Harry. Talks a lot of sense, old Harry. Except when he goes on about the moon . . .'

Brylo put a hand up to his head, saw that the gesture had been noticed, and wished that he had not made it. What *was* it all about?

'I'm sorry, Tony, I don't get it. So you've found a nice little transistor radio and you know what Harry Baines was saying. All right, now what?'

'I didn't hear what old Harry was saying,' said Tony. 'Only the first bit. Then I switched off.'

'All right, you didn't hear. So *what?*'

'Flippin' moon . . .' said Tony. 'Raving on about the flippin' moon . . .'

'Who wants to go to the moon?' giggled Di.

'Look – stop messing about. You're not drunk, Tony . . .' began Brylo.

'Not so thunk as you drink I am!' said Di.

'What's all this about, Tony?' said Brylo, trying to sound calm but succeeding only in sounding desperate. 'What's so marvellous about the radio?'

Tony leaped to his feet and poked his head close to Brylo's. Then he yelled: 'IT WILL MAKE THE KIDS LAUGH!'

He's gone mad, Brylo thought. He even looks mad!

'Make 'em roar!' hooted Tony. 'There's old Brylo the Brains locked up in Control, working away at the radio, right? OK. Then there's old Brylo making a fool of me – me! – because he got the radio going and I didn't. Oh yes, I admit it – I must have looked a right Charlie after that meeting . . . but you wait till I just pull out the old transistor and get them the Light Programme! Who'll look a Charlie then?'

'You mean, all this is in aid of making the kids laugh? Simply so that you can say "Look, I'm cleverer than Brylo, I can get Earth on a transistor"?' asked Brylo, astonished. Tony did not answer. He walked up and down, poured himself another glassful of wine and drank it at a gulp.

'Look, Tony, I don't like you either. If you want to make a fool of yourself by playing charades with transistor sets, do it and be happy. All I care about is getting this ship to the moon . . .'

'He's doing it again, Di!' said Tony. 'The moon! Old Brylo and the moon! What's all this chat about the moon, Brylo boy? What makes you think that we'll end up on the moon?'

'Because that's where the Moon Station is and that's where the landing is going to be!' shouted Brylo. 'Surely your precious transistor made you understand that?'

'Moony, Loony,' said Di, winking at Tony. Brylo felt lost.

Then Spadger rushed in. 'They're calling you, Brylo!' he shouted. 'They want you on the radio! Come to Control, quick!'

Chapter 31

Brylo and Tony ran to Control to encounter a double disaster and the beginnings of a third.

The TV screen spattered with spark-like traces, telling them that they had run into another patch of cosmic debris: and the voice of Harry Baines over the loudspeaker was barely audible over the mad racket of interference. They could just distinguish the repeated words.

'Come in, Brylo! Come in, Brylo! Over!'

Brylo flicked the switch and began sending to Earth. 'Harry, this is Brylo. Harry, this is Brylo. Are you receiving? Over.'

After a pause – less than two seconds now – the voice from Earth replied. 'I heard you, Brylo. Just. I will test, starting now. One, two . . . five . . . seven, eight, nine . . .' The other numbers were blotted out by the shrieks and howls and gunshot noises of the interference. Brylo raised an eyebrow at Tony, flicked the switch, and replied to Harry: 'Harry, this is Brylo. Brylo speaking. Your test gave me "one, five, seven, eight, nine". That is bad. Reception is bad. I will test, starting now . . .' Like Harry, he spoke the numbers one to ten and awaited Harry's check-back.

'This is Harry, Brylo . . . Harry speaking. I received only "four, five, six" and "over". Doesn't look too good, Brylo . .' Brylo and Tony picked up a few words and sentences that made some sense: 'sunspot activity . . . Mount Palomar reports solar . . . worried about damage to the ship . . .'

Brylo replied briefly and asked for instructions. The strain of listening through the noise to Harry's voice hurt his head.

Harry said, 'We're bringing you in, Brylo. Bringing you into Moon Station as quickly as we can. No more lessons, repeat no more lessons and instructions. We must get you out of the belt of debris . . .'

Brylo glanced at the TV screen. The trails of sparks were frightening. He noticed that Tony's eyes were shifting from the sparks to the red lights, still unlit, and back again.

Harry began to shout a series of instructions, repeating each three times. Brylo had no time to be frightened of their meaning. He merely obeyed them. A quarter of an hour later, Harry went off the air for a few minutes to consult with his advisers. Brylo thankfully cut off the radio entirely.

But the usual silence did not greet him. Instead, the sound of thunder filled the Control cabin. 'Look . . .' said Tony, pointing at the desk lamps. The pools of light they cast were shimmering and shivering.

'We're going at a fair old lick?' he asked.

Brylo checked the dials in front of him. 'We're going pretty well flat out on the space drive – the nuclear reaction drive. And we've turned. We're going like – like I don't know what. I suppose it must be as fast as anyone has ever travelled . . .'

'That's why we're vibrating?'

'I suppose so. Just listen to the noise . . . And, of course, we're not travelling in a straight line – although I don't know if that makes any difference. We've changed course.'

'Changed course!' said Tony. 'You mean we're not heading for the moon?'

'Oh, yes, we're heading for the moon all right – but they've put us on an arc, a curve. I suppose they want to get us out of the debris belt.'

'But they're still heading us for the moon?' said Tony, thoughtfully. He muttered something that Brylo did not catch, then looked hard at the TV screen. The sparks were still intermittently filling it, and Tony made a face. 'Try the radio again, just for a second.' Tony switched on. The noise was as bad as ever.

'I don't think they're connected – the debris and the noise,' said Brylo. He found it difficult to keep his eyes off the dull red dots of the warning lamps. He expected, every moment, that they would light. And then –

Earth flashed them. Brylo switched on the radio and the thunder of the reaction drive was once again flooded out by the din from the loudspeaker. They heard little of what Harry said, but what they did pick up made them exchange glances.

'Eight hours!' whistled Tony. 'In eight hours, he said! We'll be hitting the moon in eight hours!'

'Not hitting it,' said Brylo, with an uneasy laugh. Tony thought, then said : 'Dead right, Brylo boy ! That's one thing we won't be doing !'

Before Brylo had time to try and work out what Tony could have meant, Harry was on the radio again and Tony had left the room.

Chapter 32

Tony held a meeting in his cabin. Everyone attended. He told them, clearly and without his usual dramatics, that they might be landing within twelve hours. He explained the difficulties they were having with communications and cosmic dust. He told them what they were to do as soon as the landing signal, a siren that sounded in every part of the ship, was sounded: they were to come to his cabin, sit in the chairs, and use the straps fitted within the chairs to secure themselves.

'We'll try it now,' he said. 'Each of you go to a leather chair. No, it doesn't matter which one, Spadger. But when you've chosen your chair, remember it and go back to it when the time comes for landing. Right you've all got chairs? OK, put your hands in the holes in the arms and you'll feel the straps and buckles. No, don't fiddle about – let's start again, watch me!'

He showed them how to wear and fix the straps, which were very like a full harness car safety-belt. Brylo noticed that he remembered every detail of the straps – which part of the harness went on first, how the locks operated, just how tightly the straps should be secured. I wonder if he's been practising? he thought, then decided against it, and realized yet again what a good brain and memory Tony had.

'All right, the release.' Tony hit the buckle and the harness fell apart. 'Now, we'll all do it. Sandra, you can do Beauty's when the time comes, and Billy, you can make sure Ashley's all right. Brylo, you and me will be in Control, but we might as well get all the practice we can, so let's go through it.'

He's even being tactful, thought Brylo. Not making Ashley look small. Not trying to make me look a fool ...

'No, Sandra, do your own strap this time. I'll attend to Beauty.' Tony moved over to Beauty who looked at him uncertainly. But Tony gently went through the business of strapping her into her seat and said, 'OK?' when he had finished. She nodded, reassured. 'All right, let's see you get out,' said Tony. Beauty hesitated. 'You remember,' said Tony, 'all you do is give it a bang! Go on, you can do it!'

'Go bang!' said Beauty, hitting the buckle with her little fist. She laughed delightedly into Tony's face as the straps fell away and smiled after him as he ruffled her hair and moved on to help Ashley.

Friends again, thought Brylo; then felt mean for having had the thought.

'All right, do it as often as you like, you might as well get used to it,' said Tony, returning to his chair. 'But listen to me while you practise. First, about eating. No one is to eat or drink after tea. Billy, you lock up the kitchen. You can't land on a full stomach. Right?' They nodded.

'Second, stay in your own cabins whenever possible until the siren goes. I want everyone to be in their usual places so that I – or Di, or Billy – know where to find you. When you hear the siren, come to this cabin and go to the chairs you sit in now.'

He stood up. 'Third,' he said impressively. 'I don't want anyone in Control. Nobody. Nobody at all! Nobody, that is but me, and Brylo and Di ...'

'Di?' said Brylo, shocked.

'Yes, Di,' said Tony, pretending to be surprised at Brylo's tone. 'She's our go-between. We've got to have someone connecting us in Control with the others outside, haven't we? Well, *haven't* we?'

Brylo muttered, 'I suppose so.' Too late he remembered that there was a loudspeaker link from Control to all the cabins. Why did Tony want Di in Control?

But by now, the meeting was over and the children were dispersing.

'It's fantastic!' whispered Brylo. 'It's the most fantastic thing I've ever seen!'

'It's the most fantastic thing anyone's ever seen,' said Tony, hoarsely. 'I mean, for flip's sake . . . just look at it!'

It was the moon. It filled the TV screen, then spilled over its edges as Tony lengthened the focus of the lens. He turned the knob to its utmost, but the picture lost sharpness. 'I suppose it's a freak picture, we're lucky to get it this far out . . .'

'Bring it back again,' said Brylo, still whispering, and gazed at the reformed picture with awe and wonder.

'Can't see the Man on the Moon!' said Di pertly, jarring him out of his mood. Brylo wondered whether it was worthwhile suggesting that they could do without Di, and decided not to. Too late again . . .

Harry Baines' voice came through. The reception was still apalling. 'Within an hour, Brylo, you'll be resetting the computers for the Approach phase and adding manual corrections,' he said. It seemed unreal to Brylo. Everything seemed unreal to him since he had seen the moon.

'Start Approach procedure!' said Harry Baines. His voice was almost metallic now, as hard and precise as a machine. He began to dictate a series of co-ordinates. Brylo fed them into the instruments in front of them.

'Down to 38,000. Three Eight. Over,' said Harry.

'Three eight. Three eight. Over.' The thunder that had shaken the ship for so many hours softened a little: the pools of light from the lamps steadied.

'You're showing a drift from No. 3 computer. Over.'

'OK, am correcting drift, will read the first threes as I correct. Two four one, seven three one, nine four five. Hold for five seconds . . .'

Brylo glanced at Tony and was astonished by the fixity, the complete concentration, of his face. Tony's lips moved as he repeated the figures Brylo had just read: Brylo could see that he was reading them, correctly, from the crossed pointers. Suddenly Tony felt or saw that Brylo was watching him. Immediately, he switched on a loose grin and wagged his head. 'Too brainy for me, Brylo boy,' he said, clownishly. Brylo knew very well that he was lying.

'All right, Brylo,' said Harry's voice. 'Your set of first threes will do for five minutes. No drift now, you are on corrected computer course. Keep those readings for five minutes. Over and out.'

'How close are we now, Brylo boy?' Tony asked.

'Another hour and we'll be thinking about the actual landing. Don't you want to go round the ship and warn the kids?'

Tony beckoned Di. 'Go and find out what the kids are doing and tell them to stop it,' he said jovially. 'Make sure they're all where they ought to be. Then get back here fast.'

Di returned three minutes later. 'They're all right,' she said. 'That stupid little perisher Ashley is sitting on his bed pretending to talk to Mummy, as per usual. He gives me the willies...'

Harry's voice came over the loudspeaker. 'Brylo, how about the touchdown drill? Anything you want to go over again? Over.'

'No, there's nothing ...' began Brylo. But Tony took the microphone from his hands.

'Captain Tony speaking, Harry. Look, why don't you give us a brief run through on the touchdown procedure? It can't do Brylo any harm to hear it again and – well, you know, in case anything happens ...'

Brylo took the microphone and said, 'There's really no need, Harry. Over.'

Yet Tony had his way. For seven minutes, Brylo half-listened while Harry went through the drills he knew so well. Tony listened avidly to every word. Again Brylo found himself asking, *why*?

And now, the TV screen showed the face of the moon so clear and so near that Brylo thought he could pick out the Moon Station itself.

'Those dots – that could be it!' he said, pointing to minute specks near the centre of the screen.

'Could be,' said Tony lazily, not bothering to look.

'But don't you see – we're looking at the very place we'll land! From now on, the screen shows only the exact area we're interested in. The nearer we get, the more detail we will see!'

'Stone *me*,' said Tony. Then he leaned over to Di and asked her to go and get them a hot drink.

He's not interested at all, thought Brylo. *Why*?

Ten minutes later, the screen showed so distinct a picture that you could pick out small, individual irregularities on the moon's surface.

'I suppose we're seeing an area about the size of a smallish town!' said Brylo, craning forward to peer at every detail.

'Looks a pretty dull old town,' commented Tony.

'Well, that's the whole point, don't you see? They want to land us on the most featureless place they can find. No hills, no valleys – everything flat.'

'Yeah, dead flat,' said Tony and actually yawned. 'Any more of this poison, Di?' he said, holding out his cup. 'I'm parched.'

A little while later, Brylo said, 'It's about time we alerted the kids – we ought to get them into your room and see they're ready for the landing ...'

'No hurry, Brylo,' said Tony.

'But for heaven's sake, Tony!'

'Doesn't old Brylo get excited?' Tony asked Di.

'Yes, doing his nut just because we're going to the moon!' said Di, picking at one of her fingernails. 'Never fancied the place myself . . .'

The loudspeakers crackled and Harry Baines came in. 'Brylo, you're getting to the last stage. This is just about it. As soon as the computers say so, switch in rocket drive and then follow the drill. Follow the drill, Brylo! that's the thing that matters most. Don't get panicky. Don't do anything violently. Remember the enormous forces under your control. But above all, remember to follow the drill! Over.'

Brylo turned to Tony. 'Get them into their seats, Tony,' he said flatly. 'You've only got five minutes before I cut the rockets in. Please get started.'

Both he and Di rose to their feet and stood over him, Tony smiling and Di with an odd, set expression on her face.

'Sure thing, Brylo boy!' said Tony. 'I think we'll start with – *you!*'

Just before Di held him and Tony hit him, Brylo thought to himself, 'Now all my questions are answered. Now I know why!'

Then the blow fell and he was unconscious.

Chapter 33

When he came to, Tony was hard at work. He heard Brylo groan and then speak, but did not bother to turn round. 'See to him Di !' he said, casually.

Brylo found that he could hardly move. Tony and Di had lashed him to his chair not only with the safety harness but also with bits of webbing. This did not surprise him in the least.

'So we're not going to the moon, Tony?'

'No, Brylo boy. Di doesn't fancy it.'

'That's right,' said Di, mopping the bruise on Brylo's head with a cold cloth. His head and neck were very painful.

'You're heading for Earth?' said Brylo.

'Of course, Brylo boy. Good old Earth. You and your flippin' moon ! Who wants to land on the moon, for flip's sake?'

'I think you're barmy,' said Brylo, in a despair so complete that he did not bother to raise his voice.

'I'm surprised you didn't cotton on, Brylo boy,' said Tony, studying the instruments in front of him. 'But you're only brainy in certain ways, aren't you? You don't really know anything about anything, do you? And when you learn, you learn too late, don't you? Brainy Brylo – don't make me laugh !' He gave a false laugh, but still continued to survey the instruments.

'What about Harry . . .'

'Oh, he's gone over and out until I'm ready for him,' said Tony. 'Switched off at the mains, so to speak. He didn't half carry on, didn't he, Di?'

'Alarming,' said Di, rinsing out the cloth in cold water.

'We told him you'd had a nervous breakdown,' she added, casually.

'How much longer until we get close to Earth — close enough to use the rockets?' said Brylo miserably.

'Seventy three minutes.'

'*Seventy-three minutes!*' Brylo jerked in his chair and his mind raced. 'But that's not possible!'

'You've had a nice long byebyes,' said Di, holding a small bottle in front of Brylo. 'Hours and hours. I found these in the medical room . . .'

'And if you don't shut up,' interrupted Tony, 'we'll give you a few more!'

There was silence for a minute. A light flashed on the console. 'That'll be Harry,' said Tony. 'He never seems to learn, does he? Still can't remember who's captain of the ship . . .' He flicked a switch and the light went out. 'No interruptions, please!' he said to the light. 'Captain's orders!'

'That's what it's all about, isn't it Tony? What a fool I was not to have known! Captain Tony. *Captain* Tony! You and Di — all you want is the big film-star reception! You can't get it on the moon, so we've got to go to Earth! There'll be the press cameras and the TV cameras and the film cameras — and then the door opens, and out comes Captain Tony, the boy wonder!'

'And what's wrong with that, you chocolate coloured git?' screamed Tony, swinging his chair round. 'Look, I've had enough of you, you . . . bright boys, you brainy kids! . . . Yes teacher, no teacher! . . . You make me *sick*! Because you don't know from *nothing*! Who done all the things that really matter on this trip? *Me*! Who just sat and did his lessons like a good little boy and expects to get all the credit? You! Well, you flippin' won't get it, because I earned it, I want it, I'll get it! I'll show them! I'll show them all . . .'

He spun the chair round violently to hide his distorted face. Di, keeping her face completely neutral, said, 'Well here you are, Brylo boy. Captain Tony wants to be It, and

I want him to be It and you're strapped up in a chair. Looks as if he's going to get his way, doesn't it?'

There was silence until Tony said, 'Well, it's time I called old Harry. Almost rocket time, Brylo boy, and even old Harry has his uses.'

He operated the controls of the TV. On the screen, Brylo saw Earth – a great curve that filled the screen, patched with light areas that could be clouds.

'But we're close! We're too close!' said Brylo, suddenly sick with fear.

'We can't be . . .' muttered Tony, frantically jerking his head at one dial then another.

'Get Harry!'

Tony's fingers lashed at switches. The loudspeaker hummed – then stayed humming. Tony started at it, his mouth open. 'We're not getting a signal!' he muttered.

'It's that little perisher Ashley!' screamed Di. They ran out of the room and Brylo could hear them in the distance pounding on the Communications door. Then Beauty came in.

Chapter 34

'It's being dull,' said Beauty. 'I can't find anybody! Why are you all tied up? Oh, I know. Tony said you were bad . . .'

'Get me *out*!' said Brylo.

Beauty stared at him uncertainly.

'Beauty, you've got to get me out of this chair! Help me undo these straps! You *must*, Beauty!'

'Tony said you were silly!' said Beauty. 'He made a joke, it was about a – a transistor, and everyone laughed.' Brylo heard the Communications door open, and a shrill wail from Ashley.

'I laughed,' said Beauty, as if in proof of what she was saying.

'Please, Beauty, please!' Brylo hissed. 'Undo these straps! These straps round my arms!'

Beauty did not move. What argument would make her act?

'They're hurting me!' said Brylo.

'Oh dear,' said Beauty. 'Which ones?'

'Please, Beauty! These ones! Undo these ones! The ones round my arms!'

Brylo watched the smooth, pretty, useless little hands pull and tug. At last a strap gave, then another loosened. 'It's hard,' said Beauty. And at that moment, the loudspeaker boomed out Harry's voice and Tony and Di ran back into the room.

'What the – !' shouted Tony, striding over to Beauty, his hand raised.

'Don't hit me!' said Beauty, with a tiny dignity that stopped Tony. 'You hit me before!' she said, then lost her courage and ran from the room.

Tony glared at the loudspeakers, at Brylo, at Di. 'Get after her! Find out what the kids are doing! For flip's sake...'

He ran to his chair and listened to Harry: '...dangerously close, you have only minutes! Come in, Tony! Come in, Tony! Over!'

'It's me,' said Tony, his voice shrill. 'It's Tony speaking! Give me instructions! Over!'

'Thank God! We thought you'd ... Never mind, here are your instructions. Set these co-ordinates on the displays marked F, G and H. Are you ready? Over.'

'Ready! Over.'

The numbers poured from the loudspeaker, cold, clear and incessant. Tony worked fast to begin with, then began to lag. 'Steady on, steady on!' he shouted. But he had not switched the microphone on and no one heard him but Brylo.

Brylo watched, tugged at his bonds and tried to understand what Tony was doing or failing to do. Tony's missing some of them! he thought, he's not setting them, he's not relating them to the computer readings, he doesn't know the drill ... In an agony of impatience, he tore the flesh of his wrists on the straps. They did not yield.

Suddenly he noticed that Control was filling with the children.

'You're too late! Too late! Bring in the rocket drive, Tony, bring in the rockets! I'll give you the settings, are you ready, over!'

The children clustered in the centre of the room, gaping at the TV screen. Now, it was filled with an image of dark and light, cloud and land, that very slowly tilted and swung.

'Are you ready? Are you ready? Acknowledge and over!' shouted Harry's voice.

'I'm ready! Over!' said Tony. Again he forgot to operate the microphone switch, then remembered too late.

'... on your left to 320, three two oh, then synchronize

with the computer readings on the same console! Got that? Acknowledge and over!'

Tony was almost sobbing. 'He's going too flippin' fast, the stupid great git – too *fast* ...'

The children were staring at him. Sandra drew Beauty close to her.

The picture on the screen showed the same steady swing of what could be cloud and could be land – a meaningless picture that nevertheless showed them the shadow of death. For now the picture seemed closer ...

'Tony, for God's sake, let me take over!' Sandra moved to Brylo's side as he spoke, and stood ready to set him free, her face turned to Tony. Tony rose to his feet, his eyes glittering.

'Don't you touch him!' he screamed. 'Don't any of you touch him! I'll do the one that goes near him! I'll smash his head in! I'm the Captain! Can't you understand, *I'm the Captain!*'

His voice cracked into a screech. Not one of the children moved.

'Leave him alone,' said Di, huskily. 'He'll do what he says. He'll kill you.'

The scene was frozen in time. The lights inside Control made the alloy tube that Tony held glint in his hand. The loudspeaker hummed almost soothingly. Only the picture on the screen moved with a slow, uninterrupted, gentle swing. And each swing seemed to bring them nearer.

It was Beauty who broke the spell. She firmly removed Sandra's hand from her shoulder, and walked, very upright, to Brylo's side and began tugging at the straps. Tony made an inarticulate sound: she turned to face him and said, 'They hurt him,' and went on with her work.

Spadger silently joined her. Then Billy Bason, then the Tiddler, then the others. The straps were off. Only the harness remained. 'You have to bang it,' said Beauty, and tapped it with her plump, honey-coloured fist. The harness fell away.

There was a clatter as Tony let fall the alloy tube: then

complete silence as he slumped into another chair and Brylo took over.

'Give me the co-ordinates, Harry, Over.'

'Brylo? Thank heaven! Right, set these: three one eight and lock in your laterals. Interrupt me when you want to . . .'

'Laterals locked. Over.'

'Three one five and hold. Now integers only: five, five, four, four, four, three . . .'

'Give me a time elapse. Over.'

'Time elapse nine, but you've got that showing here anyhow. Fine! Three, three, two, two, two, two, one . . . Three-ten! Don't confirm, just follow the integers . . .'

The TV screen showed the face of Earth, steady now and advancing. By the light of the screens, the silent children watched Brylo's face. It too was steady. His brown hands moved almost lazily over the console; but with complete sureness.

'Is it going to be all right?' asked Beauty.

'Yes,' said Sandra. 'Quite all right. Now, shh . . .'

Chapter 35

In the evening sky, there appeared a golden dot – a disc that caught the evening sun. It grew in size and the world watched it grow. It made the sound of thunder, and the world listened and trembled. There was the roaring of a thousand express trains and the shattering blast of a thousand cannon: grass withered to grey ash instantly, and a tall oak that had grown for more than a century was made carbon and dust in seconds. The world clasped its hands in a frantic prayer: and the space ship hovered, dipped – and at last, landed.

For a time, the world forgot to talk of wars and strikes and politicians and scandals. For the heart and mind of the world had for once been left to itself and had reached out to the children, high above Earth, adrift in the endless enormity of Nothing. But now the world found its breath again and wagged its tongue and talked the usual nonsense.

'They're all barmy,' said Brylo to Sandra, a week after the landing. 'But it isn't until after a thing like this happens that you realize just how barmy.' He rolled over in the long grass and watched Spadger showing Billy Bason how Red Indians squat on their heels.

'They can keep it up for hours,' said Spadger.

In the middle of Little Mowlesbury's meadow, Tony swung his bat in a ferocious swipe. As usual, it connected – this time with such violence that he didn't bother to run. Instead he strolled over to Di and Brylo and flung himself down beside them. 'Got my twenty,' he announced, rather too casually. 'Did you read the papers today? Make you flippin' sick. "*The Angels of Space!*" Read that one, Di?'

'Dead right I'm angelic,' said Di, fluttering her eyelashes.

'I've got one here that's a giggle!' said Billy Bason, pulling a piece of newspaper out of his pocket. 'Listen to this: *"The heroine of space is six today!"* It's her birthday, Beauty's birthday, get it? Heroine of Space . . . !'

Tony and Brylo exchanged glances. Tony said, very quietly, 'Come to think of it, Brylo boy, that's something near the flippin' truth.' It was an admission: and an offer of friendship.

There was a long pause. Then Brylo winked and said, 'Look at Big Chief Spadger giving himself Red Indian cramp! Go on, Tony, you're nearest!'

Tony stretched out a foot, delicately inserted it under Spadger's knee, and lifted.

Sure enough, Spadger fell over backwards.

On the Flip Side

Bunjy

Lucas said, 'Oh, come *on*, Lettice. You did ask for it.' But she just snivelled into her handkerchief and pulled her rabbit, Bunjy, closer to her. 'It's not fair,' she whimpered. 'Not fair.'

Lucas's mouth opened but he closed it. Better not say anything. Better just to think it.

Lettice! What a name for this gangling sister of his! Twelve years old, almost as tall as he was at fourteen, purple-nosed with crying, blue-fingered with the cold – and crying like a child over a Rex rabbit called Bunjy. *Bunjy* . . .

'You'll soak Bunjy, crying like that,' he said, trying to jolly her along. A mistake. 'Oh, poor darling Bunjy!' she moaned. 'Darling, darling Bunjy! Does nobody love poor darling Bunjy, then . . .'

'You can't expect anyone to love poor darling Bunjy when he's not house-trained and makes a mess on the rug in Mother's bedroom,' he pointed out. 'A lambswool rug,' he added.

But of course, Lettice skidded away from this commonsense point. 'Nobody loves Bunjy!' she cried. 'Only me. Only Lettice.'

'Rabbits love Lettice, Lettice loves rabbits,' said Lucas, still feebly trying to be jolly. But still fighting against his inescapable dislike of his sister. He disliked her so much that they seldom quarrelled; quarrelling meant some sort of contact, some sort of closeness.

'Well, I can't help you,' he said at last. 'I don't understand you. You bring the stupid bunny in when you've been told a million times not to; you let it make messes in people's bedrooms; you get yelled at and kicked out; and now you want sympathy. I just don't understand you.'

'Nobody understands, do they, Bunjikins!' she said to the rabbit. 'Nobody understands me but you, nobody understands you but me.'

'Oh, my *gawd*!' said Lucas, and walked away fast, muttering a falsetto '*We* understand each other, don't we, *Bunjikins*?'

Left alone, Lettice wiped her eyes with her hair then held up Bunjy with both hands around his chest. 'We understand each other,' she repeated softly.

She brought the rabbit closer and closer to her face, slowly, until they were eye to eye. At first the rabbit twitched; then it was still.

She looked into its eyes for a long time and said, 'Oh, yes, Bunjy. We understand each other . . .'

'A worry,' thought Mrs Rideout. 'Both of them a worry.' She looked through the kitchen window at her son Lucas, striding along with shoulders humped. He paused to kick the head of a border pink hanging over the path. The flower head snapped off and arced through the air. Mrs Rideout flinched.

Worry. Lucas was a worry. He read and read and read, strange books, scientific books. But not science itself, not proper science, nothing useful, oh no . . . He was going to fail his exams if it went on like this. He was very clever, very clever indeed, they said so at school and in his reports. But he wasn't getting anywhere. All theory, nothing practical. The sort of books he read would never get him through. Science fiction, psychology, genealogy. Never anything practical. Never the things the examiners wanted.

And Lettice. Oh dear, Lettice. Lettice was named after Great Aunt Lettice who was very well off and took a great interest in the children, a *great* interest. One day she would be gone, but all that money would still be there . . .

She picked up a stainless-steel vegetable chopper and began to chop celery very fast. Lettice! A pretty name, certainly, a feminine name, but not the right name for her Lettice, not the right name at all.

What would have been the right name, she wondered, looking across the lawn at her large daughter. Some rather shocking names suggested themselves. 'Really!' said Mrs Rideout sharply, and chopped away at the celery faster than ever.

Lucas went to his father's room.

'Bunjy at it again?' said Mr Rideout, raising one eyebrow at his son. 'A mess in the bedroom this time, wasn't it? Bunjy and your sister Lettice. Oh dear, oh dear, oh dear . . . Don't come in, I don't want you, I'm busy.'

Lucas said, 'I'll come in, then.' He entered the 'study', and his father settled back in his armchair and glowered at him. But Lucas knew he was delighted to be interrupted; if he was careful, he might trap his father into playing a game of chess. Lucas had started playing two years ago but already he beat his father six and a half times out of ten – the scoreboard on the wall showed that.

'Bunjy,' said Mr Rideout, gloomily. 'Bunjy and Lettice . . .' he settled deeper in his chair. 'If I were a proper scientist,' he began, 'instead of a science correspondent – that is, a hack – I would be able to tell you, in scientific terms, what's wrong with your sister.'

'Your daughter,' Lucas said, slyly. His father disregarded him.

'I'd have a name for her condition, a long scientific name,' Mr Rideout said. 'But as things are, I'd just say she's barmy. Nuts. Loony.'

'Slipped her trolley,' Lucas said, in an American accent. 'Blown her stack. Flipped her lid. Can I have a sherry?'

'None left,' his father said, blankly. 'All gone.'

Lucas picked up the bottle and held it to the light. It was half full. 'White man speak with forked tongue,' he said in his Red Indian voice. The two of them were always harking back to the half-century-old radio and TV plays. Mr Rideout had dozens of them on cassettes.

Lucas poured sherry into dusty glasses. They drank silently. Then Lucas said, 'You ought to clean this place up. If you don't, Mother will.'

'Your mother's losing her steam,' said his father. 'She hasn't been round here for months. Still, it could do with a wipe round or something.'

'Fumigation,' Lucas suggested. 'Or a major fire.'

Mr Rideout looked round the room at the piles of manuscripts, the spilling files, the used cups and glasses, the dictating machine rimmed with dirt on the surfaces his fingers didn't touch, the big old I B M typewriter. 'Soon, very soon,' he said, in the high, whispering voice of the High Priest of Infinite Space, 'I must ascend to a higher plane ... What you humans call Death. And then – and then – all this will be yours, my son!'

'Golly gee!' Lucas said wonderingly, taking the role of the Stardust Kid. 'You gotta be kiddin', Pops! All this *mine?*'

'Lettice,' said his father, in his own voice. 'Do you really think she's barmy?'

'I don't know. There's lots of girls like her, mad about ponies and rabbits. Anything with fur on it.'

'One pony, eight rabbits,' Mr Rideout said. 'And that stoat. The one that bit her. Hamsters, dogs, that hedgehog with the eye infection –'

'That's gone, Dad. Dead and buried. You remember, Lettice cried –'

'Don't remind me. I never knew the human body had that much moisture in it.'

'She's a good weeper.'

'Four solid days. And she kept saying that she'd never been able to *talk* to it.'

'Well, that was the eye infection. She can't talk to them if she can't look into their eyes,' Lucas told his father.

'Just what is this business about looking into their eyes? She spends hours at it. Just gazing. I've watched her. It puts me off my stroke.' He waved a hand at the littered desk. Then he said, 'It worries me, it really does worry me. Does it worry you?'

'Everything worries me,' said Lucas, prodding at the dictating machine. He was tired of the subject. '*I* worry me.'

'With reason,' said his father, suddenly angry. 'I wish I knew where the hell you're pointing, Lucas. I don't want you to end up like – like –'

Lucas could have supplied the missing word – 'me!' – but didn't. His half-brilliant, half-successful, half-baked father was the person he loved, the person he could talk to. Yet he despised his father in some ways. He despised himself in just the same ways.

'I don't know,' said Lucas at last. 'I don't understand Lettice at all. I don't think I want to understand her. I don't go for this fur-and-feather thing of hers. It's not my scene.'

'I wish you'd speak English,' said his father, still angry.

But then he too became tired of the subject and said, 'All right. I'll give you a game. Best of three, no more.'

They got out the chessmen. Shadows lengthened in the untidy garden. The room filled with smoke. Downstairs, Mrs Rideout made telephone call after telephone call about a jumble sale.

By the rabbit-hutches, Lettice sat immovable, holding up Catchmouse, the Rideouts' short-haired tabby cat. The faces of the girl and the cat were separated by inches. The cat was almost as still as the girl; only the tip of Catchmouse's tail twitched from time to time.

The air grew colder. The sun was down.

In the study, Mr Rideout moved his queen diagonally right across the board and took a rook. Lucas began softly to whistle between his teeth; his father had him this time. Next the knight, then he'd bring out his rook. Check, check again, mate.

Downstairs, Mrs Rideout, at the telephone, said, 'No, she hasn't telephoned, she said she'd telephone and not a word. I suppose *I'll* just have to phone *her*, it's too bad.' She drank her cup of tea before it got too cold.

By the rabbit hutches, Lettice said, 'It's no good, Catchy, I just don't understand. You can't mean that, you simply can't.' The cat got up, stretched until its whole spine quivered and walked off, tail high, into a currant bush.

'Come back, Catchy!' Lettice called after it. But it was gone, the tip of its tail flicked and disappeared between stalks and leaves.

Lettice shivered, crossed her arms over her chest and slowly walked indoors.

She could not believe the frightening things the cat had said.

*

That evening, the family sat together in the living-room watching television. Catchmouse watched too, unblinking and perfectly content. But then, Catchy watched television even when the set was turned off and there was no picture. If she wanted the set turned on, she sat on top of the set and craned her neck and head over the screen, dabbing at it with her paw.

Old Duff, the Dalmatian, lay with nose between paws. He was not asleep. His experienced old eyes were looking straight ahead at nothing. His breathing was like long sighs. Lettice thought to herself, 'He's remembering,' but dismissed the thought. Duff never said much to her and she couldn't really tell what he was thinking these days.

Duff's eyes closed. He gave a long, wheezing sigh. Sleepy, Lettice thought. The dog's sleepiness made her feel sleepy too. She blinked.

Catchmouse leaped to her feet and stood arched and bristling on the round pink mat with the faded flowers. The cat glared.

Mr Rideout said, 'Ah, here we go again! "Look where it stands! In the same likeness as the king that's dead! Question it, Horatio!"'

Catchmouse leaped sideways, and spat twice.

'Hamlet's father's ghost,' explained Mr Rideout. Nobody listened to him. Everyone watched the cat.

Catchy moved backwards, flinching her head in little twitches, tiptoeing and curvetting, jaws arched and dagger-teeth ready.

'It's the invisible mouse again, isn't it, Catchy?' said Mr Rideout. 'After it, gal!'

'Not a mouse,' Lucas said. 'More like a mastiff.'

'Whatever it is, it's a big one this evening. Isn't it, Catchy?'

273

'If Duff were a gentleman he'd go and help her,' said Mrs Rideout, smiling at the outstretched dog. Hearing his own name, Duff jerked and snarled and uneasily shambled to his feet, looking about him. His old legs trembled, especially the hind legs. He growled deep in his throat, then walked cautiously towards the vacant space at which Catchy was glaring. He stretched his head forward, still very carefully, and sniffed – shook his head and sniffed again – growled, in a final, 'Don't say I didn't warn you,' sort of way and lay down again where he had been before.

Catchy too seemed to have reached a dead end in her battle with the invisible enemy. Now she tiptoed forward, placing her front paws neatly one in front of the other on the same line. Her head went back and forth, very carefully, as she prodded her nose at whatever it was.

'They all do it,' said Mrs Rideout. 'Cats, I mean. Seeing ghosts or whatever it is. It's funny how they all do it. When I was a little girl, we had a cat called Sooky and she used to do what Catchy's been doing, I can see her now ... Then she gave that up and took to just staring at one particular spot by the corner of the fireplace. She'd stare at it for hours, growling, happy as can be.'

'Dogs do it too,' said Lucas. 'And horses. You know, suddenly rearing up. Baulking at nothing. Rolling their eyes. Throwing their riders.'

Mr Rideout jabbed a finger at the television set and said, 'Do we have to watch this drivel? Because if we do, I'll tell you the ending right away. It wasn't the son that took the car keys, it was the son's mother –'

'Oh, let's see the end of it now,' said Mrs Rideout. 'It's quite good really. Don't you think so, Lettice?'

'I'll just go to my room for half an hour, Mummy,' said Lettice. 'I don't really want to watch it at all.'

As she left the room, Lettice picked up the cat and

tucked it under her arm. Lucas and his father exchanged glances.

'Gone to have a chat with the cat,' Lucas said.

His father shrugged and they watched the end of the play.

The Blob

Lettice lay on her bed with Catchy crouched on her chest.
Catchy's breath smelled of milk – Lettice had given her
a saucerful on the way upstairs to put the cat in a good
temper. Catchy would never talk to Lettice when she was
hungry or thinking of hunting or sleepy, hot, cold, twitchy
– there were a hundred times when Catchy wouldn't talk.
But she was talking now, talking better than she usually
did. Lettice stroked the top of Catchy's head and listened.

Or rather, she saw. Their eyes were locked, the girl's sleepy
and seldom blinking, the cat's eyes wide and slightly squint-
ing. 'Show me again, Catchy,' said Lettice.

Yet it was quite like talking, too. There were pictures, of
course – but also something that could have been a voice, an
inner voice, words inside your head. The voice had no tone,
no sentences, nothing like that – you just knew you were
being told something. First the cat's eyes seemed to grow and
grow; the two eyes became one big yellow blur; the pictures
formed; the story started . . .

It looked like a sow, Lettice decided, the thing Catchmouse was letting her see. That big black sow she had
seen last spring on the farm down the road when – no, concentrate, don't let go, Lettice told herself, it's so easy to let
go . . .

A sow. Anyhow, something big, humped, slow A Blob.

276

But Lettice couldn't see a face or feet, just a bulk. 'Can't you show me any more, Catchy?'

The Blob wavered. Its shape seemed to be crisscrossed with lines, it wavered and changed shape a little between the lines. Its outlines were vague, always moving a little.

'More, Catchy! Tell me more!'

'Can't.'

'But you must have seen more than that.'

'No more. I saw that.'

Lettice looked again, concentrating hard. There was the rug with the flowers on it. There was the TV set. There was a glimpse of the fireplace. There were her father's feet, not in focus, but there all right.

'Oh, I understand,' said Lettice, feeling frightened. It *was* frightening: the rug wasn't wavering, the flower pattern wasn't crisscrossed with lines – but the Blob, the sow thing, was. Then it did something else – it began to flicker and fade, then reappear. Lettice felt her heart beating.

The cat felt it too: the one yellow eye suddenly became two eyes as Catchmouse moved, annoyed by Lettice's heartbeats. There was no picture any more, only Catchy's mind inside her head saying unpleasant things about her heartbeats. Lettice stroked the cat's head trying to calm it and make it stay. Catchy settled down again and began to purr loudly. The pictures went and all that was left was Catchy saying, 'Very good, oh yes, very good,' because Lettice was stroking her correctly.

'About that thing, Catchy?'

'That's nice, that's the place, stroke me there –'

'No, I want to know about the *thing*. The big thing on the rug. Have you seen it before, Catchy?'

'Yes.'

'Lots of times?'

'Often and often. Sometimes in the other rooms, sometimes in the garden.' This was Catchmouse's message – but it came through as pictures mostly, sudden snapshots of a bedroom, a kitchen, a flowerbed; always with the big Blob somewhere in the picture.

'Did it frighten you, Catchy?'

The question was too difficult for Catchy to answer. Streams of pictures entered Lettice's eyes, a hundred sentences formed in her mind – but none of them made much sense. Lettice kept asking '*Did* it?' to make sure that Catchy wouldn't just shut off, as she so often did. But then she realized that Catchy wanted to tell her, was anxious to communicate. This was unusual.

'You were frightened, weren't you, Catchy?'

Catchy said, 'Yes.' Yet the cat seldom admitted to being frightened, or to any other emotion that made the cat look a loser. Catchy always had to win at everything. Usually, thought Lettice, if you asked Catchy if she were frightened of something – a dog, say – the message you got was full of spittings and claws and furious rage; which meant, 'That dog had better look out, I'll tear him to pieces!' Yet now, Catchy was admitting to being frightened. But then the cat suddenly recollected her dignity and sprang off the bed.

'Oh, Catchy, don't go!' said Lettice. She was wasting her time. Catchmouse was already scratching at the door and mewing. When Lettice let her out, she walked away without a backward glance, tail up and spine slightly arched to make her legs look longer and stiffer.

Lettice lay down again on her bed to think. She could make no sense of Catchy's messages. They were not the messages she was used to. She liked talking to Catchy more than any other animal because Catchmouse was, in Catchmouse's own eyes, the centre of the whole world – and it was a wonderful world. Catchy was an empress, a goddess, anything you like so long as it is sufficiently grand and glorious. Catchy has drunk a bowl of milk? Loud cheers from the assembled populace! Catchy has stalked a bird? Roars of applause the world over! Catchy feels sleepy? Throughout the universe, lights fade and the stars in the heavens go out!

Thinking of this made Lettice smile, but with affection. After all, Catchmouse was magnificent, from her own point of view or from anyone else's. She did everything well and everything her way.

Lettice thought of the sad little guinea-pigs, their messages full of anxiety; take them out of their cages, they were anxious; put them back, they were anxious. So many of the smaller animals were like that. And the ponies and horses – what fools they could be! They suffered agonies of anxiety, Lettice remembered, most of them centred on people. Would Lettice come and see them or not? When would she come? Why hadn't she come already?

Yet when she did come, even as they told her about their terrible anxiety, they began to forget what they were talking about. They were so easily pleased, so easily diverted. You couldn't, thought Lettice, really talk with horses and ponies. But you could be consoled by them, which was strange considering how anxious they were themselves.

Dogs? Slaves, thought Lettice. Nicer than anyone, nicer than humans, nicer – a million times nicer – than any cat. But slaves all the same. She soon got bored talking with Duff, for instance. Not only because he was old and all his thoughts were really memories; but also because everything he let her know ended with an unspoken question, a request for approval, or permission.

Yet for all this, some of the happiest moments of her life had been spent seeing what dogs saw, feeling what dogs felt, smelling what dogs smelled, running as dogs ran. Even poor old Duff could still take Lettice tearing through the undergrowth, nose down – *'Richness! perfume! stench! Over there – follow it, track it! – over there! Crash and bash through!'*

Yes, Duff could still fill her with loves she never felt of her own accord. The trouble was that these heartfelt loves became sickly and left a taste. *'Fondest mistress, worshipful young mistress – I love you and you love me.'* Followed, of course, by the inevitable anxious question – *'You do, don't you?'*

Unlike cats. Unlike Catchmouse, anyhow – only two other cats had ever consented to talk to her, and they soon got bored with human conversation. Cats didn't care, that was their magic. Cats took what they wanted and walked away. Cats used humans and human possessions and comforts, and gave nothing in return. Cats permitted some people to stroke them, dogs begged anyone to pat them. Cats knew they ruled the world: dogs knew humans ruled it. Cats feared nothing –

She sat up and said, 'No, that's not true. Catchy was afraid of the sow thing, the Blob. She was afraid, really afraid.'

She went downstairs and helped wash up. She did not feel the dishes and cups and saucers and knives and forks as they passed through her hands. She was thinking hard about Blobs.

New York, midsummer

'Hey, lookit!' said Tal. The whole Brooklyn teenage gang, Eddie, Merv, Little Pete and Bronx, stopped what they were doing – throwing nickels into an empty cola can, winner takes all – and looked at the cat.

It was standing in the gutter of the stifling street, bony back arched, scraggy tufts of fur bristling, spitting at the nearside front tyre of a derelict Plymouth convertible. It leapt back, arched again, spat again at nothing. Nothing, or a shadow.

'Some crazy cat,' said Little Pete and threw the can at it. He missed, but only just. The can banged and clattered and rolled. Yet the cat took no notice.

'Like it's spooked,' said Merv, and threw his peaked cap at it. This time it moved, leapt sideways. The gang cheered, the cat ran away, Merv put the can back at the right distance for nickel-throwing.

'All the mogs,' said Bronx, 'All weird, you know? Spooked!'

'So who cares?' said Tal. 'Cats! . . .' As he was the gang's leader, they all decided not to care; and concentrated on throwing nickels into the can.

Warsaw, autumn

The cat was glaring and staring and spitting.

'It's the cold,' said old Mrs Breslaw.

'Don't tell me it's the cold,' said her husband. 'With you, everything's the weather – too hot, too cold, always the weather, the weather always. It's not the cold.'

'Don't tell me it's the Devil!' said Mrs Breslaw. 'With you, it's the Devil, always the Devil.'

'The Devil made witches,' said Mr Breslaw, 'and witches have cats. Who ever heard of a witch with a dog, a rabbit, a sheep? A cat, it is always a cat. The Devil's beast – the cat. That cat has got the Devil in it.'

Mrs Breslaw looked at the cat. It was arched, malignant, wicked, staring at nothing – or was there a blurred shadow? – and hating it. She knew her husband was right, it was the Devil all right, but she would not admit it.

'Witches have *owls*,' she said. 'Don't try to deny it! They have owls also, as well as cats! But you don't see owls doing mad things, bad things. Only cats!'

'*Owls . . .!*' said Mr Breslaw. 'So now it's *owls!* Forget your owls. Look at that cat. That cat has the Devil in it. It's looking at the Devil!'

Mrs Breslaw knew he was right, but said, 'It's the cold. I keep telling you.'

Paris, early winter

'Stop that!' shouted Françine. 'It makes me sick, it makes me giddy! Stop it!' She threw her expensive English cashmere sweater at Minou, but the cat took no notice: it just went on staring, spitting, glaring, each hair erect, all its claws sticking out like thorns.

'Stupid creature!' yelled Françine, bending down to shout in the cat's ear. 'Imbecile! Have you no gratitude for the pretty things I give you? Stop it! Stop it, stop it!' She threw one ear ring then the other at the cat, hurting her ears as she tore them off. But the cat took no notice.

Françine began to cry. Her nerves! All cats were always doing it, always and always, nowadays. The dogs too – that was why she had got rid of Hirondelle, her toy spaniel with the beautiful long ears. He would bark and bark and bark, darting and snapping at something invisible, bark and bark and bark until her poor head could stand no more.

She cried and felt her eye-liner run. In a sudden fury, she kicked Minou with her stockinged foot. The cat jumped sideways, glared at her, then walked fast to the door, tail up. 'Go, then!' cried Françine.

But at the door, the cat paused, turned, poked its head forward to look again at the invisible thing in the middle of the room. 'Go, GO!' shrieked Françine. Through her tears, the middle of the room was indistinct and shadowy.

The glaring cat said, right from the back of its throat, '*Mrrrraow!*'

Françine stopped crying and began to shiver with fear

instead. She would not have minded if that horrid sound had been meant for her, but she knew it was not. It was meant for IT, the invisible thing in the room with her. The thing that, sometimes, she thought she could see as a big, humped, shadowy shape. A Blob.

Animal Crackers

At school, Lettice got into trouble with Miss Langham again.

Miss Langham was the Biology mistress. She was young, pretty, dark, small, straight-backed, crisp-voiced and invariably right about everything. You could imagine her as the perfect secretary – the boss's secretary; as an air hostess, saying, 'Kindly do not panic' as the airliner crashed; as a fashion model even. 'I can't see her as a nun, somehow,' one of Lettice's schoolmates had remarked. 'I mean poor old God . . .!'

Miss Langham was disliked and feared by Lettice: and Lettice annoyed Miss Langham. 'Lettice!' said Miss Langham, 'I don't think you are attending!'

'Oh, I was, I was just looking for my –'

'Lettice, tell me why the larger land animals are necessarily vertebrate,' said Miss Langham.

'Because,' began Lettice. 'Because,' she repeated. Then she changed her mind and plunged to disaster by saying, 'Oh, but Miss Langham, you can have big animals that *aren't* vertebrates. I mean, even apart from crustaceans and molluscs – I mean, you could have a big animal that *isn't* a vertebrate –'

'Name one,' said Miss Langham.

'Well, you probably wouldn't agree with me, but –'

'*Name one*,' said Miss Langham.

'The Blobs,' said Lettice, speaking more or less to herself.

'I beg your pardon, Lettice?' said Miss Langham.

'Blobs,' repeated Lettice, hopelessly.

'Come to the front, Lettice,' said Miss Langham, 'and tell the class about *Blobs*.'

For the next quarter of an hour, Lettice faced the class and told about Blobs. When she faltered, Miss Langham goaded her on again. When she did not falter, Miss Langham interrupted her with questions so that she faltered. It was a good quarter of an hour for the class and perhaps for Miss Langham, and a very bad one for Lettice.

Yet Lettice did not break down. Indeed, as her hopeless recital staggered on, something unusual happened to her. She felt, growing inside her, a determined lump of considered dislike for Miss Langham and what she represented. So instead of collapsing into dampness and snuffles, Lettice actually hardened herself through the whole endless quarter of an hour.

At the end of it, Miss Langham had drawn out of Lettice the whole story of the Blobs (giggles from the class!) – the talks with Catchy (smothered laughter!) – and Lettice's belief in a race of large animals that nobody could see properly, or touch, or hear . . . and this race had something to do with all the stories about odd animal behaviour (outright laughter!).

So Lettice made a fool of herself. Yet, for perhaps the first time in her life, she somehow managed to keep tatters of dignity about her. She had not given in, or shifted her ground, or let Miss Langham walk all over her. Indeed, the last word was Lettice's. Miss Langham, now made prettier than ever by an angry brilliance in her eyes and a flush of colour on her well-placed cheekbones, said, 'I think that is all, Lettice. You may return to your place.' And Lettice, walking back to her desk, said – quite steadily and without her voice going funny

'It may be enough, Miss Langham, but it isn't all. It's only just started.' The class did not snigger.

When the bell rang, Miss Langham said, 'Please stay behind, Lettice.' So Lettice did.

'Lettice, your work is unsatisfactory. You are sloppy in everything you do. And now your behaviour is becoming ridiculous.'

'I only did what you told me,' said Lettice.

'You wasted a lot of class time with your absurd –'

'You *made* me do it, you *told* me to stand in front and tell them –'

'Lettice, I'm warning you! –'

Then they both paused, having got nowhere. The pause lengthened. At last Miss Langham said, 'Lettice, you can't be as stupid as you pretend. You put yourself in these ridiculous positions – making up this story about invisible animals – saying you can talk with animals –'

'They're *not* invisible. Just very hard to see. And ordinary animals can see them all right.'

'You don't really believe any of the things you have been saying, Lettice?'

'Of course I do. It's all true, I wasn't just making things up.'

Another pause.

Miss Langham said, 'Lettice, you are rather a – a strange girl. I cannot pretend that I like you very much or approve of you, but, then, I don't have to. I am simply one of your teachers. Liking and approval need have little to do with our relationship.'

'Either way,' Lettice interrupted defiantly. She was surprised by her own bravery.

'Either way,' said Miss Langham, raising one eyebrow. 'But I won't put up with too much nonsense from you, Lettice, because I mustn't. Being a teacher means more than just teaching.'

'Form our characters,' mumbled Lettice.

'Quite right,' said Miss Langham. 'I'm supposed to form your characters, which may sound very old-fashioned and unlikely to you, but never mind that. My character and yours are very different. I am a vertebrate creature; I have a backbone, which no doubt you despise. You seem to be one of the Blobs you described – things without backbones. Invertebrates. And you don't want to change, do you? So what do you think I should do, Lettice?'

'You can do anything you like!' said Lettice, coming to the boil. 'Lots of punishments you could give me . . . A bad report, anything you like!'

'I could, but I won't,' said Miss Langham. 'Listen, Lettice. You insist that your Blobs – your strange animals – really exist, don't you?'

'Yes, I do. I do.'

'Then your "punishment", if it is a punishment, is going to be this. You are going to produce a properly documented statement of the things you were talking about in class just now. You are to persuade me, by any means you choose, that you are right; that animal behaviour has changed, that there is real evidence for your Blobs. But no sloppiness, Lettice, I want the job done properly and tidily and completely. And *cleanly*, Lettice. None of your usual finger-marks and stains and messiness.'

'All right.'

Miss Langham looked closely at Lettice's downturned face, trying to make herself feel some sympathy and warmth for the girl. She made her voice lower and softer when she said, 'You are very fond of animals, aren't you, Lettice?'

'Yes. And I know a lot about them. Probably more than you in some ways.'

'You insist that you can talk to them?'

'Yes. I can. I do.'

'All right, Lettice. We'll leave it at that . . .'

As it turned out, Miss Langham was punished more than Lettice. Miss Langham worried, for days after, about her treatment of Lettice and her attitude towards a girl she could not like.

Lettice, however, had no need to worry. She had always disliked Miss Langham; she continued to dislike her; but she did not think about her. For, largely due to Miss Langham, she had more interesting things to think about.

That very evening, Lucas threw the newspaper over to Lettice and said, 'There's a story for your pongy old scrapbook. Animal crackers or whatever you call it. Down at the bottom of page eight. Your furry friends seem to be going ape.'

She found the paragraph. It was a small one headed

SHEEP DIPPY?

A flock of two hundred sheep turned on Mr John Haslett, farmer, of Corfe, Dorset and pinned him against a stone wall for two hours. Mr Haslett attributes the incident to chemicals in a new sheep dip. Mr Haslett was unhurt, 'But my dinner was cold,' he complained.

Lettice said, 'I read that yesterday, in the evening paper.' She did not tell her brother that she had already assembled a pile of such clippings. Later, lolling on her bed, she opened her scrapbook and re-read them.

'KILLER DOG PACK ROAMS STOCKBROKER BELT' . . . Residents of Leatherhead and Dorking, she read, were being kept awake at dusk by the howling of between fifty and a hundred dogs, hunting in a great pack. The story did not tell what they were hunting.

'SO THE VET CALLED THE DOCTOR!' A very short story about a vet who one evening attended a little girl's sick pony and was attacked by other ponies. A doctor had to be called to treat the vet, who was kicked.

'WIDOW'S MERCY BID FAILS — ROVER MUST DIE.' An eighty-year-old widow's little mongrel dog turned savage and bit her. This story had not interested Lettice because the dog was very old and old dogs can turn 'funny'. It interested her now, however, because of a paragraph she had not really bothered to read before:

> 'He'd just stand and stare and sort
> of tremble,' said Mrs Henning. 'It
> happened every evening. Well, I
> got sick of it, you know, so I said
> "Come on, Rover! Talk to
> Mother!" and he wouldn't listen, so
> one evening I just patted him and
> then he went quite distracted, he'd
> got his teeth in my wrist and
> nothing I could do would make
> him let go. And now he's got to be
> put down,' she added tearfully.

'Every evening,' thought Lettice. 'Every *evening* . . .'

She flicked through the other cuttings. 'THE INVISIBLE MAN?' Story about a dog that stared at nothing for two days.

Similar stories headed 'CAT-ATONIC TRANCE!' . . . 'COME OUT, COME OUT, WHATEVER YOU ARE' . . . 'DO PETS SEE GHOSTS?' . . . 'SEEING THINGS!' . . . 'HOW CRUEL CAN WE GET?' (family abandons dog on motorway 'because it would keep staring').

None of the stories was given much space. The widow's

story was the longest but not because of the dog's behaviour; it was the 'human interest' that mattered to the journalist, the poor old lady who had to say goodbye to her dog.

She read through the stories again. 'Evening,' she murmured. '"Later that evening . . ." "The family was watching TV when . . ." Always in the evening!'

Duff shuffled into the room and rested his chin on the edge of the counterpane, looking soulful. He wanted to be allowed to come on the bed with her. 'Oh no you don't!' said Lettice, then changed her mind.

'All right, Duff,' she said. 'You can come up. But only if you talk. You understand, Duff? Talk.'

The dog clumsily jumped up, tail wagging, and turned round three times on the bedclothes, making itself a hollow. But Lettice took hold of his front legs and pulled him towards her until girl and dog were eye to eye. 'Come on, Duff,' she said. 'Come on, come on, tell me things.'

Duff's Story

'You like me, don't you?' Duff said – but there were no words, of course, just pictures in the amber-brown eyes, and a knowing between them.

'You do like me, don't you?' he insisted. 'Because I love you, I'd do anything for you, anything at all –'

'Tell me about the things you see, then.'

'Oh, yes, anything at all, I'd do anything you asked me. What was it you asked me?'

'Tell me about the things you've been seeing.'

'I saw a new mess in the garden, another dog has been here, a strange dog –'

'I don't mean that sort of thing. *New* things.'

'It was a new mess. A new dog. I don't know that dog.'

Lettice shook Duff gently. 'Listen, Duff, stop being a silly old thing, tell me about the new thing you don't like, the thing you bark at, the thing that makes Catchmouse frightened.'

'No one must be in our garden but us.'

She shook him again as if to shake new patterns into him. Duff's mind was like a kaleidoscope, lots of brightly coloured, meaningless things forming patterns that jogged and scattered. 'In the house, Duff,' she said. 'Is there something new in the house? Something you don't like?'

'I do like talking with you,' said Duff. 'You are my friend. My best friend. My dearest, closest friend. Please, if you don't mind, stop squeezing my front legs.'

'Something new in the house, Duff. Tell me about it.'

'Oh, that's not new, the thing I bark at. It's the same old thing.'

'*What* thing?'

Duff rolled his eyes, trying to think, and said, 'Oh, you know. It. I T. *That* thing, the thing I bark at.'

'Describe it to me, then.'

'I can't, it's changed, it's not the same as it always was.'

'But you said it's the same old thing.'

'Oh yes, it hasn't changed. Yet it's different. But it's I T all right.'

Lettice said, 'Tell – me – about – I T.' She accompanied each word with a little shake of his legs.

'Which one? There's more than one.'

'All of them.'

'But they're all the same It.'

'Then tell me about them.'

'Well, they're always there, aren't they? Blobby.'

'Concentrate. *Show* me.'

He made a picture. She saw piano legs. They went out of focus. At first she thought it was Duff's fault, but then she realized that the blobby blur was right. It was what Duff meant her to see. It was Catchmouse's sow thing.

The picture jerked, faded and was gone. 'That's what It's like,' said Duff, pleased with himself.

'Show me some more, Duff. More of them. Show me how they're changing.'

'They're different, they're getting clearer.'

'Clearer? Show me!'

Duff tried, but Lettice saw no clear pictures. 'You couldn't see them at all before, they just made a haze like heat,' the dog explained. 'But now It – they – are clearer. But I can't remember properly . . . Oh, and now I can smell them!'

'What sort of smell?' Lettice demanded.

'They smell ... wrong, so I bark. I often bark,' he said, virtuously.

'All right, Duff, you're being very good. They're getting clearer –'

'Darker. And they flicker. And they smell worse.'

'What do they smell like?'

'Foreign.'

'What do you mean? Foreign like the new dog in our garden?'

'No, foreign. I told you, foreign.'

He was getting impatient with her, Lettice realized. She understood why. To a dog, smells were everything. The language of smells was the one language Duff spoke instantly, fluently and comprehensively. He couldn't understand her lack of education about smells, any more than she could tolerate his slowness in putting thoughts together, or keeping to the point.

'Please explain "foreign",' she said humbly.

'"Foreign" means – it means – it means *not us*. Not dogs, cats, fires, carpets, cars, you – not anything. It means something from somewhere else, not a proper thing.'

'A thing you can't lick or bite?'

'Yes, I suppose so, I suppose that's it. Let me tell you about the new dog that was in our garden –'

'Is the smell of the new dog "foreign"?'

'No of course not, it's a dog. Dogs are us.' He tried to get up and move away, but she held him and said, 'Duff! Duff! Down, Duff!' He gave in, unwillingly, with a soft, annoyed woof.

'What else is foreign, Duff?'

'Nothing else. Only the blobby things. Oh, the noise boxes are a bit foreign, they smell foreign, but at least you can see they're there.'

'Ah,' said Lettice. She let him go because she wanted to think for a moment. Anyhow, he was tired by now, his mind and his legs were twitching.

She understood what he meant by 'noise boxes': she had glimpsed the television set, the radio. He often described things he did not understand as 'boxes'. There was the howl-box (vacuum cleaner), blankbox (ancient washing-machine rusting away under the house), foodbox (the fridge), badbox (telephone – Duff feared it because people talked at it to something invisible).

But the box he had shown her was the television . . .

Evenings, she thought. Always, things happened in the evening.

It was in the evenings that people watched television. It was in the evenings that the animals began behaving in their strange new way. The sheep ganging up on the farmer, Duff's outburst, the widow's dog biting her, Catchmouse's glaring and staring – always in the evenings. Always at television time.

She had relaxed her hold on Duff's legs. He looked at her sideways, cunningly, and sneaked out of the room.

Kalabza

Miss Langham said, 'Very well, Lettice. Let me see your work.'

Lettice handed over the file. It was two inches thick and solid with her own writings, newspaper clippings and pages cut from magazines. Miss Langham managed to keep her expression unchanged. She might at least have raised an eyebrow, thought Lettice.

Miss Langham began reading, turning over sheet after sheet with her taper-nailed, pretty fingers. Lettice admired her eyebrows, which formed two perfectly equal brush strokes, level and elegant. Her lashes were long, her hair had that springing liveliness from the parting that spoke of vigorous health, perfect cleanliness. Lettice tried not to think of a big, fat custard pie – a custard pie, with plenty of frothy eggwhite on top – jammed right on top of Miss Langham's lovely, healthy head.

Miss Langham said, 'When did you begin compiling all this material, Lettice?'

'I was thinking about it before we had – before –'

'Before our row. But you did not begin cutting out the pieces from the paper until two weeks ago, is that right?'

'Yes. When you told me to.'

'There are a great number of cuttings.'

'I told you there would be. I told you that the animals were behaving funnily –'

'Yes, I remember you saying so.'

She continued unhurriedly to turn the pages. She read Lettice's own handwritten pages with care. At last she said, 'You have done a very thorough job, very neatly. I congratulate you, Lettice.'

Lettice wanted to say, 'Is that all?' but said nothing.

Miss Langham bent down to pick up her own briefcase. She opened it and produced a file not unlike Lettice's. She turned the pages to a cutting identical to one of Lettice's and looked up. 'Snap!' said Miss Langham, and smiled. Her smile was unexpectedly charming.

'What do you think about it all, Miss Langham?'

'I think I was wrong and you are quite obviously right.'

Lettice, amazed, said, 'But that day, when you made me stand up in front of everyone –'

'That day, I thought you were wrong and I hoped I was right.'

'Hoped?'

'Oh, I don't mean "hoped" about the animals . . . I mean, I hoped I was doing the right thing as your teacher. Discipline and character and all that sort of thing . . .' She stopped for a moment, embarrassed, and said, 'I'm not all that much older than you girls, you know. It can be very difficult sometimes, particularly with –'

'With people like me? Untidy people?'

Again Miss Langham smiled. 'Yes, that's just what I mean. People who make me nervous; people like you, Lettice.'

'Nervous! *I* make *you* nervous?'

'Yes. Because I can feel your dislike for me. Because we are so very different. If I were not your teacher, it would not matter. But I am, so we are bound to be – enemies, in a way.'

Lettice thought about this and found it to be true. Had Miss Langham been merely a neighbour, she would have been just Miss Langham. Miss Langham, teacher, was something else.

'That day in class,' Miss Langham continued, 'I thought you were being stupid, untidy-minded, fey, whatever word you like. But you've proved your point. You've proved yourself right. So now, I hope, we needn't be enemies. Perhaps we can become colleagues?'

'Colleagues,' said Lettice. The idea was not unattractive. 'Colleagues in what?' she said. 'I mean, we're both agreed now that something's happening with the animals, here and in lots of other places. But we don't agree about the Blobs, the Its – the things you made me tell you about in class.'

'Don't we?' said Miss Langham.

'But of course we don't. You remember in class –'

'It's like ghosts and spiritualists and all that sort of thing as far as I'm concerned,' said Miss Langham. 'I didn't believe you when you said that you could talk to the animals that day: I don't *believe* you, not properly, now: but I don't *disbelieve* you any more. Look, we've got to be frank with each other. That day, I thought you were just playing an act of the sort I particularly dislike. Now I think differently. It wasn't an act, I know that now. But nor is what you say necessarily the truth.'

'I know. I quite see that, I didn't expect you to believe me –'

Miss Langham had been fiddling with her handbag, not listening to Lettice. Now she said, suddenly, 'Do you know of a man called Zafar Kalabza, Lettice? Doctor Kalabza?'

'Doctor Kalabza! Of course! I mean, he's always on TV. Showing off, waving his arms about. Those science programmes –'

'Yes, those science programmes,' said Miss Langham, pursing her lips with distaste. 'Those awful programmes . . .'

'I don't actually know him, of course,' Lettice said.

'I do,' said Miss Langham. 'I once knew him rather well.'
She sounded almost guilty.

'Is he as phoney as he looks?' asked Lettice. 'The way he
dresses and everything . . .'

'He is even *phonier* than he looks,' Miss Langham said.
'And what is worse, Lettice – he is not phoney at all!'

'What do you mean?'

'I honestly believe him to be a genius. Did you know he
won the Nobel Prize, Lettice? The highest international
award a scientist can gain?'

'Oh, that. He never lets you forget it,' Lettice said. 'Always
drags it in somehow, on T V.' She paused and said, 'What
about him, Miss Langham? Why did you ask me if I knew of
him?'

'Because,' Miss Langham said – and now she looked guilty,
even furtive – 'Because he knows of *you*, Lettice. I've told him
about you. You and your interest in animal behaviour. And
communication with animals.'

Lettice stared at Miss Langham, too confused and angry to
speak.

'I didn't mean to do it,' Miss Langham said, hastily. 'It
just – *happened*. You see, we correspond – I was once one of his
students and he insists on writing to me, and – oh dear, he has
such energy, he is so persistent, Lettice, once he gets an idea
in his head he won't let go –'

'Why did you mention *me*?' Lettice said, coldly and
angrily.

'Because he's like you, he's deeply interested in the strange
ways animals have been behaving recently . . . and talking to
animals . . . I'm afraid I let slip the things you said. And he
pounced on everything and telephoned and kept writing me
letters –'

'What letters?' Lettice said, stonily. 'What have they to do
with me?'

'Oh dear, I suppose it would be best if I showed them to you,' said Miss Langham. She opened her handbag and produced a bundle of airmail letters. Her hand shook. The letters spilled.

Lettice bent down to pick them up. One of them had fallen open and Lettice could hardly avoid reading the big, clear handwriting. The letter began, 'Charmingly Curvilinear and Utterly Desirable Schoolmarm, object of my Forbidden Fantasies –'

Miss Langham blushed as she took this letter. 'His prose style is rather lurid,' she said faintly.

'What does he say about *me*?' Lettice said.

Miss Langham recovered rapidly. Her blush faded and her hand was steady. 'Read the letter,' she said. 'Read it aloud.'

Lettice read it. 'It begins, "My adorable . . ." Oh, I'll skip that. It goes on in French, I'm not much good at French –'

'How fortunate,' said Miss Langham, tightly. 'Read the second paragraph. The typewritten part.'

Lettice obeyed. '"Dr Kalabza's dictation,"' she read. '"Regrets unable continue personally, packing for New York Nobel Convention. Says, very interested in the girl Lettice. Does not consider the girl's claims unreasonable. Many reports of human–animal communication throughout history. Dr K. has personally conducted encephalograph tests to attempt to establish reality of such communications" – What does that mean, Miss Langham?'

'An encephalograph is a machine that records brain patterns. If a human could indeed communicate with animals, the encephalograph readings would echo each other in some way.'

'You mean he does horrible experiments on poor animals?'

'I mean nothing of the sort. There is nothing horrible about taking such readings. Do go on with his letter.'

Lettice bit her lip and read on. '"Dr K. will send results of his own and other researches using dogs, horses, cats, dolphins. The most recent experiments are the most interesting and promising, he says; latest equipment producing extraordinary results. He has no doubt that such communication is and always has been possible: but today, meaningful communication may soon be shown and proved.

'"Dr K. now making a joke about breathing up nose and will follow you anywhere. Point of joke not clear.

'"Dr K. says, your girl particularly interesting because she says she *sees* images or pictures in animals' minds. She receives real information, not just emotional messages. This claim most unusual and must repeat must be investigated.

'"Dr K. says, do not dismiss girl's theories about recent examples of odd animal behaviour. He says, odd behaviour documented worldwide, the girl is right and you are wrong. He says you are adorable when wrong.

'"Dr K. getting very excited (you know him) and says coming to Europe soon, must repeat must meet the girl Lettice, perhaps she holds the key to –"'

'Now the letter finishes in his own handwriting,' Lettice said. She glimpsed a large, untidy row of hearts and kisses and a huge, sprawling signature, ZAFAR.

'He sounds a bit . . .' said Lettice.

'He is a bit . . . whatever you were thinking,' Miss Langham replied. She was looking rather pink again. 'It doesn't mean anything, of course. He's a sort of – sort of box of fireworks . . . Always exploding and whizzing about and getting wildly excited. But the thing is, Lettice, that he *does* things. He doesn't just appear brilliant, he is brilliant. He *achieves*. When you meet him –'

'Meet him?' Lettice said. 'I'm not going to meet him! Ever!'

'He says he must, repeat must, meet you,' Miss Langham reminded her.

'He can say what he likes! I won't meet him!'

'You won't?' said Miss Langham. She raised one eyebrow and put the letters neatly back in her bag. 'Hmmm,' she said.

A day later, Lucas visited his father's den.

'Chess?' Lucas said, persuasively nudging the board towards his father across the cluttered table in the study.

'No. Shut up for a moment. I want to hear this. You should hear it too.' Mr Rideout fiddled impatiently with the radio. One side of the room was filled with ancient electronic gear. There were tape-recorders, relics filled with relics – he was always listening to terrible old radio plays, half a century out of date. There was the radio he had made himself from junked transistor sets. A mess, this radio. But it gave him what he wanted. It brought in Russia, America, Rome, broadcasts from anywhere.

'Got it!' he said, contentedly, as voices suddenly cleared and filled the room. 'New York! Listen, Lucas .. The Nobel Convention. Should be worth hearing. They're bound to talk about animal behaviour.'

'Oh, *that*,' Lucas said, without interest. He'd seen and heard enough about the strange behaviour of animals. The dogs and cats and horses and pigs and rats and mice were going mad. So what? Still, his father was a science correspondent and had to be interested. Lucas lay back in the shabby armchair – it reeked of Duff – and half-listened to what the world's scientists were saying.

The bored, grating, American voice that translated the words of a Russian scientist said, 'He's saying, the agenda is being departed from. He objects to that. He says they should be discussing the wheat rust, not these general matters. He objects to that. He says they should be discussing Russian scientists' work on symbiotic parasites of grain crops. He says, he objects to –'

Lucas said, 'Dad, are you really listening to all this? Wouldn't you rather play chess?'

'Shut up,' his father muttered, fiercely; and leaned closer to the speakers. Lucas knew why. For suddenly it was Doctor Kalabza speaking, cutting across the Russian's words, ruthlessly interrupting the dreary blur. It was unmistakably Dr Kalabza's voice: piercing, high-pitched, cutting, vainglorious, speaking too-perfect English.

'Oh, cannot we talk of something *interesting*?' Doctor Kalabza's voice said, very loudly. 'Must it always be our Russian friends, and their so unfortunate problems with wheat? Russian *corn*, always Russian *corn* . . .' The 'corn' was an insult.

The radio speakers brought the sound of muffled uproar. Mr Rideout grinned. Lucas rubbed his hands together and sat forward.

The American voice, very close to the microphone, said, 'The Russian party is saying that they object. Now three of the Russians are standing on their chairs waving order papers. Doctor Kalabza is smiling at the Russians and waving right back at them. The Russians are objecting some more. Doctor Kalabza is smiling some more. Now Doctor Kalabza seems to be conducting an orchestra, he's kind of conducting the Russian choir –'

The harsh, flat American voice suddenly broke up. Its owner was laughing. So were Mr Rideout and Lucas.

'*Animals*!' cried Doctor Kalabza, loudly and clearly. 'Farmyard animals! Oh, not *you*, my dear colleagues! – do not mistake me. I was merely suggesting a better subject for consideration. The behaviour of animals – the dogs and cats, the other animals, the way they are behaving – surely that is the most important and absorbing matter for us to consider? Such extraordinary changes, dear friends, such extraordinary reports from every quarter of the globe! Think what has happened!

302

'Always, until now, man has told the animals what to do and always has been more or less obeyed. Man has said to the pig, "Be a long-backed pig with more bacon" – and the pig has obeyed. To the greenfly, man has said, "Die when I spray you" and the greenfly has obediently expired. To the horse, man has said, "Have great muscles for hauling" or, "Be slender and long-muscled for the racing!" and the horse has obeyed. Sometimes Nature has revolted and said, "No, my greenfly shall become used to your sprays!" or, "My rats shall resist your poisons!"; but even then, man has understood his own mistakes . . .

'But now – so suddenly! – so mysteriously! – the animals have decided to say, "NO!". And this presents us with a problem, a very great problem. What if the gentle cow refuses to give us our milk? What if the lamb refuses to go to the slaughter? What –'

'What about the Doctor telling us of a cure instead of describing the disease?' interrupted an English voice, good-naturedly.

'Communication,' replied Doctor Kalabza, instantly. 'We must ask the animals what they are doing and why '

'And how does the Doctor intend to do that?' said the English voice. 'Can he *talk* to the animals?'

'Alas, no. I cannot do that. *But – but*, my friends! – I think I know of someone who can!'

And then the Russians were shouting and the President was hammering for order and there was nothing left worth listening to. Mr Rideout switched off.

Lucas said, 'Who is he? That Doctor Kalabza?'

'Anyone who's ever watched T V knows who he is, so you know who he is. You never stop watching T V, you're glued to the goggle-box –'

'No, I mean, who is he *really*? All the box shows you is a sort of show-off superstar person . . .' Lucas could see this person in his mind: vaguely Indian looking, but not dark – yet with waving, glossy black hair, worn quite long, and with Indian-looking eyes that flashed. He could see the neat, slim body, the flourish of the narrow hands, the endless movements of the mouth (Doctor Kalabza never stopped talking), the teeth like a toothpaste ad. . . . He could see all this, yet had no idea of the real man, the man beneath the public man.

His father told Lucas, 'He's a superstar raver who also happens to be a first-rater. Someone who is deservedly pre-eminent in his field.'

'Zafar Kalabza . . .' Lucas said. 'Sounds more like a stage magician. Is it his real name, do you think?'

'Of course not. He was probably born Sid Sausage or Fred Fryingpan.'

'Is he an Indian, or what?'

'I've no idea. And it wouldn't be much use asking *him*.'

'You mean, he's a liar?'

'No, he simply avoids inconvenient truths. Even in his science. Once he's got an idea in his head, he simply bangs away at it. That's how he made his extraordinary discoveries about amino acids and genetic –'

'You mean, everyone else thought he was wrong? But he was right?'

'Astoundingly right. He changed the whole course of – Look, why this sudden interest in Doctor Kalabza?'

'Well, obviously, because of Lettice.'

'*Lettice?*'

'He said something just now about communication . . knowing someone who can talk to animals. Wouldn't it be funny if he meant Lettice?'

Mr Rideout regarded his son with wide-open eyes and shook his head slowly from side to side. 'What an incredibl stupid boy you are!' he said at last.

'I can still beat you at chess,' Lucas said. And he did.

Violence

While Lucas talked to his father, Danny Matheson scowled and felt lonely.

Danny Matheson was ten years old. His interests were playing soccer, watching soccer on television, going to soccer matches and talking soccer. In summer, when there was no soccer, he practised his soccer skills with a tennis ball and waited for autumn, winter and spring – the real times of the year, the times when there was soccer.

Outside soccer, Danny lived an ordinary life. He went to school, came back again, ate, slept and messed about. He was a perfectly satisfactory sort of boy in all these occupations, who seldom caused trouble or felt troubled.

Now, he felt troubled. It was mid-evening. He was alone in the house and his parents would not return for another hour and a half – they were with neighbours, Mr and Mrs Elphin, three doors down the road. To reach his parents, Danny had only to pick up the telephone and dial a number he perfectly well knew, or go down the road and knock on a familiar door. He felt unable to do either of these things, however, for what was there to say when they answered? He imagined the conversation . . .

'Mum, there's something in the living-room.'

'What's in the living-room?'

'Something. You know, *something*.'

'Dad, speak to Danny, he's gone bonkers. He says there's "something" in the living-room.'

Dad speaking: 'What's all this, son?'

'It's the living-room. There's something *in* it . . .'

'Something in the living-room!' thought Danny; that wouldn't do for sensible people like his parents. 'And it won't do for me, either!' Danny said to himself. So he turned the TV volume knob down a bit, and looked more closely at the Something.

There it was again! Over there! It had moved. It was nearer the door, further away from the TV. As he watched, it moved again: the pattern on the carpet shifted and wavered, the legs of a chair went hazy and somehow muffled, the panels of the door went out of focus. There was a greyness. Danny picked up the heavy poker from the fireplace.

How big was the Something? Six feet, at least. Six feet of nothing-very-much, six feet of disturbance and slight darkness. Perhaps it was his own eyes? Danny looked at a picture on the wall: clear as a bell. He looked at the TV picture: clean, sharp, the same as usual. He looked at the Something: no, it wasn't his eyes.

And it was still moving! It was moving by the door, *through* the closed door! It was half out of the door and half in! No, it was coming back again, moving, still moving, moving very slowly.

Vaguely moving and wavering and flickering. But it was there all right.

Danny lifted the poker and brought it down, not hard, on the Something. He gave a sort of yelp, because he thought he had felt a semi-solid resistance to the blow. When the poker touched it, he thought the Something had flickered.

It moved away from him. He followed it and hit it again harder.

A chair went over with a clatter. The Something had knocked it over, it must have done, he was nowhere near the chair. He hit it again. The Something moved on like a slug-shaped patch of mist, wavering, flickering, putting things out of focus, darkening the view. He hit it again, and again.

It was getting darker, he could almost see it. It was humped, long, legless, heaving, moving!

Suddenly Danny threw down the poker and ran out of the room. He ran upstairs to the bathroom, slammed the door and locked it. He stood by the door, listening, but all he could hear was his own panting breath. He went to the mirror on the wall and looked at himself. His white-faced reflection looked back at him, wide-eyed and worried. He put his tongue out: so did the face in the mirror. He said, 'Up the Arsenal!' and clasped his hands in a boxer's handshake: so did the Danny in the mirror.

He sighed, let out a long breath, turned on the cold tap and rinsed his face with a minimum of cold water. 'There you are, then!' he said cheerfully, 'You still don't like cold water, do you? Do you?' He and his reflection nodded and he carefully inspected the drops of water on his face before leaving the mirror and wiping the moisture off with a blue towel. Then he put his head against the door and listened. Not a sound.

He walked down the stairs slowly, listening to the TV set. It was saying, 'For the *real* flavour of *real* coffee –' then a girl's squeaky voice said, 'Reeelly?' Danny could see the advertisement in his mind. His lips formed the rest of the dialogue –

Down in the living-room, another chair went over.

He retreated three or four steps up the stairs, then checked himself. 'Go downstairs, Yellowbelly!' he said, out loud, and went down the stairs.

In the living-room there were now two chairs on their sides and the Something was still there, moving faster. It brushed against a little table and a plant in a pot went down with a crash. Danny picked up the poker and hit and hit and hit. Then the thing blundered against the TV set.

The set went down and there were flashes and a line of fire showing through the perforated guard at the back and then smoke and bursts and pops of fire. All the lights went out. As they went out, Danny saw it, almost completely! – the definite shape of the humps, the scarred texture of it, the livid crisscross that suddenly faded as the TV set went dead, the swing of what might have been a head! –

Then it came towards him, fast, and he kept hitting and hitting and hitting but it got him against the wall. He would have been crushed if it hadn't knocked the wall down. Danny fell through the great hole with all the lath and plaster.

By now he was screaming and the smoke was everywhere and the phone was ringing in the hall. He fell over something trying to reach the phone and landed flat on his face. He could feel *it* near him, he wanted to roll one way or another to get out of its way but the hall was very narrow and he didn't know which way it was coming –

Then the front door slammed open and his father was flicking light switches that didn't work. The phone kept ringing. His father got the big battery lantern from the hall cupboard and swung it round. He said, 'For God's sake . . .!' There was smoke and plaster dust everywhere, he didn't see Danny at first, he picked up the phone and said, 'Bob? Something's happened, it's a madhouse, yes, yes, ring you back!' Then he did see Danny and said, 'What the hell –' and knelt down beside his son as Danny's mother came rushing in.

Danny couldn't answer their questions at first. He could hear himself sobbing and whooping and hear them asking questions and the phone ringing again ('Mrs Elphin? Yes something's happened, yes please, yes, come over right away') but he couldn't stop the noises he was making.

By the time he could talk and listen, Mrs Elphin from number fifty-seven was there and a policeman too. The lights were on again – his father had mended a fuse. The policeman was saying, 'When you get a dead short like that, the spark can jump and then the other fuses can blow. A dead short, you see.'

They made no sense of Danny's story. The two chairs, the little table, the plant pot, the TV set – they could understand them, but not the hole in the wall. Danny's mother began to repeat to herself, 'He's a *quiet* boy,' she said, 'Quiet. It's not as if he were, you know, *excitable*, he's a *quiet* boy ...!' The policeman made notes, Mrs Elphin made tea and Danny's father made a face that meant 'we'll get to the bottom of this later, my lad.'

'I knew something was wrong,' said Mrs Elphin. 'I heard noises from *this* house when the Mathesons left *our* house ... then all the lights going out ... That's why I phoned, Officer.'

'A dead short,' said the policeman.

So they neither believed nor disbelieved Danny at the time. Later on, of course, they believed him.

Hoppicopter

An amazing Aston-Martin limousine, painted metallic gold, slithered like an exotic serpent down the modest road and settled, purring and whispering to itself, outside the Rideout's house.

From the amazing car emerged an amazing chauffeur: a girl. She wore a proper, old-fashioned chauffeur's peaked cap, brilliantly polished leather gaiters and a plum-coloured uniform. Her unnaturally blonde hair hung down to a waist encircled by a leather belt so tight that she appeared to be cut in two, like a wasp. Her heavily made-up blue eyes were like a doll's. Her small, scarlet mouth was doll-like too.

This chauffeur walked briskly to the Rideouts' front door, which was opened by Lucas. The chauffeur said, 'Rideouts?' and sniffed noisily. Lucas said, 'Yes.' The chauffeur said, in a strong Cockney accent, 'Gorrer fridge?' Lucas replied, 'A fridge? Have we got one? Yes.' He watched her, stunned, as she turned on her high heel, marched down the drive, opened the boot of the Aston-Martin and took out a hamper. 'Cop hold,' she said to Lucas. He helped her carry the leather-and-wicker hamper to the kitchen. Mrs Rideout watched in dumb amazement.

In the kitchen, the chauffeur sniffed violently through her little round nostrils, opened the hamper and said, 'Gorrer corkscrew?' Wide-eyed, Mrs Rideout offered th corkscrew. 'I forgorrer corkscrew,' the chauffeur explained. 'Goes spare when I forget fings, Doctor does. 'Ave my guts for garters.'

Expertly, she opened a wine bottle labelled Sancerre; put the bottle to her lips to take a small swig; made a disgusted face and swallowed; and said, "At'll do. Pop it in the fridge.'

Mrs Rideout, stunned, started to obey: then, collecting her wits, said, 'Wait a minute! Who *are* you?'

'Doctor Kalabza's chauffeur, o'course! 'E's coming 'ere! Didn'tcher know?'

'No.'

'Cor. Well, 'e likes 'is wine chilled.'

Lucas found courage to ask the chauffeur, 'Where's the doctor?' She pointed a red-nailed finger skywards and sniffed. 'In 'is 'oppicopter,' she explained. Lucas did not understand the explanation but was afraid to speak again. The glittering presence of the chauffeur in the everyday kitchen overwhelmed him. And anyway, the chauffeur was busy doing complicated things to little jars, tureens and terrines from the hamper. From a small stone bowl, she scooped a sample with her fingernail and gobbled it. 'Muck,' she said, and apparently satisfied, laid a tray. The tray was the inside of the hamper's lid and had a surface of smoked glass. Lucas wondered how much the hamper cost, and the little pots inside it. 'About five years' pocket money,' he concluded. But then he heard the noise in the sky outside, and went out to discover what caused it.

It was a very small red and white helicopter – the 'hoppicopter' the chauffeur had mentioned – over the field at the end of the road. He ran to see it land.

It took a long time descending, dipping and swaying and going up and down like a noisy yoyo.

The chauffeur was beside him now, watching. 'Kill 'imself,' she said, and gave a satisfied sniff. Then – 'Berrer meet 'im innis car, I spose.' She strode away on her over-long legs to get the Aston-Martin. Lucas went back to the house. He wanted to hide.

All too soon, the car was at the front door, the chauffeur announced, 'It's 'im' – and there stood Doctor Zafar Kalabza.

He stood lower than any of the Rideouts had imagined. TV makes famous people appear big. In fact, the Doctor was shorter than Lucas or Lettice – yet somehow enormous and room-filling, like sudden blazing sunlight. His golden-brown face was almost hidden by a huge bunch of radiant hot-house flowers. He peered from behind them with glittering dark eyes that darted from person to person – found the terrified Mrs Rideout – and cried, 'Darling Lady! Flowers! They match you exactly, I knew they would, they are yours!'

He pressed the flowers to Mrs Rideout's cardiganed bosom, raised his arms high above his head and shouted, 'Home! At last I feel I am at home! An English home! They say I am more English than the English, they are so right, only the English understand how to – Where is that stupid chauffeur girl, that Polly, where is my food? Polly! Here she comes, the dove, the throstle . . . put the tray down there. Ah, here is Mr Rideout, a scientific, a brother! I shake your hand! And now, food.'

The Doctor thrust himself at the food, cramming his mouth with spoonfuls from one little pot after another, pausing only to shout for wine. 'I'll bring it,' said Mrs Rideout, faintly and got the bottle from the kitchen.

'Sancerre!' cried the Doctor. 'Oh, dear lady, how did you know? Empathy! Telepathy! Sancerre!'

'Actually, it was your chauffeur that brought it –' began

Mrs Rideout, but the Doctor was not listening. He flourished his white napkin, pushed little nuggets of expensive food into his mouth and bellowed, 'But to business! Waste not a moment! Where is she? Where is the enchantress, the so-gifted one, the holder of the key, the moulder of destinies? Where is Lettice? Polly, stop sniffing, you disgust me! It is her septum, Mr Rideout – the little bone in the nose, Mrs Rideout – take away this tray, I am finished, you must undergo surgery, Polly, a very minor operation, I will arrange everything – Lettice, where is Lettice?'

Lettice, scarlet-faced, was pushed forward. She towered above the Doctor as a dockside crane looms over a racing yacht.

'So!' shouted the Doctor, seizing Lettice as if he would climb up her and kissing her loudly, twice, once on each cheek – 'So! It is she! The little fair lady with the fair name, Lettice! I love you, Lettice! And you shall love me! Waste not a moment! Sit beside me, dearest Lettice and tell me of your talks with the animals! Wine, wine, first take some wine!'

He thrust a glass of Sancerre at Lettice's stiff lips. '*I* cannot talk to the animals, dearest girl, I can only listen, sometimes, to their voices . . . To the dolphins, and the singing whales, did you know they sing, Lettice? And sometimes I listen to the brain itself –'

'I know,' Lettice muttered. 'You use those machines with electrodes. You tie them down, the poor animals, and drug them and scrape patches of fur off them –'

'To receive the language of the brain!' cried the Doctor, hearing nothing Lettice said. 'So very beautiful! But so puzzling for your poor friend the Doctor, who seeks to know all and knows – poof! – nothing!'

Lettice stared disgustedly ahead of herself, feeling her face begin to sweat. The Doctor thought she was looking at the string of beads round his neck – strange beads, not really beads at all, little images and emblems.

'Ah, dearest girl, I see your eyes are drawn to my necklace! You understand, of course you understand, are we not twin souls? Yes, perhaps these little beads contain the secret we both seek! Here are Amrithar and Thoth-ge, and Sambiranda the All-wise, whose kingdom was ruled by the Guardian Cats!'

Lettice's expression was such that even the Doctor noticed it. 'Or perhaps they are just silly little carvings,' he said; 'carvings that bore you. Ah, dear Lettice, forgive me – look, I am putting them away, hiding them in my shirt – for you are of today, Lettice, you wish to talk of science, the newest and greatest science, the science of the mind, the perceptions! Your science, Lettice!'

'You shouldn't do experiments on animals,' muttered Lettice, almost speechless with dislike and embarrassment. 'It's horrible.'

For a moment, the Doctor was stopped short. In that moment, Lucas thought he saw the computer-fast workings of the Doctor's mind – its lightning reception of facts, its instant Go/No-go decisions, the expert and in this case damning judgement of himself, the determination to bounce back and win the next round.

'Chess!' shouted the Doctor, jumping to his feet and removing himself from Lettice. 'I see a chessboard! We shall play, Mr Rideout! Immediately!'

'I play too,' Lucas said.

'I will play you both at once!' said the Doctor. 'It is easier for me, I am so very impatient – and I have a board Polly, get the little chess set from the car, do not sniff, such an ugly habit – it is in the locker facing the front seats – quickly –'

An hour and a half later, five simultaneous games had

been played. The Doctor played like a pouncing tiger, with perfectly controlled ferocity. He beat Mr Rideout five times out of five and Lucas four times.

'You let me win that game,' Lucas complained.

'Win, lose,' said the Doctor, flourishing an arm. 'What does it matter? Or perhaps it matters a great deal. Always there is this matter of win and lose. In all games it is the same, don't you think so, Lettice? Win or Lose, Live or Die. There is no escaping it, Lettice. Is there?'

'Why ask me?' Lettice said, not looking at the Doctor

'Oh, but Lettice, think! Here are the animals, your lovely animals, doing strange things all over the world. Such strange games they play . . . What are we to make of them? Tell us, Lettice! What is the game?'

'I don't know,' Lettice muttered. 'Not chess, anyway.'

'And you don't want to know, Lettice. Because of the other games, the cruel games men play with animals. Vivisection, so ugly a word and so ugly an act. You would never play that game, Lettice.'

She looked at him sullenly and said, '*You* would.'

Her father said, 'But he never has, Lettice. Have you, Doctor?'

'"Scientist" is a dirty word to our Lettice,' said the Doctor. Lucas noticed that he was speaking quietly now, for the first time. It was as if he had changed gear; as if his gaudy clothes, even, had suddenly become serious and sombre; as if he radiated the authority of sheer intelligence. 'A dirty word, 'scientist", is that it, Lettice? Or is she the new scientist herself? The greatest scientist? Because she speaks to the animals, the animals who are playing such a strange game.' He leaned forward, making her look at him. 'Do you speak to animals, Lettice?'

'Yes . . . No. I think so. In a way. I don't know.'

'You *do* know, Lettice. And you must tell me.'

'Why should I tell you?' she said, staring him full in the face.

'Because of the game, Lettice. The new game the animals have invented. We must join together to find out what sort of game it is. Is it a game of jolly fun, between friends? Do you think it is, Lettice? I see you do not. Your face tells me. Is it a game of Win or Lose, quite serious but not a war? Or is it, do you think, a game of conquer or perish, Live or Die?'

'All this talk of win or lose, conquer or die,' Lettice began, floundering, 'It isn't like that at all! You've got it all wrong in your mind!'

'Go on.'

'It's not the *animals*. They're not doing it, they're not doing anything! It's *them*! *They* are doing it. Doing it to the animals!'

'Them? They?'

'The Blobs, the big shapes they see and we can't see! That's the important thing to find out about! The animals don't matter. Find out about the Blobs and you'd have the answer to everything!'

'Does this answer matter very much, Lettice? Is it a case of Win or Lose, or is it Live or Die?'

'How do I know? Why ask me?'

'I ask you because you are the only one to ask,' said the Doctor. 'You say the animals are merely witnesses in the case, is that right? You are the only one who speaks the language of the witnesses, Lettice! Only you! So tell me, you must tell me: is there a criminal in the case? Is there a crime? What have the witnesses been saying to you, Lettice?'

She stood up, her mouth working. 'You just talk and talk!' she burst out. 'You don't *understand* ... And *I* understand ... ' She was almost in tears. 'Nobody takes any notice of me!' she accused. 'Everyone just laughs and – and jeers – and makes fun ...'

'Is there a criminal? Is there a crime?' the Doctor insisted. 'Name it, Lettice! Name it!'

'Television!' she said. The word burst out of her. '*Television*! Oh, it's so obvious, they've *told* me about it ... Catchmouse, poor old Duff, frightened out of their wits ... It's *television*!'

Suddenly she'd had enough. She ran upstairs, the door of her bedroom slammed. Mrs Rideout came in, her face twisted with worry. 'Oh, dear!' she said. 'I hope she wasn't rude –'

'I think I know what she meant,' Doctor Kalabza said. Yet again, Lucas seemed to see the stern computer behind the gaudy mask. 'I think she means Raster.'

Raster

'Raster?' Lucas said. He was alone with the Doctor now. 'What is Raster?'

The chauffeur, Polly, bustled in before the Doctor could reply. She slapped a tray of delicacies and a glass of white wine in front of the Doctor, and said, 'There you are then. I'm off.'

'Off? Where off?' said the Doctor.

'Have a swim. I can be down at the coast in twenty-five minutes.'

'But dear good girl! – I do not pay you to take my car and go swimming –' began the Doctor. Polly simply said, 'That's all right, then,' and left.

'It's always like that,' said the Doctor, rolling his eyes. 'They despise me because I am physically small, you see. Take my advice, dear Lucas: grow up to be big. A six-footer, definitely. Even two metres will not be too much in the near future. People are growing all the time, did you know that? King Arthur and his knights, were, what is the word, titchy.'

'I might not grow up at all,' said Lucas stiffly. He wished the Doctor would not clown.

'But why not, dear friend?'

'The things Lettice calls Blobs. And the animals going mad. It might be the end of our world. The Blobs and the animals might make it impossible for us to live in our own world.'

'Tck, tck, tck!' said the Doctor. 'That is a counsel of despair, is it not? But of course you are not serious. The great plagues that decimated our civilizations, the scourges and upheavals and wars and weapons – they come, they go. Mankind survives.'

'But how can we live with the Blobs?'

'How can we fail to live with them? What alternative is there? We will learn about these Blobs; understand them, control them, conquer them!'

'But suppose we *don't*!'

'Compromise,' said the Doctor.

'What do you mean, compromise?'

'Compromise. Make different arrangements. Live and let live. Peaceful co-existence. Any phrase you like, dear Lucas, that means sharing this planet with a new tribe, these Blobs.'

'But suppose they won't let us share! Suppose they want everything!'

'Then we would make a move away, like moving house. There will always be regions, in this planet or another, where the Blobs do not occur. The sky is full of planets!'

'But that could take centuries. Suppose we have to move fast, move now!'

'Suppose, suppose, suppose!' laughed the Doctor. 'Here is a glass of wine, it can do you no harm. Drink!'

Lucas said, 'Cheers,' in a dismal voice, and drank the wine. Then he remembered something. 'Raster,' he said. 'You said "Raster". What does it mean?'

'Ah!' said the Doctor dramatically, at his worst again. 'All will be revealed! – tonight! – on your television set!'

The Rideouts switched on the set, settled themselves in their chairs, and waited to be amazed. 'Here he comes!' said Lucas. And there he was: beaming, gaudy, cocksure.

Everyone else seemed so normal compared with the Doctor. And his TV manner was appalling.

'. . . an opportunity to welcome a man celebrated in at least four scientific fields,' began Ivor Mitcham, the host of the show.

'Five,' said the Doctor, stopping Ivor Mitcham in his tracks.

'I'm sorry . . .?'

'Five scientific fields,' said the Doctor. 'Five I am celebrated in, not four.'

'Five it is, Doctor Kalabza, five it is. And now –'

'And now,' said the Doctor, taking over, 'let us talk about the so strange behaviour of the animals! And about the Blobs, as a friend of mine calls them. A very particular friend: a young lady, a blonde young lady!' He rolled his eyes roguishly at the cameras.

'Oh!' cried Lettice. '*Oh!*'

She heard little more of the programme. Fury made her face burn and her mind churn. She did not properly hear the Doctor talk of animals or Blobs.

Neither did the studio audience. A white-haired man in the second row of the audience kept barking 'Nonsense!' 'Prove it!' 'Unscientific!' A woman at the back produced a poster reading:

SAVE THE ANIMALS
ALL GOD'S CREATURES

She shouted something in a strangled, high-pitched voice that no one could understand. Ivor Mitcham busily kept smiling. The Doctor kept moving, bobbing up and down, kicking the table with his toe so that the microphone picked up a drum sound.

'*Raster!*' said the Doctor, loudly and suddenly.

'What was that?' said Ivor Mitcham

'Raster, my friend. That could be the answer, do you not think? I think so. My very young blonde lady friend thinks so. It may be so, do you not think?'

'I'm sorry, Doctor, I don't know this Raster –'

'My dear good friend, you *are* Raster! And me! And our friends in the audience! But most of all, dear Mr Michelin, *this* is Raster!' – and the Doctor lunged forward and poked a finger at the lens of a TV camera.

The picture on the Rideouts' screen darkened as the approaching finger became a great obscuring blur. There was confusion for a moment in the studio until the director cued in another camera. Then the Doctor could be seen, smiling broadly, apparently tickling the lens of a camera. One of the crew was flapping at his hand trying to get rid of him. Ivor Mitcham was pulling at the Doctor's free arm.

The programme settled down again. The screen was filled with videotapes showing animals behaving strangely. Ivor Mitcham's voice gave a commentary. There was nothing very surprising in the clips – the world was used to freakish animal behaviour by now – until there was a brief shot that showed something truly unpleasant.

A field of woolly sheep ... their heads lifted as if at some signal ... the sheep move back uneasily, jostling each other, coming nearer to the camera ... some sheep are jostled and fall from the flock but rejoin it ... three sheep lose their nerve and break away, running towards the camera – and then a sequence almost indecent in its unlikeliness; the sheep face the camera, looking at a point to one side of it – their lips raise and wrinkle, their eyes roll – and then the long yellow teeth are bared, the terrified animals are snarling at something. Sheep, snarling!

In the studio, there was a shocked 'Ooooo – oh!' from the audience; the same sound the Rideouts made at home. Sheep, snarling!

Doctor Kalabza's face filled the screen. It was alert, unemotional, fascinated. Ivor Mitcham said, 'Well, Doctor Kalabza, what do you make of that?'

'My dear friend, it is nothing new, there are many such incidents . . . Over the whole world we hear of such things. Even the sheep –'

'But what do you think it is, Doctor Kalabza?'

'I have told you. It is Raster.'

'Raster, Doctor?'

'The name given to the patterns formed by the television transmissions which themselves form the pictures on our television screens. That is Raster, my friend. You should know that, being in the industry of television.'

'And Raster accounts for the behaviour of those sheep?'

'Oh no, certainly not that, not at all! But I have a belief that Raster explains the behaviour of the phenomenon that causes the behaviour of the sheep.'

'*Nonsense*!' said the white-haired man in the audience. '*Unscientific*!' The camera picked him out. A military-looking man, peppery and impatient; but not a crank.

'*Chemicals*!' he shouted. 'Never mind Raster. Chemicals. Pollution. Chemicals. Fertilizers, antibiotics, genetic manipulation, pesticides! Chemicals!'

People in the audience were standing up and shouting. Most of them seemed to be supporting the peppery man but the woman with the placard was hooting something about 'all creatures great and small . . .' It was getting very noisy again.

'Chemicals! Poisons! Driving the animals mad!'

'Save the poor dumb creatures! Save them, save them!'

The programme director lost control. Shot after shot came on the screen, face after face. Then the woman with the poster put things in focus by fainting.

Now the cameras had something to hold on to. They showed unlikely pictures of her being passed over the heads of the audience. Her poster followed her, passed from hand to hand.

Ivor Mitcham's face filled the screen. His smile was as perfect as ever. 'Well, there you are,' he said, 'the animals are behaving oddly. Even the *human* animals!'

'Wrong about Raster,' shouted the Major. 'Chemicals and poisons.'

'You should meet,' the Doctor shouted back, roguishly wagging a finger, 'my little blonde lady. She would tell you most differently, my friend!'

'BRING HER ON!' shouted a voice from the audience. People laughed and applauded. Ivor Mitcham said, 'Well . . .? Can you produce the lady, Doctor?'

'Of course!' said the Doctor. 'At any time!'

In the Rideout living room, Lettice let out a scandalized, agonized 'Ooooh!'

It was almost as if Doctor Kalabza's television appearance had acted as a trigger mechanism for an international bomb. Next day, from all over the world, the reports came in. The Blobs were on the rampage. They were running wild. And they were, increasingly, becoming visible.

In the small town where the Rideouts lived, there were enough Blob stories to fill the next edition of the local newspaper – not that the townspeople needed to wait for the newspaper; they told each other their strange tales.

In the supermarket: 'First it was my new kitchen units, you know, the ones Rod put in only two weekends ago – well, they're all smashed and ruined now, you've never seen anything like it, this great sort of wobbly shape going around just smashing and bashing and knocking all the fronts in, the whole lot's just matchwood now, and Rod put in so much work ... Well, I just sat down when it was all over and I just cried and cried, I couldn't help myself...'

In a pub: 'So when I get home, that would be twenty minutes after closing time, not late, I slip the key in the door quiet-like, you know, and I hear the missus up the top of the stairs in the dark and she's shouting and cursing. "Oh, you drunken beast!" she says, "Oh, I'll kill you for this tomorrow, see if I don't!" and suchlike. So I just stand there with the key in my hand, wondering what she's on about. I mean, I'm not drunk and it's not late...

'Then I hear this thumping and bumping and crashing in the lounge and I goes in to see what's up and switch on the light but there isn't any light – and *there it is*, blobby like they tell you and all striped, lurching round the room and breaking everything. So I back out, sharpish, and creep up the stairs, and when I get to the top – she lets out a great scream and says, "Oh, Tom! It's you! I mean, it wasn't you!" And then she passes out cold, and who's to blame her?'

In a hospital: 'No, *you* listen to *me*, Constable! I was driving buses before you got issued your first pair of size thirteens! – No, *listen*, and write it down in your little notebook. Right, we're approaching the request stop at Shadbrook Road and the Library, right? And no other traffic and the road's clear, but it's dark, right? And I'm already slowing down a bit, to say twenty-five, because I think I see people at the stop, right? But I don't see people at all, it's one of them Blobs, and I hit it with my nearside front, and that sends us right across to the wrong side of the road, right? – and that's when we roll over, and I get this broken arm, and lucky it wasn't my neck, a smash like that, right? Now, you got that all written down?'

In a school playground: 'They're all trampled flat, Dad's cabbages, and all the bean poles snapped off too. It was trying to get in again, see. Through the back door. It went

324

out the side door – went right through it – and then it was the dustbins, one of them's squashed almost flat. And I could see the stripes, like it says on the telly. It smashed the telly first go off. It was like a big see-through slug, you know, no proper shape at all, just something big and humpy. You ought to see the front room, it's fantastic. Stripes? No, no stripes . . . Not after it smashed the telly . . .

'Know what, I never thought of that! Once it had smashed the telly, it didn't have stripes! I mean, that's the first thing I'd have noticed when it was rooting about in the garden in the dark. I'd have noticed the stripes, they sort of flicker. But after it'd done up the telly, there weren't any stripes on it . . .'

Lettice and Miss Langham looked at each other across the pale oak table in the school library room and, simultaneously, shrugged. Then they laughed because neither had known the other was about to shrug. Lettice was, for a moment, surprised to find herself laughing with Miss Langham: their relationship these days seemed very easy and casual, almost friendly.

'There's no point in this any more,' said Miss Langham, pointing to the fat scrapbooks they had been working on. 'There's simply too much material. Too many Blobs reported from too many countries, too many reports and stories.'

'We're just keeping the scrapbooks for the sake of it,' Lettice agreed. 'They don't *mean* anything anymore. Besides, we've been doing it all wrong.'

'What do you mean?'

'Well, when we started, every story we pasted in the books seemed . . . significant. As if it might prove something. But now –'

'Now your case is proved. Proved a million times.'

'I wasn't trying to score a point, I just meant . . . Miss Langham, our books aren't any good because they don't make the *difference*.'

'What difference?'

'The difference between the stories about Blobs and the stories about animals.'

'You mean, we should have started out to keep one set of books for Blobs, and the other for Animals? Yes, I see. But why is it important?'

'What I mean is, the animals are familiar things behaving in a funny way. But the Blobs are unfamiliar, new things. Oh dear, I don't really know what I mean. Except that animals are animals, Blobs are Blobs!' said Lettice, helplessly.

'But the animals didn't start behaving oddly until the Blob business started. So surely the two things are connected?'

'Connected, but not the same. And now they're not even always connected. I mean, the things that happened here in our own town, last night – they didn't have anything to do with animals, did they?'

'No,' said Miss Langham. 'You're perfectly right. They didn't. It was all Blobs. So you're trying to say – now, the Blobs are on their own? But there are still stories from all over the place about animals doing strange things. That zoo in Berlin –'

'Oh, don't, it's awful, it's dreadful! Those poor monkeys!'

'And the poor keepers . . .? One was killed, you know. Torn to pieces by gibbons.'

'Oh, don't!' repeated Lettice. There had been a photograph in the newspaper of a cluster of gibbons, like swarming bees, forming a knot in one corner of the cage. Invisible in the centre of that knot there had been a man, imprisoned against the bars by hundreds of little hands – hands that were pulling the man to pieces. The man was dead now and so were the gibbons. In her mind's eye, she saw the other newspaper photographs: keepers with rifles braced against iron bars. And one grainy photograph of a gibbon falling backwards from the pattern of bars and mesh at the top of the cage: falling spreadeagled, clutching at nothing. This was the picture she could not forget. 'Why,' she asked herself, 'why that picture? Why aren't I haunted by that poor keeper that was killed? He was a human being, like me.'

Lettice looked down at her own body. It was changing fast. Her arms were rounder now. Her hands were no longer bony, the unbitten nails were oval. Her thighs were rounder, her knees no longer raw-looking. 'I'm growing up!' she thought. 'Then why can't I think like a grown-up? As if all the gibbons in the world mattered as much as one man!'

But she could not convince herself.

Miss Langham, she realized, was still looking at the press cuttings and talking about them. Lettice shook herself to attention.

'. . . very important indeed,' said Miss Langham crisply. 'You are quite right – the two subjects, the animals and the Blobs, *need not* be related now, even if they were related in the first place. I wonder . . .'

'Animals – afraid of the Blobs – animals angry: Blobs – fear of television – Blobs angry,' said Lettice, startled by her own precision and decisiveness. 'That's what I think is happening.'

'But even if you're right,' said Miss Langham, 'what do we *do*? Doctor Kalabza –'

'Oh, wonderful Doctor Kalabza!' snapped Lettice. 'He's coming back soon and he'll start all over again being –'

'Being impossible and embarrassing?'

'Yes.'

'And right about everything?'

'Yes! I mean, no. Oh, I don't know. He's so *awful*. And yet . . .'

'And *yet*. I know exactly what you mean.' Miss Langham smiled ruefully. 'He'll turn out to be right, Lettice. He always is.'

'Well,' Lettice said, 'he's certainly not right about me appearing on TV! I couldn't! Not ever!'

Lettice on TV

'I think you're being very silly,' Mrs Rideout told Lettice. 'I mean, it's the chance of a lifetime! You can't just say, "I can't, I'm too shy" –'

'But I *am* shy,' said Lettice. 'I mean, appearing on television! Me! It's all right for you and all the neighbourhood, you don't have to *do* it. And I don't see why I should!'

'And there's your friends at school,' added Mrs Rideout. 'What will they say if you don't appear? After all . . . all *this*?' She pointed a finger at the pile of press cuttings on the table by the sofa.

There were dozens of them each day; ever since Dr Kalabza's TV appearance. 'THE BLONDE AND THE BLOBS –DOES LITTLE LETTICE HOLD THE CLUE?' . . . 'BEAUTY AND THE BEASTS' . . . 'SHE TALKS WITH THE ANIMALS: WHEN WILL SHE TALK TO US?' Mrs Rideout collected the cuttings, cut them out neatly and stuck them in a large scrapbook with a paste that smelled of cloves.

All this sickened Lettice, as did the journalists who kept ringing the front door bell. Lettice hid, but it did no good. Her mother told the journalists, 'I know she's somewhere around, she was in here only a minute ago . . . Lettice! *Lettice!*' (this in her mother's special, ladylike, cooing, all-happy-family voice). 'Do come down, dear! Some gentlemen here *particularly* want to meet you!'

Almost always, Lettice would have to go down and meet the journalists; feeling a fool, looking a fool and muttering words that she knew to be foolish as they left her mouth.

And now they wanted her to make a fool of herself on television! 'I won't!' said Lettice. 'I won't and that's final!'

Nevertheless, two weeks later, she found herself sitting in the large limousine sent by the TV company, with her brother, mother and father. She was on her way to the television studio – Doctor Kalabza would be there – to make her starring appearance in *Fenton's Forum*, the biggest talk show of them all.

She felt little or nothing of their reception at the TV centre – only a dim consciousness of blue lights from camera flash-guns – of her mother's fixed smile and constant glow of maternal delight – of her father's insistence on knowing, precisely, the names of everyone introduced to the Rideouts ('You're who? What? Jamie Sinclair? Jamie? No, doesn't ring a bell. Programme Director? What's that? Oh, I see. No, wait a minute, I don't quite see . . .')

At last, after a long period of sitting in a small cell like a shrunken hotel room, she was taken to a sort of dentist's chair. A make-up girl called Fiona put a towel round her neck. Fiona was quick, clever, and heavily and excellently made up. 'Big pores here, luv,' she said, touching Lettice's nose. 'Fill 'em in with goo. There. Gone.' She dabbed and smeared away industriously at Lettice's face, which slowly became almost unrecognizable to Lettice.

'Split ends,' she said, holding up a lock of Lettice's hair. 'Me too. I've tried egg, beer rinses, everything. No flipping good.'

In another chair, the famous face of a current-events commentator was being seen to by a girl called Tricia. The famous face's eyes were closed and the famous nose was snoring very slightly. 'He shouldn't be here,' Fiona said, 'but I don't dare wake him. *Scenes*. You are the one that talks to the animals?'

'Yes,' said Lettice. 'That is –'

'You should talk to him, then!' said Fiona. 'Real old beast, he is! Free with his hands. There you are, luv. All done and wiped Whatever you do, *don't touch*.'

Lettice said, 'Oh, you mean –' and touched her face.

Fiona pounced on her, dabbed at the mark Lettice had made and said, 'That's what I specially don't want you to do, luv *Right?* Right.'

And somehow Lettice found herself in a studio. She was so busy telling herself not to touch herself – under the hot and brilliant lights, she could feel sweat trying to make its way through the make-up - that she heard or sensed nothing at all of what was going on. She was being rehearsed, they told her. It meant nothing.

Then suddenly the programme was live! – on the air! – actually happening! – and Larry Fenton was poking his face at her across the chrome and glass table with the microphones on it, and asking her a question.

'I'm sorry . . .?' she blurted, overwhelmed by several things all at once – the piercing eyes of Mr Fenton, glittering with intelligence, warmth, interest and a sort of knowing inner depth of ruthlessness and self-love; the sickening lurch of a TV camera, its lens pointing straight at every nerve end in her body; Doctor Kalabza, much too at ease, smiling encouragingly; the perpetual smile on her mother's face, showing white in the blur of the audience; and the utter hopelessness of her own position. She was lost. Completely lost.

'. . . in other words, Lettice, you are able to *converse* with animals?' said Larry Fenton. Seeing that Lettice was still incapable of answering, he added, 'I mean, not converse *rationally*, with *words*, but attain a degree of *communication* . .?'

'I don't mind this choking,' thought Lettice – her throat was stuffed with a ball of wool and her ears seemed to be hissing and Mr Fenton's face was swelling before her eyes – 'But why can't I die? Why don't I die?'

At this moment, there was a thump and a scuffle in the audience – a ripple of exclamations, a sudden yell and some high pitched shouting – a camera lurched and its operator swore and fell to one side – and the big, dark, wavering shapes were thrusting and plunging in the studio.

The Blobs had come.

Larry Fenton was the quickest to react. He grabbed Lettice by the wrist and pulled her to a clear place. With his other hand, he made furious signals to the control room which overlooked the studio behind a flat, darkly glimmering plate-glass wall. Figures were bobbing up and down in the control room. Larry Fenton shouted, 'Keep it live, for God's sake, keep it live! You! Back on your camera! Keep shooting!' A young cameraman shouted 'O.K., O.K.!' and his camera moved about like a Dalek. The noise and confusion were getting worse.

A big blurred shape heaved against a lamp pillar and the falling lights exploded. A woman began to scream. 'Mother?' thought Lettice. 'No, there she is!' Her mother and father were trying to make their way to Lettice, but there were overturned chairs and lumpy Blob shapes and heaving knots of people in the way. For a moment, Lettice's and her mother's eyes met: incredibly, her mother switched on the social smile.

Now Doctor Kalabza had Lettice's other wrist and was shouting something in her ear. She felt absurd. The Doctor was tugging her one way, and Mr Fenton the other. 'What?' she yelled. 'What? I can't *hear* you! Oh, do leave go!'

Then her father got to her, his face set in very much its

usual inquiring, quizzical expression, but with a malicious twinkle underneath. He took hold of Larry Fenton's free hand, shook it and said, 'Very nice programme. What's on next?' Fenton was sufficiently taken aback to drop Lettice's wrist. 'Must dash,' said Mr Rideout, and led Lettice away, with the Doctor dangling behind.

Slowly the family linked up and found the way out. They turned and looked back.

The whole studio was being churned by the Blobs. Larry Fenton still held a hand microphone and was still talking into it. A big board with a stylized picture of the world on it suddenly cracked, fell and crumbled noisily as a Blob trampled it. Another Blob, heaving and turning, was making a snake-pit of cables around itself. There was a bang and a mauve flash, and the crisscross pattern on the Blob brightened for a moment. Then blue and mauve and yellow electric flashes began to invade one corner of the studio, as if someone had thrown fireworks – firemen were rushing down the corridor – people were stampeding for the exits. The Rideouts and Doctor Kalabza got out of the way.

Twenty minutes later, in the hospitality room, Lettice asked the Doctor, 'What were you trying to say to me?'

'I thought, dear child, that one of the Blobs had features,' said the Doctor, 'You know, almost a face. A snout, a place for ears and eyes, perhaps . . .? I was hoping you had seen something similar?' He was at his most serious.

'Oh,' said Lettice. 'No, I didn't see anything like that.'

'Perhaps I was mistaken,' said Doctor Kalabza. 'Even the Doctor makes mistakes.' Some excited TV people burst in, making apologetic noises. '*Not*,' said the Doctor, out-shouting them, '*Not*,' he claimed, deliberately becoming the flash celebrity, 'that your good friend the Doctor would make such a mistake as this.' He held up his glass. 'A *horrible* wine. A *deadly* wine . . .'

Miss Langham's Encounter

Next day, the newspaper headlines were all about Blobs. The television story was prominent but had to share space with similar reports from all over the world.

At school, the girls rushed up to Lettice and drowned her in questions. She barely heard them, for someone had told her that Miss Langham had had an accident and was in hospital. Lettice left school without another word and went to see her.

The Sister said, 'Only ten minutes. No more, mind.'

It was a little ward. There were only two beds in it. One was empty. In the other was Miss Langham, hidden by a curtain except for an arm and hand.

Lettice was reassured by the hand. It was so unmistakably Ann Langham's hand, smooth, neat. Lettice moved forward, said, 'Hello, Ann, it's me, Lettice,' and pulled aside the curtain.

The first shock was Ann's sleeping face. The plasters and bandages were bad enough – but the face was worse, swollen and blotched, misshapen and pulpy, with a short line of hideous black stitches running upwards from one side of the mouth.

Lettice gulped, repeated her 'Hello' and got her second shock.

Ann's eyes opened, took in Lettice's presence – and stared wildly. Her uninjured arm went up as if to ward off a blow

Her voice said, loudly and harshly, *'Don't! Don't let them!'*

A moment later Ann was properly awake and herself again. She said, 'I'm all right really, I'm just in a sort of mess, that's all. I look much worse than I am, ask the Sister.'

'Doesn't it hurt you to speak?'

'Oddly enough, no. You see, Lettice,' (Lettice noticed, with amusement, the schoolmistress tone in her voice), 'in speaking one moves one's lower lip far more than one's upper.'

'Unless you're French, of course.'

'Unless you're French,' agreed Miss Langham; then, seeing how ridiculous the conversation had become, she laughed and hurt her mouth very much indeed. Lettice flustered around her trying to be helpful; and when the flurry was over, they felt close and companionable.

'I'm so glad *you've* come,' said Ann, touching Lettice's hand for an instant with her own. 'You're the only person I feel capable of talking to about that day. That Thursday evening . . . I was in my digs, doing the homework corrections. By some extraordinary coincidence, I was just picking your work up Lettice, when it started happening . . .'

'The Blobs?'

'The Blobs. Bumps and thumps. They'd arrived. Anyhow, I kept on with my work, thinking how awful your handwriting still is –'

'I know,' groaned Lettice.

'When just like that, the whole wall fell in on me. Well, it didn't fall: it was pushed. And there they were, two of them, two great Blobs covered all over with a grid of flickering lines. They started lurching about breaking everything . . .

'Oddly enough, Lettice, I didn't really mind this too much. The Blob thing can happen to anyone, and now it was happening to me and all one need do is keep out of harm's way and watch them smashing up the place. Which they did very

335

thoroughly. By the time they were halfway through, I suddenly realized that the television was on in Josie's room – she's the girl who shares with me, she'd gone to the launderette and left the set on. I realized it, I may say, because the Blobs had by now removed the wall between my room and hers! Anyhow, I switched off the set and the Blobs didn't flicker quite so much. No stripes. Then the really unpleasant part started . . .

'The Blobs began behaving a little differently – more slowly, less actively destructive. They just stood in what remained of the room, lurching and flickering and nosing about.'

'Did they have noses, then?'

'Funny you should ask that. Yes, I began to think I could see some sort of features . . . nothing definite, just a feeling of – of ugly features; thick snouts; dull, hidden eyes . . . I don't know, I don't know.' She fell silent and looked out of the window.

When she spoke again it was in her best schoolmistress voice. 'You must understand, Lettice, that, until that very moment, I had regarded the Blobs as . . . as senseless, unpleasant, ugly, mobile *things*. Merely things. But now I was made to realize that the Blobs are not impersonal things after all. They have their own intentions and they make decisions.'

'How do you know that?'

'Because,' said Ann Langham 'they positively and definitely attacked *me*. They more or less put their heads together and seemed to come to some decision.'

'What decision?'

'To beat me up,' said Miss Langham. 'They took a sort of run at me, one on either side . . . I got out of the way, the first time. But they kept on doing it – kept on lurching towards me and trying to trap me between them and pushing and shoving and moving forward. Deliberately. Wanting to hurt me ••

'Anyhow, they got me down on the floor, and I think that's when I got some ribs cracked. It was very painful so naturally I tried to get up. But they wouldn't let me. They more or less hovered about above me, both of them, like great wavering balloons of *dark*, and they kept nudging me down to the floor again. I became rather frightened . . .'

'*Rather* frightened!' Lettice exclaimed. 'I'd have screamed my head off! What did you do?'

'Screamed my head off!' Ann confessed, 'to begin with. But it hurt my ribs. I seem to remember crying for a considerable period of time. I even swore. It was all rather pointless, I'm afraid. Not at all,' she added, with an attempt at a joke, 'what I would have expected of me!

'They stood over me, the Blobs,' Ann continued, 'not doing anything in particular but not letting me get up. Then I heard hammering at the door of our flat. It was a policeman, the people next door had reported the rumpus. He was hammering away and I was shouting, "The key is on the ledge over the door!" but he was hammering so loudly that he couldn't hear me. I suppose,' said Ann wanly, 'it was quite funny, really.'

'Uproarious,' said Lettice, taking Ann's hand. It trembled.

'At last,' Ann went on, 'the policeman heard me and took the key – Josie really shouldn't leave it there, but it was fortunate this time – and came to rescue me. But he simply couldn't reach me. The Blobs wanted to finish me off, it seemed. He could reach my hand and he tugged away at that, but the more he pulled, the more heavily they leaned in on me. And I swear they do have faces, Lettice! Faces of a sort . . . snouts, eyes . . . But all vague and flickering . . .'

She began to cry. Lettice said, 'This isn't doing you any good.'

'No, I will finish. The policeman was as desperate as I was. He kept saying, "Miss, what can I *do*?" – he always called me "miss" – but all I could do was scream, because I could feel my ribs trying to snap and my ankle was trapped. They injured it quite a bit, did I tell you? Anyhow, it went on and on until Josie came home and she and the policeman had the brilliant idea of switching on the television and bringing it very close to the Blobs. Apparently the luminous pattern, what Doctor Kalabza calls "Raster", began flickering all over their bodies – and the Blobs started to heave about and lurch this way and that to get away from the television radiation. I think they became striped, I can't remember. Anyhow, I got clear at last and here I am.'

The Sister opened the door and said, 'Out. You've stayed too long. O-u-t.'

Lettice rose. Ann said, 'Oh, Lettice, there's one thing more that you ought to know, and tell other people.'

'What?'

'Hate,' said Ann. 'The Blobs hate us, Lettice. Warn people.'

It turned out that there was no need, after all, for Lettice to deliver the message. During the next twenty-four hours, the Blobs made everything perfectly clear in every corner of the world.

In New York, the Brooklyn gang lost two of its members when a wall on the seventh storey of a tenement house exploded outwards, as if there had been a bomb inside the building. Several tons of brick, plaster and furniture smashed down on the flight of steps leading to the front door. The gang had been sitting on the steps. Merv and Little Pete died instantly. The 'bomb' was Blobs.

In Warsaw, Mrs and Mr Breslaw at last agreed about the Devil.

338

They were queueing together for a tram. When it came, the Breslaws elbowed and shoved and swore their way to the second of the tram's three steps. They were jam-packed in a press of people. So they never really saw what hit the tram and themselves. They heard the screams, felt the unbearable force of bodies, knew that the tram was swaying and toppling – but they could not see the wavering grey shapes crushing them because the shapes were behind their backs and there was no longer room in the crush even to turn one's head.

'It's the Devil!' screamed old Mr Breslaw, before the huge pressure of the Blobs flattened his lungs and stopped his heart.

'With you, it is always the Devil!' shouted his wife. But then she saw what was happening to her husband and knew it must happen to her. And with her last breath, she cried, 'You are right! You were always right! The Devil, the Devil, the Devil is come!'

In London, Doctor Kalabza was faded out in the middle of a TV chat show. He was warming up nicely when things went wrong – leaving his chair, walking about out of camera range, interrupting everyone, and even, when a dull speaker went on too long, performing elaborate exercises. Then the picture broke up, screens filled with snow and zigzags – and that was that, for the rest of the evening. It happened quite often recently.

The Doctor loaded his folding bicycle into the hoppicopter and visited the Rideouts. 'Peace!' he shouted, shattering the living-room peace. 'Tranquillity! Change and decay in all around I see – except here, in the bosom of the English home!'

'Your chauffeur girl, Polly . . . she isn't with you?' asked Mrs Rideout, hopefully.

'No, we have dismissed each other. I am not sad, her sniffing was becoming unbearable. Now she is to be a pop star. I have arranged it all.'

'What went wrong that evening on TV?' Mr Rideout asked.

'Ah, that is more interesting. *Most* interesting. Havoc in the basement! Cables, wiring, all that electronic knitting – damaged, destroyed, mutilated!'

'Blobs,' said Lucas, knowingly.

'No, that is the strange thing! Not blobs. Something as bad, even worse –'

But then Lettice came in – she had been avoiding the Doctor – and he said no more. Indeed, he quietened immediately when she entered. Quiet, he was at his best. To Lucas, he seemed to treat Lettice as if she were recovering from an illness. Gradually she warmed to him, even talked with him.

'Ah, the animals,' he said to her. 'Yes, it is all very strange and becoming stranger. A new phase, I think. Can animals be evil, Lettice?'

'Of course not! They just do what they're born to do . . . I mean, it's ridiculous to hate snakes and that sort of thing, they're not *evil* –'

'I do hope you are right, Lettice,' said the Doctor. 'I do so hope you are right.'

The Animals' Revolt

'All right, then!' said Mr Rideout, pulling on his gumboots. 'Everybody out! Sons of the soil! Daughters too, Lettice. And kindly don't clodhop all over the ground I've just dug. That's a *fine tilth* you're trampling on.'

Lettice picked up a garden fork and vaguely put it down again. She hated gardening.

'A fine tilth,' said Mr Rideout, happily. 'That's what's needed. Aerate the soil. Organic matter. Minerals, trace elements.' He began to sing: ' "We plough the fields and sca-a-tter, the good seed o'er the la-a-and . . ." '

Lucas took up the song: 'It really doesn't ma-a-tter, I'd rather buy things ca-a-nned!'

'It does matter,' said Mr Rideout. 'And you can't buy things canned.'

'You can,' said Lettice. 'Mother got all sorts of tinned things last week –'

'She won't get them much longer,' said Lucas. 'Everything's falling to pieces, everywhere. Our whole civilization's going up the creek. Bust. Finito.'

'We'll look back,' said Mr Rideout, 'and remember tinned ham and newspaper deliveries, and petrol, and battery eggs, and rashers of bacon and roast beef – we'll look back at these things and we'll *marvel*. Marvel! When you two have children of your own – that is, if the Blobs let you – they'll cluster round your knee and lisp, "Did you really eat *meat*, Mummy?

And Daddy, what were pork chops like?" And you'll look down at the little eager, upturned faces, and you'll remember Yorkshire pudding and roast beef and gravy and you'll reply, "Belt up, you little morons!" and burst into tears of self-pity and nostalgia. And then you'll go out into the garden, and pick up your nasty gardening tools, and dig and rake and hoe and weed. Just as we're going to do.'

They shouldered their tools, walked down the garden and started work. Mr Rideout continued digging up a corner of the lawn, soon to be a vegetable patch. Lucas worked with him, picking up the turves on a fork, banging the soil out and carting them away to the compost heap. Lettice gawkily prodded at the vegetable bed they had prepared the day before.

'You really do think,' said Lucas, 'that we'll never see meat again? I mean, eat it regularly?'

'Never!' his father said. 'Well, hardly ever. God, my back's killing me already!' He straightened up, glad of an excuse to stop work and deliver a lecture. 'How can you have meat if the animals refuse to stay in their fields, or go to the slaughterhouse? How can you have beef if the cattle try to kill the man holding the humane killer? And even assuming you can breed the animals, and raise them, and slaughter them for meat, how can you get the meat to market when the railways won't work and the lorries can't use the roads?' He started digging again, but soon stopped. 'You read that newspaper story about the lorries in France, didn't you? And the same sort of story about the cattle on the motorway?'

'I read them,' said Lucas. 'Here, let's swop. I'll dig and you do my job for a while.'

As Lucas dug, he thought about the French disaster. The newspapers and television had been full of it. During the night, on one of the major motorway routes, Blobs had appeared. Suddenly the road was blocked. Drivers of the great *camions*, the long-distance lorries, had been forced to slam on the brakes. There had been a few pile-ups. Some cars and light vehicles were able to work through, but the big lorries had to wait. More Blobs – and the queue built up: at first, for a few kilometres, then for fifty, and at last endlessly. No vehicle moved.

When day came, the drivers got out of their cabs and argued and shrugged. White-helmeted motorcycle police blew whistles and waved arms. The engines of the great lorries were started and the front of the queue moved forward.

But then the animals came. Mild-eyed, wet-nosed cows solemnly trampled hedges and fences and ambled along the roads. They looked innocent and silly. Occasionally a cluster of cows formed round a lorry and butted against it, slowly and regularly. The panelling was left bruised and dented: no real damage was done.

But sometimes, a driver who thought he knew about animals was trapped by the cows – pressed against the metal of his lorry by a shoving mass of heavy bodies and hard horns: when this happened, there was a cry from the trapped man – more cries from the men who came running to help him – the thrashing of sticks against unyielding bodies – and at last, the amiable herd of cows would move on, leaving a silent knot of humans standing round a crushed, silent, misshapen body.

The pigs were worse. There was a horrible intelligence and determination about the pigs. When the cows came, the lorry drivers grabbed sticks or jack handles and, half humorously, smacked and thwacked at the animals, expecting to drive them away. But when a horde of pigs burst through a hedge, their heads lowered and their mouths slavering and their long, fleshy bodies packed solid and coming fast, the drivers leaped into their cabs and slammed the doors.

The cabs of these great lorries were a long way from the ground. All the same, the pigs would reach up, standing on their hind legs and probing upwards with their dripping snouts. Sometimes, the knot of pigs round a particular lorry was so dense that more pigs could climb over the heaving backs and scrabble at a window or windscreen with their cleft feet. The drivers cursed, blew horns, even started the engine and rocked the lorry back and forth to shift the animals.

Generally this worked. Once or twice it failed. Windscreen glass shattered – the great body hurtled into the cab – the man's screams and the pig's screams became one – and then the man's voice was silent and from the cab came new, muffled sounds, slobberings and gruntings and gulpings. Outside the cab, there was a mounting crescendo of squeals as the whole heaving, thrusting mass of pigs tried to climb over itself to join the feast.

Yet even this was not all. Rats scurried over the tops of lorries. The little field animals, usually never seen, were everywhere. The TV cameras picked up a worried looking old horse, rolling its eyes and tossing its head, trotting aimlessly up and down the line, stumbling sometimes on little furry bodies. The horse did this for half a day, ever faster and more anxiously, then, when a Blob emerged from nothing in front of it, the horse dropped dead.

There were dogs barking at nothing – more dogs, forming groups that attacked the cows and pigs – still more dogs forming great packs that patrolled the lorry lines, or suddenly streamed off across country to attack people in villages and towns.

The French story was, so far, the worst of many. In England, the Blobs and the animals had seriously interrupted not only the production but also the distribution of food. Farms were in chaos, trains were derailed and motorways closed. There was a twenty-five mile queue on the Luton stretch of the M 1. At the airport nearby, an airliner crashed on take-off – a Blob appeared on the runway. The Dover ports and roads had been paralysed for three days and there seemed very little hope of sorting out the confusion.

In America, beef cattle were quite simply refusing to be killed. Blobs made the vast herds of animals hysterical. They burst out of the stockyards. Steers roamed the streets of Omaha. While throughout Europe, and in Asia, and Russia and –

'I thought you said you'd do the digging,' said Mr Rideout.

Lucas stopped thinking and started working. 'I don't know why you want the beans here,' he said. 'I mean, beans grow almost anywhere, don't they? This is good soil, why don't we save it for the tricky crops?'

'I don't give a damn what we do,' said Mr Rideout, suddenly angry, 'so long as we get the blasted seeds in the ground. Any crop, I don't care. Just let's get the ground *dug* and the seeds *planted*. You don't seem to realize – oh well, perhaps you do, but lots of people don't. You know there's already a shortage of seeds?'

'And a shortage of gardens. I wonder how people without gardens will get on.'

'Perhaps,' said Mr Rideout, 'they simply won't get on at all. And perhaps we'll be mounting guard over the cabbage patch a few months from now. Night-long vegetable vigil. Imagine that.'

Lucas imagined it: and dug.

That night, horses from the nearby riding stables broke loose. They blundered about in the Rideouts' garden, trampling flat the newly dug and planted ground, knocking over the toolshed, breaking fences.

Next morning, Lucas and his father surveyed the damage. 'I don't suppose it matters,' said Mr Rideout. 'And if it does, to hell with it. My back's a disaster area. I just can't face starting all over again.'

'Look at those rats!' said Lucas. There were half a dozen of them, poking their noses in the dents made by the horses' hooves. Sometimes a rat found a seed and ate it. After a time, the rats got bored. They moved away when stones were thrown at them.

'Rats!' said Mr Rideout. 'Coming out into the open like that! In broad daylight! Bet you never see a sight like that again!'

Next day, the rats came not in half-dozens, but in hundreds and thousands.

The rats were the beginning of the end.

The Rats

There can be no creature on earth more efficient than a rat. Before the Blobs came, the efficiency of rats – the unceasing rapidity of their breeding, their ability to thrive on almost any diet, their countless ways of making a living – had mattered very little to mankind. As far as man was concerned, rats were ugly, dangerous animals; eaters of filth, breeders of plagues and carriers of disease. But for most people, unpleasant as they were, rats had one virtue: you seldom saw them. You seldom if ever had a rat 'experience'. You shuddered when you read that rats in such-and-such a town had run wild and were pouring through the streets like a dirty river. You wondered at reports on the failure of the latest, most vicious poisons – apparently the rats had grown used to them, even grown to like them, so what could mankind do next? But you yourself seldom *saw* rats, because rats knew their place. You did not wish to meet rats; the rats did not wish to meet you. So the two societies – rats and men – lived apart.

The Blobs brought them together.

Suddenly, the rats left their hidden places and came out into the open. They erupted from the ground like lava from a volcano. They invaded.

As rats outnumber humankind by nobody-knows-how-many hundreds or thousands to one, the rat invasion was, from the first moment, irresistible. There could be no question of failure.

The behaviour of the rats themselves showed the certainty of their success. If a man faces a bison, or a lion, or a bear – and if the man stands his ground, or better still raises a rifle – the animal will, most probably, pause, turn and go. If you torment an animal much stronger and more powerful than yourself – an elephant, a horse, an ox – most probably you will get away with it. Even tigers can be taught to jump through hoops.

But nobody was going to tame the rats.

The day the rats came, Lettice saw the news on television. The news was about rats, rats, nothing but rats: a whole world of rats. Earlier, she had watched the rats in the garden. She had seen them eat her guinea-pigs, overturn the dustbins, form heaving knots and rings of grey bodies fringed with writhing, naked tails. Nobody had dared leave the house, for only in the house could you feel safe. Sickened and silent, Lettice made her way upstairs to the safety and isolation of her bedroom. She would go to bed and stay there.

She opened the bedroom door, unzipped her dress and screamed.

There were rats on her bed, three of them. They were eating a piece of chocolate she had put on her bedside table. One rat was sitting up like a squirrel, its yellow-brown teeth industriously nibbling through the paper wrapper and the silver paper beneath.

Lettice kept screaming. Lucas was the first to reach her. He saw the rats and felt a great bubble of nausea inside his chest. The sickness turned to a sort of trembling hate. He took his shoes off and flung them, one after the other, at the rats.

The first shoe missed and sent the bedside table lamp smashing across the room. With his other shoe, he hit a rat so hard that it was knocked off the bed. It squeaked loudly when it was hit and fell to the other side of the bed.

Lettice still screamed and Lucas yelled curses while he looked for something else to attack the rats with. He picked up Lettice's hockey stick, seized it and went towards the two rats still on the bed.

With unwinking red eyes, they watched him come. Their backs were humped. Their long naked tails twitched. The rat holding the chocolate did not drop it.

'Get *out*!' shouted Lucas. Or tried to shout: his voice would not work properly. He knew why. He was afraid – afraid of the two rats on the bed, terrified of the third rat that he could not see. Where was it?

Lettice was gone now. He heard her run down the stairs, screaming and sobbing, and his parents' voices. He wished his father would come upstairs. Where was the third rat? He was too frightened to approach the bed while the third rat could not be seen. He knew how rats attacked: the sudden darting run, the bunched, coil-sprung leap, the snap of the two long, fang-like front teeth ... he had plenty of time to learn about their habits during the day. Particularly when they had got to the guinea-pigs.

Where was the third rat?

There! By the edge of the bed! Despite himself, Lucas let out a yelp of fear and backed away, terrified of the sudden spring and the fastening of the hideous teeth in his ankle.

But the rat had nothing of the sort in mind. It looked at Lucas for a long moment, then scrambled busily up the bed-spread to join the other two. It reached out its obscene front paws for the chocolate bar, snatched it away and started to nibble and crunch, tearing at the wrapping.

When its mouth was full, it paused. All three rats stared straight at Lucas. Lucas felt his face reddening. His first thought was that he was embarrassed – embarrassed, if you please! – by the staring eyes. His second thought was, 'I am ashamed. Ashamed of being afraid. But I *am* afraid, sick afraid . . .'

These thoughts took only split seconds – and then his father was in the room, pushing past him and gasping, 'Get out of the way, I'll *kill* – I'll *kill* –' He was carrying a few yards of nylon garden netting, strong, light stuff. He opened out the net and threw it over the rats. Immediately they began to scream and fight and scramble. Mr Rideout gathered the net together until he was holding a dangling bundle that writhed and heaved and squeaked and gibbered and thrust out jerking grey-pink limbs.

He clattered down the stairs, Lucas after him, making for the kitchen back door. 'In the garden,' he muttered. 'Kill them outside.'

His wife stopped him. 'Don't open the door! You'll let more of them in!'

'Boiler room,' said Mr Rideout and opened the little door leading from the kitchen. Lucas made to follow him into the small, bare room but his father said, 'Keep out! Out!'

So they kept outside and listened to the swinging thumps. At first there were squeaks and screams as well. But long after these were over, the swinging thumps went on.

When he came out, Mr Rideout's face was pasty and sweating and his nostrils were white. He was trembling and panting so much that he could barely speak. 'Filth!' he said. 'Filth! And the whole place could be full of them . . . Lucas, get me a whisky and make it a big one. Filth . . .!'

There was a pause while Mr Rideout washed his hands, then washed them again, in the kitchen sink. Lucas came in and said, 'I'm sorry, Dad, you're out of whisky, there's only sherry. I'm sorry . . .'

His father looked at him furiously, but as he looked his eyes became sane again. 'It was a good idea of mine, that netting,' he said, drinking the sherry. He went to the window and looked out into the darkness. By the dustbins, there was scuffling and squeaking and the noise of a lid rolling about as the rats scampered over it.

'A good idea,' he said. 'But, not good enough. There isn't that much netting in the whole wide world . . .'

The next day, Catchmouse was not there. Lettice was the first to notice. She called from the kitchen window – 'Catchy! Catchy!' – but there was no chirruping mew or sudden scurry of paws, followed by a plunge of the furry head into the food bowl.

Nobody said anything, not even Lettice. Everyone assumed – everyone but Lettice – that the rats had killed Catchmouse.

But Lettice had 'talked' with Catchmouse. She thought differently. She did not speak her thoughts.

Miss Ann Langham sat in the Rideouts' living-room with her legs – one ankle strapped – neatly crossed and her elegant hands folded in her lap. She made a picture of repose, relaxation and control. The picture was completely false. Without moving a muscle, she yet managed to radiate an almost hysterical tension.

The family pretended not to notice it. Mrs Rideout knitted, Mr Rideout fiddled with an unreliable pocket electronic calculator he had bought cheaply, Lettice stared at nothing and Lucas wiped oil over a Mark III Webley air rifle.

Mr Rideout had bought the air rifle second-hand many years ago for plinking at targets in the garden. Tiring of it – the Webley was so accurate that you could hardly miss – he had smeared it with Vaseline, wrapped it in brown paper and put it in the loft.

Now the rats had come, the air rifle was part of the Rideouts' life pattern.

Miss Langham had arrived earlier in the evening. She had been an increasingly frequent visitor to the Rideouts' since her flat-mate Josie, made hysterical by the rats, had left for Scotland. In the small country town where her parents lived, things were better.

This particular evening, the sound of the front-door bell ringing had started off the usual rat routine: Mr Rideout, hearing the bell, shouted 'Blast! – oh, all right,' went upstairs and poked the air rifle and his head out of his study window. 'Oh, it's you, Ann. Just coming. Keep moving.' The family heard Ann Langham making beating noises with a walking stick while she waited to be let in. Lucas went to the front door – waited for the shouted 'O K!' from his father – opened the door and hurried Miss Langham inside.

Nowadays, this was normal procedure, because of the rats.

Mrs Rideout said, 'Oh, hello Ann, it's you . . .' Ann replied by staring through Mrs Rideout; opening her still slightly scarred mouth; giving a single, sobbing scream; and falling forward in a faint. Luckily, Mrs Rideout broke her fall.

When Ann recovered, she told the Rideouts what had happened. Going back to her flat after the day's teaching, she had gone to the bathroom and found the lid of the w.c. at an odd angle, neither open nor closed. So she lifted the lid – to reveal a rat draped over the seat. It had eaten a poison that made it crave water.

'Unfortunately,' Ann said, 'I thought it was dead, but it wasn't. I got the dustpan and brush and when I'd scooped it into the dustpan it woke up and tried to bite me. But it couldn't move very fast, and so it was more or less limping around the room after me, opening and closing its jaws and leaving a trail of – stuff – behind it . . . and I felt rather sick.'

Lucas exchanged glances with his father, who said, 'Well yes. You would.'

Ann said, 'I really felt unable to stay in the flat so I decided to come here. So I put my coat on again and went to pick up my handbag. And when I picked it up, it felt heavy, so I looked inside – and there was *another* rat, eating the lining or something –'

She shuddered and started to cry. Mr Rideout said, 'Well, that's rats for you, they'll eat anything,' and nodded his head violently at the cupboard where the drinks were kept. Lucas got Ann a drink and she began to recover. Now she sat tidily, like a well-disciplined nightmare.

The front-door bell sounded again and Mr Rideout said, 'Blast! – your turn, Lucas.' Lucas went upstairs with the rifle and eventually the new visitor was admitted. This time it was Doctor Kalabza, with a moped.

'I am come!' he announced. 'And how do you think I came? By pedal and mo! By moped! Despite the rats! Gumboots, you see. My new chauffeur left me – how can there be loyalty in these times? – and so I must pedal and mo – but what is this, can it be my lovely Miss Langham, my dearest student!'

She smiled whitely at him. Her face was so changed that even the Doctor was quietened.

The Option

They sat and talked. They talked, inevitably, of the Blobs, of the animals, of the breakdown of everyday life, and of the new horror, the plague of rats.

'What,' said Mrs Rideout, 'are we to *do*? What *can* we do? People won't go to work – can you blame them? The lorries and trains are stopping, the food shops are staying shut, the stuff we grow in the garden is eaten, our houses are infested, the electric cables are being bitten through, the old people are dying like flies . . . What can we do?'

For the first time, Lettice spoke. 'Opt out!' she said. 'Go! Leave! Pack up and get out!'

Everyone rounded on her. 'You *can't* opt out, it's the same all over the world!' 'Where would you pack up and go *to*?' 'Trust Lettice to come up with something absolutely *stupid* . . .!'

Lettice said, 'Catchmouse did and Duff's going to.'

'Going to *what*?'

'Emigrate!' said Lettice.

'Emigrate *where*? Emigrate *how*? Emigrate *when*?' shouted Lucas.

'Just emigrate!' said Lettice. 'It's obvious! Catchmouse has gone already, she told me. And Duff's going any time now, aren't you Duff? You're leaving us all and going, aren't you Duff? Even leaving me!' She cuddled Duff and buried her nose in his neck.

'What's she babbling on about?' said Lucas, disgustedly.

'Wait a minute, friend Lucas!' said Doctor Kalabza. 'Wait a very little minute! Let us hear more of this emigration, Lettice! Tell us everything about it!'

Lettice explained.

'I was talking to them both the other night,' she began. 'First Catchmouse – but she got in a huff and walked away – then Duff. They both said the same thing. As I keep telling you, Catchmouse has done it already. Being a cat, Catchy doesn't really care about us, not like darling Duff –'

'Never mind about lovey-dovey darling Duff,' said Lucas. 'Get on with it.'

'The rats got Catchy,' said Mr Rideout, gruffly. 'You know that, Lettice. We all know it. So don't start making up silly stories.'

'*Is* it a silly story, Lettice?' said the Doctor.

'I'm not making up a story. I'm just telling you a fact. Catchy's chosen to go.'

'Where?'

'Wherever it is they go,' Lettice said. 'To some other time, or some other place. I *know*.'

'How do you know, Lettice?' said the Doctor

'Catchmouse told me,' said Lettice. She was getting pink and angry, but it was quite obvious that she was convinced of what she was saying. 'She sat on my chest in, you know, the usual way, and I was trying to find out what she thought about the rats. But it only made her angry, she bristled and stuck her claws in, you know. But I kept on at her, because I thought that she, being a cat, might know more about rats than we do. I thought she might have some sort of answer to them, I don't know. But she said there isn't any answer to rats. She went on and on about killing *a* rat and how she killed *single* rats. She was all bloodthirsty. But when I asked her about dealing with *millions* of rats, she just got uneasy. But I held on to her and made her concentrate and asked her what *she* was going to do about it. And she told me what I've told you: she was going to leave.'

'Another time or another place . . .' said Doctor Kalabza. 'Possibly . . .'

'I've tried to get in touch with her since she left,' Lettice said. 'You know, you lie there and concentrate and concentrate, and after a time you think you may be getting some response or contact or whatever it is – I've tried all that, but I can't be sure. I think she was with me last night . . . I *think* she was, but I don't really know, it could have been me, making it up . . .'

'Assume that she *was* with you the other night,' said the Doctor. 'What did she tell you? What did she say?'

'She simply said – or perhaps I only felt that she said – that it's quite all right where she's gone to, the rats were just ordinary rats, the way they used to be.' Lettice looked uncertain.

'Anything else?'

'Oh yes, there was another thing! She said she'd had fish that day! I remember now, she kept on and on about the fish, and how good it was! So perhaps I really was in touch with her after all! It was a flaky white fish, like cod, I'm sure she showed it to me with her mind! And it was boiled, it must have been a leftover!'

'So . . .' said the Doctor. 'Catchmouse is gone. Gone on a journey. Or so you tell us, dear Lettice. Lettice, this is most important, so think carefully – you tell us that Duff is to go very soon?'

'Yes, just like Catchy. When Catchy was with me on my chest, she got all excited – I couldn't hold on to her mind, she was too excited. So I got hold of Duff and made him talk to me.

'He was just the same as Catchy about the rats. He doesn't mind one rat, he likes going for it, but he's as frightened as we are of *all* the rats. And in the end, he said he was going to do what Catchy had done (he knew all about it, they used to talk to each other quite a lot). He said he was going. But then he got all sentimental about leaving us and started being soppy.'

'In other words,' Lucas said, 'you don't really know if he is going or not. We can't check on him, so we can't know if what you say is true or not. I mean, if he stays, you simply say, "Well, I never said definitely that he was going!" and if the rats get him and he disappears, you'll say, "Ah! I always told you he'd go!" '

'That's not fair!' said Lettice, but the Doctor put his hand on her arm and said, 'It *is* fair, Lettice, so I want you to think very carefully and not get upset . . .

'Now, if Duff *does* go, will there be a certain time when he goes? Will he choose day or night? Morning or evening? I ask you this, dear Lettice, so that we may *observe* Duff and hope to *see* him go and thus discover the very important truth underlying what you believe. And what I believe too. But what I believe does not matter, I am out of my depth. Only you can tell us, Lettice. You are the great scientist now.'

'What do you want me to do?' she said.

'Suppose, Lettice, you had a talk with Duff. Suppose you said to him, "Duff, I think you should go. Go at a certain time." Then we could observe him, see him go. Do you see?'

'Yes, but he's such a silly old thing, and he's so fond of us. I mean, he might say he'd do it and then not do it.'

'Ah, but suppose you gave him a reason for doing it! Suppose you said to him, "Duff, you should go, it is quite all right for you to go. And what is more, my good dog, if *you* go, then *I* will go too!" '

'But I couldn't say that, it would be a lie!' said Lettice.

'Would it be a lie?' said the Doctor, sitting back in his chair and putting his little hands on his knees. 'Are you sure it would be a lie, Lettice?'

There was a long silence. At last, Lettice jumped to her feet and cried, 'You could be right! I never thought of it like that, Doctor Kalabza! – I mean, I'm so used to people laughing at me and thinking me a liar, that I half think myself a liar even when I know I'm telling the truth! I mean, just suppose we all *have* to go . . .! Come on, Duff!'

They heard her running up the stairs – opening her bedroom door – calling, 'Come on, Duff!' – slamming the door shut – then silence.

'Now, dear friends,' said Doctor Kalabza, 'we will continue to talk. But very quietly, so as not to disturb Lettice. Softly, then. Softly!'

Pin Money

'You can't go back through time,' said Mrs Rideout flatly. 'Man, woman, dog or cat, it simply can't be done. So I don't really see why you are taking Lettice seriously, Doctor.'

'Funny things do happen, though,' said Mr Rideout. 'That bloke who bent forks, on TV. Indian fakirs. There was a fakir – never saw him myself – who could turn his bowels inside out –'

'Really!' said Mrs Rideout.

'And perfect pitch, that's a remarkable thing. Hear a note, name it. Fairy rings. ESP, psycho-kinesis. And what was that thing on telly only the other night? –'

'Telly,' said Doctor Kalabza. 'Ah, television. People are so strange. Here you are, Mr Rideout, a reasonable, rational, scientifically minded man – yet you believe in television and radio waves!'

'Believe in them? Of course I believe them! I can see and hear them in action any time I choose!'

'But – let us talk softly, Mr Rideout, let us not disturb Lettice – you cannot produce them, show them to me, let me handle them. Perhaps the radio wave is all belief, Mr Rideout? Simply a bit of folk-lore that we act on?'

'You mean that if everyone stopped believing in radio and television the waves would die? Like the fairy Tinkerbell?

"Come on, children! All together, now! Do you believe in telly?"!'

'Beliefs change, Mr Rideout. This generation believes in radio waves and *voilà*! – radio and television! But think back, dear Mr Rideout! Think back to witches and witchdoctors, ghosts and evil spirits, and the bell, book and candle!'

'Phooey,' said Mr Rideout. 'You have your witchcraft and I'll have my switchcraft!' He patted the TV set.

'Pins!' said Mrs Rideout. 'I've suddenly remembered. Witches used to vomit pins! It was their parlour trick. Just fancy vomiting *pins*, oh dear me!'

'Ah, but dear Mrs Rideout, do not laugh! You are forgetting your own English history! Disbelieving your own written records! Now, let me remind you: when witchcraft was prevalent in this country and when there was much gossip and constant gossip about the witches, you had a Judge Jeffreys. You know him?'

'The Bloody Assizes,' said Lucas. 'Judge Jeffreys used to tour the country trying witches - well, condemning them, anyhow. You could hardly call them trials –'

'You have read these trials, Lucas?'

'Yes, bits of them. History lessons.'

'Then you may know that there are many, many, many records and documents and evidences of women who, said to be witches, vomited pins. Vomited pins in the court rooms, before the eyes of judges and lawyers!

'Now, just consider for a moment, I beg you. Just think. Here is the stern judge in his wig. There is an old woman, said to be a witch. The judge, she knows, will condemn her to a horrible death: it does not matter what she says, innocent or guilty does not matter, for he is the Hanging Judge, Judge Jeffreys. She must surely die.

'So he says to this doomed old woman, "You are a wicked witch, do not deny it!" and she says, "Yes, I am, and I glory

in it! It is good that I am a witch, and I put my witch's curse
on you! And that you may know I am truly a witch, I vomit
pins before your very eyes!" And she brings up the little
glittering pins, and the people gasp, and the judge has her
burned – and the recorder of the court writes it all down, my
dear Rideouts; writes it all down so that centuries later, we
may see that a professional man, a legal man, has seen a
woman vomit pins . . .!

'And this,' the Doctor continued, 'at a time when pins
were so expensive that the husband had to give his wife special
money to buy them –'

' "Pin money",' said Lucas.

'Just so,' said the Doctor. ' "Pin money".'

'Well, I'm sure you know best,' said Mrs Rideout. 'But
why pins, I simply don't know!'

'But surely you must see!' cried the Doctor. 'Pins, because
– I must speak quietly, Lettice is at work – pins, because *pins
were expected*! For the conjurer, a white rabbit: for the psycho-
kinetics, the bending fork: for us, the electronic device, the
TV set: for Christians, the crucifix: for witches, cats, broom-
sticks and *pins*!'

'It was the fish, originally,' said Mr Rideout. 'For Christians, I mean. The fish was their symbol. And the chi-rho.
Then the sign of the cross. All very interesting, Doctor. Would
you like a sherry?'

The Doctor rolled his eyes upwards and shrugged his
shoulders. 'You do not seem to understand,' he said, coldly.

'I do!' said Lucas, flaming with a sudden excitement. 'At
least, I think I do! What I mean is, that today, we live in an
electronic age and we watch the TV and listen to the radio –
and we take it all for granted, though we don't really *understand*
– no, I mean, we can't actually *touch* and show someone the
power that makes all the gadgets go .. While in the old
days, they had -'

'In the old days,' said Ann, as excited as Lucas, 'they built cathedrals more wonderful than any buildings we have today! – and vomited pins! – and there are still witchdoctors in some parts of the world! – and –'

'And because they believed these quite different things,' said the Doctor, 'and because so *many people* believed those things, those things could work. The witches *could* and *did* vomit pins! We *can* and *do* snatch music and pictures from the air for our magic boxes, our radios and televisions! The witchdoctors, the man who bends the spoons – surely you must see, dear people, it is all a matter of *belief*!

'Now, in this very house, at this very moment, we have a girl called Lettice. She believes she can talk to the animals; and she believes the animals believe they can travel in time or space. *And she could be right!*'

'She could be wrong,' said Mr Rideout. 'Here's your sherry.'

'She hasn't been proved wrong about the Blobs,' said Lucas. 'She hasn't been proved wrong about talking to animals.'

'I don't know,' said Ann, slowly. 'Suppose she's right about everything, I still don't see that it makes much difference. Pins, fakirs, radio waves, religions · they could all work because, as you said, Doctor, nearly all the people believed they could work. So there was a huge power of belief to draw on. Without that amount of power *everyone* believing - what can Lettice, and a few more like her, achieve? Assuming, of course, that she *is* right. And I'm not sure yet about that.'

There were footsteps coming downstairs and Lettice came into the room followed by Duff.

'Duff's going on Tuesday,' she said. 'Before the dustmen come. You know how he hates the dustmen. So it will be Tuesday morning.'

Duff's Departure

On Tuesday morning, the road outside the Rideouts' house was jampacked. For once, the rats had to give way to the humans – and their vehicles, cameras, generators, cable runs, tripods, lighting gear . . .

The TV producer asked, for the third time, 'When did you say they'll come? The dustmen? What time?'

'I don't know,' replied Mrs Rideout, worriedly. 'Nothing works properly these days. They might not even come at all, how can I possibly *tell* –'

'Duff will leave before noon, whether they come or not,' said Lettice. Her face was set with determination. 'He expects them at noon and he'll go before noon. He told me so again, for the umpteenth time, last night.'

'Yes . . .' said the TV man, looking at Lettice with unbelieving eyes. 'Yes, no doubt . . .'

He stared at Duff and other eyes followed his. There were perhaps two dozen people – journalists, photographers, electricians, TV crewmen – crowded in the living-room. They were all there because Dr Kalabza had given them a news story, and a Dr Kalabza story had to be followed up. But not one pair of eyes showed any belief.

Which was hardly surprising. Duff, the star of the occasion, looked nothing like a star. He was stretched out on his familiar patch of rug, nose between front paws. His eyes were watery. Embarrassed by the staring humans, he looked up   found nothing to interest him – and began to scratch one floppy ear.

'I've always preferred cats,' said a cynical voice. A few people laughed.

Duff stopped scratching and turned his head, looking for Lettice. When he saw her, he got shakily to his feet and went to her. Although she was standing, he managed to lay his head in her lap. She patted his head and said, 'It's all right, Duff, really it is. Oh dear . . .'

The dog made a sound between a woof and a howl and Lettice began to cry. Some camera shutters clicked and you could hear tape recorders whirring.

'What's the time now, then?' said a photographer.

'Eleven-twenty. Not long to go. If we're going, that is.'

Duff went to Mrs Rideout and stared at her, mournfully. Again, cameras clicked. Uncertainly, Mrs Rideout said, 'Good dog, Duff. There's a good boy, then! Oh dear, *must* they walk all over the vegetable-bed? Mr – I don't know your name, but would you *kindly* tell your men *not* to –'

The men in the garden pretended to move their equipment away from the barren vegetable plot. Minutes went by. Duff stood in the middle of the people in the room, almost still. Sometimes he moved his head from side to side and sometimes he looked up at Lettice, who stood by him.

At last, he went to the rug and sniffed at his own particular place on it. 'Oh Gawd, he's going to settle down for a nice long sleep!' someone said.

He was wrong. Duff sniffed busily at the rug – turned again to Lettice – and made for the garden. The men and machines out there made room for the girl and the dog. Someone held a microphone in front of Lettice's mouth and asked her a question, but she did not seem to hear. Dr Kalabza, who had been giving interview after interview, said, 'Leave her alone my friend, be a little kind. Soon, she and her dog will b apart.'

'Too sad,' said a girl reporter, nastily.

The Doctor ignored the sneer. He was watching Lettice and Duff. Down the road, there was the noise of a car coming or going. One of Duff's ears went up, then down again. You could almost see him say to himself, 'Not the dustmen.' His eyes were wetter than ever and his tail was on the ground. He gazed at Lettice, adoring her.

'Duff,' she said, 'I think it's time. I think you'd better go. Go, Duff.'

Heads were bent, cameras were focused, settings and levels were checked.

'Go on, Duff,' she said. 'It's all right for you to go now. Darling Duff . . .'

The dog walked his old shaky walk to the far corner of the lawn; stopped; looked back at Lettice; and –

– *vanished*.

Within hours, the world was told and shown what had happened.

Within days, the arguments were beginning to peter out. What was the point of arguing? There, again and again on the screen or in the newspapers and magazines, was the proof. One moment a dog: next moment, no dog. One moment, bored and sceptical faces: the next, faces fixed in open-mouthed astonishment . . . with only two exceptions. Dr Kalabza's face, intent and interested, showed no surprise; Lettice's face, tears on its cheeks, showed only grief.

Within weeks, new stories began to come in – new, but the same. There could be no doubt about it: the animals were leaving. There were too many stories, from too many parts of the globe, to permit doubt.

Humans were leaving too.

A very old and overdressed lady in a New York hotel loudly announced her determination to emigrate. The press and TV men turned up to watch her go. She went. She vanished.

A wild-haired, bead-covered leader of a crazy religious sect in Australia announced that he and all his followers were about to emigrate in a body, all at once. They did. They vanished.

It accelerated. A tribe of Africans, starving and drought-stricken, stood chanting on a hill-top with their arms outlifted. They stood like this for hours, until the weaker-willed dropped their arms. Then their leader gave a sudden screaming shout of command – everyone jumped at once – and the whole tribe seemed to spring into the sky and disappear. Even the weak ones vanished. It made fascinating TV.

Sane, respectable, bus-catching, ordinary, reliable, dull people announced that they would disappear: and did.

Doctor Kalabza was more than ever an international celebrity. Wherever he went (and he went everywhere) he trailed cameramen and reporters. His fame had never been so great. Yet now he no longer frolicked and clowned. Sometimes, he was almost grim.

Lettice was a high priestess, a goddess. She disliked it. She went around the house sulkily, complaining of the constant ringing and banging at the front door, the never-ending telephone calls, the stacks of letters in the hall. She looked, crossly, at the pictures of herself in the newspapers, muttering 'I don't look like that at *all*!' Then she would disappear for an hour or so and come downstairs with her hair done a new way. When Ann called, Lettice grabbed her and demanded an opinion about the new hairstyle.

Her chief complaint, the one she repeated all the time, was, 'If we're *going*, why don't we *go*? I promised Duff, you all know I promised him!'

'Oh, do shut up!' said Lucas. 'We can't go yet, it's obvious!'

'Why not, I'd like to know?'

'Well, we just *can't*, I mean, the world's still going on, we can't just leave.'

'Why not?'

'Well, we can't go unless everyone goes . . . we can't just go on our own, as a family, it wouldn't be . . .'

'Wouldn't be what?'

He didn't really know what or why. Nobody did. They stayed on because – because why? Because emigration was not absolutely, completely, universally certain? Because you cannot just leave behind a whole lifetime of familiar houses and faces and work? Because no one knew what to expect when they found themselves in the Other Place or the Other Time?

The last reason was probably the real reason. There were too many mysteries to face. To find answers to the mysteries, the world asked Lettice (and a thousand fakes and false prophets who pretended to have her powers) for an answer. 'What is it like Over There? Should we go? Can we go? Is it . . . all right?' Mainly through the agency of Doctor Kalabza, she tried to give answers.

Sometimes she answered the questions in person. More than once, she gave in to the throngs of people at the front door and appeared on television, looking much prettier than she had ever looked in the old days, but still nervous and uncertain.

'You've got to understand,' she said weakly to the cameras and microphones, 'I'm not a *scientist* or anything like that, I only know what the animals tell me – I mean, *used* to tell me in the old days. Catchmouse? No, I never get anything from Catchy, I suppose she's just settled down, the way cats do. What does Duff say? Well, he doesn't *say* much, he's just lonely for me and the family, he just goes on about personal things . . . like, when am I coming . . .'

Whatever she said, and however weakly and uncertainly she said it, the results were always the same: huge headlines in next day's popular papers. If, picking nervously at her lip, she said, 'Well, I really don't know,' the headlines howled 'LETTICE'S LIPS ARE SEALED! NO NEW REVELATIONS FROM WONDER GIRL'. If she said, 'It's poor old Duff I'm worried about,' the headlines yelled 'MY AGONY'. If she said, 'I suppose we'll go eventually,' the headlines thundered 'WILL LITTLE LETTICE MAKE HER BID FOR FREEDOM?'

Reading these headlines, Doctor Kalabza roared with laughter, Lucas chortled, Mr Rideout snorted, Mrs Rideout looked dimly pleased. And Lettice turned various colours and gave despairing howls.

And the world at large believed what was said. Not the words, but the feeling – the feeling of excitement, drama, possibility and hope.

Rampage

The rats became bolder and the Blobs suddenly became worse than ever.

Perhaps it was the never-ending television viewing that stirred up the Blobs. Everyone turned on their sets to learn the latest news about the rats, the emigrants, the latest shortages and disasters – and Lettice. So the Blobs, stung by the effects of Raster, went on the rampage.

It became so bad that the Common Market countries put forward a scheme to cut out television entirely, for a trial period of a week. The Americans and Russians considered the plan. Doctor Kalabza made yet another TV appearance and supported it.

So, in nearly all those countries where TV was most used, suddenly the screens went blank. Immediately, the Blobs seemed to quieten down.

But then the week was up, and the TV programmes started again.

On the very first day, the Blobs attacked with a viciousness worse than anything before. In the streets of New York, cars seemed to heave and shudder - then topple sideways, pushed over by the rampaging Blobs. In Paris, old buildings swayed and toppled, crushing passers-by and the people inside. In London, the Northern, Central and Circle underground lines were completely stopped – the Blobs were on the tracks. Before it was cut off, the electricity burned them. A new and horrible smell wafted up the lift and elevator shafts and sickened the people in the streets.

From Berlin and Amsterdam, Brussels and Geneva, Brasilia and Corfu, the reports poured in. The Blobs had made their way to the top of a big store – the floor had given way – the Blobs tumbled and smashed their way down, floor by floor, and lay in the basement, crushing the dying and wounded humans. The Blobs flattened cowsheds, air terminals, cottages, hotels.

The Blobs had become dedicated killers: and the rats, scurrying over the dead, found what they were looking for, ate it and grew fat.

As if it were a family fallen on hard times, the human race slowly came to realize the horrible truth. The old home had to be quitted; the old ways were, from now on, just happy memories; a new, uncertain and unpleasant future had to be faced.

'The Baxter boy's gone,' reported Ann one day. Now she lived with the Rideouts. 'I don't know how his parents will manage. Mrs Baxter's arthritis . . .'

'I didn't think he'd go,' said Lucas. 'He'd only just got that Honda from that bloke who emigrated. He was crazy about it.'

'Well, that girl-friend of his left. And Mrs Baxter says when Barry read her goodbye letter, he just went straight out to the motorbike without a word –'

'Final burn-up to relieve his feelings?' said Lucas.

'Yes, just that. But when he got to the bike it was lying on its side. The Blobs, I suppose. He got it back on its stand, but some electric wires had been eaten through by rats. So he went back into the house and said, "Sorry, Mum, sorry Dad, but I've had it. I'm off." And he went.'

'Have the Baxters told Relief Patrol?'

'Yes, I saw to that. The Patrol people have been round already. Seen to the dustbins, brought in some food, blocked up holes where the rats could get in, and all the usual things. But of course, the Baxters can't carry on . . . she says they're leaving. Mr Baxter doesn't want to –'

'He's bone idle, that man,' said Mrs Rideout. 'He never does *anything*. Do you think they'll go?'

'Yes. Probably today.'

'Should we say goodbye, or anything?' said Mrs Rideout. 'No, I don't suppose so,' she answered herself. 'We never really *knew* them. And besides . . .'

'And besides, we'll be going ourselves!' said Lucas. 'All I want to know is, *when!*'

Conversations of this sort took place all over the world.
At first, people had said, 'We might.'
Later, they said, 'We could.'
Recently, they said, 'We will.'
Nowadays, the only question left was, '*When?*'

The Rideouts had not yet found it possible to answer the question.

Mr Rideout didn't want to go. Nor did Mrs Rideout. Both were old enough to fear change – yet feared the changes taking place every day as the rats and the Blobs took over their world, their country, their village and their home. Mr Rideout was worried because his money was going fast and he could earn no more: yet money was no longer needed. You got what you could when the government vans called; bought whatever the shops still had to sell. Perhaps what really worried him was that his occupation was gone. 'I was always a luxury,' he said. 'A parasite. A *scribbler*. And now there's no place left for me.'

'So we're going?' said Lucas.

'Ah,' said Mr Rideout, 'I didn't say *that* . . . I wonder if that new typing paper has come? I'll cycle down to the village and find out. Where's the Webley?'

He came back in triumph with a ream of typing paper. 'Look at that!' he cried. 'Last the world will ever see! – or that's the impression they gave me in the shop. Clean, white, virgin paper! The very essence of civilization! The raw material of all the most worthwhile things achieved by humanity!' He chuckled and took the package upstairs to his room. The family heard the typewriter going.

'Well,' said Mrs Rideout, 'I'm glad he's happy for an hour or two. But I can't really see what a difference it makes, his clean white paper.'

'He'll run out of steam soon,' Lucas said. 'Then we can use the paper in the loo. It's flimsy stuff, I could tell by the thickness of the package.'

Next day, however, Mr Rideout thumped downstairs in fury, holding a sheet of tattered typing paper with a corner missing. 'Look at it!' he shouted. 'Just look at it! Eaten by rats! They've spoiled the lot! – gone right through the whole pile!'

Emigration moved one step nearer for the Rideouts.

Days passed.

Now there were only five houses occupied in the Rideouts street. Mrs Clavering would never leave. She was eighty. 'I've had my life,' she said, 'and it's been a good one. The Patrol people are very kind. Oh yes, I've had my life and don' regret a minute of it. So what have I to worry about?'

The Patrol people found what the rats left of her two day later.

That left four houses with people in them.

Doctor Kalabza arrived. He came in a car he had picked up. His Lagonda could not be reached: its garage was flooded by a sea of rats. But there were abandoned cars everywhere, many with keys in the ignition and petrol in the tank. You just took one and ran it until the tank was dry. Lucas had already 'owned' four cars. It was not safe to walk, of course, because of the rats. But it was not safe to drive either because of the Blobs.

Doctor Kalabza's car was a Lotus, very low and sporty. They could hear its gears clashing long before he arrived. He was clean-shaven but the rest of him his clothes and even the whites of his eyes – was dirty.

'Dear people!' he cried. 'Still here! But that is a mistake, a terrible mistake! I have been thinking of you so much, in all the many places I have been! in Tokyo, Dublin, Los Angeles – in all the places, I think of you! But why are you still here, how do you exist?'

'I've been waiting for the Rideouts to go,' laughed Ann, 'and they've been waiting for me!'

'But that is so ridiculous!' said the Doctor. 'Why do you not go? For me it is different, I wish to observe unto the very last – but for *you* to stay, what purpose can there be?'

'You used to say,' Lucas said bitterly, ' "Leave it all to me! I'll find a way!" '

'Oh, but I was always a fool,' said the Doctor, lightly. 'A wise fool. And I am still a fool and that is why I am still here. But you, you must go!'

Lettice had said nothing. Now she spoke.

'We are going,' she announced flatly. 'Tonight. I promised Duff and I broke my promise, but now I'm going to keep it. Tonight.'

'Lettice!' cried Mrs Rideout, scandalized.

'Tonight, Mother,' said Lettice. 'With or without. I've spoken to Duff and he says it's all right where he is.'

'Spoken to Duff?' said the Doctor.

'Yes. Well, I think so. You can't really tell. But if we *did*

373

talk, it sounds much better over there than it is here.'

'But dear child, what did he tell you?' said the Doctor.

'All sorts of things. More than ever before. I got sort of pictures of the people and places ... I don't know if they're true or not, the pictures show what a dog sees, not what we see –'

'Past or future, dear Lettice?' said the Doctor, urgently. 'Tell me – Do we seem to travel backwards in time or forwards?'

'It seems to be backwards,' said Lettice. 'Women in long skirts and men wearing tall hats. Dark clothes. And there are horses everywhere.'

Mr Rideout snorted. 'Impossible!' he said. 'All this talk of moving forward in time, or backwards – a logical impossibility. You can't go to the past. The past has already happened and you can't make it re-happen. And even if you could, you'd go through a cycle of history that would bring you once again to the present –'

'Please, please, let us hear Lettice,' Doctor Kalabza insisted. 'At least she speaks from experience.'

'Oh no she doesn't,' said Mr Rideout, beginning to lose his temper. 'She speaks through the mind of a stupid old dog who may or may not be in touch with her. Look, Doctor travelling backwards in time is a particularly pointless exercise in impossibility. Logically, it ends up with someone trying to put on his slippers and finding he's already in them. Surely you can see –'

'Mr Rideout, Mr Rideout, I see very clearly! By objecting to impossibilities, you make yourself sound as I sounded, poor foolish Doctor Kalabza, only a few weeks ago. Blobs are impossible, you say? But there are Blobs. They cannot come into our world and try to share it? But they have done so, they do so. It is impossible to talk to animals? Your daughter proves that she has done so. We cannot move ourselves

374

another dimension or time? Thousands of people do it every day.'

'Not to the past,' said Mr Rideout, stubbornly.

'I never said the past. It is you who keeps insisting on that. I asked Lettice, "Do we *seem* to travel backwards?" –'

'You should say what you mean,' said Mr Rideout, red with temper. 'Just what *do* you mean?'

'Backwards, forwards – I agree that such travelling may well be a logical and physical impossibility. But Mr Rideout, has it not occurred to you that we may be able to travel *sideways?*'

'*Sideways?*' said Mr Rideout contemptuously.

'Sideways! We may be able to move to parallel lives, lived along parallel lines.'

Lucas said, 'I know one thing about parallel lines: they never meet.'

'That was before Einstein,' his father grumbled. 'Nowadays, parallel lines behave like courting couples, apparently. Always cuddling up to each other . . .' He was growing tired of the argument. But the Doctor was not to be stopped.

'Parallel lines, parallel lives!' he exclaimed. 'Surely you can see it? Was there another Shakespeare, identical to your Shakespeare, except that he was a busy French farmer who never had time to write plays? –'

'Or a Burmese Bugs Bunny who hates carrots,' grumbled Mr Rideout.

The Doctor did not hear him. 'In this parallel world, must television be invented and accepted? Perhaps not! And then, without television, would the Blobs be content to stay in their own parallel world? Very probably!'

As if the word 'Blobs' had been a magician's 'Abracadabra', the whole house shook. The ceiling began to collapse. Everyone ran to the bay window. In the garden, they could see

Blobs. There was a herd of them, flickering and wavering and heaving. They pushed their great crisscrossed flanks against the walls of the house. More of the ceiling fell.

Some of the herd seemed to concentrate on what they were doing. These creatures stopped, turned and butted themselves against the kitchen wall. There was an appalling, long-drawn, smashing, tinkling, clattering, thundering uproar as the kitchen and everything in it was smashed.

The Blobs lost interest and moved on.

Doctor Kalabza, Ann and the Rideouts brushed the plaster dust off their hair and clothes. Ann said, 'I'm going,' and left. More plaster fell from the ceiling. 'In the garden, everyone,' Mr Rideout said. 'Safer out there.'

Outside, he said, 'Show of hands. Family decision. Go now, or later?' His voice was very grim. Hands were raised. Mrs Rideout's hand went up last. She was crying, silently.

'Unanimous,' Mr Rideout said. 'We go. Very well. We'll drink a toast to the future, if there is a future. I've got a bottle of champagne somewhere, I know I have.'

'The Blobs have broken all the glasses,' Mrs Rideout said, through her tears.

'Then we'll have to pass the bottle round. If I can find it.' He stumped off.

'And you,' Lettice said to the Doctor, 'what about you? Are you coming with us?'

'My dear Lettice, I wish I were. I am sure it will be most exciting. And of course you are right to go, you must go. Everyone should go.'

'Then why didn't you raise your hand?'

'Ah, well,' he began. She stared at him. He had run out o words – something she had never seen him do before. 'Ah well, I am not family. And in any case, it would be difficul for me to go. Almost a matter of loyalty . . .'

'*Loyalty*? Loyalty to what?'

'To my science,' he replied. 'You will laugh at me, dear Lettice – laugh at me and my old-fashioned, out-dated science –'

'I'm not laughing! How could I laugh? But I don't understand.'

'Oh, I'm sure you do. It is simple. My science, the old science, is very simple. You look at things and try to see how they work – try to *see*, with a telescope, a microscope, an X-ray. So many ways to see, so many things to be seen –'

'Come with us,' she muttered.

'But then,' he said, ignoring her, 'there comes along something completely new, something that cannot be seen; only felt and known. By a new sort of scientist. You, Lettice! The new scientist for the new science.'

'That's silly,' she said. 'Please come with us. Please.'

Lucas joined them. 'You'll be killed if you don't,' he said, in a very low voice.

'I must stay,' said Doctor Kalabza. 'I must be here to see the end. I must live it, record it, make a record, a sort of tablet of stone –'

'A gravestone,' Lucas said. '*Your* gravestone.'

'No, dear Lucas – a stone for the whole world. I must inscribe it carefully, scientifically, faithfully. It must be a thing of – of –'

'Dignity?' Lettice said, softly. She could not see the Doctor's face, her eyes were full of tears. But Lucas could see it clearly. It was all there in the Doctor's eyes – the fearlessness, the dedication, the thrust of raw intelligence. And the fear.

'Found it!' cried Mr Rideout, flourishing a bottle of champagne. 'The rats have been at the cork but no harm done. Hope the wire broke their teeth. Here we go, then!'

The cork popped, the wine frothed. 'You first, my dear,' Mr Rideout told his wife. 'Take a good swig, don't just sip at it! Then pass it round.'

The Rideouts drank, avoiding looking at the familiar sights all round them – the trampled garden, the roofs of the deserted neighbouring houses, the gnawed posts of the old garden swing, the green watering can under the always-dripping tap. They drank and tasted nothing.

They put on layer after layer of clothing. If there was weather in the new place, it might be bad. If there was a new place.

'Well, Doctor,' Mr Rideout said, with an awful heartiness.

'Go!' he replied.

They went.

On the Other Side

It was an overcrowded room, rather too hot, filled with knick-knacks and framed photographs, potted plants and china figurines, glaring mirrors and dark wallpaper, carpets and rugs, doilies and trinkets. A Victorian family would have been quite at home in it.

Mr Rideout sat in the largest of the elaborately carved and padded chairs. His feet, in slippers decorated by his wife's careful needlework, rested on the brass surround. He was half-reading the local newspaper he owned and edited; but was constantly distracted by Lettice's piano practice. Her touch was lumpish and her sense of time and tone uncertain. As note followed note, each exactly wrong, his free hand fidgeted with the watch chain across his waistcoat. He wished himself elsewhere – preferably at the public house down the road – but could feel his wife's eyes glancing at him, imprisoning him within the family circle. He frowned and stuck out his lower lip.

Mrs Rideout, too, found the piano's noise irksome. There was a slight jerkiness to her hands as they drew the coloured threads through her tambour. Nonetheless, her brow remained serene beneath the centrally parted wings of shining hair drawn back from her brow. In that other world, her hair had been loosely dressed in careless waves. In this parallel world, she looked a different being: tauter, harder, more determined.

'That will suffice, Lettice,' she said. Lettice, relieved, stopped playing instantly. Duff, by the fireside, gave a long wheeze and settled his nose on his paws. Now he could sleep, undisturbed by the din from the big black noise-box. Catchmouse, sleeping, stopped flicking one ear and settled into a still more luxurious position.

'I wish I did not have to continue with my piano lessons, Mama,' said Lettice.

'So do we all,' said Lucas, saucily, not looking up from the pile of stereoscopic photographs at his knee. They were all familiar to him and boring. You soon get tired of landscapes. A boy down the road had pictures of musical-comedy actresses, showing their legs. Golly!

Mrs Rideout ignored her daughter's complaint, as Lettice knew she would. Young ladies played the pianoforte. *All* young ladies. And that was that. Lettice sighed and said, 'Shall I attend to the bovos, Mama?'

'Yes, Lettice. But do not take too long. And wear your coat and overshoes.'

'Yes, Mama.'

'And do not let the lantern flare so that it blackens the glass.'

'No, Mama.'

Gratefully and gladly, she donned her outdoor clothes, lit the lantern, adjusted its wick, and went out of the back door to the bovos. Their shed made a bold, dark shape against the night sky: a shape repeated all down the road. Behind every house there was a bovo shed.

The door of the shed grated open on the cobbles and the bovos clumped their feet and grunted in welcome. The lantern's yellow light was reflected back, redly, by their eyes. There were twelve of them, the usual number. Lettice spoke the traditional greeting: 'Bless the animals that bless us!' They grunted back.

Lettice smiled. She walked down the central aisle of the shed, enjoying seeing what the light of the lantern revealed: the simple stalls, mere dividing rails on posts – for bovos were always docile; the heavy, round, friendly backsides, covered with the thick, short, woolly fur – you could twine your fingers into its warm, springy depths; the great, blunt heads, straining round on the short necks to look at her. Cow-like hooves clattered on the cobbles in mild excitement at her presence. Cow-like eyes gazed mildly and contentedly at her. But of course, bovos were not really like cows at all.

'What would I do without you!' Lettice murmured, as she patted the big round rumps. She entered the stall of one of her favourites, Rosie. Rosie made way for her and lifted her clumsy head to be stroked.

'And what would *we* do without you?' said Lettice, to herself. The light of her lantern came from bovo oil. The gas light in the house came largely from bovo excrement. Her shoes were made of bovo leather, her coat contained bovo wool, the meat she ate –

She shuddered and switched off her thoughts. 'Fancy *eating* you!' she murmured to Rosie. 'How *can* people do it?' She pursed her lips primly, congratulating herself on being a vegetarian. Eating poor darling bovos! How disgusting! Yet everyone did it. And no one thought about it.

'*I* think about you all the time,' Lettice told Rosie, quite truthfully. Other people didn't. Lucas didn't even bother to give the correct greeting when he entered the bovo shed. He just muttered, 'BTBTBU' instead of 'Bless the beasts that bless us.' It was dreadful, the way people took bovos for granted.

Outside in the road, she heard the rumbling wheels of a cart. Probably the oilman. He sold candles, lamp oil, nightlights, lubricating oil, polishing leathers. 'All from bovos,' Lettice thought. Bovos pulled his cart – he said they were steadier than horses. Bovos gave the oil that lit the cart's flaring lamps. Bovos gave the hides that covered the cart. Why weren't people grateful? BTBTBU, indeed!

Something rubbed at Lettice's ankles. Catchmouse. She put the lantern down and picked up the cat. 'Your catfood comes from bovos, Catchy!' she told the cat. She put the cat's nose against her own. 'Aren't you ashamed to eat it?' Catchmouse did not answer. She was cross. She wanted food, or attention, or to get back into the house – something of that sort. 'You sulky, greedy, fat old thing!' she said. 'I wish I had your life! No chores, no piano lessons, no school! Why won't you talk to me?'

But the cat's head and eyes were straining from side to side, looking for mice. 'How nice to be a cat,' Lettice said. 'Mice everywhere! Poor little things.' Even as she spoke, Catchmouse clawed and scrambled, trying to escape her. She had heard a rustling in the straw over there: she wanted to get at the mice that caused the rustle. A world that kept and fed bovos was overrun with mice. Every house had at least one cat and every cat had unlimited mice to hunt.

Catchmouse got free and ran to the straw. There were squeaks and scuffles, then a little scream that made Lettice feel sick. Why was the world so cruel? Poor little mice! And Duff chasing rats, trying to kill them. He dreamed of rats, Lettice knew. He told her so.

'You never harm anyone, do you, Rosie?' she said to the bovo. Rosie clumsily tried to lick the hand that stroked her. 'You'd never harm anyone, would you? I wonder what you think about, Rosie. Do you get bored, just being useful and good? Don't you ever wish . . . Oh, I don't know. Why won't you talk to me, Rosie?' Lettice crouched down in the corner of the stall, her eyes level with the bovo's eyes. That was how you made cats and dogs talk to you. And horses and cows. 'Talk to me,' she whispered.

But Rosie only stared back, dimly, lovingly, stupidly. Bovos never talked.

Lettice's knees and thighs began to ache. She stood up, sighed, took the lantern and walked between the double line of bovos, patting each one, and calling it by name.

At the door, she took the halter of the latest addition to the herd – Rosie's seventh son, Septimus. She led the calf, already almost as big as a cow, to the floor troughs at the end of the shed. Septimus had to be toilet-trained. 'Go on, Septimus,' she said. 'Do your duty. Clever boy.'

Septimus swung his head uncertainly, but eventually obeyed. Then, without further guidance from Lettice, he began to amble back to his stall. 'Come back, you bad boy!' she said. Uncertainly, he turned. 'Pull the chain, Septimus,' she said. 'That's right! A good hard pull!' The animal obeyed, tugging solemnly with his big wet mouth. 'He's learning fast,' Lettice thought. 'We take them for granted. We call them stupid. You're not stupid, are you, Septimus? You're a clever boy! You're learning to pull the chain!' He looked at her with his great mild eyes. There was no expression in them.

She sighed and prepared to leave. She called out, 'Bless the beasts that bless us,' then closed the door. At once the warm, mystical smell of the beasts was gone and the night air struck chill at her. 'Cold common sense,' she murmured.

It was a favourite phrase of her father's – perhaps because he showed so little common sense himself. He would never make a mark, never succeed, never win his own wife's approval. Did it matter? Perhaps not. The Lord would provide, the Lord and the bovos. No family could starve or even face discomfort provided that the bovo shed was kept filled with healthy, obedient animals.

'I won't succeed either,' Lettice decided. 'Why should I? I'll just be kind to the animals and try to make them talk to me. *Really* talk to me.'

She shivered in the darkness yet delayed returning to the warmth of the house. Mama would say, 'Why were you so long, Lettice?' and Lucas would say, 'Been talking to the animals again, Lettice?' or something like that. But she *did* speak to the animals, she was sure she did.

Or did she dream it? She had such strange dreams, sometimes. Dreams of another place, a place with lots of machines ... metal machines that ran on fat wheels, going very fast; machines that talked to you, or that you talked at; machines everywhere, all so smart and clever, machines that did everything. There were no bovos in this dream world. Perhaps the machines took the place of bovos?

She shivered, entered the house, put her overshoes on the rack and her coat on its peg and went into the living-room. Her mother said, 'Why were you so long, Lettice?' and Lucas looked up, his eyes alive with malice, and said, 'Had a good chat?' This remark made Papa lower his paper to look at her and everyone started on her, as they always did.

Septimus

In the shed, the bovos talked.

Rosie said, 'She is good and kind. And she likes me best.'

Hector grumbled, 'Fools! You females are all fools! But I . . . I have plans, great plans, wonderful plans!'

The male who came second to Hector said, 'Hector and his plans!' and snorted loudly.

Septimus, Rosie's calf, took no notice of the words of the old ones. He blinked his eyes to make himself concentrate, lowered his head and pushed. The stout wooden boards forming the wall of the shed creaked.

He pushed.

A particular board bulged.

He pushed.

The board split. The jagged edge raised splinters that hurt his nose.

He ignored the pain and pushed.

The splintered board gave way and suddenly something strange and wonderful rushed into his nostrils – cold, clean, night air, scented with grass and trees and starry skies.

Septimus filled his great lungs with the magical stuff – it made his brain spin and glitter – and pushed.

Stubbornly, unhurriedly, he pushed and pushed until at last there was a big, jagged hole facing him. The others pretended not to know or hear; for they were old and stolid, perhaps afraid. Septimus was young. He walked through the hole in the wall. Young, free and angry.

He lumbered quietly down the road till the sheds and houses were left behind him. Now there were hedges and fields, glowing grey and silver and blue in the moonlight; and smells – such smells! – that led him on and on until the hedges were gone too and the neat fields, and there was only IT, the boundless world showing no signs of Man. There were grass and thistles, a scurrying rabbit, a big mushroom palely glaring in pearly grass. And always, the smells, the smells! that led him on.

Nostrils wide, his steaming back dewed, he journeyed on. Clouds in the sky parted and suddenly there was a thing up there, bright and blazing; a round thing, frilled with luminous-edged clouds. Septimus stopped, raised his great head and stared at the moon. It offended him. It stared at him. He thrust his head at it and blew loudly through his nostrils, challenging the moon to come down and fight. But the moon was afraid, it stayed up there in the sky, staring and staring. Septimus shook his head sideways to show his contempt. The clouds closed over the moon and the cowardly enemy was gone. Septimus had vanquished it.

He decided to journey on. He had to pull his front hooves out of the ground. His great weight had sunk them. He heard the sucking noises as he pulled himself clear, and snorted again. 'Big!' he thought. 'I am big!' And now, as he walked, he swung his head deliberately, blowing through his nostrils. When he breathed out, there was a spray of liquid and a fine, loud noise. When he breathed in, there was the smell – a new smell: the smell of his new self, himself washed by the dew, purified by the boundless air, strengthened by every movement of his great muscles. A fine, new, acrid, warlike smell . . .

He began to run, hugely and clumsily, tossing his head

snorting, thundering. The pounding of his heart made drum-beats and the roaring of his breath was power and glory.

And there was the moon again, broken free from the clouds, the great luminous eye staring at him! Septimus reared on his hind legs – flailed his hooves – and tried to butt the moon.

Septimus was not the only one to escape. Other bovos broke out and wandered into the wilds, seeking other places, other times and tracks.

Nearly all were recaptured and returned to their proper lives in the bovo sheds.

Nearly all, but not all.

More Puffins by Nicholas Fisk

GRINNY

Great Aunt Emma is no ordinary old lady. For a start, she just appeared, grinning, on the doorstep, as if from nowhere. Soon Tim and Beth start noticing more and more odd things about the great-aunt they've nicknamed 'Grinny'. And before long, they make a horrifying discovery. She isn't even *human*: she's as dangerous as a time-bomb, and has a fearful task to perform which involves them.

MINDBENDERS

At first, Aunt Craven's gift of a formicarium seems just a useless present – what kind of fun could you have with a portable ants' nest? But as time passes, Vinny and Toby find themselves uncontrollably drawn to stare and stare into the glass case and to concentrate on its magic occupants, and suddenly they are doing wonderful, magical things that should have been impossible: Mindbending is incredible! And then the ants decide to grow . . .

A RAG, A BONE AND A HANK OF HAIR

After a terrible nuclear accident, the birthrate has dropped dramatically. The only hope appears to lie with the Reborns – new people made chemically by scientists. But the Reborns have been given free will and no one is quite certain how they will behave . . .

WHEELIE IN THE STARS

Life as cargo strippers on Terramare 3 was boring and ugly.
Even so, it seemed crazy for Noll and Niven to dream about
driving their beautiful smuggled-in motorbike, Wheelie.
Machines that ran on petrol were banned nowadays, but Noll
and Niven would not give up. 'Something willhappen, some-
hoe, sometime,' Noll said, and indeed it did, though it was
rather more than they had bargained for.

YOU REMEMBER ME!

Timothy Carpenter, a cub reporter on the local paper, is caught
up in the huge rallies and the dazzling hypnotic world that sur-
rounds the TV personality Lisa Treadgold. But . . . why does
Lisa continually eat chocolates? What happens to the chocolate
wrappings? Why does Beth hate her so much? What's wrong
with following the three D's – Decency, Discipline and
Dedication?

SWEETS FROM A STRANGER AND
OTHER STRANGE TALES

Little children know not to accept sweets from a stranger, but
do they know why? Wicked, inquisitive Tina couldn't resist
finding out what would happen – and found herself held
hostage on an alien planet light years away.

MOONDIAL
Helen Cresswell

Minty has heard stories of strange happenings in the big house across the road from her Aunt's cottage. And when she walks through the gates, the lodge-keeper knows it is Minty who holds the key to the mysteries. She has only to discover the secret power of the moondial, and she will be ready to carry out the dangerous mission which awaits her.

HALFWAY ACROSS THE GALAXY AND TURN LEFT
Robin Klein

Learning Earth customs causes all sorts of problems for the crazy alien family from Zyrgon, even with their extraterrestrial powers. X, as Family Organizer, tries hard to keep things running smoothly, but with Father's compulsive gambling habits, her little brother's formidable IQ, and her sister's absent-minded powers of levitation – not to mention the unexpected arrival of wild Aunt Hecla in her home-made space raft – who could say what might happen?

THE CHANGES TRILOGY
(The Devil's Children, Heartsease *and* The Weather-monger)
Peter Dickinson

England in the future: but an England less rather than more civilized. The whole country seems under a magic spell. This is the time of The Changes, when the people, hating machines, have gone back to leading primitive lives and are caught up in a web of hardship and fear. An absorbing, terrifying and gripping read.

MOMO
Michael Ende

The sinister men in grey have arrived and are silently taking over the city. They are drawing life-blood from the unsuspecting habitants. They are the time-thieves. It is Momo, the ragged little waif, who discovers what is happening. And it is Momo, with her uncanny ability to listen, her simplicity and honesty, who holds the key to salvation. She is the only one who can resist these soulless, corrupt creatures. In this intricate and compelling story of a fantastic country, Momo sets out to destroy the enemy, and the mysterious Professor Hora and his strangely gifted tortoise, Cassiopeia, will help her.

THE TRIPODS TRILOGY
(The White Mountains, The City of Gold and Lead *and* Pool of Fire)
John Christopher

Massive, alien machines, the Tripods had ruled Earth for hundreds of years and enslaved the minds and bodies of most adults through the silvery caps they made them wear. Determined to escape the ritual Capping ceremony, Will Parker runs away, heading for the distant White Mountains and the small rebel camp there, hoping to join their desperate attempts to overthrow the rule of the Tripods. The journey is long, the missions dangerous and the hope of survival very slim . . .

WHEN THE TRIPODS CAME
John Christopher

The story of Earth as it was – before the invasion of the Tripods. Laurie and Andy witness the exciting and terrifying arrival of the first Tripod ever to land on Earth. As more and more arrive, these sinister machines begin to take over young people's minds and Earth looks set for Tripod domination. How can one family survive?

A compelling story and superb introduction to these legendary science-fiction monsters, taking us back before the events of the Tripod trilogy.

UNDER THE MOUNTAIN
Maurice Gee

Rachel and Theo Matheson are twins. Apart from both having red hair, there is nothing remarkable about them – or so they think. Imagine their horror, then, when they discover that only they can save the world from dominance by strange, powerful creatures who are waking from a spellbound sleep of thousands of years . . .

IRON CAGE
Andre Norton

Jony and the young twins face an awful choice when the sky ship lands, for ever since Jony and his pregnant mother escaped from the alien Big Ones' space ship laboratory, they have been protected and cared for by the large, gentle, wise creatures they call the People. Can Jony, knowing how he and his mother were used to experimental animals by the Big Ones, stand by and allow the People to suffer the same fate at the hands of his own race?

THE MINERVA PROGRAM
Claire Mackay

Here at last is Minerva's chance to be out in front, to be really good at something – computers. That's where her future lies. But that future is threatened when Minerva is almost too clever for her own good. Suddenly she is accused of cheating and is banned from the computer room. It takes the combined talents of 'Spiderman' her brother and her inventive friends to solve this intriguing mystery.

THE GUARDIANS

John Christopher

On the run, after the tragic death of his father, Rob Randall risks capture, punishment and even worse when he crosses the Barrier into the open fields of the Country. Life there is idyllic, almost feudal, and as long as Rob can hide his secret past, then he is safe. Or so he thinks . . . A chilling story of life in the not-too-distant future when power is held by a few and rebellion crushed mercilessly.

DOLPHIN ISLAND

Arthur C. Clarke

Johnny Clinton has stowed away – almost by accident – on an enormous hovership. But even before his hideout is discovered, the *Santa Anna* is shipwrecked and Johnny finds himself at the beginning of an exciting and dangerous adventure. Dolphins, killer whales, a hurricane and an underwater conspiracy all add up to a thrilling tale, set in the twenty-first century from a master of science fiction.

THE CRYSTAL GRYPHON

Andre Norton

Kerovan of Ulmsdale is born different from other children: he has small hoofs instead of feet, and his strange eyes are the colour of amber. Fearful tales spread about him – but is he really a monster, or has he inherited some of the power of the mysterious Old Ones who inhabited his country long ago? And what about the potent magic of the crystal globe he sends to the bride he has never seen?